A LINK IN THE CHAIN

○━○━○

"What do you have?" Captain Walker sat down, closing a Missouri State Patrol convention brochure and its intended agenda.

Julie pulled a two-page report from her binder. "A disappearance seventeen years ago. That in itself is not unusual, but three others took place over a period of ten months—all within a couple-hundred-mile radius. At the time, they were thought to be runaways."

"Females, I presume."

Julie nodded. "Tracked a mother of one of these women to a trailer park. When I phoned her, she says, 'It took you near a decade or more to get back to us. Why you botherin' now?' I asked Mom if the girl took any items with her when she left: clothes, toiletries, anything. She said, 'Marylou left cocky, naive, and naked as a jay.' That doesn't sound like a runaway to me."

Walker puzzled with a ring of keys, dropping them in an ashtray. "The problem with cold cases is they're just that. People just don't give a damn. Tell you what. Pursue the three runaways, but keep it to yourself. If the commish finds out, I'll be down in the basement with you, and I am way too old for that. Good luck, and, of course, not a word of this to anyone."

Critics praise Gene Hackman, an author who "takes aim at a clear target: telling a good story. He hits it, too."

—*St. Augustine Record* on *Payback at Morning Peak*

ALSO BY GENE HACKMAN

Payback at Morning Peak

Available now from Pocket Books

GENE
HACKMAN

PURSUIT

POCKET BOOKS

New York London Toronto Sydney New Delhi

Pocket Books
A Division of Simon & Schuster, Inc.
1230 Avenue of the Americas
New York, NY 10020

This book is a work of fiction. Any references to historical events, real people, or real places are used fictitiously. Other names, characters, places, and events are products of the author's imagination, and any resemblance to actual events or places or persons, living or dead, is entirely coincidental.

First Pocket Books paperback edition December 2013

POCKET and colophon are registered trademarks of Simon & Schuster, Inc.

For information about special discounts for bulk purchases, please contact Simon & Schuster Special Sales at 1-866-506-1949 or business@simonandschuster.com.

The Simon & Schuster Speakers Bureau can bring authors to your live event. For more information or to book an event, contact the Simon & Schuster Speakers Bureau at 1-866-248-3049 or visit our website at www.simonspeakers.com.

Interior design by Lewelin Polanco

Manufactured in the United States of America

10 9 8 7 6 5 4 3 2 1

ISBN 978-1-4516-2357-4
ISBN 978-1-4516-2359-8 (ebook)

PURSUIT

Prologue

A *brisk fall* day in 1995. The oaks and cottonwoods battled for color rights in the annual October leaf display.

The wooded path wound east across two rock-strewn creeks, through a grove of walnut trees, and out into a slight rise overlooking a hundred acres of sweet corn.

"I'm Cleopatra's handmaiden—prettier, of course, and smarter, but always demure." Betty's schoolbooks were piled atop her head. She swayed her hips along the dirt path in time to a dum-ditty-dum-dum beat.

"Yes, of course, and I'm Amelia Earhart flying across the Pacific." Beverly, the younger of the two sisters, had always been more levelheaded and astute.

"Ah yes. And we know what happened to her, don't we? While others fritter away their time on adventurous nonsense, I, on the other hand, reign supreme gathering my awards and accolades."

"You got a B in gym class, for heaven's sake. Give it up."

"Give it up? Hardly. Mr. Scott says I could go all the way."

"Mr. Scott, I think, means the *two of you* could go all the way. You're almost seventeen, get with it."

"Oh, Bev, you're no fun. Every time I do well, you beat me down. Go on ahead."

He parked not in his accustomed dirt road spot but farther on in a wayside picnic area. Dodging into the wooded expanse between the road and wetlands area, he found the animal trail that led him back to a knoll and his favorite dogwood.

Arriving early had been the plan, not just to get settled but to convince himself he would be doing the right thing. He needed time to think, not about what he was going to do but the consequences. His past deeds had been easy. The planning, execution, all a snap. He watched, off and on, for days, under this particular yellowed tree. The anticipation when the distant school bell rang. The delicious wait as the two girls emerged along the bushy path. He felt he knew them, shared their silly rhymes and school songs. Others crowded his past life. Drifters, thumb trippers, but now a different grander path, a different set of prey.

They came right on time, their incessant bickering a dreary habit. The two of them, though dressed in identical clothing, were not twins but made a handsome pair. The older and taller of the two was also prettier, while the other, more thoughtful. It would be difficult convincing them he was injured and needed help. Using a long oak branch as a makeshift crutch, he braced the gnarled cane against a large stone and recited in his head the memorized plea. *"Help, please help. I'm injured and can't walk."* It needed to be just right. Not too much hooey and not overdone.

The two of them would be a challenge, but they would keep each other company at his Bait Shack. Down on the path from school, he could hear them arguing.

"I need to go, I can't wait."

"Hold it til we get home. I'm leaving, stupid. See you at the house. Remember, chores."

The younger girl moved on.

He saw her through the gap in the trees. She, flouncing her golden hair and sprinting away. It just got so much easier. Charlie's day brightened with opportunity.

Other than a few errant scratches around his throat from the older girl's stupid protests, he was fine. Wearing a turtleneck to work would quiet any nosy questions.

Later, sated and filthy from digging, he felt regret. Not for his happening, as it were, but for the missed chance of a double conquest. *Maybe later.*

Saturday afternoon, and Julie Worth parked at the Westside Mall to shop for her teenager's birthday. Despite leaving her Jeep close to the entrance, she would still have quite a walk. As she started across the vast macadam lot, the air held the crispness of a perfect late-fall day. Near the mall entrance, the early rumblings of a disorderly crowd, with several people rushing through the electric doors. A woman fell, trying to push through the slow-moving exit.

"A man, with a gun. Inside."

Julie helped the woman to her feet.

Others rushed past her.

"Jesus save me!"

"Move it, bitch!"

She pressed against the rough brick surface of the mall entrance. Part of her wanted to stop, seek cover, and wait for backup. But she knew that was so 1999. Columbine changed everything. Old rules—call it in, wait for a Special Weapons and Tactics team—still applied to a barricaded badass. But this situation looked like an active shooter, someone still racking up a body count. And the orders were simple—go stop him. About 30 percent of the time, the first cop in would get shot. So she knew she would have a two-out-of-three chance of going home tonight.

A woman clutching a child stumbled and grabbed Julie by the waist. "He's killing people, call the police."

I am the police. Julie stepped through a broken glass door and pushed against the human stampede. With one hand clasped on her holstered 9-millimeter Sig Sauer, she held her badge high above her head and moved toward the corridor wall.

Once firmly inside the mall, she saw only a few people remaining in the wide hallway, some crouched in store entries. Julie signaled them to slip away. She waited and listened. Halfway down the mall at the junction of another hallway, a body lay sprawled on the floor.

Julie stayed to the extreme left side of the wide passageway. Stepping lightly, she stopped at each store entrance to assess the situation. Echoing effects of shouts and cries for help played tricks with the direction of voices.

She took a deep breath and called 911. "Sergeant Worth. Missouri State Patrol. I'm at Westside Mall. Active shooter on scene. Man down in center of corridor. Condition not known, send an ambulance. I am armed."

She put her phone on vibrate and once again eyed the corridor before her: a man in a pale green security guard shirt and navy blue pants, splayed out in front of an information kiosk. A distant siren drew close; someone else must have called 911 first. Julie secreted herself in each storefront, checked the area and moved on. Her phone vibrated. She didn't recognize the number. "Sergeant Worth, who is this?" She stepped deep into the vestibule of a shoe store, her hand cupped over her phone.

"Lieutenant Mac White, city police. Sergeant, I suggest you get the hell out of there while we assemble our SWAT team."

"Due respect, sir. I got caught in the middle of this, but now that I'm here, we have what looks like a security guard down in the center of the mall. I'm fairly close to him, probably safer here than trying to make my way back out. Hold, please."

Across the X shape of the concourse she saw movement. Behind the counter of a fast-food stand, a man with one arm hooked around the neck of a screaming boy. The man's other hand held a sawed-off shotgun.

"Still there, Lieutenant?"

"Just heard from my captain. Listen, Trooper, he wants you out of there. Now."

"Tell him I don't work for him. I just saw the suspect. Looks to be forty-five to fifty, white male, dark blue T-shirt, red-and-blue baseball cap. Heavy beard, long brown hair, five foot ten, one eighty. He's got a hostage; kid about fourteen. Suspect is armed with what looks like a sawed-off shotgun."

"Hold tight." The officer was on the radio, a garbled voice coming back at him. "State your name again, Sergeant."

Before Julie could answer, a loud shotgun blast came from the fast-food stand. Broken glass rained hard on the terrazzo floor. A sign above the information booth knocked lopsided on a chain. Then a scream.

"Anybody around here better listen up! I'm gonna kill this little bastard!" He raised his voice. *"You listening?"*

Julie tucked down low behind the window valance. If she crept along to just one more storefront, the information booth would hide her from view of the food stand on the other side. She whispered into her phone.

"Subject will kill his hostage. How long before SWAT?"

"Ten minutes tops."

"Kid will be dead by then. I'm going in."

"You are not to—"

She closed the phone.

The gunman's voice faded and then grew loud as he paced. She waited until the sound cut back; then she slid around the corner of the storefront and lay flat on the stone floor, pushing her way forward, ranger style, with her elbows. She smelled old floor polish and dirt from thousands of shoes. When she reached the next store, she turned 45 degrees to her right and continued to crawl across the open center of the concourse, toward the pagoda-like stall in the center.

The man in the security uniform, blasted in the face. Julie, still prone, searched for a pulse. None. A half door on the booth left open, describing someone's hasty exit. A sliver of light edged through the far side of the hexagon-shaped structure. She crawled in and surveyed the food stand from the top of the cracked board.

From somewhere, a woman cried out a prayer in Spanish. A dull thud came from the food stand. Julie peeked through the splintered board as a man with a head wound and blood-splattered white chef's gear stumbled out of the stand and fell to the floor.

Shotgunman still paced, his head bobbing, the young boy still secured by his crooked arm. Through the opening to the kitchen jutted three sets of hands, all stretched toward the ceiling. The man continued to pace and then stopped to slap the boy. He wrapped his arm back around the kid's neck.

Julie's phone vibrated against her pant leg. She whispered, "Go."

"Where are you?"

"Kiosk."

"We're at the end of the corridor. SWAT is on the way."

"Hold." She crawled into a corner where someone had left a jacket on the back of a chair. She bundled it up in front of her mouth, almost gagging from a heavy, perfumed scent. She pulled the phone under her makeshift muffler. "This guy's berserk, Lieutenant. He's beating the crap out of a kid; three other hostages are in the kitchen. If he sees you guys, he'll really snap. He's yelling. Wait." Julie pulled the phone from the muffler.

"Somebody better hear what I got to say, or there's gonna be shit to pay!" he shouted even louder. "Get it, goddamn it?"

Julie once again wrapped the phone close to her mouth. "Hear that, Lieutenant?"

"Yeah, made out some of it. Nuts."

"He whacked one of the cooks on the head. Needs help."

"We can't see him from where we are. Can you?"

"He's about thirty feet from me. I've got an idea."

"Don't do anything stupid."

A loud slapping thud came from the food stand, followed by the boy's cry for help.

"Gotta go. I'm gonna stand up, so if you have your sniper scopes on the kiosk, I'll be wearing"—she held up the coat into the light—"a pale blue jacket. I'm in the middle of the concourse in the info booth. Pale blue jacket." She slid the barrel of her Sig an inch to make sure a round was chambered. Then she tugged the tight-fitting, wrinkled blazer over her broad shoulders and clipped the mall ID badge higher on her lapel. She grabbed a pair of tortoise-rimmed reading glasses from the counter and ruffled her hair. The front of the jacket lost its button, but she still concealed her pistol in her left waistband.

"I'll talk to you, sir!" she yelled. "Hey there! Help! Don't shoot!" If he was going to fire, it would probably be in the first couple moments.

"Who the fuck is it?" The man's head popped around the stand's swinging door. He still had the kid in a neck hold.

Julie took a deep breath, her hands high overhead. "Please, I have two babies at home." The lie seemed to work; she had his attention. "Sir, can I just walk away? Promise I won't tell a soul." Hands still overhead, she cleared the booth and got to within twenty feet of the food stand, in good pistol range. She gestured toward the corridor, which would bring her even closer. "If you'll just let me get to my car"—she pointed down the hallway toward the back of the mall—"I'll be out of your hair and on my way."

"Hold up there! Damn it all and shut the fuck up! Come over here." He let go of the boy's neck and pulled him in tight to his side. He brought the shotgun up to belt level, the short barrel and chopped-off stock piece looking like a stretched-out handgun. "I ought to blow your girly brains out—"

"I just want to get to my car." She shifted from foot to foot. "I hurt my side when I fell down in the booth, and I have to call the babysitter to tell her—"

"Close your mouth, for Christ's sake. One more word, and I'll blow this shit-for-brains' head off." He brought around the sawed-off shotgun and pressed it against the boy's head.

Julie held up one finger as if asking permission to speak.

The man looked down both long corridors. "Take that jacket off, or I'll make a mess here. Wanna see if you're armed. Do it." He turned on an evil grin and lowered the gun slightly, waiting for his show.

Julie slipped her right arm out of the jacket and took off the glasses. "What do you want to see?" She reached across and slowly pulled her left arm sleeve free of the jacket and pinned it against her hip. Her right hand now held the Sig behind the coat. She stood feet together, head bowed, submissive.

The man gestured with his 12-gauge weapon. "You work here with the rest of these bastards?" The end of the shotgun rested on the counter, pointing down the long corridor, away from Julie.

Without a view of the man's head and upper body, she would not have a shot, and neither would SWAT. She would have to draw him out. Julie dropped the jacket and glasses. Her weapon flashed across a short arc and leveled on the man's chest. "Police officer. Release the child and slowly take your hand off the weapon."

His eyes turned into fiery red orbs. "I'll kill you, bitch! I'll—"

Julie secured her 9-millimeter with both hands, her left foot slightly in front—classic shooter's stance. "I'll say this for the last time. Take your hand off the shotgun." She watched the air slowly drain from the suspect's body, his lips bunched into puffy regret.

His fingers began a slow retreat.

He's going to give it up.

The kid screamed and jerked away. When he did, the man's left hand flew toward the scatter gun, firing a round as he leveled the barrel at her.

He never heard the sound or felt the two .9s as they dug through his body. The third left a dime-sized hole in his forehead.

Julie saw the blood on her left leg, midthigh, and just below her knee before she felt the sting. She lifted the still-connected phone. "Scene secure. Shots fired. Subject down. Officer down." She backed against the information booth and slid to the floor.

T*he Dragons will* do it this year. God is my witness."
Todd, aka Big Man, fancied himself a hot ball-
player.

Todd Devlin, Julie's partner, and several other troopers enjoyed a lunch of burgers and fries at Wing's Diner.
A couple guys agreed about the local team's chances. Julie
listened to their heated discussion but couldn't commit
to the conversation except to say that she'd spank all their
butts in a one-on-one and spot them *h,o,* and *r,* in a game
of Horse.

There began a chorus of oohs and aahs, as if she were
goddess of the court.

She made a quick fake to Todd's right and mimed a
one-handed three-pointer. "Swish! She shoots and scores!
Give it up, boys. You're outclassed."

They enjoyed her performance, but her thoughts were
on the lieutenant's words to her as she left the station for
lunch. "Captain wants a word with you at one thirty."

"What's it about? Any idea?"

"He seemed pissed. Wear your raincoat."

After lunch, she had a half hour, so she decided to take

a slow walk back to the station. She had been lucky with the shotgun pellets. The skin was punctured, but no bones were struck, and no nerve damage. She just needed to keep moving.

"You sure you want to walk? A girl can't be too careful."

It was her first day back, and Julie knew that Todd was more concerned about her injuries than she was, but she played along with him. She patted her hip, her short leather jacket hiding the Sig automatic tucked high on her waist. "I can manage, thank you."

She liked Todd. He was a good worker and loyal to a fault. Maybe a bit too easy, as her father used to say.

A brisk fall day, she couldn't imagine a nicer afternoon—if only the threat of having to speak to Captain Walker in a pissed state wasn't looming over her.

"By the way, according to our beloved Dr. Crankenstein . . ."

Walker held a typed memo at arm's length for her to see. His wide shoulders sloped from years of heavy decision making, his lined face having tracked the many miles of police toil. "She says you never . . ." he scanned the paper to pick out the appropriate line. "Subject is not completing her psychiatric examination after the shooting incident. I deem this treatment crucial and necessary for the safety of said patient and others who may in the future prove to be at odds with the aforementioned patient. Miss Worth shows a combative nature when confronted. Dr. Heidi Cranstein."

"She'd love hearing you call her 'Crankenstein,' Captain."

"Oh yeah? I hear she's a piece of work. The commissioner thinks you're exploiting your newfound celebrity in order to get out of seeing this doctor. I don't agree, but there you have it."

He gestured toward the door for her to leave. "Anyway, you have to go back and see her, fulfill your required number of visits. Help me out here."

"Thank you, sir, for allowing me to speak." She left his office and noticed the squad room listening in.

The following day, the captain again called Julie into his office.

"What's up on the gas station shooting debacle? Anything new?"

She brought her three-ring binder, anticipating that she would be placed on administrative leave and that some of her cases would need to be handed off. "We're close to wrapping it up. We know this heavily tattooed street guy, Lobo, was involved. Probably did the deed, just need to find him."

"That house fire BS. What about it?"

"About the same, Captain. We've got pictures of the wife going into a motel with a fellow we thought was good for that double tap up north last year." She glanced at her notes. "Swan McGee—hell of a name, but he's our guy. Todd's working on a warrant as we speak. Our favorite judge"—they gave each other a wink—"is usually good about probable cause. In any case, we've got this jerk McGee at the scene with the broad doing the nasty at the Motel 6. We're pretty much locked up."

"Good work." Walker cleared his throat. "Here's the

hell of it. I ran a couple scenarios past the commish in terms of your rehab. Doesn't help that you're blowing off your psych sessions. Best I can do is two weeks admin leave and a month of desk work, either in the property room straightening stuff or in latent."

"Latent prints?"

"No, past unsolved crap."

"How far back would I need to go, sir?"

"Up to you. You're probably not going to find anything. O'Neal and Jefferson spent a month last year dusting off all that baloney. I looked over their work. Actually, they were fairly thorough."

Julie closed her binder. "If it's all right with you, I'd like the cold case files. Is there any reg saying I can't do this as admin duty rather than admin leave?"

"I don't get it. You're being disciplined, and you want this work. Is that what you're saying?" Walker leaned back in his chair.

"That's what I am saying, Captain."

Julie was made to wait far past her appointment time before Dr. Cranstein called her in. The previous patient had left in tears nearly a half hour earlier. She decided she would get the best out of the sessions, regardless of any prejudice she might feel toward Frau Cranstein.

The woman sat next to a file cabinet, her streaked blond hair pulled back tight into a sweet-roll bun. Pince-nez glasses graced her heavy nose, as she looked, head down, over the top of the eyepiece. "You missed a few appointments, Miss Worthy. Will this be your habit?"

Julie hid her smile behind a manufactured cough. "No, of course not. I simply forgot."

Cranstein adjusted her glasses and made a few notes.

"It's my experience that dissembling, feigning forgetfulness, and being insincere are all signs of secrecy. Wouldn't you agree, Sergeant?"

Julie nodded.

"I'm so sorry. I didn't hear your response."

"My response, madam Doctor, was a nod of the head, as in 'Yes, I agree.'"

"So it would follow that although agreeing, you wish to hold your own counsel, correct?"

"I'm not verbose, and generally not a liar, either. But your questions regarding being secretive might be accurate." She paused. "Just like our last meeting. Today I was required to wait half an hour after the previous patient left, knowing full well that half of a one-hour session leaves not a hell of a lot of time. I'm here because I'm required to do so. A psych examination is required by the department. To get right to it, madam—"

"Doctor."

"All right. Doctor. Your questions of whether I enjoyed the shooting were inappropriate."

"How so? Enlighten me, please."

"How can you be serious, madam—"

"Doctor."

"*Madam*, for you to say, 'Tell me your innermost sense of joy, your feelings, over the death of a human being?' It is not only inappropriate but insensitive and rude. I killed a man to save a young boy's life. The only joy was still being able to go home and see my kid. Why don't you read the account of the incident before you ask me if I enjoyed the taking of a life?"

"When you raise your voice to make your point, do you say to yourself, 'I will be forceful to assure those listening and myself that I'm righteous, indeed'?"

"We are mixing our metaphors here, madam Doctor. Whether or not I was, to use your word, 'righteous' in God's eyes or correct in the realm of the criminal justice system is way beyond your purview to adjudicate. To ask me that kind of question equates me with a common thug. A killer. Is it your duty to suss out murderers in the department? To weed out the homicidal? Is that who you are?"

"I would remind you, Sergeant, that I'm not the one being examined here."

You should be, bitch.

The woman made a deliberate show of looking at her watch. "This is not of benefit, Sergeant. Let's be honest."

"So fifteen minutes into a one-hour session, and it's auf Wiedersehen, right?"

"You really do have issues, Sergeant. One is your inability to interpret emotion. It's possible the man you mur— shot, killed, was in fact considering a course of agreement. Your explosion of self-righteousness could possibly have been avoided if you considered the other's right to life. His family, loves, and joys in simple everyday activities, which you took away in the blink of an eye. A millisecond of thought may have changed not only the man's life but your own. In the years to come, keep in mind your power with that beloved weapon you so proudly wear. You must, at least, be honest with yourself."

"To be honest, I want to say 'Fuck you,' but I won't. I'll just say this is what I call a holy session of misinformed bullshit. If and when I'm ever confronted with another deadly armed shoot-out, I'll give you a call first, and we can discuss your book-smart theory on who dies and who doesn't in these truncated guidance sessions. It's great drive-through psychiatry, Doctor, and, by the way, do you have a dog named Blondie?"

The woman had goaded her into making an ass out of herself. Julie stopped on the street to think of what the Nazi bitch said to her about taking away the man's life in a millisecond, without thought. She asked herself if things could have turned out better—or at least different—if she'd given it more *thought*. Maybe a wounding shot, not a mortal one, would have been better? It flew against everything she had been taught. The mantra was always two rounds at center mass. A wounded man could still be dangerous.

It gave her pause, though she didn't regret the man's death. He had killed and wounded at least three people, but Frau Cranstein finagled and fucked her mind with inaccurate accusations. Niggling doubt remained. Hateful as the woman was, maybe she had a point.

4

A *careful driver,* Charles stayed five to ten miles under the speed limit. The stolen 1993 Ford Bronco, a proud symbol of American workmanship. Steady hands guided his vehicle, both in traffic and on deserted country roads. He would grin when drivers circled around him and honked past. He loved it when they'd throw their hands up in despair and laughed when they got worked up.

It didn't bother him. Charles continued with his safety-margin caravan-like ways. The Bronco was special. To say he owned it would be an exaggeration. But it was his. He used the vehicle during his tomcat hours and on those occasions when transporting female passengers, some of whom would be better left in the wilderness. So the Bronco stayed, for the most part, in a wood garage adjacent to Bait Shack. He often thought how bizarre it would be to take the auto back to Oklahoma, where he had stolen it many years ago. Each year, he would lift a Missouri tag from another car to comply with state regulations. Messy but necessary. However, maybe Charles Adam Clegg, poster child for the thoughtful traditionalist, would leave it in the driveway of the house where he had acquired it, with a note:

> *Thanks for the use of the Bronco. I have such a short memory, couldn't think of who I borrowed it from. It wasn't until watching a recent football game between Oklahoma and Missouri that it dawned on me, sorry. I filled the tank.*
>
> *All the best, your friend, the absentminded thief*

Friday evening held a hint of rain, the western sky a color wheel of darkening clouds. The stop at his one-bedroom apartment outside Morse Mill yielded the proper prescription weekend garb—raincoat and boots. He remained the careful stickler. Charles's usual grocery needs involved sojourns to two separate stores, the overwhelming Splendid Farms supermarket and Mag's family store, a mom-and-pop place.

"Evening, Mr. C. What's the news?" Mag's husband, Winston, a pleasant man who might have actually graduated from elementary school, always greeted him the same way.

"The word is rain, pardner, coming soon and plenty of it." He probed a large head of lettuce. "So batten down the hatches."

"What's that mean? Never really put a thought to it."

"Means the doors on the cargo hold of a boat or ship should be battened, sealed, ready for foul weather, to make fast."

Bits of an overripe cantaloupe spotted the narrow aisle floor between the freezer case and the vegetables. Charles picked up the larger pieces and placed them in his shopping cart.

Winston wore the same vacant look. "Why would you go out to sea if it were nasty weather?"

"Exactly." He smiled. "Why?"

"You been buying a right smart load of food lately. Having a weekend bust-out?"

"I'm expectant, Winston. As if with child, ideas, full of yearning, nostalgic for the old days prior to television's political wrangling and Washington's backbiting."

Winston seemed sorry to have asked, so he checked and bagged the mountain of produce. "They do get heated on the TV. When you gonna move out to the lake full-time, Mr. C? Hells bells, you could fish and carry on til Judgment Day." He droned on, like a gospel minister, Charles having opened the floodgates to Winnie's dull world.

He wondered why Winston spoke of God and that painful day of judgment. Even Jesus had reason to keep his miracles hidden. "You're not going to charge me for the cantaloupe, are you, Winnie?"

"Heck, no. Been busy trying to get to that mess for an hour." He took the spoiled chunks of fruit from the cart.

Yeah, right, Winnie. And the people in the South have forgotten the Civil War.

The hour-and-a-half drive out to Bait Shack, his country shanty, had been pleasant enough. A soft, steady downpour kept the wipers at their busiest. He kept his reliable 1969 Chevy Nomad in mechanically perfect condition. His other vehicle, the Bronco, he stashed away safely in the garage for special occasions. The hard-packed dirt road danced with the first slanted drops. Charles listened to his oldies-but-goodies station, knowing that the next hour would be stressful. But the familiarity of Elvis doing "Hound Dog" brought a warm anticipation.

He always pictured himself an entertainer. Given the right circumstances and breaks, he thought a career playing Midwestern bars and roadhouses as a rockabilly revivalist might have been his.

The early days of guitar picking brought him pleasure, though his small grip refused to wrap comfortably around the neck of his secondhand acoustic Gibson. He would prop his knee against the throat of the instrument, his left hand counterpressing in an attempt to make chords. The few times he tried to play at local amateur nights turned into ultimate failures. One club owner nicknamed him Camaron, which he quite liked. It sounded friendly, like he was the man's comrade. But it shook him when later at work a fellow toiler at the Drew Box Factory explained that *camaron* was Spanish for "shrimp." A questionable five foot six, Charles addressed his vertical challenge with helpful lift-enhanced shoes that still left him wanting.

The group of foster homes in various counties around the state established twice yearly trips to participating factories in the area. Chuck attended with his foster parent, the other six kids in his foster home, and several other groups of youngsters who arrived expectant and loud at Drew Inc. on a "Way Things Are Made" school trip.

The box factory vibrated with overhead cranes, forklifts, and long, noisy conveyor belts, like a giant Erector Set, a boyhood dream. Chuck and his best friend, Bink, were told a number of times by Mr. Tucker, his so-called nurturing sire, to "Stay the hell with the group, shitheads." Tuck had a way with words.

They wandered. Bink pressed a button on a yellow metal box that controlled an overhead apparatus moving on rails high in the ceiling. A heavy pallet of boxed tape for cardboard crashed down on Bink and Chuck. Bink died instantly. Chuck suffered a crushed hip and a broken leg.

He could still see Tuck hovering in the background with a wry look. Chuck heard himself scream.

"You're lucky, limp dick. You gotta sign a paper saying you'll behave yourself, but the Drew company did right by you. A lifetime job at your disposal, medical and retirement benefits as per rank and file, and a chunk of earth fit for a baron."

"What's a baron?" He understood later that Tuck's explanation of the company's generosity was more liberal than what had been advertised to him.

He didn't see Tuck much after that. The man would disappear from the foster home property for several weeks at a time, coming back tan and grouchy.

On Chuck's sixteenth birthday, Tuck drove him to the box factory. "You're on your own, tough guy. By the way, you know anything about Rat? Gloria says she found him hanging by the neck from that elm tree by the outhouse. Anything?"

"He was your cat, Tuck. You should look out for things that are assigned to you."

It didn't seem that his foster parent understood the reference but simply gave him the finger and sped away.

Charles liked his job, for he didn't have to talk to anyone. After several weeks, he bought the trashed Nomad and spent the weekends at the lake fixing up his legacy, a gone-to-hell fishing shack on a tract of uncut timber. The land was worthless—really too far from town to commute—but he liked it; it was his.

"Chuck, it's a hell of a deal," one of the older accountants at the factory said. "A real fixer-upper; we'll get the paperwork settled later. In the meantime, I'm off to sunnier climes."

He never saw the man again, learning that he had died

while on a search for a retirement spot for himself in the Tampa, Florida, area.

Several years later he ran into his old mentor, Tuck, toiling at a Conoco gas station on one of the winding back roads of the lake country.

"You don't recognize me, do you?"

Tuck glanced up at him as he filled Charlie's tank. His long black hair still swept back in a ducktail. "I see a lot of folks passing through here. That'll be nine dollars and eighty cents"—he paused—"cowboy."

Charles thought him to be the same surly bastard who took money from the county for all those years to raise him and a half-dozen other pitiful waifs.

It looked as if Tuck either owned or ran the station. Charles rode by several times over the next few weeks and saw a woman pumping gas most of the time.

It wasn't Gloria, his old foster mom, though it looked somewhat like her—floozy hair and big knockers.

The mysterious fire that burned the Conoco station a month later at three o'clock in the morning was seen for ten miles. The inferno, listed by law enforcement as "suspicious." The two bodies inside, charred beyond recognition.

Charles considered the event. On the one side, the world—as rotten as it appeared—was better off having been rid of Ol' Numb Nuts and his big-breasted partner. On the downside, Chuck had to give up his nightly prayer: "Lord, please help me find my old nemesis Mr. J. T. Tuck Gerard; I need to pay my respects."

Tuck and his big-titted friend went up in smoke for $9.80. It weren't no joke. *Cowboy, indeed.*

Charles made it a ritual to drive by the blackened remains. It made him smile as nothing else could.

5

The Show-Me State's countryside. Age-old trees, shrubs, and vines covered Julie's hillside bungalow. At the white picket fence, she waved to Mrs. Tripette and her cottage, *Serenity*. The name, a little over the top, but the woman seemed pleasant, and Julie believed each to his own. She even felt a comfort in another neighbor's perpetually broken-down slatted corral. She would keep the memory of her early days leaning over that top rung watching the colts and their mothers and wishing for a Shetland pony—not, she thought, the usual young girl's yearning for dolls or a bright dress.

It wasn't to be. Her father stated, "Ponies are expensive toys. They give you nothing back but a brief, bumpy ride and a possible bite on the butt."

Her daughter, Cheryl, on the other hand, claimed she was more reasonable for never asking for a horse, but rather, only a car. "Mom, everyone has one. You know, get to and from school, shop, go out. Hello, Earth to Mom."

It was this thinking that further upended Julie, just on her way out for a slow walk. She had given a lecture to Cheryl about their financial situation—generally, to tighten their unnecessary spending, and specifically, to allot their dollars more carefully.

In Julie's divorce settlement, desiring the least amount of ties to her ex-husband, she took no financial support from him but stipulated a trust fund for Cheryl's college education. Perhaps a tough decision to live with when these tiffs with Cheryl erupted, but Julie would arrange for a truce with her later. She had considered going back to her maiden name, but kept Worth out of respect for her daughter. Getting into this conflict with her girl also reminded her of one particular argument with her ex many years earlier.

Bart (or, as she would say, the rotten bastard she had been married to for less than a year) resisted living in their house, which her father had built after WWII. When questioned, her husband rambled, "It isn't mine, it's not something I built or paid for. Too many cute stories of your parents and all their junk."

"Junk? You didn't know my parents, Bart, how can you say that?"

"I know you and how you relate to them, your overly sweet recollections of 'Dad used to say this,' and 'Mom sat there in the rocker,' and 'the dog pooped on the rug' in such and such a corner. It's all too cozy and homespun."

She had stepped out into the fall night air, like this evening, knowing then that to stay inside with her husband would lead to trouble.

But he came out looking for her. "Jules, get your ass in here. Stop the bullshit. You don't like this broken-down shack any more than I do, so stop pretending you do. It's full of memories of your old man and when you were Daddy's *little girl*." He mimicked a spoiled brat. Then Bart threw up his arms and went in to make a call. Walking back toward the house, she listened to his shielded conversation through an open window.

"When do you want to get together?"

She watched him through the multipane front door. He stood more erect, grinning, his left hand fiddling in his pocket. She thought it wouldn't be good for her or the expectant baby to pursue this stupid conversation any further.

Julie turned and walked back to the house, her mind drifting over those past years.

Her attraction to Bart mystified Julie. She liked classical music, Broadway tunes, and dance, while Bart existed on baseball, hockey, and boxing. She granted that theirs might have been a typical girl-boy difference, but Bart made his love of sports an inherited right, his father having been a minor league baseball player who had been released for deliberately hitting another player with a ball. His defense being "He asked for it." It didn't bother him that the other player was on his own team.

Julie recalled another incident. Bart's car starting up and backing down the gravel drive. He pulled up beside her and rolled down the passenger-side window. "Going into town to see whatshisname about that computer thing I told you about. Back soon."

"Horseshit." Julie continued to walk.

"What?"

"I said you're full of shit. You're going out, pretending it's to talk over your worldwide start-up computer 'thingy,' right?" She knew at that particular moment that she wouldn't be growing old with Mr. Barton Worth.

He had sped off in a huff, only to flash his brake lights and back up some fifty yards. "You're a real bitch, you know that? I'm trying to make a better life for us with this programming idea for a better billing system, and you do nothing but piss all over it."

Julie leaned against the passenger-side door. "Doesn't it bother you even a little that I'm pregnant and you're hotfooting it around town with your computer boyfriend? Doesn't that rock your self-centered world just a little, Bart baby?"

When he slammed the car into park and got out, Julie thought that Mr. Manly Man was going to prove himself right by beating the piss out of her.

It wasn't a trouncing in the classical sense but more of a mauling, a grabbing hold of arms and scuffling on the dirt road. It took more than a "Get in the car, bitch!" and "You kiss my ass!" before Julie went down.

"Why didn't you get in the car when I told you? Now look what you've made me do. Get up." He reached down and offered her his hand; she spit on it.

"I wouldn't feel right about having you assist me up after I *made* you knock me down, so fuck off."

It was, as she got back to the house, a resolution; a sense of closure. She knew she'd reached a change in her life, one that didn't include Barton Worth.

The state patrol opportunity, though, had been the right choice, but her time as a rookie did not pass uneventfully. Her partner at the time hit with a baseball bat as they attempted a drug arrest at a dope house. Tommy had walked much too boldly into the suspect's apartment. He saw the woman, looking contrite and scared, standing against the kitchen wall, her arms cramped behind her. Tommy moved as if to walk past her, and the woman lashed out with the metal bat. He never regained consciousness. The druggie's wife swung the bat again. Julie yelled "Freeze!" to no effect. The missus continued her windup and uncoiled. Julie stepped inside the arc of the bat and cracked the woman on top of the head with her Sig. The woman went down in a thud. Julie's misgiving came immediately. A young girl stood between the parting of drapes separating the kitchen and living room.

"Mommy, why are you lying down? I'm hungry."

Every day for the next fifteen years, Julie tried to be an exemplary officer, never again wanting to hear a child's voice pleading with its mother.

The aftermath proved difficult. Because she was a rookie, her superiors and most of the older patrolmen treated Julie as an incompetent. The investigation exonerated her, but it stayed with her. The stigma of losing a partner as a rookie followed her long after others in the department had forgotten. She went out of her way to be thorough and fair, and gaining a reputation for being tough not only on lawbreakers but also especially on herself.

6

His boss, *William* Arlen Drew—or Wad, as Charles called him in the privacy of his thoughts—confronted him earlier in the day with the notion that he, Charles, should be more aware of time, taking care to arrive when his coworkers punched the clock, taking only the prescribed breaks during the days, and making an effort to enjoy his fellow drones.

He didn't use the word "drone," but he might as well have. "It's incumbent for all of us to pull together; to create a sense of commonality in the workplace."

Each time Mr. Wad spoke to him, Charles grinned like a white-faced circus jester. He acquiesced by moving his head obediently from side to side or acknowledged him with a "Got it, sir" and sometimes a condescending "Wow, that's terrific." At least he would have described his days as entertaining.

Quitting would have been easy. He didn't, only because he had signed the property settlement as a youngster, and he enjoyed his present circumstance.

Part of Charles's deal with the company included an office. A needless waste, but it amused him to still be tied to Drew Inc. At thirty-eight, the envy of most other young guys in the plant, he was named disposition manager, a cooked-up position given to him after he'd worked the floor for twelve years. He never understood his duties, but it had something to do with solving problems, being a liaison between management and union, putting out labor fires, and holding hands. He appreciated the authority of his managerial position.

He nipped a sexual harassment complaint in the bud, so to speak, when he presented the company with the woman's resignation, a letter absolving her boss of any wrongdoing and her promise to Charles personally that she would settle in a place "far removed from Drew Inc."

"Congrats on cleaning up that Russell dung heap. She's no longer a bother, right?" William Drew seemed to hate Charles and his unholy bond with the company but remained pleased with the outcome of the Russell situation.

"Yep, the fifty thousand was money well spent, sir."

"You got the usual paperwork? Everything signed and agreed to?"

"She wouldn't meet with our lawyers, but I convinced her and her people that this was all the company could do. Otherwise, 'See you in court, sweetheart.'"

"You have such a succinct way of putting things. And she's . . . left town?"

"I can promise you, sir, you will not be hearing from her or her people."

Charles took pride in his persuasive ability. It took barely an hour to convince Miss Russell to relent, her painful options being slender and nil.

The company never heard from her. Nor did anyone else.

He also made a number of friends on the production floor. Charles gained trust by playing a tricky game of "I'm on your side, dude" to "The men can be handled, sir. We just have to convince them it's in their best interest."

The pay was good, and his hours were made flexible by a series of white lies, outside meetings, and pure bullshit. No one alive, other than the senior Drew and a long-past-departed exec, knew of his sweetheart agreement with the company involving his lakeside cabin and grounds.

He was, among other things, a lucky guy.

A nice woman by the name of Deidre took care of him early on when he was just settling into his new office. If it hadn't been for their torrid lovemaking, Charles would have considered her more of a mother figure. Her fastidious handling of his inexperience as disposition manager was touching. She coddled him. His favorite pastime was watching her walk away, her tight skirt and barely perceptible swagger reminding him of earlier times at the foster home.

They played spanking games. Deidre scolding Charlie for his bad-boy behavior, and giving him numerous erotic chores to perform. While little Charlie whined and begged for his titty pie, Deidre laughed a lot. Baby Charles, though, took it dead serious. Deidre, when married barely ten months, drifted into Charles's slim arms. Their brief affair didn't seem to bother a working relationship that sustained itself for nearly five years. They never spoke of it, Charles now limiting his office flirting to an occasional pat on the behind.

He reminisced, his thoughts drifting to topic A: his current enterprise, and the overwhelming piece de resistance project in his life.

So delicious and special, he restricted his daydreaming to a paltry couple times per work session. Sometimes he would indulge himself to twice that. Why shouldn't a man have a few hushed pastimes?

On his way to Bait Shack, Charles passed the First Episcopal Church. He had attended a few times, always struck by the devoted. Their prayerful, self-conscious attitudes got the better of him. Although he liked their summer dresses, the women all stank of simple bathwater and cheap soap.

Charles stopped at his front gate, the house situated considerably back from the road. His hundred-odd acres wasn't a farm as such, just virgin timberland, and because of the lake, it seemed even larger. But most important, it was isolated.

He reheated supper, a roast chicken from Splendid Farms, half of which he put back in the fridge. A fresh salad and a container of store-bought sweet beans divided between two plates. A muffin sat on a tray along with plastic utensils and fresh coffee. Charles looked at the inexpensive bottle of red wine and decided to be generous, pouring a substantial portion for himself and, in a large paper cup, an equal amount. He had tried a variety of enticements. Maybe a special dinner and wine would do the trick. He balanced the cup, paper plate, and coffee on the tray. Next to a heavy wood door, a large key ring hung from a hook. He took the key with the flashlight attached and opened the door to the basement.

In the late evening, he watched the pundits on the Slyboots channel, admiring their preening and dismissive attitudes. The stark pale blue light of the television washed the room in melancholy. It reminded Charles of earlier days, running naked through the woods with Patty, her high-pitched laugh a stark contrast of things to come.

He bounced the remote in his hands, suppressing an urge to shatter his television.

Patty had been naive, exuberant in nearly everything she undertook. She believed the world to be dominated by truly good people. Surrounding herself with all manner of hangers-on at work, her treating friends like family became maddening. Bringing home strangers, he predicted, would bring about a cataclysmic event. To his chagrin, his childlike bride persisted in her innocent ways.

Her quick tongue and wit annoyed him. He thought people of a certain caliber seemed arrogant to those of lesser education or advantages in life. Her pertness gnawed at him; a cheerfulness in the face of devastation rattled his very being.

He enjoyed only her athletic body; a tribute to a lifetime of exercise. Patty finished her degree and went on to teach, saying to him nearly every day, "I want to experience everything before I die. The good, the bad, the sublime. I want my life to amount to something."

When Charles tried to explain to her the reality of the cold, cold world, she would laugh.

"Reality is what one makes of it; beauty can be found in a trash heap."

And that is exactly where they found her.

7

J*ulie didn't mind* the storeroom work. She devised a system, laying out files on a long worktable. Much of the text was standard procedure, dry statements of assaults leading to deaths, outright homicides, and abductions. As Captain Walker explained, most of the files were recently reviewed by other officers; their notes on the various events, self-explanatory.

She had worked briefly on some of these herself. The Herod case, a homicide ten years earlier where the wife allegedly killed the husband and then disappeared. Cops called it a "forty-nine-dollar divorce," in reference to the cheap Saturday night special handguns often favored in these killings. The woman's picture in the *St. Louis Post-Dispatch* looked provocative. Julie's daughter, Cheryl, was almost seven at the time. She recalled her asking, "Who's the pretty woman, Mommy? Did she do a bad thing?"

"Dear, we just don't know. We can't find her. When we do, we'll ask her. Okay?"

They never found the woman; she'd simply vanished. An odd part of her job—pursuing people who harmed others. Not so much godlike in terms of discipline for the community but an attempt at balance for those who had been wronged.

Julie, lugging a stack of files, knocked politely on Captain Walker's door. "Got a minute, sir? I'd like you to take a look at a couple items."

"What's up, Worth? What do you have?" He sat down, closing a Missouri State Patrol convention brochure and its intended agenda.

Julie pulled a two-page report from her binder. "A disappearance seventeen years ago. That in itself is not unusual, but three others took place over a period of ten months—all within a couple-hundred-mile radius. At the time, they were thought to be runaways."

"Females, I presume."

Julie nodded. "Tracked a mother of one these women to a trailer park. When I phoned her, she says, 'It took you near a decade or more to get back to us. Why you botherin' now?' I asked Mom if the girl took any items with her when she left: clothes, toiletries, anything. She said, 'Marylou left cocky, naive, and naked as a jay.' That doesn't sound like a runaway to me."

Walker puzzled with a ring of keys, dropping them in an ashtray. "The problem with cold cases is they're just that. People just don't give a damn. Tell you what. Pursue the three-runaways in any order you want, but keep it to yourself."

"Oh, another gal. Name's Preston. I'd like to talk to her about her sister's disappearance. Okay?"

"Keep it to yourself."

"Can I bring my partner into this?"

"Not until your admin duty runs out. Otherwise, if the commish finds out, I'll be down in the basement with you, and I am way too old for that. Good luck, and, of course, not a word of this to anyone."

"Mrs. Preston?"

A slight pause. "Who's calling?"

"My name is Sergeant Juliette Worth. Missouri State Patrol, Criminal Investigation."

"Criminal?"

"No need to be frightened. Are you Beverly Preston?"

"Maybe."

Julie thought she'd heard some strange answers to an "Are you so and so?" inquiry, but "maybe" was the weirdest.

"May I have a few minutes of your time? I'd like to come out to your place and speak with you."

"Does this have to do with Betty? It will be several months before the sun crosses the equator, so day and night are still unequal."

Julie explained the recent opening of unsolved case files and that she would like to speak to a family member in regard to the missing Betty Preston. Telephone number changes were made over the years, the victim's family having kept the police department up to date. Preston agreed to have Julie come to her home. Julie wasn't sure it would lead to anything, but it was good to get out. She got into her Dodge Charger work vehicle, appreciating the drive to Walnut Springs, a bedroom community just twenty miles west of Saint Louis. She could get to the Preston house before the spring equinox. She smiled at her own joke.

She drove down a dirt road scattered with homes that sat a hundred feet back, all of them featuring well-tended yards. Grassy expanses stretched through a culvert area right up next to the road's shoulder.

The door to the suburban cottage opened right away, answered by a woman who appeared older than her years.

"Mrs. Preston?"

The woman seemed distracted. She opened the screen door without speaking and ushered Julie into a pleasant though sparse living room. Dressed in baggy sweatpants and a faded T-shirt proclaiming she'd visited Meramec Caverns, a former hideout of the outlaw Jesse James, she gestured for Julie to sit.

"You have a nice home, Mrs. Preston."

"Thank you, and it's 'Miss.' I'm Betty's sis; she was taller." She raised her hand above her head.

"I see. Yes."

The woman then sat with knees together, hands folded in her lap.

"Miss, we, the State Criminal Investigation Unit, periodically go through our older files, trying with fresh eyes to see if anything new has developed." Julie paused.

Neither curiosity nor concern showed on the woman's face.

Julie opened her black imitation leather portfolio and pulled out her notes on the missing Betty Preston. "According to this information, your sister was reported missing on October 1, 1995, by a family member."

Nothing was forthcoming from the woman, except that now she began rocking slightly.

"It says here that Betty disappeared on the way home from school and that—"

"We took our regular shortcut across farmland through a bunch of woods."

"You and your sister?"

"She was stubborn."

"How do you mean?"

"She said she wanted to use the little girl's room. I said to wait til she got home; she went anyway. God save us, I continued on." She recounted these events as if she had gone over them many times before.

"I realize this incident must be difficult to relive, Miss Preston. Is there anything about that day that has come to you over the years that wasn't said or discussed or passed on to the police?"

She shook her head, never taking her eyes off Julie.

"Are your parents . . . still about?"

She nodded again.

"It says in the initial report that the mother of the child—your mother—at first denied her daughter was missing, saying—"

"'She wouldn't leave me, my little darling. No, she wouldn't run away from her loving mother.'"

Julie looked down at the police report. The woman repeated her mother's words verbatim. "Do you live here alone, Miss Preston?"

Once again the solemn stare, the slight action of the head. Julie busied herself with her paperwork, and then thanked the woman and started for the door. She turned at the entranceway to thank her once again only to see the slight figure turn her back on Julie and walk to a shelf of knickknacks in the far corner of the living room. Julie saw her take something and hide it in her hand.

"I walk to the spot each day; it keeps me sane." She cocked her head, and a smile crept out, allowing Julie to share her strangeness.

"The spot?"

The woman edged past her and then made several slow turns around the living room. She held out her treasure. It looked as if it were a piece of wood. Julie took it

and turned it over in her hand—a Y-shaped stick not unlike a slingshot.

"Is this from the area where your sister was . . . taken?"

"It smelled of pee-pee, so I brought it home."

Julie set the wood object back on the shelf and rubbed
her hands on her slacks. "When was this?"

Beverly Preston once again paced the living room.
"Yesterday. I have others. Would you like to see?" Without waiting for an answer, she hurried toward the kitchen
door.

Julie followed.

Standing beside a shed attached to the house, Preston
signaled to Julie as she disappeared inside.

A dark flight of stone steps led down into a cellar under
the house. The air cooled. Julie's breath floated in a white
mist in the dank enclosure. She swatted away cobwebs that
crossed her forehead. Preston stepped into the center of
the room and snapped on a single naked lightbulb hanging from a floor joist. "In the summer, I sit down here to
escape the heat."

Under the bulb, a straight-back kitchen chair faced a
long table stacked with shoes and frayed floral dresses. In
the middle of the display, a foot-high cracked statuette of
Christ, his arms spread wide as if presenting Beverly Preston's homage to her missing sister.

"If she returns, her clothes probably won't fit her."
She shrugged, her palms facing up in a "What can you do?"
gesture.

Julie walked the length of the table, observing several more Y-shaped pieces of wood, teacups, a thick, old-
fashioned comb, a toothbrush in a wood tumbler, and a
mason jar. "What's in the bottle?"

"It's his."

Julie took the offered object. Curled in a lump at the bottom of the jar, a ring threaded through a stiff, dirt-matted chain. All of it appeared as if undisturbed for a number of years. Julie also eyed insect remains at the bottom of the jar.

It struck her, the woman's way of never answering a question. "What are the holes in the top of the jar for?"

"When you catch a bug fresh from its den, it must breathe." She hummed while circling the room, her arms paddling like a dog trying to swim. "Run Betty run. The house is on fire."

Finally, a straight answer. "May I take this to have it examined?"

"He would like me to have it when he appears."

Julie replaced the jar on the table and followed Beverly Preston up the stairs. She thanked the woman and left. Once in her car, she called Walker.

"I'll get a warrant from the judge," he said. "You think she'll hide the damn thing?"

"No, I don't think so, Cap. By the way, it has a heavy chain strung through it as if someone wore it not on their finger but around their neck. And, oh yeah, this woman, she's mental, but in the end, I think she'll give it up. She just has to be handled gently. She is, to put it kindly, disturbed."

8

Cold case files appealed to Julie. The exactitude of it all satisfied her. In her regular capacity as a detective, much of the work had become routine, her years of police work at times punctuated by chaos. On the whole, she settled into admin duty in her cozy basement spot.

She asked permission from Captain Walker to drive downstate to speak to the uncle of another missing female. While polite enough on the phone, the man assured her that the police had interviewed him at the time.

"On the document, it says here, Mr. Drew, you explained to an Officer Roberts, and I quote, 'While at work, I was notified that Trudy, my niece, had gone missing. At the time, I didn't think much of it. The girl always stayed out late, disobeying her mother's rules on curfew. I tried to reassure my sister that she would show up with a lame excuse, but it turned out not to be the case.' Would you say it was an accurate reflection of the situation?"

Julie sensed hesitation.

"At the time, yes. Since then I've given it a great deal of consideration."

"Mr. Drew, would it be possible to meet me either later today or tomorrow?"

Once again the man paused. The phone clicked, another wait, and then William Drew again. "I've moved a few things around, Miss Worth. Would noon tomorrow in the factory cafeteria be convenient?"

After receiving instructions on how to get to the plant, Julie went to Walker, who reluctantly gave permission for the trip.

"When I assigned you that shit detail in the basement, Worth, you *do* realize it was an alternative to administrative leave? A low-stress, take-it-easy-and-heal kind of assignment? You got that, didn't you?"

"Yes, and I'll make the trip downstate as disagreeable as possible."

"I'll contact Adams in the southern district and let him know you're in the area," he said smiling. "Don't enjoy yourself too much, Worth, or I'll have to punish you by putting you back on regular duty. Scoot on out of here, Sherlock."

9

The plant, as described, looked like a series of older buildings—starting at the front of the property—and stretching for a hundred yards back into a housing development. The office building, however, was new and bordered a series of row houses along its fence line.

The factory cafeteria was a wing of one of the older buildings, built as an afterthought, its long single story capped with a red-tiled pitched roof.

Mr. Drew's secretary met Julie at the entrance. A pleasant young woman who pretended to be interested in Julie's work.

"How exciting for you, dealing with all the lowlifes. Lots of stories, yes?"

They made their way through the noisy seating area of the cafeteria into a back private room. She left Julie at the doorway.

"Mr. Drew got caught with a long-distance call he couldn't avoid. He'll be out soon."

The room was comfortable enough, if somewhat stark.

Photos on the walls of old white guys in suits and ties. A conference table for twenty dominated the wood-paneled enclosure. A settee and two overstuffed chairs semicircled a fake fireplace. Julie saw a setting for two arranged at a heavy oak coffee table. She was halfway through Drew Inc.'s rogues' gallery when the door behind her opened, and in walked Mr. William Drew. A nice-looking man, but he appeared slumped by the pressure of his responsibilities. His short, neat hair and tight, dark mustache complemented his navy blue suit.

"Miss Worth, so sorry to keep you waiting." He glanced at his watch and motioned for Julie to have a seat at the place setting closest to the faux fireplace. "Lunch will arrive shortly. I've taken the opportunity to order for us. Short ribs and potatoes fine?"

It was going to be a long afternoon for a white-meat-only girl detective.

"I'm a little short on time, Miss Worth. So can we get to it?"

Julie noticed that he took another purposeful look at his watch. She had reviewed the file once before this meeting and knew there weren't many outstanding issues. "After that initial phone call from your sister about your niece missing, can you tell me what transpired?"

"My sister called several times over the next few hours, each successive call more rife with hysteria." He leaned back into the leather chair. "I finally called the police for her. I must confess about having admitted to myself ad infinitum over the years that I truly didn't believe anything wayward happened to Trudy."

"What did the police do?"

Drew fussed with a pleat on his dark blue trousers.

He seemed reluctant to meet Julie's eyes. "I admit I called the mayor, who at the time was a friend and shareholder in Drew Inc."

"So it was the mayor who notified the authorities?"

"Miss Worth, how can I say this . . ." Drew picked at an errant thread on his Canali jacket to distract himself. "I explained to Mayor Bishop that Trudy was a troubled teenager, probably out on a tear, and that I hated to bother him with such a trivial matter. But, and this is the part that's difficult for me"—he took deep breaths—"I said, 'Tom, as a favor, drop the police chief a note describing the missing girl so I can say I did what my sis asked of me. Is that possible?'"

She didn't honor him with a reply.

"My sister died two years ago still not knowing what became of her daughter. And me, I've lived these last seventeen with the burden of knowing that if I'd acted in a more expedient fashion, maybe just by pushing with more alarm, Trudy might still be with us."

Julie's instinct was to reassure Drew that no, he did the right thing. That's exactly what the man wanted to hear, but she resisted the urge. "Was there ever any word from Trudy at all; any clues as to what might have happened?"

He glanced once again at his watch and pushed an intercom button on the table. "Do you need help in the kitchen, Arthur? Should I assign someone from the office to give you a hand? Expedite, please." He jabbed at the intercom. "Sorry, getting back to your question. No, there was never any word. It baffled the police. She vanished. Not a trace, no indication of kidnapping, ransom notes. Nothing."

Lunch arrived complete with salad, cooked vegetables, and rolls. The short ribs, Julie figured, could be covered with her napkin. Drew ran through the history of the company, explaining the partnership with his father's best friend and how they worked so hard in the early years to create Drew Inc.

"Are they all gone? Early employees, someone in the company who might have known Trudy? Anyone surviving the years?"

Drew turned to a large photograph over the fireplace. "That's my father, William, on the right, along with his partner, Sidney Randall, both long since gone."

"Mr. Drew, I know you're a busy man, but could a list of employees who were working here at the time of your niece's disappearance be drawn up? Those who are still here?"

She watched him making circles through his potatoes with the tip of his fork. "What would that do? How could that help after all these years?"

"I'm not sure it would, sir, but it might be a way of finding out if anyone recalled anything. Over the years, there may have been a flash of something, maybe unexpressed."

He put down his fork. "I need to hustle out. My secretary will get that list to you. Terribly sorry. Anything else? Can you find your way?"

After assuring Drew that she indeed knew her way, he left. Mr. William Drew, a heart attack in the making.

Charles Clegg had friends in high places. His oldest and dearest happened to be ensconced on the top floor of the Drew office building.

Deedee's closet-sized office was squeezed between the elevator shaft and the men's room. Pushing fifty, and having been with Drew Inc. since the beginning, she had started in the shipping department and worked her way both vertically and horizontally through the corporate maze. Her oversized chest worked for her, guiding her unerringly through a sea of wannabes as if it were a ram on the front of a huge tugboat. She weathered the early start-up days, the indecisiveness of Drew Sr., the lean seasons of cutbacks, and the happy days of acquisition. Shuffled and fired, rehired and replaced, Deedee was still there, in all of her bosomy glory.

"Hello. Deidre Watts, how can I help?"

The voice at the other end of the phone came off gruff and sexual. "I'm below you looking through the concrete floor at the bottom of your chair. If you do not obey my every command, I will increase my optic powers and bore through steel and oak to get to your innards."

"Charles, you nasty boy," she said with a grin. "What's up?"

"Price of eggs, stock market, and my favorite body part."

"That's nothing new, is it? Hold on a second while I close the door. So it's one of two things. You're horny for older women, or you want the latest in female office gossip. Or, a third unlikely possibility, you want to borrow money. What is it, handsome?"

"How about after satisfying the first two—which can be done at the same time—we discuss your paying for services rendered, which is not the same as borrowing money. What do you say?"

"I say you're full of crapola, Charles Clegg. I've got a conference call coming up, so I'll have to hightail it. By the way, Wad is pissed at your absenteeism. How do you get away with it?"

"I'm cute, smart, handsome, and have an ironclad agreement, okay?" He started to sing. "There was a new girl in town, she looked like an Elvis-ex, and she was sexy, uh-huh." He hummed, then, "Hey, been wondering about any new hot numbers I might have missed applying for work, that kind of thing. You know me, sweet stuff."

"Nah, afraid not, Bigstuff. Ah, wait, a hottie paraded through the cafeteria with Wad's secretary during lunch yesterday, headed for the exec dining room. Five nine, a hundred forty-five pounds, looked like she might have great legs. A no-bullshit type. Pretty in a tough way. Why am I going on like this?"

"No, no. Don't stop. I'm getting all lit up."

"Got to run, Hornytoad," Deedee interrupted their nonsense. "Give me a call later, okay? Oh, by the way, that toughie I was telling you about is not your type."

"Why, is she a lesbo?"

"Maybe, I don't know, but she was carrying a gun. I saw it under her jacket. She had state police biz with Wad. Gotta run. Call me, please." She lowered her voice. "I'm horny and available." She hung up.

Charlie laughed. He envisioned a mercy hump in his near future.

"William Drew, please."

"May I ask who's calling?"

"Charles Clegg."

"Mr. Clegg, nice to hear from you. Let me check if Mr. Drew is available." After the usual delays and "So sorrys," Charles was asked to call back at three o'clock, but it didn't matter, as he had lots of free time, so he decided to take a drive before the appointed call.

The woods were always a comfort to him, the soaring straight pines enveloping him in a cocoon of shade. His complex love of the timberland. The rational part of Charles knew that he was not immortal, but at times he thought that his dark, exciting secrets would live on long after he was gone. He loved his walks, especially at night. The hawks and owls calling to their brethren. The whippoorwills repeating their names endlessly.

He'd always resisted leaving his "event" participants on his sacred land; it seemed sacrilegious. But it would have been comforting to have them closer, to be able to visit as old friends would, to share more often his scarf of treasure.

"William, how are you? How's tricks?"

"I'm passable, Charles, just passable. What's up?"

"Something have to be 'up' for me to call, my friend? Just thought I would check in."

"Are you in the building?"

"Just out and about, Willy."

"Our third-quarter profits are up a point and a half. We just signed a new agreement with Local 39, which will help the bottom line."

"Did they cave on the medical business?"

"'Caved' is the right word. The recession reaped some benefits for us. These tank-busting hard-line union jokers are just as worried about jobs as everyone else. They're sneaking around trying to make covert backroom deals, mostly looking out for numero uno. What's with the phone call?"

"Just checking on the status of my favorite chief executive officer. Anything exciting going on, anybody pregnant, filing more harassment claims, sick with the flu, herpes, hiccups, anything like that, Billy? Have you got a new squeeze?"

"Please, I'm a married man."

"Thou doth protest too much, methinks. Doth thou?"

William laughed a bit at Charles's attempt to humor him. "If you must know, I did meet an attractive lady yesterday."

"Tell me quick, Billy. I'm jiggling my underclothes."

"Don't get lathered up. It was nothing; a woman from upstate, a government employee. Incidentally, how did we ever get to be so chummy? You are, I must remind you, still an underling. An employee."

"The party of the first part shall honor said agreement pertaining to—"

"Yeah, yeah, right. Got it, spare me. The poor orphan child with the boo-boo on his hip."

"Broken hip, to be more accurate. Along with a broken leg and, I might add, the loss of a sweet friend, one Bink Caldwell."

They waited through an uncomfortable pause.

"Tell me about this attractive member of the opposite sex. Was she trying to pierce the corporate hierarchy? Sexual harassment complaints in the workplace? Some people have all the fun. Were you caught massaging shoulders, pinching behinds?"

"No, nothing quite so interesting. Just an inquiry of ancient times and events." He stopped talking.

"Are you holding out on your trusted employee and loyal friend, sir?"

"A woman from the state police had a routine inquiry about that past unpleasantness concerning my niece." The conversation seemed to be wearing out Drew. "You remember that, don't you, Charles?"

He took the appropriate amount of time in answering to fortify his seeming concern. "Sorry if I made light of what must still be a trying part of your life." *Suck it up, asshole.* "Is there anything I can do?"

"No. It was all routine. They're reopening several cases of disappeared girls stretching back a ways. I'm sure nothing will come of it, just some bureaucratic bullshit busywork for a cop. Must be a slow crime week."

Charles produced a laugh, trying to cover his interest. "What's her name? I know a couple state-police types up there."

"Ware or something close. No, Worth. Yeah, Julie. Nice enough girl. Tough but still feminine. Thorough. Listen, pardner—gotta run. Call soon, will you?"

"Yeah, right. I'll do that." No need for panic. A routine tying-of-loose-ends inquiry. Julie Worth. Maybe out of caution, take a closer look.

11

He stood outside the house. The moon had not yet risen. Night birds broke the quiet evening hush. At least six hours had passed, his pace along the sparsely populated road slow and deliberate, occasionally broken by contrived jogging when the odd car approached. A billed cap helped fake an image of an avid health nut. He approached the darkened house and once again slowed. Earlier, he had watched from behind an abandoned shed from across the road. An early-model black Jeep Wrangler was parked outside the house with motor running, lights dimmed. Someone—it looked like a teenaged girl, with long blond hair—darted back and forth in front of a lit window. The car's horn sounded an impatient toot. The moon started to rise by the time the girl appeared at the front door. She carried several duffel bags and sprinted toward the awaiting SUV. Exchanging words with the driver from the passenger-side door, she swore as she ran back into the house and disappeared. Then the porch light was doused, and the silhouetted figure once again raced to the car.

He felt they were gone for the night, but he continued to pace what he now considered his nightly rounds. They'd be back; he had to be patient. Perhaps one of them, maybe both, would be introduced to his ring of *C*. The view from Cameltop.

12

B *ack in her* suite of private offices—or basement, as
most people referred to it—Julie continued her
dogged pursuit of past wrongs revisited. Three
weeks into administrative duty, she so far she had spoken
with one, and met with two of four missing girls' relatives—
diminished capacity Beverly Preston and William Drew.
The redneck woman on the phone seemed uninterested.
Gut feelings couldn't always be trusted, but in the case of
the factory boss, she was confident that he'd told her all he
knew about niece Trudy.

Pastor Garthwait, the name being unusual, sounded familiar
to Julie. His listing in the phone book came up the same
as in the 1995 police file. After listening to eight bars of
"Onward Christian Soldiers" on the phone before a human
came on, Julie readied herself for a holier-than-thou pastor.

"We are blessed on this God-given crystal day. Would
it be amenable to meet here at God's temple within the
hour, Miss Ward?"

"It's Sergeant Worth, and let's say twenty minutes."

Julie glanced at the grey muddled sky and thought it would be more likely to produce rivers and lakes than crystal.

On the way out of the building, she bumped into Walker leaving for lunch.

"Worth!" he called out over his shoulder. "Check with evidence, they've got something on the ring we picked up from your Preston gal, okay?"

Julie parked out front and let herself into the modest white frame building. "Reverend?"

Pastor Garthwait sat in the front pew of his church, a well-worn King James Bible open on his lap. He turned, stiff-necked, to Julie's greeting. "You are Sergeant Worth?" He continued, not waiting for a reply. "I've been sitting here contemplating"—he motioned for Julie to sit in the pew next to him—"why one covets. The Book states one should not covet our neighbor's wife nor his house nor—"

"Excuse me, all good thoughts, but could we speak of your daughter's 1995 disappearance?"

The man held the Bible to his forehead.

"Sir?"

"Sorry, I needed to give thanks for this message from Him, of our departed."

"To be honest, there isn't any message as such." She wasn't sure if any of this would be pertinent. "As I explained on the phone, this is just a follow-up on what we, in the department, refer to as a cold case."

"She left as she lived, swiftly and without regard. There was a man, several times seen in the back of the church." Once again the pastor stretched his neck toward the entrance of the gallery. "Just there, close to the choir loft steps. In thinking back upon it, I recall a smile, not one of warmth but of knowing a vast hidden story—an enigmatic presence."

"Did you at the time describe this man to the police?"

"Yes, I gave as his description 'a Satan-like presence, diminutive in stature.' There seemed a glow surrounding him. Others who witnessed him were blinded by his aura."

"Was there ever a composite drawn of this man?"

"I don't recall. But those who did attest to his presence now dwell in heaven. Gone the way of all flesh."

Julie read several eyewitness observations in the reports of a stranger loitering in and around the church several Sundays preceding the young woman's disappearance, but the accounts were vague and contradictory. One report detailed the man as being middle-aged and white. Another described him as clean cut with slicked-back dark hair; a third said he was definitely Hispanic. But all described him as being of less than average size.

"Was there ever any word at all from your daughter?"

"I speak to her at night when the calm envelops the earth. Her image comes to me as a shivering child spending the dark night naked without clothing and without covering against the cold, driving her sainted mother to utter distraction. The last we knew of her, she snooped through her mother's jewelry box."

"Was there anything of value missing?" Julie didn't recall any mention of jewelry in the report.

"Value, you mean as in worth? Monetary? One cannot measure what one holds dear. Did it have merit, what she took? Her great-grandmother's gift to her daughter and then passed on. Value, you ask?" His voice rose, agitated as if sermonizing. "Yes, a deep, painful keepsake; a treasured inheritance. My grandmother was an ancestor of the

American Revolution; she treasured her one true item of vanity."

"And what was that, sir?"

"A circled bangle, my child." Once again he raised the Bible to his forehead, this time with his left hand, his right reaching into Julie's lap to clasp her folded hands. He held them for just a moment, and then excused himself, walked past the pulpit, and through a paneled door.

Julie made her way to her unmarked Charger, her hands damp from the reverend's unexpected pawing. *What in the hell is a bangle encircled?* she thought. A piece of jewelry with a band around it? A bauble with a band? Baubles, bangles, bright shiny beads. *Ah, Kismet,* she mused. Truly a stranger in paradise. Considering the business she was in, "paradise" was too strong a word.

The one constant in the eyewitness accounts, a "less than average size" description. Cold cases should be left just that. Cold.

The woman in charge of the evidence locker was of a different sexual persuasion. Being rebuffed by Julie several years earlier had made her less than cooperative ever since. Rather than a "What's up?" or a "How's it going?" greeting, she met Julie with a below-freezing attitude.

"I'd like to take a peek at the evidence in that missing-child case. The name was Preston, I think."

"You think? No evidence number? You believe we catalogue evidence under 'I think'?"

Julie examined her shoes, smoothed out her belt, and sipped in air. "Check under 'Preston,' and if it's not there, give Captain Walker a call on his cell. He told me to take a look at this case. He didn't have an evidence number, but

I'm sure if you disturb him at lunch, he'd be glad to give it to you. Okay, Maddy baby?"

The woman went into the back of the cage and returned holding a file box with an envelope attached. "Sign the register."

Julie did so, noting time and date. "You might want to put this in your memory bank—one little word for the future, Madeline."

"What's that, Juliette?"

"The word is 'Sergeant.' Don't forget it."

The woman gave a halfhearted salute and returned to a table piled with bagged and tagged evidence.

The ring sat nestled in a layer of cotton. Julie used tweezers to lift and turn the piece in the light. The lab's exam hadn't taken much of the caked debris from the object. Here and there a bit of shiny metal but, all in all, much the same. In the envelope, a description of the article.

1. item 5205. Preston estate.
2. one gold ring. Size 6
3. age of item. Undetermined.
4. missing jewels on left side.
5. blurred insignia. Possible "delta" letter in ring's center

It continued on for almost a full page. Most of the information, routine.

"Do you have a magnifying glass, Madeline?"

The property clerk reached into a drawer and handed a rectangular magnifying glass to Julie. "Sign, please."

Julie looked closer at the ring and spoke to Madeline at the same time. "If I have to sign for this glass while standing at this counter for thirty seconds, I'm going to make your fucking life miserable." She lowered the glass and tossed it back to Madeline.

"Why you giving me shit?"

"I think you're aware of why. A simple 'no' doesn't seem good enough for you. I have nothing against your lifestyle, but it's not for me, and you seem to have taken offense. Get over it. That's the last I'll say on the subject. Give me an evidence withdrawal form." Julie signed it and went to her file room on the same level.

In the strong light above her worktable and with her own high-powered magnifier, she discerned an embossed, damaged *B* or *D* for the first and third letters, and in the center of the ring, a triangular shape that looked like the letter *A*, or Greek symbol for alpha.

Julie continued to consider the ring and once again scanned the item with the magnifying glass. The third letter might also have been an *R* without the bottom stem of the letter. On closer examination, she saw a spot where glue could have held the diagonal leg of the letter. But it didn't make sense, a fraternity or sorority ring with an *R*.

13

A *full moon* lit the sky in a blue-grey wash, and trees and bushes cast dark shadows against gently rolling hills.

The lone figure stood on what local hikers referred to as Cameltop, the large, rocky hump being a challenge even to the best outdoorsmen. The night climber had a series of steps that only he knew. It had been, over the years, a simple matter of moving a few rocks at the bottom of the escarpment. When he was finished with his nocturnal ascent, he would place them back, sometimes sprinkling a little dirt into the cracks. He liked the idea that his vantage point was secluded and, for the most part, inaccessible.

The view became his salvation; his only real fancy. He had been careful all these years to come only at night and preferably when natural light lit his way.

He sat on his familiar rock, a smooth-surfaced bench-like outcrop. The cool night air tingled his hands as they pressed against the age-polished stone.

Somewhere beyond the nearest hill, in a valley, a coyote yelped its eerie song. The sound repeated through the earth's canyons.

He took the binoculars from the padded case and scanned the night, the slight swaying of pines, their crooked branches spiraling upward. Near the middle of this dark panorama, nestled between a silver stream and a gentle pasture, lay a shadowed group of boulders looking as if, over the years, they'd grown tired of their loftier homes and rolled gently down into the glade below. From his vantage point looking down, they formed a large C. He felt it vain but couldn't help himself, each stone a triumph.

From a backpack, he retrieved a silk scarf, carefully folded with four corners tied. His keepsakes—the only evidence of a life filled with the complete domination of other humans. He ran his hands over the smooth cloth, relishing the objects inside. Each treasure elicited a separate but distinct pleasure. As he jiggled the contents, a wide metal bracelet pressed against the sides of the bundle. His fingers felt the cross with its jeweled exterior wrapped with a soft woven cord. A thin gold watch and a metal American flag clinked together. Missing was his most treasured of all—the ring and chain. He had searched the area where he was sure it had been lost. After all these years, maybe he would look once more. He began his ritual as an errant cloud shifted its position. Liking the unexpected darkness, he reminisced. Starting with the first, his trousers tightened. He smoothed the offending bulge several times and squeezed his eyes tight.

By the time he had finished reliving the history of his stony quintet, he was breathing heavily, his trousers at his knees. His bright celestial cousin peeked through her shaded cloud. He shouted in joy and anguish.

Each time, the same melancholy settled in his chest and then gradually spread through him. He made it a point to descend his stony pinnacle before his wretchedness got the best of him, always vowing that this would be the last. A part of him laughed at his empty pledge, for he knew there would be another pilgrimage to his site. But he would try not to; he would be strong.

His supreme hidden life. The pursuits. But maybe, just a final and triumphant event; an homage to his silent years of red meetings.

Charles knew right from wrong. No conflict there. But doing wrong had been such a part of his life that it seemed an old friend making a decision. He recalled the fall of '95, the comfort he felt when he dispatched his disciples.

The decision had been to quit, to give up his moonstruck needs, to squelch his desires in more conventional ways. As his former keeper, nee "shitso minder," or better yet, county-paid father figure, used to say, "Shrimp, face it. You'll never be a normal, desirable person. Deal with it, shit-for-brains."

He tried religion: went to a church where he made an unusual alliance. A lady who, marked by her relationship with God, had been transformed into a hedonist slave, a believer of the flesh. He then took her to the depths.

No, in fact, religion didn't work for him. But through sheer force of will, he began to taper off, his conquests became fewer and for the most part ended in simple degradation and the reduction of his captives' ability to think of themselves as decent humans.

He felt good about his progress. An advanced study in self-denial and a lot less risky, as his disciples were oftentimes not coherent enough to report what happened to them.

Charles Clegg, the happy philanthropist. He reasoned the sparing of human life to be God's will. The Almighty empowered him to give life back and make these women a symbol of his work.

Maybe if he deviated from the prescribed on occasion, he would be forgiven. Completing his ritual at the height of his special mountain, it would be only a matter of hours before he would be forced to the edge of oppression.

Anger and desire split his life. They became mixed, with desire usually winning. Early on, dreaded anger took over, culminating in what he called his Scarlet Rendezvous.

14

*H*ey, *Dev, how* about I take you to lunch?" Julie offered.

"What you hungry for, partner?"

"The Mexican joint up north where we caught that parole violator?"

"Let's do it. We'll go in separate cars. I need to make a couple stops after lunch."

Julie started to leave the department parking lot. She saw Todd with his cell phone to his ear, waving at her. He held up his left hand to signal five and pointed for her to go on. He added a halfhearted tap at his chest. She glanced once in her rearview mirror to see him going back into the station. If she understood correctly, he'd be along in five minutes along with his yearning heart. Knowing her partner, it would take a world-class prison break for him to miss an invitation to lunch. She thought a lot of the guy, but mostly like a kid brother.

She liked the drive up north. The paved road bordered with Lombardy poplar led immediately into the country. Although an isolated road, folks on the north side of town used it regularly as easy interstate access.

Julie looked forward to lunch. Rodrigo's La Playa, located next to a busy interchange, specialized in seafood. Her favorite, a ceviche-style shrimp cocktail.

It seemed quiet for a weekday. Traffic, light, on the two-lane blacktop road. Another week of basement duty, and she would be back in present-day crime investigation.

In some ways, her penance in the dark confines of the storage files proved to be good for her. Rather than being held to the strict accordance of investigation, she took her time analyzing items long since restricted to the cellar. Maybe not a quantum leap but a minor revolution.

Revolution. What if that third letter in the ring was an *R*? That would make it *DAR*, a society of women who were accepted in a special organization only after proving a direct bloodline link to the American Revolution. Like Garthwait said, his grandmother had been an ancestor. Daughters of the American Revolution. *Okay, Dick Tracy. What now?*

She wondered about the link between the Preston girl and the Garthwait kid. The reverend's daughter takes the ring from her mother's jewelry case and splits. Somehow she meets up with a bad dude who takes the ring. *And probably more than that.* The creepy bastard can't wear the ring, so he strings it around his neck. The Preston girl rips it off while trying to save her life. *Makes sense.*

Something caught her eye. A dark grey Ford F-150 pickup truck eased in behind her. Not exactly tailgating but just a bit too close. She slowed, not wanting to deal with the guy. She assumed it was a guy—she couldn't tell—a baseball cap and sunglasses completing a dark silhouette. She waved him on. Instead, he dropped back. She dismissed the person as just one more in a legion of bizarre drivers.

She passed through what was not a town or even a community but merely a wide place in the road. A general store, an abandoned gas station, and a couple grain elevators.

After slowing through the burg and then at a Thank You for Visiting sign, she accelerated back to sixty-five in the fifty-five. A cop should have some privileges. Tired of a political hack ranting about the disillusionment of America, Julie reached down to lower the radio volume as the sound of a loud, straining engine came up next to her. The driver, as he pulled even, ducked his head.

She eased up on the gas, gripping the wheel as the pickup stayed next to her, and then started to move past. When almost clear, the truck cut in front of her, crashing into her left-side front fender. Julie's car jerked violently to the right. She fought the wheel, trying to correct back to the left. The right rear wheel of her vehicle caught the gravel verge and began to lose traction.

She wrestled her Charger back onto the pavement, stomping the brakes, only to have the wheels lock up. A fleeting thought of a defensive driving course flashed to mind, but in the moment, she forgot everything. The pickup continued to slam against her left side.

A concrete abutment appeared to the side of her. The impact snapped the front of the car back toward the right and up and over the three-foot-high buttress. The car spun 180 degrees toward where she started and then plunged, cocked to one side, into the deep culvert bordering the road.

The world turned upside down. Quick-cut movie images of bending steel and shattering glass. Dirt, papers, cups, and food wrappers whirled in a cyclone of confusion. Her head bounced hard against the door post and then rocketed back the other way. She slammed against the center console, her arms flopping hard against the right-side dashboard.

A suspension in near silence as her car went airborne, and then everything was repeated. She tried to grip the passenger-side seat belt, but the loose webbing flapped at her. The car slowed, spun onto its nose, and then the noise stopped. Dazed, Julie felt the car rock gently onto its back. Her seat belt tightened; she was suspended upside down. Water from the culvert rushed into the ceiling of the car. It settled, finding its level. She tilted her head slightly to keep her nose and mouth free of the drainage.

Someone wearing pants, the legs had gotten wet, appeared where the windshield should have been. She tried pulling on the clasp of the seat belt with both hands and called for help. The legs moved. A head with a grey cap and dark glasses appeared at her side where the window used to be. Julie reached out toward the apparition and faded into a world of gauzy white clouds.

Voices came to Julie. One of them sounded like her mother.

"I don't think there's anything we can do."

"She has to be dead." Another voice, a man's.

Then a warbling unrelenting siren. More "Step back!" "Stand aside!" commands.

Julie wanted to push away from the confusion. She struggled to come from a far-off place, feeling cold water and a light continuing to brighten. She felt a force against her neck. Someone was trying to get her to do something; what was it?

"Let me through. Stand aside. Jules, it's Todd. Can you hear me?"

She tried to push away the fog; this had to be someone she knew.

"You'll be out soon." To protect her face, Todd placed a blanket over Julie's head. "Hold on, okay? Just hold on."

There began a repetitive whirring, like a motor scooter. A giant yellow claw danced before her eyes, then once again a terrible wrenching, metal being stretched and bent. A hand slipped to her neck along with the reassuring strong grip of her partner.

"He did it on purpose, his pant legs, wet. He turned his head and laughed." She came off delirious, but at least it was a sign she was alive.

Todd cradled her neck as the jaws of life continued to stretch the window opening. "Who? Who did it on purpose?"

Julie felt herself once again on the roller coaster, her stomach reaching up into her chest, her head pounding full of blood. "A grinning bastard in a dark grey pickup did it."

Someone ran a hand along the inside of her right armpit. "Can you feel that? Does it hurt?"

Several voices went back and forth in the room. "She's in what we call a fugue state—not conscious but not in a coma."

"When will she recover; come out of it?"

Julie knew that voice, someone close, a person she loved. She wanted to respond.

"Mom? Ma, open your eyes. It's Cheryl."

"In school. Why aren't you—"

"Mrs. Worth, I'm Dr. Jacob. How are you feeling?"

"Cheryl?"

"She's right here."

Julie felt her daughter's arms around her neck.

"I love you, Mom, you okay?"

Julie wanted to see her daughter. She forced her eyes open and tried to smile. Cheryl's face was close to hers. She saw a hand caressing her daughter's cheek. A faraway voice echoed as if coming from a cavern.

"She'll be fine. It will take time and rest."

That seemed like a good idea to Julie. She slipped away, feeling only a slight dampness on her hand that held her daughter's cheek.

"Mrs. Worth. Wake up."

"What?"

"You were having a bad dream. Heard you all the way down at the nurse's station. Do you need anything? Something for pain?"

"Okay, but no, I mean I'm not in pain. It was just a—"

"I'll change that damp pillowcase. You're perspiring a great deal."

"Maybe a glass of water. How long have I been sleeping? Have I been here awhile?"

The woman checked the chart at the end of the bed. "Says here you were admitted day before yesterday, so about thirty-six hours, give or take a few."

"Thank you. What's your name again, please?"

The nurse came closer to the bed and pushed her badge pinned to her chest. "Mary Ann. If you need anything, buzz me." She waited while Julie drank her water and then slipped out of the private room.

On her nightstand, the clock flashed three thirty. She dreamt of loud noises pounding in her ear, a dizzy roller-coaster ride, and a sharp pain under her ribs. A man with wet pants and a grin. Julie pulled her legs to the edge of the bed and tried to stand, her left leg bandaged in the same place where she had been sprayed with a shotgun. No real pain, just a dull ache. Her left arm and shoulder similarly swathed in white dressing.

A little rocky, she made her way to the bathroom. When she turned on the light, the image in the mirror above the sink startled her. A welt on her left cheekbone darkened her eye and the bridge of her nose. A bandage around her head kept a bulging compress above her ear in place. She was alive, if nothing else. Shuffling back to bed, she stopped at the window. Her room seemed to be at least five stories up. A bright neon hotel sign was to the east. Beyond, blinking lights of an all-night Walgreens.

Again, the image of a man came to her, defying a reaction. "Shoot me," he said. Her days had been so affected by guns, living each day strapped to a three-pound metal death piece. It had become her ambivalent life.

15

Hey, Sarge. *Did* I wake you?" Todd looked freshly scrubbed, his white shirt set off by a slim reddish tie. His hair, a modified brush cut.

"Nah, I've been awake off and on since three. What's up, Mr. Military?"

"Military? Please, those days are over. How you feeling?"

"Pretty good. Slept a lot in the last few days. In and out." *Mostly out.* Julie used the remote control to raise herself to a seated position. "Thanks for coming by. What you been doing?"

"Checking on that pickup truck." Todd pulled a chair up close to the bed.

Julie wracked her brain for a connection.

"We recovered it parked behind an all-night gas station on Central. All messed up on the right side, with paint from your Charger."

She tried faking it until she could catch up. "Was it—"

"Yeah, stolen. No prints. Belonged to a kid who worked in a body shop."

"Did he check out?"

"You have no idea what I'm talking about, do you?" Todd walked over to the window.

Julie tried to put things together. A sketchy recollection of a truck, a guy.

"You were forced off the road and—"

"Wait, wait. I got it." She sat up in her bed as Todd came back to the chair. "Some clown followed me, then pushed and forced me into a ditch or something, right?"

Todd seemed amused. "Yeah, go on."

"You're a prick, you know that? We were going on a case, in separate cars."

Todd held up his hand. "We were going to lunch, in separate cars."

Now she had it. The guy in the pickup followed her.

"The kid who owned the truck had a perfect alibi." Todd's voice soothed her. "He was on a flight from Chicago, parked in the airport lot, it all checked out. He put his parking stub in his overhead visor, typical—"

"The guy tried to kill me, Todd."

"How do you figure?"

"He came up too close behind me. When I signaled him by, he dropped back instead."

"Wonder why?"

"That bastard, 'cause we were coming up on that little farming burg. Ah, what the heck's the name." She'd gone blank again. "He waited until I sped up. I drifted off, thinking about lunch or something."

"Did you recognize him? Maybe some guy we busted holding a grudge, disgruntled con, anything?"

Julie's memory played tricks on her. She didn't know if she should mention the face in the window. And was there a gun? "Who was the first one there?"

"People were standing around looking at your car.

There was an EMT guy, but I would say I was the first one down next to you in your vehicle."

Julie thought about the man with the baseball cap. "You see anything around the car, like wet footprints?"

"Nah, it was all torn up. Mud, glass."

She still saw his image in her rearview mirror. "He came down and looked into, I think, the side window. That water from the ditch soaked his trousers. Did you hold my head out of the water?"

Todd nodded. "Yes."

"I was somewhat cockheaded trying to keep my nose above water, but he looked at me and grinned." She sighed, looking at all the dressings on her. "We need a good sketch artist."

"How much longer are you going to be in here?"

"Not long, I hope."

"I'm going to bring that fellow—you know, the fat one that works for the county. You guys see if you can come up with an image. You sure about this being deliberate?"

"Positive."

"I'll be back with him later today." Todd got up to leave. "Glad you're back among the living." He shuffled out as if there were more he wanted to say.

Todd was a good man. Too young for serious consideration, but still a heck of a guy.

16

A *day nurse* stage whispered from the door. "You have a visitor. It's after hours, but I'll bend the rules. Plus, he looks important. Keep it short, okay?"

Captain Walker appeared in the doorway. "How's our budding race car driver doing?"

"I'll let you know in a week or so," Julie said, smiling. "No broken bones, slight concussion, a few scrapes. Aggravated my leg again. Nothing too serious. Thanks for dropping by, Captain."

"Can't stay long, I came up yesterday morning, but you were out cold." He removed his hat. "I've got a couple people checking your past cases. Devlin told me both of you discussed whether this scumbag driver might have been a guy you had arrested. Did the sketch artist come up with anything?"

Julie shrugged. "We got an image of a guy in a cap and dark glasses with a shit-eating grin. Looks like a couple dozen guys I see every day."

Walker took a couple paces across the room and then back. "We find this guy, there's gonna be some serious ass

kicking. You need anything? Magazines, books, choco-
lates?"

"Thank you. No, sir." The man's caring touched Julie.
"The doctor says I'll be going home day after tomorrow.
Maybe take a couple days, if that's all right?"

He settled in closer to the bed and put his hand on her
shoulder. "Take whatever you need." He paused. "Damn,
girl. What am I going to have to do, put a chain on you?"
Walker smiled. "I've got a trooper sitting outside your door
until we can get clear on all this BS."

"Do you think that's necessary?"

"I think that I'm not going to have my people threat-
ened or run off the road while doing their jobs, is what I
think. His name is Davis. He'll be replaced at 0600, and
so forth and so on, until you're discharged. We'll see how
it goes after that." He then left, pulling his hat down hard
across his forehead.

Julie made her way to the window. A minute later,
Captain Walker emerged from beneath the overhang at the
hospital entrance. He looked distracted as he crossed the
parking lot. At one point, he stopped as if he'd forgotten
something but then continued on to his car. A big, tough
guy; bright and sensitive but always the solid policeman.
Her dad had been a similar man, having died way too soon.

She slept well, awakening only once in the night. A
brief flash about something to do with the evidence room
bothered her. She dismissed it and went back to sleep,
thinking that her life as a cop had recently become more
exciting than she would have wished for.

After lunch, Cheryl and Julie's friend Billie came to visit.
Her daughter brought news of school, boys, bullies, and
a recruiting drive for cheerleaders. "Wearing scanty pants

and tight stuff on top is so much crap. I'd much rather just wear a sign saying 'Available for sex. Apply within.'"

Julie tut-tutted a few times over Cheryl's free speech, but her daughter's indomitable free spirit always buoyed her.

Cheryl had been staying with Billie since the accident. Billie, an accountant, helped navigate the intricacies of Julie's divorce and became good buddies when they discovered they'd dated some of the same losers in high school. Billie went through a similar manner of uncoupling. Still annoyed with her own ex, she relished helping Julie and her attorney map out her divorce settlement.

"Do you mind, Willie, if Cher stays with you a bit longer?"

Wilhelmina had gotten used to Julie's nicknames for her. "Mind? Are you kidding? I wake up in the middle of the night having dreamt of cooking and cleaning up after darlin' Cher baby." She waved her chubby fingers at Cheryl and then let out a huge laugh. "Really, all kidding aside, not a prob. Right, baby doll?"

Cheryl imitated an infant and waddled across the room toward Billie. "Cherwee wants her Aunt Billwee to make her fave-fave pasta with sausage for sup-sup." She put her thumb in her mouth.

"Oh, now I know why she likes staying with you." Julie smiled. "You fall for all that baby-talk crap. So, what's going on with your latest? What's his name again?"

"My latest? I haven't a clue as to what you are speaking of, madam." Billie adapted a prim manner. "But it might be, of course, my Diet Constant. A lifestyle I've chosen to keep my figure within the boundaries of human decency."

Cheryl quieted her giggles, hand over mouth.

"Why, just today a woman at the market asked if I

knew where the sugar-free colas were kept. I took that as a compliment. A number of people stood about, and she could have asked anyone, yet she approached me." She fluttered her hand in front of her face as if she were having the vapors. "But if you're speaking of Jackass Johnnie, or Johnson, as he liked to be called, he beat it out of town after borrowing two hundred bucks from me."

Julie breathed a heavy theatrical sigh. "Ah, piss, Willie, where do you get these dudes?"

"The internet."

"You're joking."

"Yeah, I am. I met Jackass Johnnie at a gym I was trying out. One of those free workout deals. He said he was a masseur—yeah, right. Anyhow, Cher and I will be great. Don't worry about a thing, rocket woman. You just get well."

Julie marveled at her friend's humor. "If Cher misbehaves, call nine-one-one."

"*Mom*." Cheryl extended the last *m* to make the word last an eternity.

"What? I have to have your word that you'll behave. Word?"

"Yes. Word, Mom, word."

"Love you, kiddo."

The day had passed quickly, and Julie never missed feeling bliss when spending time with Cheryl. She loved her to distraction.

Twilight set in as she nestled into the chair by the window and gazed out at Downtown Saint Louis. She knew her pursuit of the truck driver would be consuming, and the cold cases would just have to wait. She smiled at the captain's admonishment of putting a chain on her. *Chain*. Why was that familiar? The chain was important because—the chain from the ring that Beverly Preston had found, the one she saw in the woman's hand, where was it?

She didn't know. It could be important. But it was too late to call the State Patrol property room and her new best friend Madeline. She'd do it in the morning.

The next day, Julie felt ridiculous being carted out to the entrance curb in a wheelchair, but no sense fighting policy. It felt great to be out. Todd picked her up for the drive home.

"Before I forget it, Big Man, can you do me a favor?"

"Sure, what's up?"

"I keep going back to this cold case I've been on. Who or why would a ring be put on a chain? If it wasn't the victim's, did it belong to someone else? A keepsake? The ring got taken into evidence, but I don't know about the chain."

"So what's your thinking about this, Sarge?"

"There might be some evidence there. The lab checked the ring and cleaned it but not the chain, at least as far as I know. Probably a long shot but worth checking."

C harles *walked through* Legionnaire's Park. Bronze statues of fallen heroes flanked the wide concrete paths. He pushed his hands into his trouser pockets, trying to get over the stupidity of his unsuccessful recon at the hospital. But doing stupid things these days seemed to be his life's blood. He just needed to see her, to glance at his handiwork, the beautiful dark bruises around her green cop eyes.

He wanted her. The brief newspaper account of Sergeant Juliette Worth's auto accident made no mention of criminal intent. Her prognosis, according to the paper, seemed good and her release from the hospital imminent.

He tried to think positively about the events; he slotted his feelings with ease. Whether successful or not, he'd manage to find something of the truth in what he liked to refer to as "the periodic arrival of the circus."

Rarely did the red-nosed buffoons appear; it was always men and women in their tights. The vision of the ringmaster thrilled him. The long-tailed jacket, flowing cape, often a white scarf draping his torso, and, of course, the hat. His fingers touched the silk brim of the topper as he turned to introduce his acts.

The bareback riders. Demure women sitting with both legs on one side of the shiny beasts, their buttocks protruding delightfully as they crouched upon the undulating hind quarters of their half-ton chargers.

His ringmaster would introduce a woman—a Rosetta or a Maria Elena—who would wrap her arm around a thick lanyard and then flange her legs straight out horizontally as stagehands towed her forty feet into the air. One foot secured into the inner thigh of her opposite leg, the vulnerable Maria Elena would begin to twirl faster and faster.

The Spanish web, a marvel of grace and sex. His hero would doff his hat and encourage the throng to applaud what he had wrought. Often in his daytime dreams, the women would follow his master of ceremony into a wooded glen, his cloak a blanket to perform upon. The white scarf for later, when dreams succumbed to reality.

He stopped in front of a seven-foot bronze soldier, hand in hand with a small boy. *How cheap.*

His rendition of the law enforcement pit maneuver had gone well, until the arrival of the first lookie-loos, and then the ambulance. He parked fifty yards down the road and then jogged back, hoping to finish the job. She saw him, but all cockeyed and jumbled through a maze of splintered glass and sharp-cornered metal. The wheels of her vehicle reached skyward, turning gently.

Not able to complete his task, he drifted back up the culvert and meandered through the growing crowd to the stolen truck, as wide-eyed late arrivals hurried to the overturned police car.

He recalled driving past the spectacle, seeing a tall,

sandy-haired young man in a dark sport coat bullying his way through the crowd. He looked like the one from the parking lot with the cell phone outside the police station. Were they lovers? He hoped so.

Then the deliberate drive back to town, to shed the illegally acquired truck. It disappointed him that his mission remained unfulfilled both on that day and the hour previous, which he'd spent wandering through the scrubbed halls of St. Mary's Hospital.

He sat under a flowering dogwood just off a well-used nature path.

Over the years, hikers expanded the winding trail that stretched for several miles across a vast wooded area, eventually leading to a rapidly flowing creek. In the distance, a small rundown community, unchanged over the years. A church steeple appeared slightly tilted, a general store and school long since abandoned by their people.

To the east, another group of houses, the road connecting the two settlements making a large semicircle around the dense woods.

He stopped along this road a blue moon ago to let the Nomad cool off.

While his overheated car sat ticking in its cooling process, the woods beckoned. He walked to a patch of berries alongside the road extending into a pine-covered wood. He thought back about the dense growth of underbrush and timberland, his several-day-long surveillance under this same dogwood.

Animated with constant chatter, their friendly arguing interrupted by genuine excitement at the discovery of an odd-shaped stone, peculiar-looking stick, or flower they couldn't identify. They seemed in no hurry to get home from school, and one of them always appeared too proud, a criticism ready to roll from her tongue. Sisters, undoubtedly. Similar but different. He tried to sort out how many years it had been—perhaps seventeen. The seasons melded into one enormous tangle.

He recalled having come back after the—what should he call it?—"occasion." But that word seemed too casual. He liked "happening." It felt celebratory, as if it had reason to exist. His mind wandered back to the search of the grounds for his keepsake, much of it having been trampled by the authorities. He blamed himself, not for the way it was lost but for his hubris—the sheer overbearing need to advertise his accomplishments by wearing something around his neck that should have been left in his nostalgic treasure trove along with the rest.

Rising now from his mossy seat, he searched once again—more out of curiosity than hope—the brush-covered area just off the hiking path. Wondering if the slight slope in the ground would, with the yearly rainfall, carry something as heavy as his prize farther toward the creek bed, he moved downhill.

The sound, when it came, startled him. A squeaky voice, an off-key song coming from the direction of the path. The key high and tremulous, full of wispy accusation.

The words seemed cobbled together. Something about a blue-eyed girl with a wandering heart.

> Come back, come back, ohh sweet little one,
> your kin doth miss you so.
>
> Oh run, please run. Blue Mountain girl,
> run home this bright clear morn.

He dropped down behind a thorny bush, the spiked branches tearing at his sleeves and forearms. A woman off the path with a stick made large circles around the area he had been searching. She scratched the earth and hummed, raising her head as if sensing the air.

> Run, oh Betty Blue, please run lest
> you be late for school.

18

J*ulie had been* home for three restless days. Her limp was only a bit more pronounced, and with her shoulder strapped and supported under a generous blouse and a cut above her ear covered by her hair, one might not have known she had survived a serious accident. They would have to overlook the discoloration between her eyes, however.

If anyone asked, she would blame it on her ex-husband. "He's six foot four, can't fight for beans, but he managed to clock me in the face. I got him good, though. A size-eight hard-toed oxford right in the man handle. Blah-blah-blah."

She called Todd. "What's doing, partner?"

"Funny you called. I was just waiting for an email from the lab before talking to you. I spoke to them this morning. Listen to this. After our talk in the hospital about ex-cons looking for tit for tat, I rechecked the debris from the stolen truck for evidence and ran a Kleenex tucked into the driver-side door pocket—mucus and a dot of blood on it. Guess what?"

"I don't know, but I'm sure you're going to tell me."

"None of the yahoos we've managed to blood-type

over the last—how long we been partnering? Seven years, something like that?"

"Yeah, so?"

"No match. The suspect has a rare AB negative blood type. One in one seventy."

"Come on, Devlin, for Christ's sake," Julie rattled. "Let's hear it. Who is it?"

"We don't know, but this blood type from the truck matches the one on traces located on the chain."

"What? You mean the chain holding the ring?"

"That's what I'm saying, Sarge."

Julie couldn't put it together. If it were true, whoever was driving the truck could have been in the woods abducting the Preston child all those years ago. But it didn't make sense. She didn't have any connection to the Preston case other than simply looking into it. How and why would the driver connect her? "Todd, this is wacky. You're saying it's a match, the blood?"

"The labs always give you that one-in-a-thousand crap but yeah, it's a match. Walker's gonna push the envelope on the lab business; splurged on a private company out of Chicago. For DNA, it'll take a while. What do you think? Does this jar your rehab efforts?"

"Too bizarre. I'll check with you later. Thanks for the info." Julie didn't believe in coincidence. In her job, it didn't pay. It was too easy. Also, how did the ring and chain get to the site if they weren't in the man's pocket or around his neck, and how did blood—evidence—get onto the chain?

Julie rubbed her thigh, trying to coax circulation back to her leg. She thought there might have been a struggle, and perhaps the kid grasped at the man's eyes or throat and came away with the chain, scraping the man's neck, leaving DNA.

Gonna get you, mister.

19

He *watched as* Julie limped to her car. He laughed, amused that she was disabled. She backed out of her drive, the right rear wheel of her Jeep bouncing over the curb, just missing the garbage can. If there were more time at the crash site, he could have rendered her persona non grata. A simple ninety-second choke hold seemed more in keeping with his intent.

Staying back several hundred feet, he tried to keep a two- or three-car separation between them. She drove across town, to a modest suburban community bordering a wooded area. Idyllic. Children playing ball in the winding streets, housewives conferring with neighbors, a genuine all-American homespun atmosphere.

He settled in next to a grassy dog park. Julie parked on a dead-end road in the midst of several other vehicles dotting the long, clean street. Taking a map from his glove box, he watched over the top of it as she made her way up the walkway to a frame house. Halfway there, a teenaged girl and a heavyset woman of Julie's age came out to greet her. A half-pint brown-and-white dog jumped around the trio as they drifted into the house. Charles drove around the nearby blocks several times, coming back to Julie's car. Continuing a bit farther to the end of the street, he parked at a For Sale sign in front of a new home. A sign reading Thousand Pines Estates, Phase Two hung on a nearby gated barrier.

While waiting, he surveyed the empty house. Trees and shrubs both in back and front provided good cover. A large yard at the rear of the house faded into a dense wooded area. He took down the name and number of the broker from the sign. He settled into his seat, keeping an eye on the street. Nearly an hour passed.

He watched the activity on the sidewalk near her car. The girl hugged his new favorite detective while the other woman looked on. It seemed as if the girl he'd seen at night darting in and out of the isolated house at North Point was probably the daughter, whom he thought might be staying with a friend while Miss Pain in the Ass Worth recuperated.

The dog scampered about, darting across the street and returning when called back by the heavyset woman. "Here, Scoot! Scooter, come boy!"

He enjoyed watching the tall woman's hampered movements; she seemed vulnerable getting into her car. He stopped at a Walgreens to call the Realtor.

"Hey, Sergeant, howzit goin'? You're looking pretty fit." Several of the officers in the unit working desk came over to say hello and wish Julie well. She tried walking without a limp or a shuffle, squaring her shoulders as if she just came back from vacation.

Captain Walker wasn't in, so she called Todd. "Devlin, what are you up to?"

"One eighty-five and holding." He seemed surprised to hear from her. "How about you?"

"Good, good. Hey, can you run me out to that Preston woman's house? I need to ask her a question."

"You want to speak to *el jefe*, or should we just wing it?"

"I'll leave him a note. Can you meet me out front in ten?"

They drove out without calling, Julie not wanting to deal with Preston on the phone. Todd was full of questions about her recuperation and when she would be back.

"I'm back. Just not officially or full-time, okay?"

They pulled up to the Preston house, which looked the same as the last visit. Tired and neglected. The yard, a combination of foot-high weeds and dandelions gone wild. She wondered how Miss Preston made do, living out in the country, so isolated, and especially after what had happened to her sister. Julie thought that Beverly Preston's run-down yard reflected the woman's state of mind.

"Hi, Miss Preston, remember me? Sergeant Julie Worth, State Patrol. This is my partner, Detective Todd Devlin. May we come in?"

Once again without answering, the woman left the door open and turned away.

Todd looked at Julie and shrugged. They followed Preston into the living room, where a musty combination of mildew and sauerkraut settled in the air.

"I won't take up much of your time. Just one question, if you will."

The woman nodded.

"Show me again, please, where you kept the ring and the chain?"

"By the by, when will I get it back—the ring? The smelly policeman that came for it with the foolish paper said he didn't know."

Julie knew she needed to tread lightly. "Miss Preston,

the items you gave up might be pertinent to an official investigation, which could lead to prosecution if we can—"

"My sister, by the way, would be thirty-three, day after tomorrow." She held her arms out in supplication, eyes moist, head cocked slightly.

Julie waited until Preston lowered her arms. "Please tell me the conditions in which the ring and chain were kept all these years."

She walked back to the knickknack stand that Julie had noticed earlier, and with her back to them, busied herself with a few items. She turned, her hands cupped around the mason jar.

"I brought the preserve jar up from the room below. I knew you'd be coming for it." She shoved the jar with its punctured holes in the top toward Julie. "Here."

"Can we take this?"

"Hoo-hah, better take it now than later when your stinky policeman comes back with another piece of paper." She paced. "As I said before, remember when you were here six months ago?"

It was four weeks.

"The slippery devil left it so he'd have an excuse to come for me. When he does, I'll be waitin'." She took a pair of household scissors from her apron pocket, making feeble stabbing motions in the air. "He crouched by the dogwood."

Julie glanced at Todd, who gestured back to her with an open hand, as if to say, "She's all yours."

"Miss Preston, what exactly do you mean when you say 'He crouched by the tree'?"

"Dogwood."

"Yes, of course, sorry. Dogwood. What did you mean?"

"I smelled him, his man scent." She straightened up.

"He stunk of sweat, piss, and men's cologne. I sang and pretended, like always." She hummed an off-key lament, breaking up the passage with a half-spoken "Fly home Betty Blue, fly home to your kin."

"And where is this area, Miss Preston?"

She headed for the back door.

Julie and Todd followed. "What is that old 'In for a penny' cliche?" he asked Julie.

"I'd give more than a penny for a pair of sneakers about now."

They walked behind Beverly Preston, Julie needing to pause every fifty yards to rest her leg. Then Preston pointed her long hickory walking stick to a dogwood tree that sat some thirty feet back from the path.

"That's where I smelled the demon, so I sang and fooled about."

Julie played along. "Let's take a look."

Todd started up a narrow path. "How do you get to a dogwood?"

Julie stopped to poke around in a thicket of thorns. "I give up, how?"

"On an animal path. Get it? Animal path. Dogwood."

"Yeah, yeah. Look at this, Mr. Funnyman." Julie examined the end of a branch, noticing dark spots on the leaves.

"What have you got?"

"Looks like fresh blood to me—not much, but enough for an analysis."

They searched the ground for footprints and then bagged the branch with the blood sample. When they looked up, they saw the back of Beverly Preston a hundred yards down the path, headed for home.

A long discussion began on the ride back to the station

about the mason jar and whether the cool basement preserved any possible DNA. They placed the glass container in a paper evidence bag. The blood sample was a long shot, and it might have been from an animal. But they would test it nevertheless.

G ood afternoon, Watson Real Estate."

"My name is Phillips. I'm interested in purchasing a home—"

"Let me put you on with one of the brokers."

He waited, subjected to a recording of Andy Williams singing something about a moon and a river and how wide the river was and—

"Hello. Cathy Watson. How may I help?"

"My name is Phillips, I'm new to town. My wife and I are interested in a home in the two-to-three-hundred-thousand-dollar-range." He guessed at the figure. "Suburban, maybe."

"Do you want a community feel or an individual home by itself?"

"Oh, definitely community. You know, dogs, cats, kids, trees, and such. Whatever, the full disaster."

"I have a couple things I could show you both. Nice developments. When would you be available, Mr. Phil?"

"Phillips. Sooner the better for us. We've got a couple of rug rats and a teenager that we need to get into school. Hold for a minute; I have to ask my wife something." He covered the phone and then came back. "Ah yeah, thanks. Excuse the interruption. Today would be fine."

"We have a three-bedroom in the Bristol Heights development, asking two-seventy-five, or a lovely two-story farmhouse-style new home in our own development on the west side."

Bingo.

"At the end of the street, lovely trees, somewhat isolated and yet a real part of the Thousand Pines Estates settlement. Large one-acre lots—"

"That last one sounds fine. When can I see it?"

"My husband and I will meet you at the office or the home at three o'clock. Would that work?"

They agreed on the time, and, given that he didn't want to sit through a half-hour sales pitch in the broker's car, they would catch up at the house.

He had an hour before the appointment to do a bit of a makeover. Tucking a compact throw pillow under his dress shirt, his jacket stretched tight over his middle-aged potbelly. A pair of mild-strength reading glasses from Walgreens and a beat-up snap-brim fishing hat.

The drive back to the subdivision filled him with expectation. Over the course of his twenty-year career of extracurricular activities, he had become many different people. Charming and polite, aggressive, and even a passive, milquetoast kind of fellow. But never in a real disguise. It should be fun. *Where's the harm?* he reasoned.

"How does this suit you, Mr. Phillips?"

They stepped out of their car, grinning like fools.

"Seems fine. May I walk around for a bit, get acquainted?"

The middle-aged couple gushed, "Make yourself at home." The house, being used as a model, was decorated with run-of-the-mill furniture spread generously throughout. The first-floor bedroom looked into the woods. He unlocked the window and pulled the curtain shut, and then inspected the whole house.

"You have done a nice job on this place. Can we look outside?" Upon first meeting, the couple had told him that they had a condo showing in an hour. He tried stretching his viewing so they would, pressed for time, lock up the front door and not reinspect the house.

"Mr. Phillips, if you would like us to show the home to your wife and children, that can be arranged. The power is on; we could meet here in the evening, if you like."

Looking at the place from the street, he took his time, stating that he would come back with his wife at the broker's convenience. It worked: the elderly man simply snapped shut the universal broker's lockbox on the front door, and they all parted.

He bought a portable radio at Kmart, using a credit card and driver's license lifted from a man in the crowded checkout line. He picked up the rest of his necessities at a hardware store, relying a great deal on having seen what he thought was a dog tag hanging from the collar of mutt Scooter.

Driving past the Thousand Pines Estates entrance, he made notice once again of the unfinished guard shack and electric gate. A half mile beyond the development, he turned right on Deerpoint and continued until he felt he was parallel to the house in the cul-de-sac. His aged Bronco blended with surrounding trailers and steel-sided buildings. He parked on the edge of the road closest to Thousand Pines, threw his backpack over his shoulders, and started his long trek through the virgin timber.

The hike through the woods reminded him of days gone by. Dampened pleas, the excellent memories of yore.

The dog whistle he bought upheld its advertised worth. Bringing on a horde of inquisitive canines, he easily curried favor with Scooter and bundled him into his arms, giving him just a whiff of sleepy time. The For Sale sign came out of the soft earth with ease. He wiped his prints and hid it behind the front door.

The window he had unlocked earlier proved difficult, budging only an inch at a time. Finally, he entered into the stillness of the house, savoring the emptiness. The dog whimpered. It did, in fact, have an "If found, call 562-1242" tag. He turned on a few lights, plugged in the radio, and, in keeping with his impression of the neighborhood, tuned into a country music station. He laid out the items of his trade on the kitchen counter: the bottle of sleepy time, gauze, tape. Rope for that all important calming effect and cloth hoods for his new friends, to be used against the glare of the rising moon.

"Hi, I'm new in the neighborhood. I have one cute but homesick puppy." He gave his voice a lilt, his inflection leaning toward the benign.

"Oh God!" Cheryl called out. "Aunt Billie, someone on the phone says they've got Scooter!"

"I twisted my ankle at work, have to hobble around, can you come get this little rascal? Sorry. My wife will be home shortly; she can bring him to your place if you wanted to wait."

"Ah, thanks, but I don't. Can you hold while I check with my aunt?"

"Certainly."

21

With her leg now stronger, Julie felt better. Overall, not quite a new woman but passable. Her trip with Todd to the Preston house, insightful. She couldn't imagine what Beverly Preston must have gone through, and by all indications, was still dealing with.

While driving, she debated whether to call and tell Billie she was coming over to fetch Cheryl, or just appear. Better, she thought, to alert them so that Cheryl could pack and be ready. Julie dialed but then hung up. She felt a little unsure of herself these days and wondered if she was healed enough to ensure Cheryl's safety while driving. Perhaps Mrs. Whitman from across the street could drive Cheryl to school tomorrow, and that extra day of rest would put Julie in better shape. The hell with it. She dialed Billie's number; it was busy.

Cheryl returned to the phone. "Who did you say this was?"

"Phillips. Ronnie Phillips." He nudged the dog with his boot.

Scooter half yelped, half growled.

"There, there, baby. What's the matter? You want your

mommy, don't you? This little rascal is so cute. I don't know where you live, but you're welcome to pick up—"

"Scooter."

"Ah yeah, Scooter the tooter."

"Can you hold on for a minute? I should tell my aunt—my mom's friend. She'll be right here. Oh, is that Scoot barking?"

Reaching down again, he squeezed the neck of the little spaniel. Scooter bellowed.

"I think I can hear him without the phone." She laughed. "You're down the street. Are you in the house that was for sale? At the end of the road?"

"Yes, I'll be going to bed soon. I hate to be a pest but—"

"Be right there. I just have to tell my aunt Billie. "

Charles went out the back of the house to the front door and snapped off the broker's lockbox with oversized cutters. He left the door open a good foot and turned up the radio a notch. Scooter was held by a short length of newly purchased clothesline. It was a straight shot from the entrance through the living room and into the galley. The swinging kitchen door was propped open for a clear view of the chopping block in front of the refrigerator where the dog had been tied. He stood behind the door waiting to deliver his sleepy time.

"Hello, I'm here!" She rang the doorbell several times. He waited.

"Mr. Phillips, hello! Come to get the dog. Howdy-ho, knock, knock!"

He cupped his hands around his mouth and turned toward the wall. "I'm back in the laundry room, come in, please."

"Sorry about Scoot." She came down the hallway and stepped into the kitchen.

He grabbed her around the waist from behind and pressed his nighty-night cloth over her nose and mouth. He felt the girl's air leave her body. Holding her tight, he breathed against her neck.

A voice came from the street. "Cheryl, you in there? Do you have Scooter? Cheryl?"

He cursed his luck. Now the older woman was on her way. He tidied up the last few knots of rope and then hid once again behind the kitchen door.

Julie let Billie's house phone ring seven or eight times until voice mail picked up. She tried Billie's and Cheryl's cells, with the same fruitless result. She'd thought that Billie and Cheryl were eating in tonight. After the third phone call, she headed for Thousand Pines.

22

He stood behind the door, the girl's inert form at his feet, the impatient calls of the woman getting closer. He poked the tied-up dog with a broom handle.

"Scooter, is that you, baby? Scooter, hello. Cheryl, you in there? Answer Aunt Billie, please. *Cheryl!*"

"Come on in!" he called out, snorting a friendly chuckle. He stepped toward the kitchen, his back to the front door. "Come in, come in. We're just having a—" He stopped and looked back toward the kitchen wall. "Ha, ha. Cheryl says Scoot wants to stay here." He waved a casual invitation and stooped down to speak to the dog.

"May I come in?"

"Yes, of course," he continued, on a pretense of petting the dog. "We're just telling Scooter the perils of running away from home." He stood up and in sweeping fashion gestured a "Welcome to my humble kitchen" just before she entered.

He saw the woman glance down at his feet. A pair of bound hands snaked between his shoes. The woman bellowed when he struck her on the forehead. She held her hands to her face as blood splattered onto the tile floor.

His plans had definitely changed. He now had two potential subjects, and he didn't want either. But a lure was still a lure. Miss Julie's missing brat would stir the very foundation of that woman's soul. The older woman would serve as simple R & R and then be disposed of.

A car made a U-turn in the cul-de-sac. After turning off the lights in the kitchen and the living room, he stepped to the door. He looked up the block to see Julie get out of her car and step carefully up the walkway.

A country singer on the radio lamented lost chances and roadhouse bars. The neighborhood slowly came alive, with porch lights flicking on. A streetlamp halfway up the block cast a dim bluish glow over the dampening pavement. A light rain began to fall.

He had to hurry; there might only be fifteen minutes before a search of the neighborhood ensued.

Julie made her way up to Billie's front door. The quaint coziness of the Pines had its appeal, but it was sad to admit that a playground across the street was no longer in the realm of Cheryl's interests. It seemed mere months since her girl had hung upside down on their backyard swing set.

She heard music down the street.

The door was wide open.

He stuffed their mouths with washcloths from the freshly decorated powder room and placed muslin cloth hoods over their heads, securing them with tape wrapped under their chins. Clothesline extending from tied hands to their necks joined the captives five feet apart. They were both drowsy, and he considered leaving the older woman behind in the house, but she had seen him.

"Listen to me."

The teen, lying on her side, pedaled her legs, searching for purchase.

"Listen, dammit. Stop thrashing, or I'll make you stay still. Got it?"

The hood shook up and down.

"You're going to get up now. You're tied by the neck to this other woman. If you make a sudden jerk, you'll strangle yourself or break bones. Hear me?"

Once again the nod.

He repeated his instructions to the woman, who got to her knees then struggled to a standing position, whimpering like the mutt. The only light came from the laundry room with the door cracked open. Leading the two women by their leash, he opened the back door.

This would be the most dangerous moment. Although dark out, they would be visible crossing the yard, and conspicuous if hooded and led by a short length of rope. The girl in the lead tugged on her tether but stopped after he snapped the rope, hard. The light rain turned into a harsh downpour.

Halfway across the yard, the woman tripped, and they both fell. Before he could get them on their feet, a rear door opened down the street, and light flooded the fence surrounding the property. He crouched down, his arms encircling his two captives. The fence might have saved him, the horizontal and angled boards creating a mixed pattern of shapes in the darkened yards.

Distant lightning whitened the sky. He waited until it was dark again and pulled his charges back on their feet, hustling them into the edge of the woods.

Scooter barked twice, his sharp voice dulled by heavy rain. He had locked the pest in the powder room. Now he wished he had strangled the little bastard.

The trio made its way into the woods, the two females stumbling while being led through the rock-strewn forest. Charles glanced back at the development. In the distance, through the trees, he saw the revolving blinker lights of a police car. He damned his luck. He had to either cut and run or lighten his load.

The younger of his two burdens stood head down, almost calm, while the older woman struggled with her bindings. He walked to her side. "Stop your infernal Hoochie McCoochie, or I'll place a rock upside your head, hear me?"

He led them onward through the slash and rocks of the dank forest.

In the near distance, Charles saw the dim house lights he'd noticed when he parked earlier, off to the left, several light poles away. He waited, uncertain if he should proceed with both his prizes. The heavyset woman continued her weeping and pulled against her rope restraints.

"Either quit your blabbering, or I'll put an end to it for you. You choose." Charles yanked on the lead rope hard, pulling both his captives off their feet and onto the rock-and-weed forest floor.

The older woman bucked, making wet choking sounds as Charles cut the rope between them. He pushed the girl toward the road, leaving the woman behind on the ground. The older one was more dangerous to have around than any benefit she would have provided later.

He retrieved his vehicle and secured Cheryl in the back. Settling into the driver's seat, he reconsidered leaving the woman in the woods. If she talked, it could be difficult for him later. He eased himself out of the truck and headed back into the tall trees.

Billie was lying right where he'd left her. Legs pulled up tight to her chest, her head turned into the earth.

"You had to kick up a fuss, didn't you?" he whispered. "Had to show your hind side, be all whiney, right?" He poked her with a long stick. "I'm talkin' to you. Shake your head."

She lay still.

He stepped closer, nudging her with his toe. "You playing possum, hefty?"

The smell of corroded earth and animal death penetrated Charles as he walked back to the truck. He felt no guilt about the lump of humanity lying soaked and still in the blackened forest. She had caused her own demise by being desperate and unruly. After all, he was only having a bit of fun.

Julie searched the house and took a quick look into the backyard. Neither Cheryl nor Billie answered her calls. Julie thought the dog might have strayed and they went in search. But they would have gone on foot as Billie's car was in the drive. She stood by the front door, watching as the rain eased.

She got a flashlight from her car and headed for the playground. She met up with a couple and their son crossing the street.

Julie aimed her flashlight down at the wet pavement. "Excuse me, I'm looking for my daughter and Miss Cooper from across the street." She gestured toward Billie's house. "Have you seen them?

"That hefty gal with the pesky dog," the man said to his wife. "Haven't seen them. That cur was yapping a while ago down the street toward the end there. Who wants to know?"

"Just a friend, thank you."

"'Friend'? We're careful around here about strangers."

"I'm an officer. Just concerned; the door was left open." She took out her badge and turned to walk away. "Thanks for your help."

"Ma'am, would you like me to accompany you?"

"Thank you, no!" she called out. Just what she needed. A neighborly vigilante. It didn't make sense. If Cheryl and Billie were in the vicinity, they would be calling for the dog. It was too quiet. She walked deep into the playground and then rested her leg on the pipe supporting the teeter-totter. In the back, toward the lit street on the other side of the development, she saw picnic tables and trash cans. A gully separated the green area on the near side from the backyards on the other street. The only way to check out the rest of the development would be in her car.

Driving, she moved her flashlight back and forth across the street and pointed it toward the end of the cul-de-sac where she had turned around earlier. Nothing.

Somewhere from behind, she detected whining. Then a crisp bark.

She picked up her phone. "Todd, listen to me. I've got a problem. I can't figure it out."

"Where are you? I'll come over."

"Would you? I'm out at my friend Billie Cooper's in Thousand Pines."

"Be there in fifteen."

Julie went to the end of the street and saw no signs of a dog. Going back through her friend's house, there were no indications of struggle or violence. She stepped outside. Once again a light drizzle slicked the black asphalt before her.

Todd arrived sooner than expected. They stood in Billie's living room.

"What worries me is her car is in the driveway. I've been here for almost an hour, maybe less, and—" Julie noticed lights blinking. "What's that?"

Todd parted the curtains. "Police. Local guys. Let's go

cool them down." They took out their badges before meeting up with two officers pulling up in their patrol car.

"State troopers, fellows. Not sure if we have a situation here or not."

"We got a call from a guy who says he lives here in the development." The lead officer seemed receptive.

"That's me, Officer. I called. It seemed suspicious." The ever-vigilant home owner walked up behind them.

The policeman assured the fellow that all was under control, though Julie wasn't too sure.

"My daughter and friend are missing. Would you go with me to spotlight the cul-de-sac? I was down there earlier and thought I heard my friend's dog, but then nothing. Weird."

They followed the patrol car. The officer scanned the neighborhood and parked at the end of the street. The light beam cut through dense trees, creating an eerie display.

"Scooter, come boy!" Julie called out. "Hey, Cheryl! Billie!"

They waited; a dog yelped from the direction of the home behind them.

"That house is empty; has been since they built it." Like an unwanted fly, the busybody had followed them to the end of the street.

Todd and Julie stayed near the police car while the local cops knocked on the door and walked around the house, aiming their flashlights into the dark rooms.

"Think we have something back here."

Todd and Julie tracked the policeman's voice. "I can't see in this high window; might be a bathroom, but there's definitely a dog in there."

Julie once again called out to Scooter, who answered with a yelping fuss.

"There shouldn't be an animal in there—"

All four of them once again looked at the neighborhood fellow.

"This house hasn't sold. I saw the brokers here today showing the place. I'm part of community patrol; we look out for things."

"Thanks," replied the older officer. "Wait back in the street. We'll call you if we have questions."

The man trudged back toward the patrol car.

"Listen guys, I'm really getting anxious," Julie said. "I know it's not protocol to enter a house without a warrant, but something's wrong. There's no way in hell that dog should be in that house. Couldn't we use probable cause? Bust a window, force a door?"

The older cop flashed his light around while trying to make a decision. "Let's see if there's a door or window open; maybe someone broke in."

The two locals went toward the back while Todd and Julie checked the front.

Julie rattled one of the porch windows.

"Door's open!" Todd shouted. He walked to the side of the house and saw the lockbox lying behind a porch chair. "Officers, we've got a break-in."

Guns out, the two local cops went in first. Julie followed and flicked a switch on the wall, bathing the front room with light from a chandelier shaped like a wagon wheel. Hearing Scooter scratching against the door, she started to open it.

"Better not until we check everything, okay?"

Julie knew she shouldn't handle things, but it made her feel like it would put her in touch with Cheryl.

From the older patrolman in the kitchen, "Hold it, guys. We've got a long smear on the floor. Looks like blood."

Julie took deep breaths, pacing the front porch of the house. She called dispatch and brought Captain Walker up to speed. Todd then took over the call. Three police cars and a crime scene van blocked the street. Held back by yellow tape strung up between two trees and the boundaries of the house, residents lined the far curb and milled about in the cul-de-sac.

Julie watched the man on duty. She thought him oblivious to what was taking place. He wasn't derelict, just doing what he'd been told to do, waiting for his night watch to end so he could traipse on home to Molly and the kids. Julie waited, wishing her evening could also be that simple. She caught herself glancing at her watch once again, wondering if these events on this rainy night with its wispy haze in the distant pines were, in fact, real.

She walked to the opposite end of the porch. Sitting on the broad wood bannister, she tried to calm herself between heavy gulps of air. She smelled damp grass, a warm breeze stirring the pines in the woods. A potted plant swung from the porch ceiling, the creaking noise running counterpoint to the murmuring crowd. She thought this had to be the work of that grinning wet-pants son of a bitch. She was sure of it.

Todd snapped the phone shut and tossed it to Julie. "The captain is on his way out with a couple investigators. He suggested you go home. I told him I didn't think there was any way that was going to happen."

"Got it. Right. How about a canvass of the neighborhood? What do you say?"

"I'll tell the local cops what we're up to. What side do you want?"

"I'll start next door; take the other side of the street, okay?"

"Be careful, Sergeant."

They parted, Julie went to the first house. She stepped onto the porch.

"Can I help you, ma'am?" a woman from the street called out.

"May I speak with you? I'm with the police."

"Of course. Please, come in."

The house was an exact duplicate of the one she had just been in. Julie introduced herself and asked the woman if she'd seen anything out of the ordinary that afternoon.

"I work late and don't get home until dark. Paid the babysitter, had supper, and then this." She pointed outside to the growing crowd of observers and patrol cars.

"Do you have a number for your sitter? I'd like to speak with her."

"Hold on; number's on the fridge."

The woman went to the kitchen, and a voice from the stairwell called out, "Mommy, can I have a soda, please?"

"No, dear. Go back to bed, it's late."

Julie saw a child on the stairs, wide eyed at the flashing lights outside. She wore pj's that reminded her of a younger Cheryl. *Damn.*

"Who are you?"

"My name is Julie, and you are?"

"Rose or Rosie, sometimes Pumpkin, and most times 'Don't do it.'" She smiled.

The woman came back into the room. "It's late, please." She pointed upstairs to the child. "Here's that number." She handed Julie a piece of paper. "She'll be cooperative, I'm sure."

"What's happ'nin, Mommy?"

"Just the police looking into something. It's nothing, honey."

"It must be Halloween. Is it Halloween?"

"No, Rose, please go back to bed."

Julie turned for the door.

"Must be Halloween. I saw people with scary masks jumping round all fun like."

Julie moved toward the woman. "May I ask your child a question?"

"Sure."

"Sweetheart, when did you see these Halloween people?"

"When it got dark, out my window. Where I make up my stories. In the back, they were playing and wrasslin'. It was raining and thundering."

"Could you show me that window from your child's room?" Julie asked the mother.

"Follow me." Halfway up, she turned around. "I hear there's a kid missing. Can't imagine what those parents are going through. Christ."

Julie swallowed hard.

The child's room looked out onto their backyard, with portions of other properties visible on both sides.

"Where did you see these Halloween people?"

The girl pointed toward the middle of a heavily treed backyard at the cul-de-sac house.

"How were they dressed?"

"The man—I guess the daddy—didn't have anything on."

Julie and the mother glanced at each other.

"I mean he didn't have on a mask like the others."

Julie waited. She wanted to shake the information from the child.

"I think it was a girl with a mask." She stopped as if searching for a word. "No, it was a . . ." She looked to her mother for help, and then got her pillow and slipped the cover over her own head. "Like this." She cranked her head around. "They were tumblin' on the ground and then they marched off all funny into the woods. It was flashing with lightning."

Julie felt light-headed and realized she was holding her breath.

"He led them with a rope, Mommy."

Julie needed to leave. She wanted to break into a full run to get to the house next door.

The house teemed with police officers and techs dusting surfaces for prints. She felt they were stealing glances at her. It grew humid; the noxious air felt dense. Her clothes grasped her underarms and bound her thighs.

Someone tapped her arm. She jumped.

"What's going on, Sergeant? Talk to me." It was Captain Walker.

"I'm revved up, sorry. A kid next door saw someone lead Cheryl and Billie—hooded and tied—into the woods."

He put his hand on her shoulder. "Let's go have a look."

They stepped out the back door of the house into the yard and scanned their flashlights across the grassy area. Fresh footprints half filled with water led a serpentine-like trail into the woods.

Walker took a quick call on his cell. "We have K-9s on the way in five. Chopper dispatched, also five to ten minutes out."

24

It was always the same. The rush of adrenaline from the pitiful trust that seemingly bright people extended to perfect strangers. In this case, "perfect stranger" would be well placed.

The girl stirred in the back of the Bronco. As if he would harm her, heaven forbid.

He smiled, thinking of the young one. It would take planning to explore the possibilities of his newly acquired Teen World.

He kept right below the speed limit—not too slow, not too fast. He recalled a recent scare when stopped for an extinguished taillight. How close the officer had been to his human cargo. "It looks like a lens might have slipped out. Get that fixed as soon as possible. You never can tell; wouldn't want to get rear ended, would you?"

No, and neither would the young lady tied up and covered in the back of the car. He had driven two hundred miles south before leaving that particular love mate. She lasted nearly two weeks before he tired of her. Annie or Angie—some stupid high school name—a would-be hippy hitchhiker learning the hard lessons of the road. He left her standing on a deserted country lane, shivering on the gravel shoulder. He thought it comical. Her all naked with a hood over her head, looking as if terrified to move. He made a U-turn and watched her pan her head in syncopation to his car's 180-degree maneuver. The figure in his mirror appeared wistful; probably missing him so very soon.

25

T*he Watson couple* arrived at the cul-de-sac. "Oh my God. The house. It's a mess. Look what they've done."

Walker got permission from the local police to interview the brokers. Julie stood off from the trio, having been told by Walker that she was in no state to involve herself in the interview.

"You are, I understand, not only the listing brokers but also the owners of this house. Is that correct?"

The elderly man pulled off his raincoat and hung it over the porch bannister. "Dammit. All you people traipsing in and out making a pure chaos out of—"

"Do I have to ask you again? Are you—"

"Yes, yes, we own this place. We're also the listing brokers, and we'd like to know what's going on."

"When did you last—"

"Who's she?" Mr. Watson pointed at Julie. "I've a right to know who's in our house, dammit."

"This is Sergeant Worth. She's . . . helping in the investigation. Detective Devlin, take the wife down to the other end of the porch." Walker turned to the man. "Can we get back to the facts? When did you last show the house?"

"Today. Earlier, a nice gentleman from—" He called to his wife. "Where was Mr. Phillips from?"

Walker interrupted. "Answer the question, please."

"I don't think he said." He paused. "Such a pleasant fellow. Why would he break into this house?"

"I'm going to have you accompany me throughout the house except the kitchen and—"

"What happened in the kitchen?"

Walker didn't answer; just guided the man into the living room. Julie followed.

"I'd like you to tell me if you see anything missing. Don't touch, please."

They walked up the stairs, checked the bedrooms and baths, came back down, and looked into the dining area. The man tried a quick peek through the swinging door into the kitchen.

"Please don't, Mr. Watson. Anything different, moved out of place?"

He cruised around the living room as Todd walked the woman up the stairs. Walker wanted them gone, so he ushered the man toward the front door and called to Todd to come downstairs.

"Would you please have your men take all their paraphernalia?" Mr. Watson asked. "It will take us days to clean this."

Mrs. Watson came down the stairs. "I'd think your people would have better things to do than listen to music." She stopped in the front hallway.

Julie whispered to Walker.

He called to Mrs. Watson. "What do you mean?"

"You said, 'abduction.' That's a pretty serious thing to

be investigating while entertaining yourself listening to a radio."

Walker looked at the small unit on the hall table. "That doesn't belong to us. It isn't yours?"

She shook her head.

The buzz of a helicopter swept over the crowded street. From the porch, Julie watched the couple disappear down Tranquil Pines Way. The hum of activity surrounding the house at the end of the street gave lie to its rustic name.

"I realize I'm probably more a hindrance than help, but I just can't leave." She tried to show restraint. "She's my baby. I've gotta find her." She looked around. "Would you allow Devlin and me to take a look in back?"

"What do you mean? The woods? We've got the chopper and the dogs. Come on, Worth, you know better. Go home, wait for my call. That's an order." Walker held a stern look but then melted. "Damn, what a mess," he said, putting his arm around her shoulders and walking her off the porch.

"Devlin, take care of your partner. She wants to explore the woods out back. Think it's better to wait til daybreak so we can see, for Christ's sake."

The hounds from the K-9 unit raised hell in the playground area up the street.

"You have flashlights, Devlin? Radios, first aid?"

"We're prepared."

"Take care of her." Walker glanced down the street in the direction of the barking. "Too damn wet for those dogs to pick up a scent. Shit." He gave a resigned gesture toward the woods. "Officially, you're off this abduction, Sergeant. I don't mean to be a hard-ass but gotta say it. I'll be assisting the locals on this while you—" He hesitated.

"While you make your way home. If Devlin leads you on a detour that has to do with that cold case, then that's on him." He made his way back toward the house.

"So if I got this right," Todd said, "we're cleared to look into past transgressions? Let's go, Sarge."

Julie brushed her elbow against her handgun before walking to the corner of the house.

"I'll get you a coat. I've got an extra one in my car."

"My daughter was in short sleeves, I'll be fine. And yes, we are cleared."

Halfway across the wide expanse of tended lawn, from her right, she noticed someone with a flashlight looking at the location where she and Walker had discovered footprints. The beam moved across the lawn and came to rest on her face. Julie shielded her eyes.

"Who is it?" Todd asked.

"I spoke to the lady earlier in the street. I'm part of the home patrol."

Julie waved her arms. "Get that fucking light out of my eyes."

"Oh, sorry. I guess with all the excitement, I've lost my manners."

Todd walked toward the man. "What are you doing out here? Do you realize this is a crime scene? You could be destroying evidence."

The man pulled himself upright. "I have a right as part of the community to—"

"Get your donkey ass back on the street, or I'll get the locals to lock your inquiring butt in one of the squad cars for as long as we need to, got it?"

"Well . . ." He hesitated, almost stomping his foot, but then headed for the street.

Julie turned north toward the dark silhouette of the

woods. In the beginnings of the tall pines, the slash had been cleared, their flashlight beams bouncing off the vertical tall timber. They trekked in silence, Julie now off to the left of Todd. The undergrowth thickened, slowing their progress. In the distance, the chopper, its light source scanning the lawns behind them close to the house. Moving over the heavy wooded area, the beam swept the forest through the rain and tangled crisscross of shadows.

They hiked on, Julie's light attempting to cover every inch of the location. She searched every ditch and behind each tree, her calls to Cheryl and Billie dampened by the wet forest. Julie heard Todd breaking his way through the undergrowth, coming toward her.

"Sarge, what do you think, should we turn back?"

"I'm going to push on; you do whatever you want." She panned her flashlight through a 180-degree arc in front of her.

"Sorry, just thought we might be doing something more useful back at the house or headquarters."

"Yeah, I know. I just have to keep moving; feel like I'm doing something." She traversed left and right some twenty yards and then maneuvered forward. "Cheryl! Billie!" She knew the chance was slim of them being left in the woods. After ten minutes, they reached a road, with nothing in sight except a dim light a hundred yards to their left.

Julie rubbed her eyes. "Let's walk this way a bit and then turn back; make another sweep."

"This time let's stay closer. I'm worried about you." Todd followed her down the country way. He sprayed his light on both sides of the muddy dirt road. After fifty yards, Julie, without a word, dove back into the woodland,

Todd keeping a safe distance to her left side. They hadn't been but a couple minutes when Julie called out.

"Devlin, get on the horn! We need an ambulance!"

Todd radioed for Walker and backup. He moved toward Julie's direction and came upon her crouched over a partially hooded figure on the ground.

"It's Billie!" She tucked her flashlight under her chin and put her hand to her friend's neck. "I can't find a pulse." She ripped the hood the rest of the way from Billie's head. "She's got something in her mouth." Julie pried the cloth muffler from between Billie's teeth and then with her fingers cleared her passageway. She turned her friend's body with Todd's help and applied rapid pressure on her chest.

"I think she's gone." He played his flashlight on the woman's face. "Probably choked on her own vomit."

Julie continued compression on Billie's chest, screaming at her friend. "Billie, goddamn it, breathe! Breathe!" She applied full weight. "Jesus, kid. Please, take a breath!" She heard Todd say, from somewhere, that the EMTs had arrived.

"Let her go now, Sergeant. Let her go." He rested his hand on Julie's shoulder.

She crawled away on the soggy earth, her hands and knees buried in the mud.

The traffic lights on the drive home seemed rigged. Double for the time while waiting at red, and half the time for green. Everything a conspiracy. She had nothing to do but worry.

Julie once again went through the multitude of arrested bad boys who had sworn revenge. None seemed capable of anything more complicated than tying his shoes. Orchestrating an abduction of two women in the middle of a thriving community like Thousand Pines was beyond them.

Walker instructed Todd to follow her home. She saw him in her mirror.

He had been sweet as he led her to her car. "I want you to know that whatever it takes, I'm there for you, understand? We will find Cheryl, I promise you." He squeezed her arm and then embraced her.

Traffic was thin at this hour. A loud, oversized pickup truck with spinning hubcaps and drunk young men pulled up next to her at a light. A bearded guy with muscular, tattooed arms and wearing a black wifebeater leaned out of his passenger-side window. "Excuse me. I need directions."

Julie glanced at him.

"Could you tell me the way to get into your pants?"

She raised her window and waited for the annoying rigged light. The wiseass had gotten out of his car and was doing a suggestive dance next to her door, arms gyrating above his head, hips pumping. His buddies were clapping in unison as he rubbed his pelvis against her left side fender. She saw only a blur as Todd, coming from behind her car, drove his shoulder into the guy and took him to the ground. He applied an arm bar and wrenched it up in back of his shoulder blade, all the while shouting, "Stop resisting!" The other badasses, including the driver, piled out of the red truck and surrounded the two men on the pavement.

Julie wondered when this day would end as she put her car in park, pulled out her Sig, and climbed into the street. "Don't anyone move, got it? And I mean anyone! I'm with State Patrol. No smart-ass talk, just shut the fuck up! Todd, you okay?"

Todd came off the ground with the tattooed guy in cuffs. "You're going to jail, fella."

"What charge, tough guy?"

"Violation of probation!" This shouted phrase came from behind Julie's car.

A uniformed local policeman Julie had seen at the Thousand Pines house hustled up to the fracas. His squad car's blinking lights vibrated the night sky.

"William 'Junior' Gaddis, all-around disturber of the peace, general nuisance, and recent graduate of our modernized state facility of incarceration. Say good-bye, Junior."

The officer locked him behind the cage in his patrol car, and then came back to Julie with the cuffs. "I'm aware of what you're going through, Sergeant; sorry about Junior. I'll write it up in a way to keep you out of it. This guy with you?"

"Yeah, he's also a trooper." Julie handed Todd his cuffs. "Works with me. Just seeing that I get home okay. Thanks, Officer."

The patrolman raised his fingers to his brow in a polite salute and went back to his car. On the way, he signaled the driver of the muscle truck to take off. The late nighters trundled through the intersection with a couple loud, protesting engine revs and then drove off into the deserted night.

Julie pulled to the side of the road and went back to Todd, who was clipping his cuffs back on his belt. "What you got there, partner, a dinged elbow?"

"No, no. I'm fine." He shook out his arm. "My pleasure, believe me."

They contemplated each other.

"Why don't you head on home, Mr. Jiujitsu? I'll be okay."

"Not a chance in hell. No way, zip, zero, zilch, nada."

Julie nodded, got back in her car and headed toward the highway. She had never seen Todd in any real take-

down situations. There would be the occasional undisci-
plined lout at a warrant serving or a citizen who wanted to
express his rights in a confrontational manner, but nothing
like the beatdown of the dancing Junior Gaddis.

The incident served to distract her for a few minutes,
but now she was back to reality. Her daughter was missing, her dear friend dead.

At the house, Todd insisted that he was spending the rest
of the night. "In my vehicle, on the porch, up a tree, I'm here,
Sarge." He smiled and bowed politely. "Get used to it."

"I don't think this prick will contact me tonight. Go on
home. I'll be okay."

Todd folded his arms over his chest.

"Okay," she sighed. "I've got a couch; you can use the
bathroom off the kitchen."

She pulled a pillow and blanket from the hall closet and
placed them on the couch. "Good night and thank you,
pard."

Julie passed by Cheryl's darkened room. She wanted
to peek in her room, sleep in her bed, but she only pushed
open the door a few inches to let in the hall light.

In her own bedroom, Julie slipped out of her slacks and
blouse and put on an old flannel bathrobe. She propped
herself up against the filigreed metal headboard, knowing that sleep would be an impossibility. She reviewed
the outlandish group of events in the previous weeks. The
mall, the truck incident, her hospital stay. Cheryl having
to be with her friend Billie, and the guy Phillips—she was
sure that wasn't his name. On top of it all, being accosted
by the four tough guys at the stoplight.

She allowed herself to think of Todd. It was impres-
sive to watch him in action. She knew that he had been a

Special Forces guy—or maybe it was recon or Navy SEAL. She got them confused. But she was embarrassed to admit that she'd always thought of him as a gentle soul.

The moon was at an angle to the west, veiled by a thin grey cloud. The light dimmed. She fought her heavy eyelids and recalled the delighted squeak of joy from that little girl swinging by her knees in the backyard.

26

Cheryl felt vibrations from below. Rattling, whirling, then smooth. The street. She must be in a car. If she were dreaming, she would like for it to be over.

She could think only of a suffocating rag being clamped over her mouth. A threatening voice.

Her shoulder hit hard as the car braked. Something in her mouth couldn't be spit out. Stay strong. Had Billie been with her when she felt woozy and went to sleep?

Soon after they were hooded, she remembered falling. Then a long trek through damp weeds, the man's voice sparked with anger. Heavy rain fell, and the occasional snap of a rope around her neck, and then the clumsy pushing and groping to get into a vehicle. Billie may or may not have been with her when they got in the car.

It felt as if she were lying on her side for hours, her hands and feet numb from being bound. She sensed a cloth covering her head, wet from the rain and ripe with the scent of laundry soap.

The ride got smoother, the engine noise a bit louder. What did the man want? What would he do to her? Cars passed to the side of her. A freeway? She couldn't see. She willed herself to fade away, to sleep.

They jolted to a stop. "Pull your legs toward me." The same voice.

A hand grasped her ankle and pulled hard, and then fumbled and tugged at her waist. She felt herself falling onto damp, clean grass, sweet and safe.

Once again the voice, "Roll onto your side, pull your knees up to your chest, then straighten up."

She complied the best she knew how. Her head felt stuffed, the man's legs against her back, his searching hands clasped across her breasts and armpits. A sharp tug, and then she was standing. She thought owls squawked through what might be a wooded area.

Once again the rope looped around her neck. In the near distance, water lapped against a shore. They trudged up a stone path.

"Two steps up."

Her right foot searched out the first step. After a slight stumble, the warmth of a room. Beyond the scent of the hood, she smelled the remains of a wood fire and maybe bacon. Then the man's rough grip on her arm.

"Steps going down. If you fall"—laughter—"you're dead."

Her foot thumped on a hollow wood step. She continued down until the air cooled, and she landed on a hard, rough floor. Then the screech of a door opening. A different smell. An artificial floral scent. And a slight hum, like a fan. Once again the man's hands caressed her arms. She felt him too near, tugging on the ropes around her wrists. A knife cut through her restraints.

"Stay," he ordered. "Do not move." He continued to

work her bindings. "When you hear the door close, you can take off your hood. Not until, understand?"

Cheryl nodded.

The heavy door slammed. Cheryl yanked off the hood and pulled the cloth from her mouth. "Billie, where are you?" Her voice trailed off.

Cheryl rubbed at her wrists, looking around the eight-by-ten-foot room lit by a bulb hanging in a wire cage over the door. Above the bulb, an electric fan had been installed behind a rectangular grate. No windows. Pushed against one wall, a cot with blanket, wrinkled pink sheet, and thin mattress. In one corner, a commode. In the opposite corner, a small refrigerator. Next to that, a faucet jutted out from the wall with a circular floor drain below. Images of children dancing through a fantasy woods papered the walls, all set off with a ceiling painted black.

27

Chuck and Bink played in the woods next to the Tucker "spread." Father figure Tuck liked calling the foster home a spread. He said it harkened back to the old days when ranches covered miles and people were limited to their acreage only by how far they could see.

Tucker's double-wide mobile home sat cockeyed on concrete blocks. Three abandoned cars were parked next to a junked motor home along with a two-wheeled truck, all in mixed stages of disrepair. Most of the vehicles sported bullet holes in their windshields from the responsible Mr. Tucker's target practice. A bent wire fence contained a dozen chickens and a hutch for rabbits. A second, temporary corrugated-steel building housed the boys. The girls occupied a run-down cabin.

"You and Bink stay close. Did you do your chores? Your homework? Brush your teeth?"

He recalled infuriating Tuck by answering only with a quick nod.

"I will teach you a passel of manners, little smart-ass. You and your asshole buddy Bink Boy will toe the line, got it?"

Chuck answered with an "Uh-huh" grunt.

Among the other six kids at the foster home, two were girls: one fourteen, the other seventeen. Chuck and Binky called them Boots and Saddle. Boots had big feet and was awkward, but she was sweet and compliant. Saddle was built tall for a seventeen-year-old. She had a funny way of speaking—always a little too knowledgeable about almost any subject.

She wasn't fat but carried a protruding stomach and a swayed back; hence the name Saddle. Chuck, on many a night, snuck around to the windows of the girls' hut to peek. One night on the way to his private show, he turned the corner of the house to see Mr. Tucker spanking the monkey while bent over a gap in the window blind. He laughed. Tuck turned, monkey in hand, as Chuck ran.

He paid dearly for that little indiscretion. Tucker escorted him into the woods the following day, where he was forced to drop his pants. While bent over a fallen tree, he was beaten with a switch until he wept. Months later, he took out his revenge not on Mr. Tucker but on Saddle. She mocked him and his palsied gait. It was easy for him to transfer his anger. She paraded around the bottle-strewn yard swinging her right leg stiffly in front of her left. "I'm midget Charlie, and I have a mighty leg that I throw about when I want to gain sympathy! Yo-ho-ho and a bottle of rum!"

The rest of the kids laughed and pointed. Chuck thought she looked ridiculous.

On her eighteenth birthday, she announced her righteous departure. "I'll see you jokes—I mean *folks*—down the road. I love you all and wish you good fortune. I'll miss you, I mean it. I'll miss the heck out of you. Everyone except Creepo Charlie."

"Creepo Charlie! Creepo Charlie!" the kids chanted.

His face reddened while the rest of the kids, including Bink, kept up their chant.

Saddle saved pennies from her meager allowance and had enough to buy a trashed bicycle from Mr. Tucker. Her plan was to ride the bike south through the Ozarks into Arkansas and on to Little Rock to complete her emancipation.

The kids gathered to see her off. All except Chuck, who, after lunch, had snuck off into the woods. Mr. Tucker stood waving as one of his moneymakers pedaled off.

Chuck waited a mile from the spread in a shrub-filled area next to the country road. When he spotted her, he felt a thrill, seeing her pumping hard down the slight incline. Her hair lay straight against the wind. A small pack with straps flying bobbed on her crooked back. The long, heavy fishing pole he'd stolen from the work shed jammed easily into the rear wheel spokes as she passed. Saddle went flying over the handlebars. She lay looking like an *S* curve groaning in the middle of the asphalt road.

When he envisioned this little adventure, Chuck wasn't sure what he wanted to do with her. But from the moment of her first profane retort to him while sprawled on the two-lane blacktop, it all became admirably clear.

Years later, when he built the "spa," as he liked to call it, in the corner of the basement, he dedicated it to Saddle. "A wonderful ride."

He lined one side of the stone cellar with vertical two-by-fours sixteen to twenty inches apart, filling the spaces with heavy insulation; then he did the same to the adjacent wall. The small basement window, hidden in a similar treatment. He covered the interior with thin plywood instead of the soft wallboard. It was not quite a square. In one corner, he tapped into the septic line and installed a toilet. An overhead water line strapped to the ceiling joist was easily diverted inside the wall down to the toilet and a faucet. He ran an extension cord through the wooden studs to join the refrigerator with the house circuit. An electric fan and energy-saving lightbulb with the switches on the outside of the room completed his private little spa.

These guest quarters had served him well in a number of trials over the previous few years.

28

A dog barking in the distance awakened Julie. She had drifted off, and her back and neck hurt from the awkward position in which she'd fallen asleep. The illuminated dial on the clock read four thirty in the morning. Two hours. She'd slept too long; it felt disloyal. Where was Cheryl? She would not allow herself to think of the possibilities; the odds of Cheryl being harmed. She knew the pinch that Captain Walker was in—local police had jurisdiction—but, still, she'd wasted so much time before convincing her boss to let her search the woods. She might even have saved Billie if she'd gotten there sooner.

Having a man around the house felt different. Todd had been adamant about staying. He was probably right. The abductor was coming out of nowhere. Targeting Cheryl didn't make sense.

Wandering around the bedroom, she stopped at each passing of the window to look out as if the answer would be hidden among the trees and hills along her country road. She ran her hand along the rough edge of the windowsill. The weathered house held bittersweet memories.

The birth of her daughter, a failed marriage, the deaths of her parents.

She stood at the sink in the kitchen, waiting for her coffee to brew. She thought about Billie. How in the world had she gotten involved? Surely by accident; wrong place, wrong time.

"How about a cup of joe?" Todd had rolled off the couch, slipped on his trousers, and stood in the kitchen doorway.

"Sorry to wake you. Can't rest, can't get this craziness out of my head. You don't have to be here. You know that, right?"

"I know. I've been lying there thinking how strange this is, starting with your being sequestered in the basement at work and then the nutty business with the truck." Todd got his coffee and sat at the kitchen table. "And your interviews with the known relatives of the missing girls."

"They're long shots to be involved, but this all has to be connected. Has to."

Julie sat across from him, taking slow sips of coffee.

"The lady Preston. What's her name? Beverly?"

Julie nodded. "She's different but harmless."

"I didn't meet the other guy you told me about."

"Preacher. Garthwait. A touch on the defensive but okay. The executive at the factory whose niece had gone missing, Drew, got upset when I spoke to him. Felt guilty about his not calling the cops and seemed apologetic. That low-life bastard."

"Who, the factory guy?"

"No, the bastard who took Cheryl and Billie." Julie stood to get more coffee, wanting to crush her cup. "It's about me, isn't it?"

"What do you mean?"

"He wants me, right? Why? He wants me to know he's coming for me or he's going to bargain with me?"

"You think all of this is connected?" Todd tapped the spoon in his cup.

"Yeah, I do. How? No idea."

"Preston has to be eliminated as a suspect. No car, I doubt she can drive, and she's not capable of any of this. Maybe connected unwittingly through circumstance. Your preacher man could be the fellow, but unlikely." He looked at Julie.

"Yeah, right. Doesn't have the balls. Our factory guy seems an unlikely candidate, but he's surrounded by a lot of working types. Pickup truck potentials. How in piss sakes does the guy who forced me off the road have anything to do with this abduction?" She stopped, the word having come from her mouth so easily. *Abduction*: the act of taking someone against her will—or in this case, two someones. "Then there's that angry bitch I've only spoken to on the phone. Probably should visit her. But she seems to be just another victim's relative." Julie gazed out the kitchen window. "We have to assume it's a guy. After all, how would a woman handle both Billie and Cheryl through that rain-drenched forest?"

Setting words to the event cast a realistic pall on the conversation.

"Hold on. We're going to prevail here, trust me. Go see Pastor Garthwait again." Todd paused. "Also, why don't we call the lab in Chicago, have them take pictures of the ring from all angles, see if the good reverend recognizes it as his grandmother's?"

"How will that help us?"

"If we can establish a connection between what's going on with you and what happened to these other girls years ago, maybe there's a way to put this guy in the picture. Some sort of coupling, a nexus."

"I hate that word, but I get where you're going." Julie looked at the still-darkened sky. "It's early. I hope my Cheryl's all right." She covered her eyes. "Sorry." Her mind worked on the possibilities. "I still don't get it. What's my link to this guy? It has to be me, Todd. He took her because of me." She paused. "You're right about talking to Garthwait. I look into these cold cases, and suddenly my life gets dangerous."

Todd phoned dispatch and got the number for the lab in Chicago. "We still can't do anything for a couple hours. Let me ask you—who might be the most relevant?"

Julie had no response.

"Okay, let's concentrate on Garthwait. We've seen Preston recently, and what's your factory guy's name?"

"Drew. William Drew. As I said before, I don't think he knows more than what he's already told me. But today we'll probably find out who has been there since Drew's niece went missing."

Todd looked surprised.

"I'm sorry, maybe I didn't tell you. We asked for a list of people who were around when the kidnapping occurred. If, in fact, that's what it was."

Julie took her cup to the sink. She put her hands on the edge of the counter and stretched. The pain in her upper body was still intense, but she welcomed it. It put her in touch with her baby. That smiling cherub years ago. Pigtails waving as she sang, "You are my thunshine. My only thunshine."

ngie Hogar, here."

Cheryl pulled the cot away from the wall. It looked like someone had lain facedown on the cot and with an outstretched arm over the edge scratched the words into the concrete floor. The woman must have carved the message with a piece of metal, something hard. She peeled off the dirty sheet and stuffed it between the wall and the faucet. She vowed to wash it, but later. Cheryl curled up on the flimsy mattress, a mere token of protection from the wire stretched across the frame of the cot. She didn't know how long she had been there or why.

In all of the trekking through the rain, stumbling falls, and angry man retorts, Cheryl never got the idea that this had anything to do with her. Or Billie, either. She wondered what happened to Aunt Billie. The man's attitude echoed that of a workman going about his chores, doing what he had to do. His initial sense of excitement gave way to a dogged firmness.

She wrapped the blanket around her like a cocoon. The light stayed on, as there wasn't any way to turn it off. The fan hummed, once in a while going off center and creating a metal-on-metal screech, mixing the cool basement air into her cell.

Cheryl stared at the opposite wall. In the corner, a piece of the children's nursery wallpaper buckled slightly, forming a rectangular protrusion. She eased off her bed and moved her hand along the length of the bubbled wallpaper. Then she felt the short side of the wall. There was a difference. Was it just the texture, the sense on her fingertips of the rough, thick paper? She felt it again. No, the temperature. The area where the paper bulged was cooler. She shut her eyes and did it again, this time going in the opposite direction. She lay back on the cot and looked at the wallpaper's shape. It began high in the corner of the room, stretched two feet across, and a foot and a half down. It looked like the size of a picture frame, maybe an earlier installation of the fan that was now over the door. Or perhaps a window.

She continued to look at the swollen wallpaper, and she was sure that it covered a window. Basement windows were placed in that way, under heavy beams that held up the floor above. Whoever made the room—probably "the voice"—covered the window. It made sense. Why build this prison cell and have a window through which one could escape?

She eased into a light nap, thinking about what her mother used to say about adversity, "Don't bellow until you're out of the woods."

A man's muted voice awakened her. "Hey you, move over here, close to the door."

Cheryl positioned herself where a waist-high slot in the wall had been opened. She glimpsed a man's belt looped through dark blue trousers, a white shirt, and the tip of a tie. "Are you listening? *Are you listening?*"

"Yes. Where's my aunt Billie?" Cheryl saw the man's waist and the back of his shirt as he paced.

It was a while before he spoke. "Mind your manners, and you won't end up like your auntie, you hear? I'm going to pass you food." Five apples and a loaf of bread were squashed in the pass-through. Then three tins of sardines, a package of potato chips, and two sealed Styrofoam Cup Noodles soups. "My advice, make it last. I'm not going to wear myself out hiking up and down these stairs to feed you."

In the past, he'd tried to gain favor by feeding his guests substantial meals. Now, let them eat cake. He flashed the lights off and on several times, working himself into a fever. "What do you expect of me? Lazy bitch, sitting on your butt, like a teenage pig! I'm telling you, I don't want to hear a peep out of you!" Once again he flashed the lights and cut the fan on and off. He stomped up the stairs, his voice high and angry. "If I hear a whisper, I'll come right back down and *beat the living hell out of you*! Got it?" His voice trailed off as he slammed the basement door.

Before the sound finished reverberating around the concrete block walls, he was back. "And, if there's anything you need, sweetie, just tap on the door." His voice, coming from the top of the stairs, had changed to that of a gentle soul. "A light, pleasant knock will do."

She thought he was more than strange.

He hummed a few notes. "By the way, you can call me 'King,' or 'the King.' A-wop-dah-a-doo-dah, a-wop-wop-wop!

"Should I avail our guest of the full spa treatment? Massage, pedicure, a refreshing cold shower under the tap? Naked, of course." He laughed. Still in a fit of self-congratulatory merriment, he forgot to close the food slot and once again slammed the door shut. Cheryl went to the wall and pressed her head against the slot, holding her left hand tightly to her ear. After several minutes, a car revved and drove off.

She waited five minutes. Her head and hands rested on the ledge of the food slot. *"Hey up there!"* She heard only the faint *whir* of the fan above the door. "Hey, King! If that's your name." She pounded her clenched fist on the ledge. Nothing. She sat back down. He was gone. She made a pledge that she was going to get out.

"How?" She startled herself by speaking out loud.

She would use the tops of the sardine cans to cut through the wallboard, certain that there was a window up in the far corner, noting also a bulge in the wallpaper where it looked water-stained, as if there were something behind the paper. She would cut through to the window but try to preserve the wallpaper in case he came back and looked in the room. She wasn't even certain a window was back there, but she was going to find out.

Cheryl took the wrapper from the loaf of bread and emptied the can of sardines into it. She wasn't crazy about sardines, but maybe they would save her. She took the oily can and climbed on top of the fridge.

Once the paper had been pulled away, about twenty inches from the corner could be seen, with a couple nails perpendicular to each other. Tapping her knuckles on the wall, and then on the upper portion, it sounded different, more hollow. She scraped a line next to the nails and then a horizontal one at the bottom, where the wallpaper had been. Taking a dish towel from the top of the fridge and wrapping it around the empty sardine tin, leaving a sharp edge exposed, she cut away. She created a long, horizontal line and worked for what seemed several hours, making a pitiful amount of progress against the wallboard. The sardine can began to distort, the constant sawing pulling it into a more elongated shape. Her hands cramped. Shifting positions, the tough-minded teenager worked on the vertical line next to the nails.

30

While *heading into* town for work, Charles thought about his life. He enjoyed his multiple-residence routine. A modest one-bedroom flat served him well from Monday night through Friday morning, and then he would be off once again to his "pied-à-terre." A real estate lady used the expression once while giving a talk at the factory. French. He liked the idea of it. "A foot to the ground."

He relished his acts of authority; they gave him great joy. The banal patter with his captives lifted him like nothing else.

Somewhere, others might say that what he was doing was wrong, but he reasoned that they would be the cowardly; the meek sisters of ho-humdrum. Those do-gooders who raise the prescribed number of children, attend church, and vote for the candidate with the biggest grin.

He vowed that his days would be filled with more worthwhile endeavors. A foot to the ground indeed. Or, closer to accurate, a whole body itself to the ground. Or how about a half dozen to the earth? But he had to admit he'd lost count, now with quality being the essence of the work.

Laughing out loud, he wondered if motorists around him thought him to be at all exceptional or queer. No, not queer. That, he knew, would not be accurate. His relationship to women would no doubt deem him heterosexual. He might be thought of as different but not fairy-like or lame. He and his mighty stallion implement would prevail, with never a hint of light-footedness. He sang:

> I have this grand opinion
> that I'll always rule my dominion.
> Women will beg to be incarcerated
> in my basement room, inebriated.

31

Julie contacted Captain Walker and discussed her theories on how the cases connected.

"Okay," said Walker. "Meet me at the office. We'll start pushing some of these interviews again. See who we can shake up."

When Julie and Todd pulled up to the office, Captain Walker was outside, talking to two very serious-looking men in dark suits.

"Who are these guys?" Todd asked.

"I'd say feds," guessed Julie, not too excited about the development.

Walker made the introductions as they approached. "Julie Worth, Todd Devlin, this is Supervisory Special Agent Jason Tyler and . . . " He trailed off, having already forgotten the second agent's name. "Agent Tyler was just offering his support." Walker gave Julie a look that clearly meant "Play nice."

"Sergeant Worth, we are sorry to hear what you're going through. We are here to offer the full resources of the Bureau."

"Thank you."

"Such as?" asked Todd.

Tyler flashed a quick and easy smile. "We're not here to take over your case, Officer. We've been talking to Captain Walker, and he was quite clear." He shot Walker a quick glance. "This case is being directed personally by him and the Missouri Highway Patrol. And so far, we have no evidence to support that Sergeant Worth's daughter has left the state, so it is still not a federal case. We want to offer to handle this with the other potential victims around the country. Captain Walker says this guy might be a serial—"

"Abductor," offered Devlin.

"Yes, sir." Tyler smiled again. "We are staffing a command post in Saint Louis as we speak. We've requested copies of your cold cases, as well as others around the region. The Behavioral Analysis Unit at Quantico is already opening a case, building a profile. The crime lab already has a file open and is searching other pending unsolved cases. And we have agents around the country who can chase down interviews, so you guys can focus on finding Sergeant Worth's daughter."

Julie nodded. *This might not be so bad after all*, she thought.

"We also have an Amber Alert issued. Anyone traveling with a pretty sixteen-year-old blonde in the Midwest will probably be interviewed. If they are not moving—"

"You mean if she is already dead?" Julie interrupted.

"No, ma'am." Jackson Ross spoke for the first time. His face was solid and strong, and, unlike his supervisor, smiling did not come naturally for him. "We mean if he is holding her, in a room or a basement somewhere."

Julie shivered at the image involuntarily.

Ross continued, "And if he is, we can bring Hostage

Rescue in from Quantico and get her back." He held her eyes, his confidence undeniable and a little contagious.

"Special Agent Ross will be the case agent on this," explained Tyler.

"Have you worked abductions before?"

Ross nodded. "Maybe a dozen."

"How many have you solved?"

"All but one."

"How many victims did you get back?"

Ross continued to look into Julie's eyes. "Alive? Four."

Julie looked away. Jesus, she'd had better odds in the mall.

Tyler interrupted. "If we could get those files, we'll get out of your way."

As the captain and Tyler walked off, Julie asked Ross, "So how did you get stuck with us?"

Hearing the question, Tyler stopped and turned. "Because he is the best I have at this."

Julie looked at Ross, who nodded briefly, as if to confirm his supervisor's assessment. For the first time in a couple days, Julie smiled. "Then let's go find this motherfucker."

And for the first time, Ross's face broke into a broad, engaging grin. "Yes, ma'am. Let's do."

# 32

Todd, Julie, and Captain Walker stood at the wide double doors of Pastor Garthwait's church. Makeshift tents and large cabana-style beach umbrellas crowded the yard next to the church parking lot.

Walker scuffed his new black combat boots on the rough concrete. "Of all the fucking—" He stopped and looked around. "Of all the days to have a church bazaar, they gotta pick this one."

When they arrived, a man identifying himself as a church deacon assured them that he would round up the good pastor. A scratchy "Onward Christian Soldiers" recording blared from somewhere in the crowded Bedouin-like encampment.

The reverend came from within the church. He appeared in a tight-fitting black suit, white ironed shirt, and patterned tie. Julie's eye caught his polished black shoes.

He looked as if he had been eating, wiping his hands on a delicate handkerchief, which he stuffed back into his pocket. "What, pray tell, may I do for you?"

"We'd like a few minutes with you in private, if we may."

"And you are?" The reverend looked perplexed.

"Captain Walker, Missouri State Patrol."

The man paced across the broad concrete landing of the church steps. He brushed lint from his suit jacket. "This is not convenient for me now, Captain. As you can see, we are in the middle of a celebration."

Walker made impatient clicking sounds with his tongue. "You've been interviewed by Sergeant Julie Worth recently, do you recall?"

"Yes, so? And?"

"We're investigating a kidnapping."

"She told me, and I relayed to her—"

Walker held up his hands to stop the clergyman. "It's not that kidnapping. Do you have an attorney?"

"Why do you ask, my good man?"

"Because if I have to get a court order to speak to you, you're probably going to need counsel, understand me?" Walker took a step toward the man.

"Sir, may I?" Julie asked.

Walker signaled for her to speak.

"You recall my having spoken to you, correct?"

The pious man blinked.

"We have something we think is relevant pertaining to a recent kidnapping. It may have a link to your daughter's case."

"As I attempted to tell this elite member of the"—he tapped his heels together in a halfhearted salute—"I'm in the middle of a financially important church function."

"Listen to me." Walker turned his back to the tented crowd. "I'm going to tell you something confidential. Sergeant Worth's sixteen-year-old daughter was abducted last evening, and the sergeant's friend was ruled dead at the scene. That death, because it was connected to the kidnapping, is believed to be a homicide."

Julie took in a sip of air at the spoken words.

"We also have evidence that it is related to your daughter's abduction. We want to show you a few pictures."

The reverend paced again and then nodded.

Walker looked him in the eyes. "Not here."

Garthwait stepped aside and opened the double doors to the church foyer. Set up at the back of the gallery, a long table piled with plates of fried chicken, potato salad, and corn on the cob. A young woman sat alone at the far end of the banquet table.

"Excuse us, please." Walker gestured for the woman to trot along.

Todd moved aside a plate of salad and opened a manila envelope, spreading five eight-by-ten-inch photos on the table. "Any of these look familiar?"

"Where did you get these?" The reverend adjusted his glasses and leaned over the table.

"Let's just stay on point here, okay? Where we got these is not important." Walker pushed the photos closer. "Any of these look familiar? Do you recognize the ring? Can you answer the question? Please, we're pressed for time." Walker tapped at the table's edge.

"That's my grandmother's ring." Garthwait pointed to the center photo.

Julie resisted putting her hand to her mouth.

Walker stepped closer and lifted the photo close to his eyes. "How can you tell? The letters on top are broken."

"Look at the bottom, inside of the ring. My grandmother's initials in Old English script."

Julie stepped forward to take a look. The initials *DG* appeared more like worn scratches. Todd gathered the photos, slipped them back into the envelope, and headed for the door, with Walker and Julie close behind.

The reverend shuffled his feet. "What does this mean vis-à-vis my situation?"

Walker stopped at the door. "It means, vis-à-vis, that you are to remain quiet about this discovery. Understood? Even a hint of a rumor that gets out will be on your head, not to mention your soul. Good day"—he slammed the door—"sir."

They burst into the morning light. Behind them, Reverend Dr. Garthwait. "Thank you. The Daughters of the American Revolution thanks you." His voice rose to a gospel-style head tone.

"That ass." Walker slapped the top of his squad car. "I didn't handle that well. Sorry."

"If no one else will say it, I will." Julie hesitated. "We are dealing with a serial"—she almost said "killer"—"abductor."

Walker's phone buzzed in his breast pocket. He held up a finger to them while he answered with a series of uh-huhs.

Todd and Julie waited in silence.

Walker ended his call and looked at his two underlings. "That was UltraTest in Chicago. Prelim work on the blood from the branch you gave them the other day and the specks in the mason jar show identical blood type. No DNA yet, of course, but I don't think we need it."

"Why is that?" Julie said.

"The guy has a rare blood type."

"How much so?"

"Very. AB negative. One in a hundred seventy. It's not DNA, but close enough for now. Probably a white male."

Todd leaned against the fender of the squad car. "That links the Garthwait and the Preston mur—" He stopped and looked at Julie. "Sorry. The blood on the leaves and branch puts him recently visiting the Preston abduction scene that happened seventeen years ago. But how does that link—"

"He saw me in one of the interviews," Julie blurted. "Probably not Preston; her house is too isolated."

"When you went to the factory, who saw you?" Walker asked. "Were you identified?"

"Yeah. I walked through the cafeteria with the secretary, nosed around a little after my lunch with Drew. That's William Drew, sir. Head honcho at Drew Inc. Do you know if the box factory has come up with that list of employees yet? The ones who were working at the plant when the niece was taken?"

"Nah, let me check." He phoned his secretary and stepped away from the squad car.

Julie and Todd had nothing to say to each other. They both paced, Julie watching the chosen as they arrived for the church social, waiting for Walker to return from down the sidewalk. She thought of Cheryl and her early days of antipathy for Sunday school.

When the captain returned, he did so with a sober expression. "Jan says she received the list of workers who had tenure in 1995, and we can look at that later at the office, but, this is unreal—I called UltraTest again and pushed them a bit. They say samples from the truck with the blood drop is AB negative."

Todd's look told Julie that he would agree with her suspicions that this abductor and the tormentor who'd driven her off the road were, in fact, the same person.

Walker headed for his squad car. "But kids, here's the capper. Sergeant Worth—" He took a deep breath.

Julie knew she was in trouble from that hesitation.

"There's a gentleman at headquarters who wants to

talk to me. He's with an attorney and another fellow. This gen-tle-man"—he overenunciated each syllable as if she were hard of hearing—"happens to be a certain Barton Worth. Sound familiar?"

Her ex-husband had finally made a showing in the clusterfuck. Walker signaled for Julie to step closer to his vehicle. "In my office as soon as we get back, understood?"

Julie held up her hand for him to hear her. "I've left a number of messages for him. Rather than call, it's so typical of him to just show up. Did he specifically ask for me or what?"

"More of an 'or what.' His attorney is with him, and my secretary says he's pissed." Walker shut his door and drove off.

Todd looked puzzled.

"My ex, all out of shape, just made an appearance at headquarters. Walker wants us back there ASAP."

In the car heading to the station, Todd and Julie kept to themselves. They never shared family matters. Julie busied herself by trying to get comfortable with the assorted impediments on her service belt. "This is going to get messy, Mr. Devlin. Watch out for flying glass."

"Is he that violent?"

"No, I am." Julie gazed out the passenger-side window.

33

*C*rowded *as usual* at headquarters, several cuffed and seated suspects were being questioned at multiple desks. Walker's office sported a huge glass partition where Julie observed a number of people, all of them on their feet. Most prominent in the group, her ex, dressed in a two-thousand-dollar suit. She took out her Sig and locked it safely in her desk drawer, not trusting that sixteen years down the line would be enough to cool her jets when it came to Captain America. She approached Walker's office and heard Bart.

"Where is she? We want answers."

"Am I the 'she' you're referring to, Barton?" Julie didn't wait for an answer but asked Walker permission. "May I come in, sir?"

Walker invited her around to his side of the desk, where he cleaned off a straight-back chair piled high with reading material. "The next person who raises his voice in this office is out of here! No exceptions." He glanced around at the assembled group. "Sit."

Bart Worth started pacing.

"I said sit, Mr. Worth, or leave."

"You can't tell—"

"In my office, in my headquarters building, I damn sure can." Walker waited until his command was understood by all. "First of all, my sympathy to you, sir, and your troubles at this time. Secondly, and maybe more important, what is it you hope to accomplish here?"

Worth put his hands on the arms of his chair as if to stand—until he caught Walker's eye. "I demand some answers, dammit. My child has been kidnapped. I've been getting the runaround." His level of anger made saliva accompany his every word.

Walker listened, making light circles on top of his desk with his fingertips. "This abduction, Mr. Worth, is an ongoing investigation. You cannot storm in here and demand anything. Clear?" He didn't wait for a reply. "I've extended you the courtesy of my office because of the great respect I have for Sergeant Worth, your ex-wife."

Julie's body shook as if trying to shed the relationship. She tried not to look at the narcissistic bastard, but inevitably the man's sheer gall dominated the room. She had slogged through academy training, fell in love—or, rather, lust—married, and separated all within two years, with Julie filing for divorce after Cheryl's birth. It seemed that Bart's busy schedule kept him from visiting Julie and his newborn.

On the rare occasions when they would speak, he reminded Julie of the trust fund he'd set up for Cheryl. "You don't like the idea of this fund assuring Cheryl's future?"

"I don't like the idea of you trying to justify your dick slinging by mentioning this fucking trust fund each time we speak. Got it, Mr. Wonderful?"

"You are one mean bitch, you know that?"

Lawyers' voices startled Julie, and she took a moment to catch up.

"Mr. Walker, uh, excuse me; Captain Walker, may I?"

"And you are?"

"Walt Abrams. Mr. Worth's attorney."

"And may I ask why you are here, Mr. Abrams?"

The attorney attempted to make a grand show of moving his briefcase onto his lap as if the contents held the secrets of the lost Mayans. "Mr. Worth's concerns are well founded, Captain. His wife's—excuse me, ex's—lifestyle and dangerous work have precipitated this abduction."

"Hold it, Abrams. You don't know that. You don't know Sergeant Worth's routine, her relationship to the work—and what does that mean, 'lifestyle'? How can you come in here and say that Sergeant Worth's work caused this?"

"What has she been working on?" This question from the third man, who hadn't been introduced. A lanky, grey-haired fellow with mean, dark eyes. "By the way, Captain, I'm Mark Issen of Issen Security, recently hired by Mr. Worth to help in this investigation."

Walker had a knowing smile as he stared down the private investigator. "What has she been working on, you ask? Do you honestly expect an answer to that question?" The captain scanned the room. "Do you folks have any idea how hard we're working to get this young lady back with her mother?"

"That brings up an interesting question." This from lawyer Abrams. "We've been working with Child Services recently to reverse the divorce ruling on custody. Our initial responses are encouraging and forthcoming."

"How long?" Julie inquired.

"How long what? How long are we going to sit here? How long before we see results from the police? How long before people stop stonewalling this distraught father?"

Julie edged forward in her seat. "How long have you been dealing with Child Services about custody?" She saw his eyes shifting, knowing it to be a sign of dissembling or outright lying.

He wrinkled his nose as if smelling something distasteful. "Sergeant Worth, I understand your anxiety. I know what you're going through."

"You haven't any idea what I'm going through, so don't say you do."

"You're being difficult, Sergeant." Abrams raised his hands in protest. "Your manner, although somewhat understandable, is completely without merit and nonproductive. I, for one, think it might be beneficial if you would excuse yourself from this meeting."

"Not going to happen," Walker said. "Let's stick with topic A."

Julie settled back in her chair, determined to stay calm. "And I, for one, would like an answer to my question."

"Which was?"

"How long? When did you contact Child Services. When were you hired?" She noticed the PI, Issen, duck his head. An "Oh shit!" moment. "Both of you, when did you begin this long arduous quest for truth, justice, and custody?"

The attorney leaned over and whispered to Bart Worth.

Captain Walker rested his fists on the hard surface of his oak desk. "Okay folks, I'm going to call a halt to this. It's total bullshit. You come in here talking truth and visibility, and it devolves into a veil of accusations. Sergeant

Worth is not on trial, get it? Now answer her simple question if you expect cooperation from this department."

Abrams fiddled with his briefcase at the side of his chair and then eased up from his seated position as if the universe were his. "I'll be in touch with my friend the district attorney, of course. And—"

Walker grabbed the sleeve of Abrams's suit coat and led him to the door of his office. "Get out. You dare come into my headquarters building and threaten me with your DA 'friend.' We're investigating a murder and abduction, and you have the balls to hinder our time by jamming my office with this shit? This personal vendetta?" Walker opened the door.

"All right, all right, dammit." Abrams shook Walker's hand from his sleeve. "It was this morning."

"What? What happened this morning?" Julie was right on top of it.

"Our meeting with Judge Hancock on the custody issue. And your proximity to dangerous people."

The captain dropped his arms to his sides, his neck stretching out from his collar. "She's a sergeant in the police force, for Christ's sake. Dammit. That's law enforcement." Walker turned and shouted for the open squad room of eavesdroppers to "get back to work!" He returned to his office, signaling for the others to leave. He rattled the glass door as he slammed into his workplace.

Julie caught up with her ex in the hallway. "You must be proud of yourself, mister. Dragging in your minions, trying to portray yourself as the long-suffering parent, when, in fact, you've been absent for years."

"Now, wait just a minute." He reached out and waved a finger in her face.

Julie slapped away his hand.

"Bitch," he hissed.

Bart, the lawyer, and Issen swept out of the building as she turned toward the ladies' room. After splashing water on her face and composing herself, she searched for Todd, who had already left.

The parking lot buzzed with groups of officers huddled in conspiratorial conversations. Julie ignored them and hurried toward her car. She saw Bart smoking a cigarette, leaning against it.

"Is this another of your ambushes, junior?"

"No, it's not, Miss Righteous. I wanted to explain to you my concern for Cheryl."

Julie paced up and down the lot's driveway, her throat contracting almost to the point of strangulation. She stopped between two vehicles. "You were so concerned for her that it took hours and hours to hear from you."

"I happened to be in New York on business."

"No, you happened to be in Mexico with your secretary, you lying sack of shit! Doesn't that fancy resort in Cabo San Lucas have telephone service, Barton?" She knew he hated for her to use his full name. "I left a half dozen messages for you. The temp at your office here said you'd left word not to be disturbed. You'd think that after the fourth or fifth 'Urgent, call home immediately' alert, you would respond."

He showed Julie his woe-is-me, put-upon attitude. "The girl never said it was—"

"Oh, stop the bullshit. You come here with your yes-men proclaiming a long, drawn-out attempt to get custody of your daughter, when, in fact, it just happened this morning. That's when you made the initial inquiries." She fought for self-control. "Rather than get in contact with me, you go the legal route. You are such an ass."

"I visited her when I could. I provided her with a trust that was quite generous."

"Who mentioned money, Barton? Why the lawyer and PI? Why didn't you at least call and inquire of any developments in the case?"

"I called. I was put on hold."

"Oh, poor baby. Put on hold? How dare they! Didn't they know they were speaking to Barton Worth, the most powerfu—"

He stepped in close to Julie and slapped her face hard.

The blow spun her around and knocked her to her knees. She got right back up, covering her face, both arms up on either side of her head in a boxer's stance. She two-stepped in toward Bart. "You chickenshit piece of garbage."

A number of shouts came from nearby officers. Julie made a show of her right hand and then kicked Bart's knee hard with her left foot. As he went down, she ran her knee hard into his groin and struck him with her elbow across his face. She reached for her handcuffs while several officers behind her asked if she needed help.

"I got it, guys." Crowded between two parked cars, she cuffed Barton's right hand and twisted his elbow. She rolled him onto his stomach and gave him his "You have the right to remain silent" Miranda warning, and then added, "I've been wanting to say those words to you for years, Mr. Chickenshit. Get up."

Julie's nose bled, and the left side of her face was red and swollen. Her leg felt heavy. But she felt good. Lately, getting the shit knocked out of her was becoming an occupational hazard. She heard more running footsteps and backed off as two officers dragged Bart between parked cars.

"Let me go, goddamn it! Don't you know what's going

on here? My girl's been kidnapped! Why are you doing this? I've got a lawyer!" Bart struggled as he was perp-walked back toward the station. He looked over his shoulder at Julie. "I've never been anything but a loving father, you rotten bit—"

"Shut your mouth." The larger of the two officers spun Bart around into his face. "You assaulted an officer. You're under arrest."

Julie massaged her thigh a bit while brushing off her slacks. The officers marched Captain America into the station. She was thankful that she'd left her 9-millimeter locked in her desk.

he streets were deserted. The time of night when bar hoppers called it quits and working stiffs were an hour away from their rude awakenings.

A misty rain polished the pavement as Charles made his way west toward Bait Shack. The idea of his newest captive intrigued him. As always, he would proceed with caution, but he loved the possibilities. A teen would give rise to untold exploration and fun. He would go against his previous vows and make an exception in her case, wooing her with all the drama of a torrid high school tryst. It all seemed ideal, but for that three-letter word always getting in the way. Perhaps he would just frighten her, sticking closer to his promise of abstinence. His vow. Treat her rough but with the hope of—dare he imagine—romance.

His performances these past few years made him proud, but only when he was dominant; the subjects had to be his absolute captives. Depositing his guests hundreds of miles away after the honeymoon period seemed safe and provided entertainment.

Having done no real harm to most of his "girlfriends," as he liked to refer to them, he would drive them the opposite direction from where they were acquired, while being careful not to establish a pattern.

Leaving the city, the wet asphalt country road made his tires hum. He kept time, whistling through his teeth as the blacktop emitted its steady whistle.

He considered his present female houseguest to be his most daring to date. The exposure at the real estate development and the subsequent abduction became dodgy. When the older woman, Billie something or other, came waltzing into his coop where he had his little chickadee tied up, he didn't know how he would handle it. Her death solved that problem. He sped up, longing for the love and comfort of the young one. He would calm her fears with a bit of reason, assisted by a slight dose of sleepy time and his standard short lecture on reciprocity. *It will happen, my sweet. Relax. Let it wash over you.* If she turned out to be volatile or cocky, he would repay her in kind. In time, he felt she would take him as her prom escort. He thought of himself as an incurable romantic, not someone who could never be loved. A flower for her hair, their evening full of dance, laughter, and a wrestling match in the backseat of the car.

If none of that worked, then he would have to consider squeezing his current visitor into his ring of *C*. It had been quite a while since his halfhearted promise of abstinence; he felt he could give up his pledge and rekindle his scarlet rendezvous.

He would have no choice. The Cheryls of the world would force him into his former mischief. The devious slut.

By the time he arrived at Bait Shack, he was livid.

35

*C*heryl awakened from a dream in which an enormous bird trapped her in a cave of twigs papered with old comic books. In the smoking, vaporous atmosphere, the bird pecked his way into the nest as Cheryl tried to cover herself.

In the dark, a sliver of light sliced through her escape gap in the plywood wall. Cheryl had figured out a way of unscrewing the pesky lightbulb so she could sleep. She stretched out on the thin mattress.

She thought about the last few moments. A dream, with its fantasy bird screeching to get to her. The slamming of a car door. She hesitated, realizing that the door was not part of the dream but her reality. He was back. Her four-walled universe was about to resume.

Her escape hatch, only half done. She'd made progress, but there was still a ways to go. The noise made by the wooden barrier changed, the solid resistance became more resonant. In certain places, her makeshift knife pierced the patterned rectangle and went through the wood. While squinting through the slight hole, she saw something that looked like glass. She remained quiet.

Cheryl knew she had to once again get to her job at the window and reminded herself about the lightbulb and the fact that the shithead might pop in at any minute. She rolled off her mattress and went to the door. Bracing her right foot against the corner of the papered wall where she suspected a concrete block made a convenient bulge, she levered herself up until her left foot was atop the doorknob 90 degrees from the corner wall. She poked her right index finger into the wire cage that protected the now-extinguished lightbulb. Initially, she'd unscrewed it a quarter turn. She hooked her finger into the curlycue low-energy bulb again and relit it, hopping down just in time to hear the basement door bang open at the top of the steps. King was singing his rendition of "Heigh-Ho, Heigh-Ho, It's Off to Work We Go."

The pass-through for the food slid open. "Buckle up, Snow White. We're going for a ride," hissed the no-nonsense voice.

Cheryl saw just a bit of the man's face as he bent sideways to look into the room. The light blinked on and off several times as King played with the switch. The door opened, the light switched off.

"Put on the hood, sweets. It's time to earn your keep."

The light coming from the stairs helped Cheryl see a dark outline of an undersized man in the doorway. He tossed the hood toward the cot.

"Let's hustle now. Don't give me trouble. I'm not in the mood."

Cheryl picked up the hood and then positioned herself against the far wall from the cot. A soft flake of light shining down at an angle across the floor crept halfway up the wallpaper. Her efforts on the window escape were showing up too nicely on the basement wall. She stepped forward, trying to position herself between the light patch and the man at the door.

"Where you going, dumpling girl? I didn't tell you to shake it. Are you anxious to trot upstairs with Ole man Studley? Your time is coming, darling." He laughed. "Put on the hood, cheerleader." He shuffled back and forth in front of the door.

Cheryl pretended to struggle with the hood.

"Who fight? We fight. Red and gold, fight, fight!" He laughed. "Thank you, thank you ver mush."

She waited. The man slid closer into the room.

"I don't want to take away any of your recreational privileges, my dear, but—and this is a big one—if you don't get your cute butt out of this room in the next five seconds, I'll beat your rosy-cheeked face to a pulp. *Do you hear me?*"

Cheryl took another step toward the man to hide the light streak and then jammed her finger down her throat, attempting to throw up as King came scuttling across the room. He grabbed her by the shoulders as Cheryl doubled over trying to stir her bile. She coughed several times and then pulled the hood farther up toward her nose and projected her warm vomit into his face.

He screamed and jumped back from the green mess. "You dirty, stinking little bitch! I'll kill you! I'll kill you!" He swatted at his face, wiping off the sardine-laden slop. He beat his hands on his legs and staggered around her.

King slipped on the vomit, letting out a less than manly yelp. "Why did you do this to me? Dammit! I've been decent with you. I've fed you and offered my physical self to you in a gentlemanly fashion."

Cheryl would not let this slug of a man dominate her. She placed her hand on his arm. "Oh, please, Mr. King.

Have mercy on me. Just give me a moment; I truly will cooperate."

He yanked his arm away from her.

"Could you find it in your heart to allow me a few more days to adjust?" She clasped her hands to her knees and choked as if to vomit again.

"No one has ever . . ." He turned to her half-hooded face. He couldn't finish.

The door closed, and the caged light went back on. The fan and motor switched on and off, back and forth. The light blinked a few times.

Cheryl realized he was beginning to lord over her simply by his presence. She wanted it over. If she confronted him, maybe he could be shamed into allowing her to leave, but she knew her fantasies were childish. She resolved to keep at her work, to sardine-can her way to freedom.

She opened a Cup Noodles container and ran tap water into it. It would take about an hour of soaking in cold water for the noodles to become palatable.

Other than her hands blistered raw from the constant sawing with the makeshift knife, the cans worked well. After a great deal of sawing, the cans would lose their body and collapse, but they were still effective. She had used a couple of tins so far, depositing the empties into the refuse bag so that King would not become suspicious. She had no idea how long she had been in her tight little quarters. It seemed more than a week; maybe less than two. Once again she climbed onto the efficiency refrigerator and traced the carved scratches in what she thought of as her "life's work."

Cheryl toiled at the plywood panel. She promised herself early on that she would not be violated by him. She would stash her sardine knife in her sock, or wedge it into her hair, or somehow take it with her up those high, dark stairs.

He came down the steps. Again. The food slot opened, and he tramped back to the top of the steps. His shoes sounded as if he wanted to make a point. *I'm here. Listen to this. What do you think of these boots?* And then guitar music. It was just humming, melodious guitar chords that couldn't be sustained, and then the inevitable story.

> Oh, Charlie Wiggles lived down the way.
> Sittin' on the porch most every day.
> Oh yeah, dum ditty dum dum. Oh yeah.
> Charlie had an ugly wife.
> Dangdest thing I'd seen all my life.
> Oh yeah, dum ditty dum dum. Oh yeah

It went on for too long, the words as bad as the music. Cheryl clapped, but with each meeting of the hands taking twice the normal time.

"Wake up, little Susie, wake up! Get your lazy backside up!" he shouted.

If he left tomorrow, she would saw her way out.

The last several sessions became less confining. She called them "sessions" instead of days, since only fragments of light messaged the passing of time.

She turned out to be the worst guest he'd ever had. Smart aleck and mean-spirited, not content and resigned like the others. He knew he would have to dispose of her.

He grew restless; the girl, a nuisance. Going through his collection of movies, he came upon an always-enjoyed snuff film reenactment. It looked as if it had been shot in Mexico or the desert. The lead actor strutted about naked except for his black Western hat and boots. These boots reminded him of his own special midcalf walkabouts—not exactly Tony Lamas but bought online for $49.99, with a false set of laces in front that took the onus off the three-inch heels. That, along with the disguised thick soles, gave him an eye-to-eye advantage he had not enjoyed previously. His fists clenched when he thought of the vomit cleaned from his boots after Miss Nymph greeted him with her earlier projectile display. He mused that she wasn't worth the trouble if there wasn't the potential of a true romance—which he doubted in his imagined generous heart. Maybe it was time. He'd think upon it tomorrow and come home to do the deed.

36

Julie and Todd checked out where they thought the abductor might have parked when taking Billie and Cheryl. Julie took the right side of the run-down housing development. No answer from the first two shacks. She stood on the rickety wood porch of the third.

"Good morning. Sergeant Worth, State Patrol. We're looking into an incident that happened on the other side of the woods in the Thousand Pines development."

The man's unkempt beard and filthy wifebeater undershirt matched his well-used hut. "If it happened over at Snobville, why you askin' me?" He moved to shut the door.

"Hold it." Julie opened the screen door and pressed her badge up close to the man's face. "Maybe you didn't understand me. The police have reason to believe that the suspect"—a sour, sweaty odor made her take a step back—"may have parked his vehicle near your residence." Julie indicated a spot across the road.

"Who am I? Houdini? Why the hell would I pay attention to some thief's car? I'm a busy man. Take a hike, babe." He slammed the door. "Gestapo bitch."

Under ordinary circumstances, she would have let it go, but these weren't everyday conditions.

A Black Sabbath anthem blared as she again opened the screen. She pounded on the door, still with badge in hand. "Police! Open up!"

Todd jogged up to the front of the house. "What's up, Sarge? You need help?"

"Check the other side of this unit. Not sure about this guy." She pounded and shouted once again. No answer. Pocketing her badge, she unholstered her weapon and cupped her hands at the door's window. She made out the torso and legs of the man using a kitchen ladder to pull himself up through a skylight door in the slanted roof.

Julie stepped off the porch and took several paces. "What you doing up there, asshole? You want to go to jail? Let me see your hands. Now!"

The man stretched out on the roof. "I don't know shit. Why you pissin' with me?"

Todd came around the back. "Did he split?"

"No. He's on the roof."

His .45 in hand, Todd stepped back to take a look at the man. "Put your hands in the air, above your head."

"I'll fall. I'll lose balance."

"Tough shit, asshole. What are you wanted for, Jack? You on probation? What's up?"

"I don't like cops."

"Yeah, right, get in line. Listen, amigo, if I have to come up there, someone's gonna get hurt." Todd turned to Julie. "How'd he get up there? From inside?"

"Climbed up through a door in the roof. Don't let him come down unassisted. He could have a weapon."

"Right. Hey, buster! Throw me your house keys. Do it!"

Julie double-handed her Sig as she watched the man fumble in his pocket. He looked all around before tossing the keys—not to Todd but at the dirt pathway in front of the house.

Todd and Julie exchanged looks as Todd retrieved the keys and let himself in.

Julie waited outside in case junior went sideways. She wondered if any of this would help get back her daughter. She watched as Todd guided the man's legs back down onto the kitchen ladder. Todd cuffed him and brought him outside.

"Bitch." The man spit on the ground in front of Julie.

"Hey, that's my sergeant, you asshole!" Todd gave the man's arms a good tug upward.

"Oh, you mean piece of tail—"

"Shut your mouth unless you're asked a question." Todd grabbed the back of his neck. "Now," Julie said calmly, "as I said, there's been an abduction." She closed the distance between them.

The man's brow wrinkled.

"A kidnapping. Someone taken against their will. You understand?"

"A two-tone Ford Bronco." The man spewed the information like a child reciting his wrongdoing. "Dented right front fender; maybe early nineties. Okay?"

"What color?" asked Todd.

"Puke green and white."

Todd went to uncuff the man. "Why didn't you say that in the beginning?"

"I'm gonna have your badge. You're gonna wish you didn't wake up this morning, *amigo*."

"I'm going to shake down this shithole disaster you're living in, my friend." Todd got up close to the man's ear.

"Am I going to find something your parole officer won't like?"

The fellow hung his head and pouted.

"What else did you see?" Julie demanded. "And speak up."

"The guy parked. About an hour later, it's raining. I was rolling up the windows in my truck when the dude comes back. Couldn't see much 'cause it was dark. Raining, like I said. They piled in."

"They?" Julie asked.

"Yeah, looked like a young hottie with a short guy. It was dark."

Julie got in front of the man. "What else? Give it up; I don't have time for bullshit."

The bearded man shuffled from foot to foot. Todd once again gave him a nudge.

"I was watching my dog program. I didn't—"

"Dog program?"

"The *Bounty Hunter* guy." He bit his lip and then blurted, "She was roped up and hooded. He put her in the back."

"And you didn't find that unusual?"

"Don't know; ain't none of my doing. The driver sat there for a while, then got back out the car and pissed off into the woods."

"Then you went back to your TV show, right?"

"Yeah, I don't know nothin' about this bullshit."

"Did you see him leave?" Julie wanted to bust him in the chops.

"Nah, yeah, I don't know. About ten minutes or so, I was up during the commercial. A door slammed, and I saw the lights of the car. He was digging his way out of the ditch. What else you want, for Christ's sake?"

Julie half listened to Todd's recommendations to the man about future behavior. She knew she should be pained by the thought of Cheryl being roughed up by a mean-spirited bastard, but she felt only a growing anxiety. Todd tossed the man's house keys back to him as they walked to the squad car.

"Early-model Ford Bronco. It's something, partner, its gotta be something."

He had her daughter bound and hooded. She needed to hold herself together. At this instant, without a second thought, she would gladly kill the son of a bitch who took Cheryl and who had been responsible for the death of her friend Billie. It became obvious to her that the reason officers were excluded from cases involving their relatives had to do with judgment, usually impaired.

37

Bronco, huh? Not many still on the road. I'll call Jackson Ross; his people can start running them down." Captain Walker tossed two pages of names across his desk.

Julie and Todd scanned the list.

"The employees at your Drew Box Factory. The ones who were there when the CEO's niece was abducted. Doubt it will lead us anywhere."

None of the names rang any felon bells or reminders of former bad boys.

"I'll call the plant. See who, if any, of their workers drives a Bronco. On another front, Jackson sent us this lead his analysts found. Old report that looks promising, from regional." Once again Walker slid the pages across his desk.

Julie shared it with Todd.

Notice. Abduction. Angelina Hogar, white female, picked up by a passerby, partially nude on a dirt road just west of Wolf Bayou, Arkansas, near junction Rt 25 and Rt 92. Abducted on April 1, 2012, east of Jonesboro, Arkansas, while hitchhiking. The aforementioned was on U.S. High-

way 63 heading to West Memphis, Arkansas. The victim
reports she was hooded and kept captive for two weeks. For
further information contact Commander Lawrence Ren-
saler, West Memphis police.

"I called this Rensaler. He says Hogar is back in Jonesboro,
tight-lipped, scared out of her mind. What do you think,
guys?"

"Normally I would think of it as a common hitchhiking incident." Julie looked again at the bulletin. "Maybe a
solicitation deal gone bad, but it might be something. The
hood, especially. He say anything else?"

"Yeah, only thing the girl said was she thought it was
an older-model SUV and described the car as 'not really,'
meaning who in the hell knows what."

"Maybe she meant it wasn't a van or an SUV but
something in between."

"Like a Bronco," Todd piped up.

Walker looked at Julie. "Want to take a ride?"

"Definitely. Jonesboro?"

"You and Todd go interview this Hogar gal, see what
you can turn up. It's only a couple hours down there. I'll
call Jackson and tell him we'll cover this one."

"You trying to get me out of your hair, boss?"

Walker tilted his head down. "It will do us both good
if you do as I suggest and leave the hair reference to those
more qualified than present company. There's nothing
you can do here. If something develops, we're in touch
by cell." He paused. "I'll call Rensaler and let him know
you're in the neighborhood."

Dvořák's *New World Symphony* thundered from the radio
as Todd drove the interstate south.

"I don't know if this is the proper music, considering your reference to Walker's hair," he quipped

"You mean, as in long-haired music and 'Get me out of your hair, boss'? Is that the segue you're trying to foist on me, Mr. Todd?"

"Sorry, that was weak. Jesus, when Walker gets pissed, he's funny." He glanced across the seat to Julie. "Hey, what's going on?"

"He's like my dad." Julie turned away, her hand going to her face. "Always so direct. Painful. How much farther? Are we there yet? Let's move it."

They checked in with Rensaler when they got close to Jonesboro. His only advice: "She's upset and difficult, should probably be in a hospital being looked after. By the way, she doesn't have a phone, so I guess you just show up. Good luck." He gave them her address.

They located the Hogar digs easily. A rented room above a workingman's bar on the hard side of town.

She wasn't home. Another tenant stuck his head out his door and volunteered that he thought she was at work, waitressing. When pressed, the Good Samaritan shrugged and suggested downstairs.

Todd spoke with Walker while Julie went to the tavern. She waited for her eyes to adjust, the dark interior a violent contrast to the midday sun. Someone played a pinball machine to her left. She noticed a silhouetted image reflected in the liquor bottles and back bar mirror.

"What's your pleasure, miss?" The barkeep, an older fellow.

"Hi, looking for a girl by the name of Angelina, works here. Can you help me?"

"You a cop?" He continued drying a cocktail glass.

"Out of state. Just want a word with Miss Hogar. She's not in any trouble, just want to talk a bit."

"Good luck on that. Our Missy Hogar is screwed up. Don't know what happened. She was gone for a spell, then reappeared and was different."

"Different, how?"

"Don't know, just different. Used to be all bright lights and grins, worked here for a while, then left. Like I said, weird. Wouldn't talk about it; boss had to let her go. Shame, nice gal. Works over at the cafeteria on Main." He glanced at his watch. "Probably still there, since it's late lunchtime."

Julie thanked the man and hurried toward the exit. The fellow at the pinball machine rubbed himself suggestively when Julie glanced his way.

"Hey, Ned, cool it. Five-O." From the bartender.

She would add the pinball fool to her list of recent candidates for bozos of the week. Todd was just getting off the phone as she came blinking out of the bar. "Sorry to report nothing new. Find out anything?"

Julie headed for the car. "Our girl works at a cafeteria over on Main—and, incidentally, bars that open at noon suck."

After several inquiries, they came upon the Mayfair. The cafeteria was half empty. In the back, a girl stood with a large tray of fried chicken. Julie watched her distribute food into the steam table and then look as if she had forgotten what to do next.

"Let's grab something to eat and wait until things thin out a bit, okay?"

Todd headed for the line. "Don't you think we should inquire if our Hogar girl is even here, Sarge?"

"She's here. Watch the kid with the food trays. She's in the kitchen now."

Julie gestured to the food line as the girl drifted back and forth behind the counter.

"I see what you mean." Todd watched her. "She's out of it."

An older man in full apron and pencil mustache came up to speak with the girl. He pointed to different parts of the cafeteria before rushing back to the kitchen. Eventually she cleaned and bussed the table next to Todd and Julie.

"Angie, how are you?" Julie asked.

The girl's eyes darted back toward the kitchen and then settled on Julie. "Ah, fine, thank you."

Julie got up and walked toward the middle of the stainless-steel food line, just opposite the doors leading to the kitchen. "Hello, Mr. Manager, hello."

"What's up? Help you? I'm the owner."

"May I have a word with you?" Julie pointed toward the end of the stacked food trays. They met behind the cashier. "Loved your chicken a la king," she lied. "Everything was great." Julie flashed her out-of-state badge and took on a conspiratorial tone. "We wanted to have a word with Angelina. She hasn't done anything wrong. But we think she could help us with something. Would that be all right?"

The man nodded but lost a bit of his hospitality.

Julie walked up to Angie. "Miss Hogar, you don't know me. I've spoken to your boss, asking if I might have a few words with you. Do you mind?" She motioned to a seat next to Todd.

"I didn't do anything. Did I?"

"No, of course not."

Smoothing her hair, Angie took a seat and then straightened her skirt. "Are you police?"

"If we were the police, would you still speak to us?" Todd gave Angie his card.

The girl studied it and fussed with a loose button on her shirt uniform. "Would three o'clock be okay? I have an hour-and-a-half break before dinner."

"We don't have a lot of time, miss." Julie smiled. "What we're dealing with is serious sh—well, an abduction. I'll speak to Mr. Mustache, get you to meet with us now." Outside, the three of them stood next to the cruiser.

"We don't want to make trouble for you, but let's talk," Julie said to Angie. "Do you want to sit in the car or—"

"I don't feel well. Could we go to my place?"

They drove the short distance to the girl's room above the tavern. Angie led them up the narrow stairwell, taking what felt like far too much time.

Julie stayed patient, thinking that with any luck the girl would give them something. Anything would be better than what they didn't have now.

"Excuse the room. Have a seat if you can find a spot."

Julie cleared a chair of old magazines while Todd stood near the kitchen counter.

"Sorry, Officer. I don't mean to be deceitful. I just don't know how to think about it. I don't even know what to call it." The girl sat on a single bed, gazing out the window at the metal fire escape.

The light caught a gleam in her eyes. "I was thumb tripping to West Memphis when—oh, I didn't even ask what you wanted of me. I assumed it was about my incident."

"It's okay. Go on."

"He hit me several times before I got settled in the car." She paused, digging her nails into the mattress. "He put me in a nasty little room, odd wallpaper, a bed—really just a cot—a toilet stool, a fridge." She continued to stare out the window. "At first he would be in the room every night. What a horrible little human being. I had to wear this smelly black hood when he came into the room, so I couldn't see him. He would leave food, and I wouldn't see him for what seemed like a week. He would be different, trying to be sweet or charming." She dropped her head into her hands.

"He talked about the stupidest things. A ring of rocks he looked down on from high places, girls who loved him. I have no idea what he meant by that. He was impossible to care about, even if you wanted to." She paused. "He smelled of garlic, mostly. I was in a basement; it was cold and damp. He was short for a man. His body, was, I guess you would say, inadequate. I thought he would kill me— he talked of it." She cast her eyes to the floor once again. "He would play sappy guitar music outside the room; the same passage over and over. It drove me nuts."

"What did he say?" Julie tried not to break the spell. "Did he threaten you?"

"Uh-huh. Said some women deserved to die. Some days there were motorboats; the house might have been by a lake. One day he made me strip and put on the hood. He put me in the vehicle, and he must have driven for hours. Then he stopped and pulled me from the back of the truck and left me on the road."

"You were hitchhiking, right? When you first got in the car, didn't you get a look at his face?"

"I should have, but he was bent over, getting something from the floor. The driver's footwell. He said something about my seat belt, so as I turned to grab it, he socked me hard. Maybe with a handle from a hammer. Wow, I don't even know why I would say that—about the hammer, I mean." She paused. "Oh yeah. Once, after one of his nightly visits, I peeked under the hood and saw him slapping a piece of round polished wood against his leg. It looked like he was going to hit me again."

She circled the room. "Dirty little bastard." She covered her face with crossed arms. "Excuse the language." She went to the window. "Once in a while he would put his hands around my throat as if he were about to strangle me. Then he would laugh as if it were a joke. I never saw his face that well except the night he let me go, and even then it was pretty dark.

"His smell, I'll never forget that." She waited, as if for permission to continue. "Cheap aftershave, sweat, and the garlic." She turned back to Julie. "Where he let me out was close to a place called Heber Springs. There's a bunch of lakes there. That's where I might have been the whole time. He just drove around those hours to confuse me. If you catch him, tell him for me, 'Angie thinks you're a coward.'"

Julie walked over and gave the girl a hug, and then signaled to Todd that they were leaving.

Listening to the hums and rattles of the police car on the way back to Missouri, the day turned out to be a long one.

"You okay to drive, Todd?" She didn't hear his answer as she drifted into a dream—Cheryl giving a speech at her elementary school graduation.

"All people—white, black, brown, yellow—are equal in my eyes, as in the eyes of the Lord." She continued her charmingly naive speech. "There is good in us all, every being has kindness that shines through, every man has the power to be gentle and decent."

Julie woke up, wondering if Cheryl's innocence would betray her, and would she be able to see there were those who didn't obey the commandments? *Be strong, baby, be strong.*

38

To be in accordance with the truth, one must also understand how ugly it can be once it makes its appearance. Being honest for most of his life had been a mere suggestion; a whiff of a passing breeze, Charles mused. Common folk were anchored to their corny "Honesty is the best policy" cliches. Charles, however, believed that truth and lies were mere tools in life, the best policy being "Whatever it takes."

William Drew called him at the Bait Shack to explain that the authorities wanted to interview all of the employees who'd been working at the plant when his niece had gone missing. "I know this is a pain in the behind for you, Charles, but it shouldn't take long."

"Would you like me to organize the whole thing for you? I'll hustle the men in and out of the interview space; be the goodwill ambassador for the company."

"Great. Especially since you are part of the management team. I'll leave the list with Deedee, and both of you can determine the best way to go with this. Oh, and we have a number of folks who worked here at the time but have moved on. If they ask for their names, tell them they'll have to hunt them down on their own. Thanks again, Charles."

"When did they say they'd be here?" Charles glanced at his watch.

"They didn't." Deedee busied herself at her desk. "I was told midmorning. You seem fidgety today."

"Oh, just another day at the mill. Nose to the grindstone. 'A man's work is never done.' Blah-blah-blah." He willed himself to relax, concentrating on his shoulders and the tension around his neck.

"Oh no, hold it, Slick-a-roonie. It's a *woman's* work that's never done. Let's keep our priorities in order, shall we?"

Charles tried to conjure up a laugh—not feeling it. "I'll get going on this group of fellows, have them come up in herds of two, since you say there will be a couple of *po*-lice."

"You should be ashamed. They aren't cattle."

"Of course not. I meant it only as a passing witticism. A mere jest to describe one's hardworking mates. Our fellow travelers on the road to . . . let me think, the well-traveled path to—"

"If it's fellow travelers, they'd be on their way to Moscow, silly."

"But yes, of course. Dressed all in pink, get it? Commie tools, headed not for Moscow but for—"

"—San Francisco," they answered.

Deedee waved toodle-loo.

It pleased him at times to play the innocent fool. He walked down the stairs into the factory proper. Wearing his best blue suit, new Van Heusen shirt, and conservative grey tie, he looked down at the names, choosing the oldest and least likely candidates first. He rounded up the men and assembled them in the break room at the far end of the factory floor.

"The police want to talk to you people about an event that took place . . . ah, let's see." He glanced down at his list as if the abduction date of William Drew's niece were there. It wasn't. But he knew the time sequence. "Well, it was somewhere in the neighborhood of seventeen years ago. You were all working here at the plant, so go on back to work and try and think of anything that might help the police. Mel Brown and Douglas Wright Vance, stick around."

The rest of the men filed out, leaving the two older fellows sitting hangdog in their hard plastic chairs.

"Wait here in the break room til I call you, okay?" Charles flinched as he walked past the factory floor area of his nearly fatal overhead crane encounter.

Deedee scurried about, straightening books, adjusting papers. "I cleared that vacant space next door. The second cop could use my spot here."

"Terrific. Now what?"

"They called; be here in ten minutes."

Charles walked along the long hall connecting the executive wing with the office staff. This, he thought, might be a real test. A day he suspected would come, but not exactly like this. He continued pacing, trying to think of what to say if asked; how to comport himself. He knew he would get through this inconvenience, as it had been seventeen years, *and* given that the girl was a tramp and more than deserving; she was hardly missed. Bring it on.

"I've taken the opportunity to alert the men, sir. And I've asked them to stay at their stations until called. Will that suffice, Mr. Todd?" Charles looked him square in the eye.

"It's Detective, sir, and my last name is Devlin."

He knew all that. He just wanted to be difficult; maybe appear naive.

"You haven't met Sergeant Worth, have you, Mr. Clegg?"

Charles had been facing away from the door when it opened. When he turned, he was pleased to see the mother of the young lady whose company he had shared the last ten days. Not in the conventional sense, but in a performer-audience-type relationship. Sitting at the top of the stairs, he had played his guitar and sang a number of times. The girl, Cheryl—whose attractive parent now stood in front of him—needed discipline after the concert. His captive's striking image was reflected in the face before him.

She looked tired, this clueless mother, her face lined with concern.

Charles called down to the break room for Mel Brown and Doug Vance. Over the course of the next hour and a half, he heard snippets of questions being asked of the eleven other men, individually, who'd worked at the factory those many years ago. "Did you know Trudy, your employer's niece?" "How did you learn of her disappearance?" "Have you ever talked to anyone about the event?" "How old are you, sir?" "Do you drive a Ford Bronco?"

When it was over, he felt confident. All the questions seemed fairly benign. The one question they didn't ask was, "Do you currently have a sixteen-year-old girl named Cheryl imprisoned in your basement?"

Charles dug into his well-worn briefcase and pretended to busy himself with paperwork. They had moved to a conference room, Julie and Todd comparing notes.

"Of the whole lot, I didn't sense much dissembling, did you?"

"No, on the contrary, they seemed like a bunch of average Joes." Todd ran his pen back and forth between his fingers. "No one seemed defensive. It's a dead end."

"Excuse me, I couldn't help but overhear your conversation." Charles spoke up from the other end of the conference table. "I would have to say that's right; these are hardworking people."

Julie eased back in her chair. "Before I forget it, Mr. Clegg, thank you for organizing this little get-together."

"How, may I ask, did you come to resurrect this ancient case?"

"We're not at liberty to give any details at this point. Suffice it to say there have been recent events that seem to indicate a resumption of earlier"—Julie hesitated—"let's just say peculiar happenings."

He delighted in her choice of words, describing the abductions as "happenings," just as he liked to refer to them.

"By the way, Mr. Clegg, do you own a Ford Bronco?" Julie phrased the inquiry as if it were a joke, laughing a bit at the end to take some of the sting out of the question.

Todd joined in. "Yeah, right, I can just see the headlines now. Top executive at Drew Inc. involved in abductions."

"Oh, but I'm not a top exec. Simply a lowly manager of sorts who has been around for a long time, and no, I don't own a Bronco." It was true, he didn't own the Bronco. He had stolen it.

Todd and Charles laughed while Julie smiled, having come to the realization that the employee interrogations were a waste of time. She looked at Clegg.

"By the way, you were here when Trudy was abducted. Can you tell us anything about other employees who may have left soon after her disappearance?"

"Such a shame, really," Charles replied. "I saw her several times touring the factory with her school friends. A cute, shy kid." He cleared his throat. "As far as employees, I wasn't in management yet, just a meager slug in production, trudging along. Don't recall anyone being in a panic or leaving suspiciously. Nope, can't say I recall anything like that." Charles stood relaxed before the two troopers, eager to answer any inquiries.

"Right. Okay, Mr. Clegg, thank you."

Julie had enough from the factory front. She didn't feel well. A malaise dominated her since she'd stepped into the building. The interviews of the factory workers, the atmosphere, the here-there whiff of overcooked food made her want to pack up and leave.

The attitudes of the men at the plant seemed consistent—a polite but bored demeanor. Clegg seemed typical of what you might call a worker bee, his constant grin annoying and phony, but probably a decent sort. Most of the interviewed seemed willing to help, their tics and furtive glances reflections of being in an unusual circumstance. One's behavior didn't always identify the accuracy of a statement, but sometimes it could be a tell.

Clegg was a good example of what she generally referred to as a cipher. Well meaning, tough to read, but, generally speaking, a nonstarter.

Julie called headquarters, reaching Captain Walker.

"How'd it go, Worth?"

"Not well. We're just wrapping, heading back. Anything new? Any word?"

"No, nothing. Why don't you stop off and interview that trailer park gal you told me about. What's her name?"

"Miss Riley. Right, I've got her info in my book. Maybe a surprise visit might produce something. Good idea. See you later."

They said good-bye to Clegg, who called out, "Hope things turn out well for you, Detective."

39

*T*en *minutes passed* on the highway when Julie turned to Todd. "Didn't you think it unusual what he said to me at the end?"

"No, what? Who are you talking about? What did he say?"

"Clegg said, 'I hope things turn out well for you, Detective.' Isn't that odd?"

Todd drummed his fingers on the steering wheel. "I know what you're going through, but he didn't say 'Detective.' He said 'Detectives,' plural."

"I don't think so. He distinctly said 'Detective,' as in one of us, and since he was looking right at me, how would he know about my situation? We didn't mention it."

Todd pulled the car over to the side of the road. "Excuse me, Sarge. As I said before, I know what you're going through. But you're reaching. That guy couldn't abduct a pussycat. He meant nothing by that remark other than what he said. He wished us good luck."

Julie's hands were on both sides of her face. "Okay. You're probably right." She seemed to collapse into her own lap. "Ah shit, why can't we get any further on this fucking thing? Damn."

Todd eased the cruiser back onto the highway. "Something will break. I feel it. So, we head in?"

She dug through her portfolio. "Walker wants us to go talk to that trailer park bitch, Venus Riley. I spoke to her on the phone." She handed him the address.

They had little trouble finding the place. Julie remembered having spoken to the woman at the beginning of her cold case hunt. She checked her notes while Todd went into a beat-up trailer where a handwritten Manager's Quarters sign hung from the canopied porch.

Todd tried to convince someone inside to give him Venus Riley's stall number.

"Ask if they have a license and proof of rabies shot for that mutt they got chained up in the side yard!" Julie shouted through the ratty screen door.

When Todd came out thirty seconds later, he waved a slip of paper at Julie as if it were a winning lottery ticket. "Funny how cooperative some people can be: one minute unmovable, and then, for no reason, they change. Ha. She's right down here at the end of the street."

Julie went to the door while Todd checked the registration on the rusted Cadillac sitting in the driveway.

To the left of the screen door, a brass-plated "If you see this trailer rockin' don't bother knockin'" inscription. Julie pushed the doorbell button, the buzzer giving off a tired response.

"Yeah, what?" A woman in a thin housecoat and faded red paisley pajamas came to the door. She held a can of Bud.

"Miss Riley? Venus Riley?"

"Who wants to know?"

Julie eased her badge out from her jacket breast pocket. "Miss Riley, I spoke to you on the phone not too long ago about your daughter, Marylou. I'm Sergeant Worth, Missouri State Patrol, Criminal Investigation. Can we have a few minutes with you?"

"We?"

"My partner, Detective Devlin, will be here in a minute."

"You people have a way of checking in at the darndest times." The woman glanced at her watch. "Come on in. What's up?"

"Nothing new, I'm afraid." Julie took the offered seat at the dinette. "I just wanted to clear up a few things about Marylou. You said she left without even taking her toiletries. Is that correct, Miss Riley?"

"Christ in a hatbox! You folks did nothing for years, now here you are pestering me about Lulu after I told you everything I knew when you called. What in hell's name is going on?"

"I'd like my partner to join us, please."

Todd came up on the wood platform that served as a porch.

Miss Riley waved him in.

Once Todd sat down on a kitchen stool, Julie again glanced at her notes, for no reason other than to give the visit an official feeling. "You said on the phone your daughter might have been pregnant. Did she have a steady boyfriend?"

The woman smoothed her fingers across the Formica tabletop. "How long is this gonna take? I got company coming."

Julie looked into the woman's bloodshot eyes.

"Ah, well, you folks don't give a shit about Lulu being

gone, do you? You just want to pester a hardworking woman."

"What sort of work do you do, Venus?"

"I read fortunes and such."

"What's the 'and such' part?"

They stared at each other.

"I'm a working girl. Okay? You satisfied? You gonna run me in?"

Julie was close to the end of her patience. She would have liked to run her in for using the word "girl" instead of "drained old woman." "I asked you a question, Miss Riley. Please answer."

"Yeah, she had a boyfriend. The cops at the time cleared him. He was nothing, a midget looking for a circus. A squirt. I met him once and told my daughter she could do better. He kept glancing at my tits. What a weasel. Trust me, a *no*-body."

"What was his name, Miss Riley?"

"Don't remember. Must be in the report. He was at work the day my daughter disappeared; the cops looked into it."

Julie glanced at Todd with a look that said they were finished there.

The woman brushed up against Todd as she opened the screen door, her breasts barely concealed by the flimsy housecoat.

As they started to drive away, Julie saw the woman wave at her as if she had something to say. "Hold it, Todd. Biggy Boobs has something on her tiny mind."

The woman pulled her clothing tight around her body as she leaned out of her trailer. "I believe his name was Rink or Tink—something like that."

40

Charles took extra caution driving back to Bait Shack. The idea of taking Cheryl as a lure to get to her mother had not been thought out; a plan did not exist as to how he would get the sergeant to walk into his world.

The wayward truck episode had been fun but, in the end, not worthwhile. The cop wasn't seriously injured, and worst of all, he had taken a big chance. Charles, in his review of adventures with the Worth family, would have to admit that he was stuck. His original plan to lure Julie Worth to his cabin at the lake now seemed far-fetched and juvenile. He needed, in his defense, a way of neutralizing Worth and her investigation of William Drew's niece. After learning of her interest in the case, he saw her as a threat. Not unlike most of the women who came into his life. Clingy, whiney, and smelling of artificial products. Womanly, peculiar smells.

The closer he got to Bait Shack, the more determined he was to get rid of his teenybopper houseguest, maybe in a new and exciting way.

He came onto the property and sped up the car. Halfway down the long, extended drive, he put the car in neutral and cut the engine. It felt special, gliding along. It became a different quiet, a rumbling tire sound as the vehicle traveled the rutted dirt, and the creaky metal-on-metal grinding, which normally one couldn't hear. Charles noticed for the first time the driver's seat squeaking in tempo with the swaying.

Human noises, or lack thereof, became a part of his life. He asked himself, *How can I change?* Not in the conventional manner, like giving up something to be a better person, or vowing to be more gracious and clean cut. He wanted a real change, to be a different person—six-foot-tall handsome in a rugged-individual way. Bright, aware, worldly. All the things that had been denied him. On a conscious level, he knew that growth to six feet would not happen. Likewise, intellect, charm, and people skills were not in his future.

So that left him with just the things he was good at: abduction and systematic mayhem.

Cheryl heard a sound. The movement of old timbers resettling after pressure and weight had been applied. Someone was walking across the floor above her. She stooped down to retrieve the wallpaper she kept under the cot while sawing the plywood panel. She barely got the heavy colored paper back in place when she heard footsteps land on the stairs.

"Wake up, wake up, my little chicky pet. Time to go to work."

The light and fan were extinguished and relit several times. The door opened to a dark silhouette, an arm moving in a slow pendulum motion. A hood was then tossed onto the cot. "Put it on and be quick."

Seated on the fridge, Cheryl gazed at the dark mask. A ray of light crept through the heavy cloth as she slipped it over her head.

"Pull it down tight. No funny stuff. Leave the comedy to me, sweets."

Cheryl tugged on the dark cloth. Suddenly she whipped off the hood and screamed. "A bug! A spider! Eek! Oh God!" She twirled around the room rolling the hood tight while searching with her fingers for the small hole that had given off the ray of light. "Oh Christ, it bit me! Ahhh!" She kept moving about the room, feigning disgust, all the while her fingers tracing the dark cloth.

"Put it on now, or I'm going to offer you a severe beating. Got it?"

She worked her index finger into the opening, making it a bit larger, then smoothed the cloth before putting it over her head. Staggering toward the door, her arms stretched out like a zombie, the tear appeared just to the side of her right eye. She promised herself she would not be harmed.

The man grabbed her arm and shoved her toward the stairs. "Up you go, Cheerleader. Time for your sex education class."

Maybe, maybe not. He hadn't tied her hands but had looped his hand firmly into the belt area at the back of her jeans. Once again he was singing his "Heigh-ho, heigh-ho, it's off to work we go" Disney theme. Cheryl's view was a kaleidoscope of images flashing across her peephole. A rustic chair next to a worn couch, a table stacked with dirty dishes, and a poster of a nude woman hanging crookedly on the front of a wood door.

"Welcome to showtime, sweets." He swung her aside and opened the door, pushing her into the room. Through her makeshift peephole, she saw an unmade bed, and a brass headboard draped with assorted ropes and leather restraints.

She felt his presence at her side.

"Itsy bitsy spider, climbing up the wall. It's no good for you to holler, scream, or call." He snorted. "Gotcha." *Snort.* "Gotcha."

# 41

S *omething, or someone,* saved Cheryl. The phone rang as the man had led her through what she thought was the living room and then into the bedroom. He locked the door while she remained staring at a wall. In the other room, King was on the phone. "But it's Saturday." Then a long pause. "Why me?" And, in a changed voice, "I'll come in, of course."

After moving the tiny hole in her hood, she peeked at a wall covered with a heavy curtain. A sliver of light pierced through where the drape caught on the windowsill. Grass and weeds covered a long stretch of backyard dominated by several large oak trees leading to a shimmering lake. The water ebbed into a basin, forming a pond-sized enclave. A wood boat, unused and in need of repair, lay on the shore, half into the finger of water.

She heard something through the thin-walled bedroom. Cheryl adjusted the drape to cover the light and hurried back to the center of the room.

"Well, Miss Prom Queen, this is your unlucky day." He put his hands on her hips, his body shaking as he gyrated behind her. "Seems I've been alerted to an emergency at my place of work, so heigh-ho and so forth, it's back to the dungeon you go."

He pushed her through the living room and stopped. "Stay, you understand me? Stay."

Behind her, a refrigerator door opened and closed, the rattle of a paper bag, and his tuneless humming. "It's now or never."

So what does that mean? He led her down the basement steps again. "Take two steps into the room, do not turn around," he said at the door. "Take off the hood and without turning, pass it back to me."

Cheryl complied and exhaled. The door closed behind her. On the concrete, a paper bag held a fresh supply of Cup Noodles, two apples, and three cans of sardines. Ten minutes later, the car and its tap-tap horn. He was gone; she had to get to work.

42

Julie's days and nights melded. Her drive into work felt long, the lack of rest wearing on her. She asked for an early-morning meet with Walker and Todd.

"Since I've come across this, I've found the young Riley girl's mom, Venus, to have all sorts of baggage."

"Like what?" Walker asked.

"Think I told you about this the other day. As Todd and I were leaving Riley's place, she runs out and spouts some garbage about someone named Rink or Tink."

"Yeah, you mentioned that. Bolstered her story about being somewhat cooperative toward the end of the meeting."

"Right, well. Todd, I didn't bring you up to date on this. It was just last night. With everything going on, it slipped by me. Sorry."

"It's okay. So what about Lady Venus and her baggage?"

Julie looked to Walker for permission to continue.

"Go ahead. I'm anxious to hear what this pissant Riley has going on. Anything besides her hooker business?"

"Yep. In mid-1995, councilman Mars Riley, cousin of

Mayor Tom Bishop's wife, was indicted for fraud, which he of course denied. He says a relative named Venus committed said fraud." Julie felt bad about not bringing Todd up to date on her findings. "It gets even better, Todd-O. At Miss Venus Riley's trial, she claimed her innocence and said she was bamboozled into this corruption by a man named—are you ready? Rhymes with kitchen sink."

"Rink."

"Close, name of Bink. Bink Caldwell. It's in the court documents and the police report."

"You mean there really was someone named Bink?" Todd glanced at Captain Walker and then back to Julie.

Julie wanted to stand on the front steps of the station and shout it out. "When Venus was convicted for fraud, in her statement to the court, she said she was forced into her life of crime by this Bink Caldwell." She let this settle in. "This same hero who had been dating her daughter turns out to be the exact guy who forced her into this misappropriation of funds and—this is the big one—at about the same time that her daughter goes missing. Odd, yes?"

Walker reached for the phone. "Get me a sector car that's in the vicinity of . . ." He looked to Julie and Todd.

Todd pulled out his notebook while Julie spouted off the address from memory. "Venus Riley, 2710 New Market Road. Unit D as in Delta."

They waited as the captain directed the patrol unit to the Riley trailer. "How'd this come about?"

"I put it together with the Venus flytrap's sudden cooperation at the end of our interview, remember?"

Todd showed her a thumbs-up.

"I got to thinking about it last night. Our girl Venus thought we would stumble upon this Bink connection, and she was trying to cover herself for later, down the road."

Walker flipped his pencil in the air a few times. "What would you have done if you were taken off the case?"

Julie raised her hand, her index finger extended above her clenched fist. "As a private citizen, a quiet talk with Venus would have been in the cards." She cocked her thumb with a loud *click*.

Julie and Todd hung out at Coffee Time Cafe waiting for word from Walker that they had corralled Venus Riley.

Todd tore his paper napkin into tiny bits. "Why didn't this idiot tell the cops at the time of her daughter's disappearance about our guy Bink?"

Julie pulled a piece of croissant off her half of their joint breakfast. "Beats me. Well, yeah, but she gave up his name at trial. She's one of those people with a perpetual hard-on for cops. Such a snot. That vitriol about 'haven't seen you people for twenty years, I know you got better things to do than find a poor kid who disappeared, blah-blah.'" Julie's cell rang. "Yeah? Okay, Cap. We'll be right there." She dropped a five on the table. "Venus is at the station."

When they arrived, Todd hung back as Julie came upon Walker shadowing Venus strolling down the corridor into an interview room.

Venus settled into the cramped space on her own slow time.

Julie spoke up. "Would you like something to drink? Soda, coffee, water?"

Walker cleared his throat. "I'm sorry, Miss Riley, there's no smoking in here. If you'd like to step outside, please do so."

She lit her cigarette and blew smoke in Walker's direction. The three of them sat around the table. Julie made notes while Walker reached over and opened the door. Venus fiddled with a gaudy necklace.

"The up-to-date is this," Walker said. "No smoking in a government building. No exceptions. Also, Miss Riley, you're here at my indulgence. You claim you're indigent. If any of this doesn't sit well with you, you'll be placed under arrest."

"On what charge?"

"Violation of criminal code 6110: pandering, solicitation. Criminal code 350: hindrance of a criminal investigation. Withholding evidence.

"I could go on."

Walker once again addressed Venus. "Miss Riley, you say you know nothing that would indicate these charges are anything but vindictive nonsense. Is that your position?"

"Yes, nonsense," Venus said with a smirk.

"Nonsense?" Julie jumped to her feet, her hands halfway across the table. "*My daughter has been kidnapped,* and you use the word 'nonsense'? Miss Riley, you have knowledge of a Bink Caldwell, were in business with him, and because of him, spent six years of an eight- to ten-year sentence for fraud, and you say nonsense? You're withholding information; *that's* real nonsense."

"Stop this bull right now!" Walker pounded the table. "Both of you! I mean it."

Julie spoke in a conciliatory tone. "Captain, may I please?"

Walker breathed hard, his face reddening. He tried to smile. "Go ahead."

"What do you say to an understanding? Huh?"

No one spoke.

"All right, we needn't verbalize it, but since we're all sitting here anyway, listen to this."

Julie shifted her attention to Venus. "Miss Riley, my daughter is being held captive as we speak. Are you going to help with this business or not? Regardless of what you may feel about me, or how angry you may feel toward the police and this meeting, would you put yourself in my position? As a mother, you know what it's like to have a child missing. Could you be objective and try to help us out here?"

Venus's hard-worn features softened, and her thin hands went to her face. "I can do that. I met this A-hole Bink Caldwell in spring of '96. He answered an ad I put in the paper for someone to share expenses on a three-bedroom house I was trying to buy; a rental with an option to purchase. I won't get into it, but it was a long, hot spring. Then Bink, the prick, I catch messing with my daughter, Marylou. He talks me into doing some rubbish with my brother's company. At about the same time, Marylou went missing. Then the company's gone, along with Bink. It's all in the local police report. Sergeant Worth, what the hell else can I tell you? I don't know anything else except what I've said."

"Did you see this fellow Bink after your daughter disappeared?"

Venus dabbed at her eyes and nose, the crumpled Kleenex leaving white specks on her upper lip. "Yeah, I'm not proud of it, but Bink was a great comfort in those mixed-up days."

"Was he ever questioned by the police? Taken in, anything like that?"

"No. By then we realized Marylou hadn't just run

away, I'd been talked to by the State Attorney's Office and was sitting in lockup trying to raise bail. Bink came to see me in jail. We spoke of going to the Caribbean or Mexico together. I told him where I buried the money from my—how should I say it?—dalliance, and he said he would need the money for my bond. Then the bastard disappeared."

"What can you tell me about where he was from, where he worked?"

Venus wrung her hands as if trying to cleanse them. "Said he was an orphan, raised in the western part of the state, had a settlement with a big company over an injury he sustained years ago, wouldn't go into it. When I asked about his name, he wouldn't talk about it. Said, 'He's another person.'"

Julie looked up from her legal pad. "'He's another person'? What do you think he meant by that?"

"I don't know. Just pillow talk. Besides his being less than average size, there was that forever-pleading bullshit singing. I never knew how long he'd be gone. Sometimes days on end, then show up in a broken-down piece a shit car or truck. Took my money and split, never saw him again. Left me in the pokey." She inspected her chipped fingernail polish. "Was a shameful period for me."

"Can you describe him?"

"Describe him, yeah. A weasel dressed in men's clothing. A would-be Hells Angel without balls. A loser."

"I mean, for a police artist, describe how he looked."

"How about a picture?"

"You've got a photograph of Bink Caldwell?"

"Oh yeah, he and my daughter had it taken a few weeks before she vanished. Got it at home; you want to see it? Hey, maybe the next time you see me, I'll be in

Lewisburg's federal lockup with the rest of the criminal elite. Shit."

"Miss Riley, you're doing the right thing, thank you."

Venus Riley's modular home, D unit, looked the same as before, a curdled-milk beige over a grey-blue, while next door it was beige over greenish yellow.

Inside, Julie smelled incense and burnt candles, evidence of a midnight get-together. She scolded herself for her judgment of Venus's livelihood. If it brought Cheryl closer to home, the woman, if she were so inclined, could stand naked on top of her mobile home and shout the teachings of Buddha.

"It's going to take a while; haven't been through these boxes in a coon's age." Venus dragged two large cardboard boxes from the drawers beneath the couch. She teared up as she leafed through the mountain of photos. Julie watched, praying this wasn't an exercise in futility.

"Here's Marylou at six. Cute, huh?"

Julie took the photo and said all the required oohs and aahs while keeping an eye on Venus rummaging through the two cartons.

"Not here. Damn. Where in the dickens could—"

"Do you ever stick photos into books? Some people use them as markers."

Venus was on her feet, darting around the kitchen, pulling out drawers and cupboard doors. "Here it is. Shoot. Greasy and bent; stuck it in a cookbook."

Julie went to her side. The picture looked as if it had been taken at a photo booth. A male, seated with a girl, presumably Marylou, on his lap. The girl's curly hair dominated the three shots. The only clear picture of the man, at the bottom, where the camera caught the fellow's mustache and goatee in a deep comic scowl, his pompadour flopped down over one eye. An oversized collar sporting a string tie hung down his chest. Julie didn't recognize him. She was disappointed it wasn't someone she had arrested or seen in the station, a lineup, or in court. She looked at the images again, sensing a familiarity, but laid it off as too many years of looking at weird-eyed bad guys.

"Miss Riley, may I take a photo of this?"

"Of course, that's why we're here."

Julie snapped a shot, made sure it came through, and walked out to her car with Venus. "What a piece of dog crap that guy was." The woman said the last part as if she were talking to herself. "So sorry, Sergeant. I honestly pray you get your daughter back safely."

"If something comes up, may I contact you?" They hugged, Julie wishing she were more benevolent, but the woman had delayed the investigation by a number of days.

"It's been years since I've felt anything about Marylou. Call anytime. I'll be glad to talk."

43

The *continued back-and-forth* motion of the sardine can on the wood panel made Cheryl's arm ache. She stopped to massage her shoulder and switch hands. From time to time, the can would twist into jagged pieces of tin. Her remedy was to place the can under one of the legs of her metal cot and tamp the oily makeshift saw back into some reasonable semblance of a handle and blade. She might have been concerned about the noise of the cot's metal leg resounding off the concrete floor, but the late departure of King seemed to leave the evening open to all kinds of opportunities.

She played mind games to relieve the boredom of the continuous scratching. At times she would make a complete circle around what she referred to as her window of freedom. One more trip, and then she'd rest. She dug into the plywood again. The toughest section—the top horizontal plane. Her reach wasn't high enough to put any real power into her scraping. As night wore on, she felt the blade break through for the first time. It happened in the lower right-hand corner, making a hole the size of a dime.

With both hands wrapped tightly around her bent can,

Cheryl pulled down hard on the vertical boundary. Again and again she ran the blade up and down the indented groove. She switched over to the other side and began the relentless routine of the left vertical line. The constant sawing raised blisters and welts on her palms. She opened another can of the pungent fish and continued.

Cheryl rested. Lying on the hard cot, she gazed at the escape hole, a bright orange light coming through the right corner. She swallowed hard and lifted herself atop the squat refrigerator, pressing her eye to the hole. A dark cloud streak blotted part of the bright light of the moon.

When Cheryl looked at the debris made while outlining the window shape, she knew it would not be possible to hide this escape attempt. It would have to be now. A full commitment over the next few hours or probably not at all.

She sawed back and forth on the bottom portion of the window, the tone changed from a low, throaty rumble to a higher reed-like squeak. She felt a roughness the last few horizontal swipes, and then she was through. She attacked the right vertical upright. A new vibration at the bottom as the sides fought to stay together. She stayed at the right upright until it broke through from the dime-sized hole to the top. Cheryl wedged her fingers into the corner. Two sides of her work were now free, but the plywood would budge apart only a few inches. She slid down off the fridge and slumped onto the cot.

The moonlight spilled in from the scarred wood frame, and she wondered how to finish this before stinky garlic man came down to fetch her. Cheryl pulled the thin mattress off the metal cot and examined the connection between the rails holding the wire springs. She saw a simple C-shaped hook on the rails and a corresponding knob on the headboard portion that secured the hook. She turned the cot upside down and stomped her tennis-shoed foot onto the connections, the cot separating into three pieces.

Experimenting with the footboard of the cot wedged under the corner of the plywood, Cheryl thought there was too much room between the fridge and the window for her to have something to pry against. She laid the metal footboard upright on the fridge and placed the cot rails on top, forcing the rail under the crack in the window opening.

When she pushed down at the other end of the mattress rail, the plywood came apart with a loud split. She moved the whole apparatus to the left—toward the wall, about a foot—and repeated her levering. Once again the large panel protested the surrender of the glued plywood. It was a hole—not yet big enough to crawl out of, but promising.

She paused to look at the wind-stroked patch of clouds from her escape hatch. Cheryl climbed back on top of the fridge and, with her hands, pried the remaining cracked pieces of wood away from the window. The latch on the metal frame gave way. The window itself would open only a few inches until she cleared away the last few stubborn pieces of the plywood. She thought a four-inch strip of wood left at the top of the window was probably nailed to a two-by-four.

Cheryl once again placed the cot rail under the strip of wood and jammed the headboard on top of the fridge to give herself a place for her lever. With all her weight on the rail, the plywood strip splintered with a sharp crack and the breaking of glass. The edge of the bed rail had punctured the window. She broke the rest of the glass and scraped away the shards from the metal frame with her last sardine can. She raised the window, hinged from the top, and noticed a hook in the rafter above her head, left over from the old days when the basement was simply a basement and not a dungeon. A number of jagged plywood pieces still stuck out into the window opening. She hooked the casement opening and breathed in the fresh lakefront air.

The sound, when it came, had the temper and dread of an atomic bomb. An automobile; her worst fear. She saw headlights flashing against the tree branches in the back of the property next to the lake. Cheryl knew the basement window wasn't visible from where he was driving. But would he check on her? It was late. Would he be tired? Maybe she should try to get through the narrow window now or wait until he was asleep.

She hesitated, knowing that if he came down the steps and opened the door for her to come with him, he would see the dismantled cot. If he saw the cot, then it followed that he would come into the room to see what was going on. She knew he would kill her if he saw her work at the window. What was keeping him from not killing her, anyway?

Cheryl slumped against the cold wall, holding her breath against the options. Another hour, and she could have been free. She closed her eyes, wondering what her mom was doing, knowing that even now in the middle of the night, she would be thinking of her. Sounds from a television or radio upstairs came through the newly made opening. King must have had a window open just above her.

There seemed to be nothing more to do but wait. She pulled the thin blanket off the mattress and wrapped it around her legs. The sudden warmth made her sleepy. She drifted back to high school.

"Girls do not normally take wood shop, Miss Worth."

"With due respect, sir, I know of a boy, Ivan Bell, taking home ec this semester."

The principal drummed his fingers on an algebra book and cleared his throat a few times. "Ivan is an honor student whose family owns a restaurant, Miss Worth. The idea of him taking a cooking class seems a good one. How do you compare to that?"

"Well, my family doesn't own a restaurant or a woodworking facility, to make the comparison, but I come from a single-parent family, and it would be a big help to my mother if I did some chores around the house. You know, fix the screen door, repair the tread on the basement staircase. That kind of thing."

The principal looked up at Cheryl from his paper-strewn desk. "This is not an attention-grabbing trick, is it, Miss Worth?"

Her answer was no answer.

"Go on, take shop class if you want. I'll okay it. But if you cut off a finger or get an eye poked out from a flying piece of metal from a band saw, don't come yelling to me, understand?"

She ended up loving shop and made buddies with a couple of the tough guys who had ridiculed her. It seemed a sweet memory until she heard footsteps on the basement stairs.

Elvis was back in the building.

44

Walker *studied the* photo-booth image enlarged and printed to four times its original size. "It's not what I would call an ah-ha moment, sorry to say. If we ever catch this guy, we can probably match him, but a picture that's, what, sixteen years old and at this cockamamie angle . . ." He set down the photo. "I don't know; just doesn't seem possible."

Todd picked up the photo. "The problem as I see it, the guy's got a lot of hair, most of it down across his face. Mustache, goatee, and sideburns, his head's tilted. Too much stuff. I don't recognize him. Sarge?"

"Yeah, right. I don't, either, except it's all we've got. The guy from the pickup truck was all shadowed out. Hat, dark glasses, could be anyone. Cap, what would you say to a little subterfuge?"

"Like what?"

"I was thinking about an article in the paper, one of those 'Police Are Working on New Lead,' 'Photo May Be Abductor of Police Officer's Daughter,' 'FBI Forensics Teams Working on Possible Link to Earlier Crimes.' Some sort of bullshit to get this animal to come after me."

"We're not in the bait business, Sergeant." Walker spread his arms, palms down, to signal the end of that topic. "You and Todd are not to do anything remotely close to putting you in danger over this thing. We want your daughter back, but not at this level of risk, got it?"

Julie acknowledged the captain and got up to leave, her gut telling her that she would continue to do whatever it took to get her girl home safely.

Todd and Julie walked the two blocks to Brisco's Beef, a cop joint specializing in keeping the police force fat and happy. Ordinarily, Julie devoured her turkey burger, but today she pushed the food around on her plate. The burger's one bite mark grinned up at her. "I've got to do something. I can't just sit around and 'What if?'"

"Let's take another run at the box factory," Todd suggested. "There are a lot of healthy-looking fellas full of testosterone down there. Might be productive."

"I'll see you in the car." Julie got up. "Take your time." She acknowledged several officers on the way out after paying her check. Most of the cops wanted to speak to her, offer their support, make suggestions of help, but almost all had already done that, and they were stuck for something to say.

The day was shiny and bright. Not too hot, just happily perfect. She wished it were miserable, to fit her mood.

Todd checked in with headquarters to report their locale. "What do you think, Sarge? Should we call that secretary at Drew and tell her we're coming down?"

As they left the city, Julie watched the rolling hills, trying to determine what approach to take when reinterviewing the factory workers. Should she lower herself, be condescending, or be the police bitch everyone expected of her? "Nah, let's just bust in, maybe take on a little different no-bullshit attitude. We've wasted a lot of time. All these MFs can kiss my state trooper ass. I want some answers." She napped, mostly in a fit, waking in an embarrassing sweat. "Pull over, will you, Todd? I've gotta walk around a bit."

They came up to a gravel turnout built as a memorial to a Civil War skirmish. Julie walked around the compact historic site. A sign acknowledging the event had been vandalized, the name of the site chiseled and covered with red paint. In the fifteen years that she had been a policewoman, it never stopped overwhelming her how stupid some people could be. She looked at the field. Rows and rows of ripe corn stretching down a slight hill. At the bottom, bordering a creek, stood a dozen hefty oaks overlooking a series of other vast expanses of corn. Julie leaned against a five-foot-high barbed wire fence. She wondered if that copse of ancient oaks had sheltered a blue or grey squad of men doing what they thought was the correct thing at the time. She hoped her desperate pursuit would be on the winning side; that justice would be served. She got back in the car.

"Todd, give me a good boot in the pants every now and then, will you?"

He put his car in gear and accelerated out of the byway. "Sure, with pleasure. And . . . what else is up?"

"The not knowing is getting to me. The self-doubt when I think of Cheryl makes me want to beat my fists against someone's face so I can feel better. I want to hear that steel door close on some don't-give-a-shit punk." She stopped. "Sorry, pard. I'm talking the woe-is-me bullshit called 'I've lost my daughter, and some douche bag is going to pay, big-time.'"

Julie wanted to lose herself in the roadside pines whipping past her window. The straight, thick trunks and spindly branches a contradiction in nature. A number of quaint farming communities popped up along the winding road, each one with its own distinct high-porched facades. No Wal-Marts or Home Depots in this vast, rolling panorama. Only Mom, Pop, and Uncle Harry passing their friendly stores down through generations of would-be merchants.

She wondered if one of these quiet retailers would know her daughter's abductor.

"I will remain on the proper side of the law, Detective Devlin. No worries." She hoped a manufactured lilt to her voice would keep Todd from thinking she had gone over the line. "And you, sir, will be the first to know if I go completely south. Okay?"

"If you go south, that large dark blue Crown Vic with the flashing lights stuck to your rear bumper will be me." He reached over and squeezed her arm.

45

S omewhere out past the lake, a wild dog howled into the
night wind. Cheryl listened to the animal's plea and
continued her work. Her idea was to quietly pry as
much of the remaining plywood out of the window area
as possible.

Voices floated upstairs. Television laughter, canned
and too loud. Her head poised toward the open window,
she waited to time the TV actor's buildup in speech and
the subsequent laugh track with the splintering of wood.
After each effort, she waited, and then resumed, having
not heard the dreaded footsteps on the steep basement
stairs. All this through back-to-back reruns of *Cheers*. She
wrapped each jagged piece of splintered plywood with
the tattered remains of her dishcloth, trying to muffle the
noise. She had long ago passed the point of worrying about
protecting her hands. It wasn't the physical effort that exhausted her, but the coordination attempts.

She listened carefully, her head bent into the opening.
Wiggling through the ragged hole now might have been
possible, but weighing the pros and cons of a major gash,

she waited. Cheryl pulled out more long slivers from her escape hatch and stumbled off the refrigerator. The noise was more of a scraping effect rather than a loud *kerplunk*. She lay still on the bare mattress, her sore back enjoying the hard surface of the concrete floor. While trying to catch her breath, the basement door opened. King's booted step sounded deliberate.

"Oh, it's now or never! Tra-la-de-da!" Halfway down, he stopped.

Cheryl put a twist in her hair and slipped her last oily sardine can into her hair bun. Once again she vowed not to be harmed by Nasty Nashville.

He sang his country lament in a different way this night, more controlled and personal. Even the guitar, not being played with its usual gusto, was only moderately awful. After too long a while, it stopped. And the heavy footsteps retreated up the stairs with a barely discernible "Thank you, thank you very much."

Cheryl breathed a heavy sigh at the departure, and then realized that she had left the curlycue lightbulb turned off. If he'd continued down and opened the food slot, he would have seen her darkness.

She scanned the room and went back to work on the remaining shards, carefully bending them back and forth until they gave way. One long tentacle stretched from the bottom left-hand corner a third of the way across the twenty-by-eighteen-inch rectangular opening. She knew the splinter would do heavy damage to her left side if she attempted to go through. Electricity hummed while a refrigerator was opened upstairs. Then the soft closing followed by a pan being knocked against metal. Her down-home Caspar Milquetoast was having a midnight snack. She heard a toilet flush and the slow, sliding creak of a window being closed. And all grew quiet. Poised on the fridge, she waited to hear a snore or a cough.

Cheryl looked around the room, wondering what she could take with her. On the stained floor next to the toilet, she eyed a plastic bag used to bring in groceries. She stuffed it into her back pocket, cringing at the thought that he had touched the bag. She wrapped her blanket into a tight bedroll, placing it around her neck and tucking one end of it into the front of her jeans. Holding the rapier-like plywood needle in both hands, she cranked it toward the broken window and then back a few inches toward the room. She heard nothing from upstairs.

She pried the piece of wood up and down until it came loose. She glanced back at her prison room: there wouldn't be anything more to take. Again Cheryl listened for something from above her. Hooking her right elbow outside the window casement, she gripped the left side and pulled. As her feet left the steady support of the refrigerator, she began to wiggle her way through the tight opening.

Halfway through, with her head and shoulders protruding into the wet grass and earth, she felt the basement window above her trip the overhead latch, bouncing down onto her back, wedging itself into the curve between the end of her spine and butt. She was stuck. Then the rain started. Cheryl reached back with her left hand to try to grasp the hinged window, to no result. The bedroll she'd fashioned caught in the shattered glass of the basement window, making the passage even tighter.

She stopped to listen again for any noise coming from the living room window just a few feet above her head. If the man had heard her struggles, he would look out that window. *Why not? Isn't that the way it goes for the good guys?*

The girl shook it off, knowing that feeling sorry for herself would do no good.

Her hips were killing her. All the weight of her body, centered in the middle of the window, had dealt her a teeter-totter position, half in, half out. The blanket was still caught. Cheryl reached down to where it was stuffed into her jeans and pulled out the other end. She looped the thin cover back over her head and shook the blanket against the glass shards, trying to dislodge it. It took a while, and her shoulder cramped, forcing her to stop. Movement came from the room above her.

King was up. A light went on, and she heard pacing in what she was fairly certain was the room with the television.

The window in the house squeaked and bounced while being raised. Cheryl smelled cigarette smoke. An off-key humming started; then once again the hollow thump of the guitar. She renewed her efforts to free herself. The guitar music faded above her head, and the window closed.

She cursed for having brought the worthless blanket. The pain against her hips and stomach grew more intense. Cheryl thought that if she pulled the rest of the blanket from her jeans, it would help her to slide out from underneath the tight space, but her hips and ribs, along with the now bundled-up cover, put her in a tight fix. The thumping of the guitar resumed and was getting louder.

He had moved to the basement steps. Of all the nights to serenade her, why now? If he opened the food slot, he would see the light was not on. She pulled her left knee up even with her hip and pushed down hard against the sharp edge of the metal window casement. Inching her way forward, something else began digging at her back: the outside handle of the basement window.

"Are you lonesome tonight?" His voice echoed in the stairway.

Cheryl hesitated to answer for fear that he would hear a difference in her voice, considering her head was outside. She pulled her knee even higher and felt a glass shard rip her denim jeans. She wanted to scream but clamped down on her teeth and pushed even harder. His voice changed. She realized he was at the food slot, and would see the light was out. She glanced over her shoulder as the light flickered on, then off. Her jeans belt buckle caught on the bottom of the metal casement as she made a last huge effort to push through. Again, the light went on and off. The fan stuttered, he was in the room.

He reached up and rescrewed the bulb into its socket. Cheryl jammed her left arm through the opening and reached a small shrub and pulled. With both arms free, she began to work her way through. A hand grabbed her right leg.

"Where you going, dumpling? The light was out. Don't you wanna see what I got for you?" His hands started up her legs. "You must be exhausted, having to pull yourself through that tiny opening, sugar." He pulled himself up onto the refrigerator.

Cheryl let go of the shrub with her right hand and clung to the prickly bush with her left. She felt King's hands reaching her hips.

"Could've asked me for a walk in the rain, didn't have to do it on your own, hon."

Her right hand felt the sharp edge of the crushed sardine can in her hair bun. Cheryl edged onto her side and waited for his hand to find her belt buckle. He fumbled with it, and then scratched her bare stomach and giggled. She moved her shoulder around far enough to get both hands on the sharp can and then reached down past his wrist. She jammed the ragged edge into his forearm. When he screamed and jerked away, her two-handed grip became an immovable knife point ripping his arm from elbow to wrist.

"You rotten little murdering whore! I'll kill you! I'll—"

The panicked effort of his having to push her from him and the tightening of her upper body broke her free from the window. She kicked hard with her legs and scrambled away from the house toward the lake, pulling the blanket tight around her waist.

A large tree loomed ahead. She tripped but kept going. With an unexpected splash, she ended up hip deep in the lake, feeling her shoes sinking into the heavy mud bottom. She turned to the right and waded into the cold water. Chest deep, she looked around. It seemed darker to her left, where silhouettes of huge trees loomed. She looked at the house and saw a flashlight beam darting back and forth. An angry voice screamed a pathetic list of harm that awaited her.

Cheryl slipped down to eye level in the frigid lake water and moved toward the darkening area of the shore-line trees.

A nightmare awakened Julie. Finding herself sitting up in bed with thrashed covers wrapped solidly around her feet, her breath came in heavy pumps. An intruder, someone in the house? She reached for her Sig on the nightstand while catching more air into her lungs.

Listening to the night sounds: a door slammed somewhere in the distance, someone cursed, heavy rain drummed on the tin roof of the utility shed behind her house, and the creaky settling of the old bungalow.

Her thoughts turned to Cheryl, the cold rain, and her own inability to do anything about her daughter's disappearance. She flopped back onto the damp sheets, her eyes penetrating the grey riot of patterns on her bedroom ceiling. Above the old brass chandelier, a jumble of shadows converged like a busy urban intersection. The shadowed tree branches from outside whipped the diagonal window designs into a map-like collage. Road-like lines led past oblong shapes of clouds. Or maybe they were balloons. Or even ponds or lakes.

Cheryl *swam a* slow breaststroke toward the tree line. A flashlight beam continued darting across the blackened landscape. A car started up. Tires shredded the gravel driveway, headlights bounced recklessly through the woods. The light reappeared briefly, searching the side of the road, the culvert. A car door slammed, an engine's high, revving protest, and spinning tires. Cheryl watched as lights from the car blinked as it passed the tall pines, heading away.

Her feet touched the slope of the shoreline. She rested, her arms and legs trembling. The moon hid behind heavy rain clouds. To her right, scrub oaks. The dreaded house and a long driveway to her left. That must be the road where the car disappeared. She wondered if it would make sense to go back to the house and get a weapon, since he was gone. Maybe make a phone call, scream for help.

No lights appeared anywhere along the distant shoreline, making it tough to gauge how far it would be to cross the lake. Cheryl felt sure in her ability as a swimmer, but once there, what would she do? As she stood waist deep in the lake, the cold water stung at her open blisters. Her dilemma got easier when she saw the bouncing lights of the car returning along the tree-lined road. She eased backward into the dark lake and kicked hard with her legs. She kept her eyes on the house and the approaching car. He turned into the driveway, and Cheryl let her head slip underwater, pulling through the water with long strokes. She waited until her breath would not hold any longer and surfaced as a beam flashed across her watered vision. A blurred light set on a tree illuminated the boat she had seen earlier. He seemed to be turning it right side up.

She arched her body and headed for the distant shore, stopping to look back every ten deliberate strokes. The light beam caught the bent figure pushing the boat into the water. Cheryl renewed her strokes, pulling even harder. The wind swept the rain across the water.

When she looked back again toward the dimly lit house, the beam had disappeared. He was in the water. She couldn't see the boat but knew it was there. She swam backward. A flicker of light swept across the lake. A drifting tree branch bumped up behind her head. The rain pelted her. In a way, she thought it to be a blessing. The hard splatter of raindrops deadened the sounds of her heavy breathing and the occasional splash of an arm or leg as it came out of the water. The boat seemed closer. She went under and swam with her arms out front, clearing the way. When she surfaced, the flashlight swept her approaching shoreline. She was closer, but the man in the boat had the advantage. The oarlock groaned against the metal prong in the oar itself.

"Oh, sweetie! Come back, come back!" he called to her. "I'm not angry."

I'll bet.

When he stopped rowing and flicked the light, she sank to eye level and waited. The beam twice swept across her face but didn't stop. The rain dotted its way over the vast lake, making little splash mounds that hid her from the light. She once again began kicking underwater, her eyes never leaving the boat or its treacherous light.

Her foot hit what felt like a rock. The boat drifted off to her left. Taking a quick glance over her shoulder, she saw the shoreline nearby. The boat continued to her left, so she went to her right, her feet now touching the rough bottom. She crouched to keep her torso submerged, skirting along the shore, looking for a place to pop out where, once on land, she wouldn't be seen from the boat. His voice again, closer now.

The deep breath she took before submerging was filled with water, causing her to choke as she fought to stay under. When she came up for air, the boat had continued along her path. It seemed to be several clothesline links away. She crawled on all fours out of the water and onto the rock-strewn mud. She kept an eye on the now-distant boat and bumpy shore.

Weeds and boulders hid her from view as she climbed a muddy bank and flopped down to rest. The light beam continued to sweep the heavily wooded shore in the distance. She crawled through weeds and broken tree limbs until she could no longer see the scattered beams of light coming from the water. She emptied her sneakers of mud and pebbles. The voice called to her from a distance. A pleading, put-upon tone a reminder of her two weeks of hell.

She watched as the boat disappeared and then reappeared in the pressing rain and the rekindled flashlight.

The flickering light seemed at least a hundred yards from her as she made her way through the woods, and she knew she had to put as much distance between them as quickly as possible.

The wind picked up and beat against her wet blouse. The bedroll she'd fashioned out of the blanket pressed heavily around her middle. She stopped to lighten her load by tying the blanket to a sapling and twisting it, until most of the heavy water drained. It did feel lighter but would soak up the downpour and become her weighty companion.

She wanted to toss the blanket but thought she might need it. Wrapping the roll back around her waist, Cheryl continued her exploration. After a dozen steps, she realized she was heading back toward the water. Confused, she saw the searching beam of light reaching much closer. Cheryl turned and headed back into the heavy woods. He called to her as if he were pursuing a dog.

Traipsing through heavy woods, she'd lost track of time. In front of her, the trees thinned out to an open glade. Through all the trembling cold, she was still happy to be free of basement hell.

Cheryl knew she had to keep a steady pace. An old fence stopped her trek. She bent it down and scrambled over, falling on the other side in a ditch with steep sides and running water. She stayed on her hands and knees at the top of the creek bed and continued for several yards, straining to see what was next.

Coming upon another severe grade that appeared to drop down to a second creek bed, Cheryl slid down, stepping across yet another stream of running water and finding herself in a long, gradual slope leading to she knew not what. The rain finally stopped, along with the biting cold. But still, she realized she needed shelter.

A number of weird events drifted to mind. Goblins stared at her from overhead branches, and guitar players serenaded her from outside a deep freeze. Her legs gave out, and she slipped on the weed-covered forest floor. Cheryl placed her fists into the wet earth. Her knees bit into the thorny bushes dotting the soaked ground. She promised that she would not be taken again, that she must move on. Head down, she vomited. Deep thunder rolled across the black sky as the rain once again pelted her.

Stumbling down the slope, she fell into another ditch, letting running water push her down the funnel to yet another stream.

Cheryl asked herself if she had gotten turned around again. Did she, in her cold delirium, circle back to his lake? She thought it curious that over the thunder and driving rain, she heard the water. Not so when swimming the lake. *Why now? Has to be a dream.* She shielded her eyes and looked out toward the dark, realizing it wasn't a lake but a river, one that was heading off to her left.

If it could be crossed, she felt she would be safe. Easing into the cold water, she stepped to avoid rocks and tall weeds. By the time she traveled forty feet, she was only knee deep. She continued, the current getting stronger. Cheryl cautioned herself not to rush into the unknown. Several hesitant steps landed her chest deep once again. When she was able to break from the force pulling her downstream, she swam for the far shore.

The moon peeked through the downpour to highlight cliffs fifty feet high bordering the far shore. The water propelled her as she dug for the distant edge. After another hundred feet, she touched bottom, the brush-lined shore within reach. She crawled onto a sandy inlet surrounded by bushes, exhausted but pleased with herself.

As if by decree, it stopped raining. The misshapen moon once again popped out. Isolated in the cove and surrounded by a river on one side and a clay cliff stretching high above her head on the other, she had used up her last reserves and couldn't go back into the water.

Cheryl looked at the river, up to the towering cliff, and then to her enclosed inlet. She worried that this might be where she would die.

She had come so close to drowning and being caught by Mr. Wonderful, yet here she was, safe—at least for now—determined to shake off any cowardly ways and survive. The cliff in the unexpected moonlight showed a yellowish brown wall streaked with towering flutes buttressing the sheer face. Close to the bottom, a dark spot the width and height of a car door. It looked like a cave.

Cheryl climbed a stout tree and rock outcropping to reach the bottom of the enclave. She pulled herself out of the elements. The cave seemed not to be animal inhabited but a weather-induced phenomenon. She propped up several branches from a long-dead tree in the opening, creating a blind. Once again she wrung her blanket and placed it along with her jeans, blouse, and underwear into the branches, providing both a doorway and a clothesline. She gazed upon the arrangement and then decided to get rid of the undergarments. Something about a bra and underwear swinging in the breeze didn't feel right. A flurry of wind rippled the damp blanket. She curled up on the dry leaves and willed herself to sleep. Visions of running in deep water, a bony hand grabbing at her, and a laughing face breathing on her neck.

In the distance, an apologetic voice. She sat straight up.

"Cher, baby, let's make up and go home! I'll fix coffee, and we'll talk!"

She thought him an idiot. Yelling in the middle of the night like a whiney ex-boyfriend. The flashlight beam was directly across the river from her cave. She saw him panning the light over the yellowed buttress. Cheryl held her breath. She pulled the damp blanket away from the broken branches. The light settled onto her jeans, worrying its way in, trying to sort out the shape. The bright beam edged on. Cheryl dared not move her clothing. She made herself smaller, curling into herself.

The light was back, at a different angle.

"Hey, kiddo, I'm gonna come over there and get you!" He cursed and threw a rock. But his aim was too high, and it bounced down the side of the cliff. Another caught the edge of the cave. The beam scanned the entrance, searched inside, and then slipped away. His voice grew fainter.

She gazed over the entrance edge and caught the flashlight beam streaking across the river, a voice behind it pleading. He came back, shining his light into each dark cave-like area along the supporting cliffside columns. At each spot, he proclaimed his love and then maneuvered on. It would have been touching if it weren't so ridiculous. He once again snaked his way past her cavern, all the while peddling his litany of endearments. Finally, a car door slammed, followed by the screech of tires and a blaring car horn that pierced the night until the vehicle faded out of sight.

A noise like an outboard motor filled Cheryl's half dream. The interruption fought hard with her vision of a warm glow in her mom's fireplace, the crackling flames sounding like a boat on a countrified lake. She woke up to see a pair of dark eyes surrounded by her blue jeans staring back at her. A squirrel paddled its front legs in her direction and then disappeared behind her dark blouse.

The high-pitched engine grew closer. Was he back? Cheryl reached past her jeans and lifted the edge of the blanket. In the dim morning light, she saw a girl on a motor scooter across the river, her hair flying behind her. The scooter disappeared behind a few trees and then reappeared. She looked to be going too fast to be in the woods. She must be on a road. Cheryl considered yelling at her, thought better of it, and rested her head back down on the bed of leaves. If King was anywhere in the vicinity, he would hear her. She rose up again and looked out; in the distance, she still heard the motor.

A road. Why hadn't she seen it the previous night? She then remembered crossing a stream, climbing a bank to a short stretch of flat ground, and then sliding down into a culvert on the other side, then the river.

She shut her eyes and curled into a ball. Her bed of leaves was now damp from her body. Cheryl reached out and felt her jeans, clammy and cold. Her sneakers, with their patented holes, were damp; socks and blouse, about the same. She didn't know if she had slept or not; she felt groggy, her eyes squinting to adjust to the pale light. The sun had not fully risen. She watched the road. After an hour, the sun began to beat down on the face of her cave. She waited.

A truck full of squawking chickens swept past, its radio blasting a rockabilly tune. Her recollection of the inlet below her was that the steep cliff face fell right down to the edge of the water. She would not be able to walk on her side of the river. After looking out of her cave both upriver and downriver, she knew that she would have to cross back over to the road.

Tugging on her jeans, Cheryl winced at a variety of aches. She realized that the plastic grocery bag from basement hell was still in the back pocket. She stuffed the denim trousers along with her blouse into the bag and tied a knot at the top of the indented plastic handles. She would leave the wet blanket for the next poor girl caught in this damp predicament. Cheryl looped her sneakers around her neck, securing them with her shoestrings. Listening for cars, trucks, or motor scooters, she pushed the branches away from her cave entrance and slid down to the single heavy branch on the stout tree and dropped back to the patch of sand. She was well hidden, and catching her breath, she looked down and saw shoe prints. It frightened her until she realized they were hers from the night before.

The water seemed even colder in the day than in the dark. Naked, Cheryl denied fear and waded in, holding the plastic bag above her head as she paddled with one hand. She lost yardage as the river took her downstream. A log grounded in a stretch of sand caught her in the side close to her hip, which was still sore from being stranded in the window. It hurt like hell. She rolled onto the rocky shore, got dressed, and put on her sneakers. Again, she started shivering. It surprised her that she was so thirsty, given how much water she'd swallowed. Her stomach felt knotted and empty. She ran her fingers through her hair, wanting to look presentable. Why that mattered now made her laugh.

At the road, she stomped her feet to squish away the river water. Looking both ways, she decided to go away from the sun, west, thinking that to be the way home. An engine came laboring up a rise behind her; a tree trunk the size of two armfuls around hid her until she was able to see the driver. A bearded man with a deep frown. She stayed hidden. Over the next hour, two more vehicles passed, each with a male driver. She needed to find a hideout that had a little more sun. As she hurried toward a lone gnarled oak along the road, a horn from behind startled her.

An old woman in a battered truck pulled alongside. "Going my way, darlin'?" She grinned a toothless display as Cheryl piled into the front seat.

She wore bib overalls and a red flannel shirt. On her head a faded yellow Caterpillar tractor cap. "Whatcha doin' out here, deary?"

"Sorry, ma'am. Thanks for the ride. I'm sorry."

"No need to be sorry, hon. You look cold. You're shivering! Lord, are you soaked?"

"I'm lost. I mean, I can't find my mom—" She struggled to pull things together.

"Were you in the river?"

Someone said, "Yes." Maybe it came from her.

"Someone you ditching? A boyfriend?"

Cheryl caught her breath and gently shook her head up and down. She shivered once again, and an avalanche of tears started.

The old lady patted her on the knee. "Why on earth was you in the river, baby?"

She knew, but the words would not come. She felt dizzy and laid her head against the tattered upholstery next to the door. "I was looking to find the dog. Then I crawled out of the basement." *I'll just shut my eyes for a moment.*

"Good Lord A'mighty. Dear, are you hurt? You feel poorly, do you?"

Cheryl didn't respond. Her arms squeezed each other. The old lady said something, but Cheryl didn't understand any of it. She felt the car stop, a door open. The sudden warmth of the truck's interior shocked her, and she didn't know if she was hot or cold. Cheryl heard the woman speaking to someone.

"She's in a bad way, Horace. I better drive her on up to Jefferson City; it's about the closest hospital." She paused. "Okay. I'll meet up with you just outside Meta, State Road B on the way to Saint Thomas. See you in a few minutes."

The driver-side door shut again. The old truck's starter ground away as the woman patted her on the leg again.

"We got a police escort into the hospital at Jefferson City, hon. How you holdin'?"

Cheryl tried to catch her breath. Her teeth chattered. The road in front of her made wiggly curves. "A sardine can in my hair, it made him mad. Would you call my mom?"

"What's the number, hon?"

Cheryl knew the number, but it wouldn't come out.

"What's your name?"

"Sc- Sc- Scoot—is he okay? Mom's gonna be angry."

"Your name, sugar, what is it?"

Cheryl slumped down in the seat. The words to a song keeping time with the truck tires drummed in her ear. "Tutti frutti! Oh, Rudy! Tutti frutti!"

48

The *logical part* of Julie's mind would not allow the instinctive Julie to take over. The thought to pursue anything as simple as just a last name on a whim would be crazy. She struggled to recall what Venus Riley had said about Bink Caldwell. "A midget looking for a circus." Did she also say "a loser"? "Orphan"? Had she actually said "orphan"?

Her cramped work space at home held four shelves of books that would be described as research oriented, but she ignored them and looked in her local suburban phone directory for "Caldwell," discovering it to be somewhat common. The only other directory she had was for the Saint Louis metropolitan area, which contained several hundred Caldwells. She then Googled "Bink Caldwell," with no success.

The house felt empty. So much of Cheryl dominated the bungalow, such as her trophies for volleyball and girls' track. A gilded frame displayed the mayor's commendation for her work on a charity that she and several other girls started. It made Julie proud that Cheryl, at fifteen, helped pull together an organization in Saint Louis that raised nearly $2,000 for Special Olympics Missouri during the school year.

She rested her hands on the heavy wood mantel over the fireplace, running her fingers over a trophy inscribed with Cheryl's name for having won the girls' 400 at a dual meet with Jefferson City. She glanced at the clock—close to six in the morning. Another two hours before it would be reasonable to make her calls. The rain continued, a brisk wind ruffled the tree limbs, driving sheets of water against the wood pane windows. Julie shivered, not knowing why. She thought of Cheryl. Her police life consisted of, for the most part, black-and-white situations handled with a modicum of emotional decision. Unlike her present dilemma.

She lay on her leather couch, the old, cracked, slippery hide sinking down and wrapping itself around her. She reached up on the back of the sofa and pulled the wool blanket over her. The covering fell to her sides and feet and warmed her. She stayed that way for several minutes, but, feeling guilty, kicked off the blanket and moved to a straight-back kitchen chair, sitting in a rigid upright position. She looked into the cold fireplace, willing it to supply answers. She overrode her rigid mind-set and gave herself up to her hunch.

She called Gina Morada at home. "Sorry to call this early, Gina. It's Julie Worth, how are you?"

"I'm fine, no problem. I was up making a pot of joe. Any news about Cheryl?"

"No, nothing." Whenever someone mentioned her daughter's name, her heart did a little hiccup. "Reason I'm calling is, I've got to run out to see a woman who might know something about a suspect we're looking into. I wondered if you could look up some info on this fellow as well? Not much I can tell you other than a name, though. What do you say?"

Gina spent most of her time as headquarters dispatcher. Officers often recruited her to research information. "Sure, what do you have?"

"Name's Bink Caldwell. Bink is probably a nickname, but it's all we have right now. Can you look into your database? You know I'm e-literate when it comes to computers. Say, white male about five eight, thirty-five to forty years old."

"Any DOB, tats, birthmarks, arrest records?"

"Nope. Just Caldwell and that weird first name."

"Will you be in cell range?"

"Yeah, hope so. If not, I'll get you on a landline. Want me to get the okay from Captain Walker?"

"No worries. I got you covered."

"Thanks. I owe you."

The department had issued Julie another Charger. She went to the station and then headed out with Todd for a surprise visit to their heavenly bodied Venus. Their route took Todd past Westside Mall. Julie realized she was not far from the lot where she'd parked on the day of the shooting. She dismissed that event as being straightforward. There had been a well-defined bad guy who'd pushed too far, and he received his justice the same way he'd dished it out—unlike her present situation, which was far more complex and without a known villain.

"Any news about your daughter, miss?" Venus was in the middle of breakfast, a bowl of half-eaten cereal on the kitchen table.

Julie shook her head. "Think back, see what comes to

mind about this Caldwell person. Anything unusual that pops up since we spoke last?"

"Nope. As I said, he wouldn't say much but always had a scam going. One of those main-chance dudes. Like I said, I never suspected him of any funny stuff with my girl, in terms of taking her. He had his sad tale of woe. 'Dad left us, Mom had to hustle.' He wanted to come back, Mom let him, Dad beat the shit out of the kids, Mom kicked him out again. 'Poor me, I never had a break.'"

Todd stepped in. "Did he ever say where he came from? Missouri, Illinois, Iowa, Arkansas, Okla—?"

"Just the western part of the state, like I said."

"Where specifically, Venus? It's important, please."

She wedged her spoon into the vile-looking cereal. "He spoke a couple times about the lakes and Clinton or Warsaw. Lived with a family; said they had a big spread."

"Not *his* family but *a* family. Is that right?"

"I'm pretty sure he said *a* family." Venus clinked her spoon against the sugar bowl. "He and some kids, maybe brothers and sisters, all together on this big ranch."

Todd spoke. "You said 'spread' at first."

"Did I? Yep, he did say 'spread'—good catch, Officer. He used that word like he'd been told it were the big deal. The promised land."

"Recall him ever mentioning the names of any other siblings?"

Venus smiled. "Nah, he wouldn't talk much about his years as a youngster."

"Take a minute, Miss Riley. Let your mind go blank. See if something else comes to you, okay?"

Closing her eyes, she relaxed her hands on the painted metal tabletop. She tapped her head gently with the palm of her right hand. "He used the word 'tuck' a couple times, almost always in a deroga . . . ahh . . . roga—what the devil, you know when you don't like something and call it a name, it means a bad word, and you meant it?"

"Derogatory," Todd stated.

Julie didn't think Todd liked Venus much. Trying to prod the woman's memory, she interjected, "He spoke of this guy or gal in a—"

"Yeah, like that. He spoke the word 'tuck,' because it rhymed with the F-word. He was being vulgar, and I told him so. The couple times he spoke of this guy, he always spit, like the bad taste would never leave his mouth. But he never said who it were. Just Tuck the mother 'F.'"

"When we were here before, you mentioned a number of things about this Bink. A 'midget looking for a circus.' 'A loser.' Anything else?"

Venus chewed her lip. "Nah, I don't think so. What? Did I say something else?"

Julie hesitated, knowing that suggestions to witnesses and suspects could lead to false statements and innuendo. "Think about it."

"I know I gave you grief about my having company on the way. Sorry about that. And what else? Did I mention he said once he was a ward of the state?" She laughed. "Fancy name for an orphan, don't you think?"

Thanking her for the help, Julie again reminded Venus, "Call if anything comes to mind; anything at all."

In the car on the way back to headquarters, Julie's cell rang.

"Hey, Gina, what's up?"

"There's a whole hell of a lot of Caldwells in this state. Nothing that pops out, and, of course, no Bink. I've got a list of people broken down by city or area. I'll leave it on your desk, okay?"

It didn't sound very different from the info that Julie had accessed. She knew she had work to do.

Thanking Todd for his offer of lunch, she smiled at his feigned hand-on-heart disappointment. She made her way through headquarters to her desk in the basement. As promised, Gina left a stack of papers for her. The girl had separated the various Caldwells by cities, towns, and counties.

The eastern part of the state seemed to have a predominance of Caldwells. The towns Warsaw and Clinton were close to Lake of the Ozarks, a vacation spot hardly suitable for what Venus said Bink mentioned as a "spread." She called the Warsaw Chamber of Commerce and got a recording that the office was currently undergoing a renovation and would reopen at a future date. The future date in this case probably meant adios—not unexpected in the present-day economy and for a town of only twenty-two hundred folks.

Clinton, however, was more than anxious to help, the warm-voiced resident spieler full of facts, figures, and historical data.

"The town square is full of shops, ma'am—over a hundred—and you must see our courthouse dating back to—"

"Yes, okay. I mainly wanted information on one of your first families, the Caldwells."

"Ah, what did you need specifically, miss?"

"Well, you know what, forget it. Sorry to have bothered you." She hung up, feeling like a fool. Some things relating to Cheryl's disappearance needed to be kept private.

She called Captain Walker and explained her reasoning. He arranged for her to speak with the sheriff of Henry County.

She dialed him, and he answered on the first ring. After the preliminaries, he got right to it. "I can't rightly say if the Caldwell I know would be able to he'p you, but I'll put you in touch, okay?"

Thanking the lawman, she stopped to think before dialing the number she'd been given. Maybe she should go in person. It was always more beneficial when she presented herself to people face-to-face, watching their tics and shifting eyes.

She called Todd. "What would you think of a little two-and-a-half-hour trip west to the Lake of the Ozarks area? Assuming I can get permission from SS Capitan Herr Walker?"

"Long as you don't use my name in conjunction with his charming nickname."

"As always, you will remain my silent partner. It's late—but can we get under way, Big Man? I'll get Captain Walker up to speed on the Henry County sheriff and meet you in the lot."

An hour onto the road, Todd asked her the plan.

"I know it may not be protocol, but it's important you understand this. I want to see if these Caldwell folks can give me some straight answers."

"How do you know you've got the right folks? You told me Gina said there were a ton of these jokers."

"I don't know. It might just be a hunch."

Todd made an odd popping sound with his mouth, keeping time with a musical sales pitch on the radio. "Hunch? Remember what SS Capitan Walker said about that."

"No, what? Refresh my tired memory, señor."

"Señor? *Sí, un error grande como una casa*. Or, a mistake bigger than a fucking house."

She thought about it. "Yeah, maybe, but it's my mistake, my inspired guess, and, as it turns out, my house."

They were quiet the rest of the way to Clinton.

When they rolled into town on West Franklin, Julie called the number given to her from the Henry County sheriff for the person who seemed to be patriarch of the Caldwell clan.

"Good afternoon, sir. Sergeant Worth, Missouri State Patrol. I was given your number by Sheriff Jonas of Henry County. I just happened to be in town. Could I have a few minutes of your time to talk a bit about your— I hesitate to use the word 'clan;' maybe 'relatives' would be less intrusive. This *is* Walter Caldwell I'm speaking to, correct?"

"Yes, correct. Ma'am, is someone in trouble?"

"No, sorry if I gave that impression. Just that we are doing an investigation of an abduction, and the name Caldwell came up—more than likely unrelated, but we're just checking. Could we meet?"

The gentleman gave Julie his business address, and they settled on a time. Julie and Todd first had lunch at Golden Valley, a quaint eatery near the outdoor pavilion, and then walked to the Caldwell Firm, a modest real estate office.

After Julie took a seat, the elderly gentleman behind the oak desk rested his elbows on the oversized blotter. "You were saying?"

Not wanting to be the one under focus, Julie moved out of a bright stream of sunlight coming through the second-story window. "We're investigating an abduction and what is being called a homicide. I now can't give you more facts because of the ongoing nature of this case. The name Caldwell has come up. Does the name Bink Caldwell mean anything to you, sir?"

"No, there isn't anyone by that name in the Caldwell group, at least that I'm aware of."

"What about another name for something with a *B*? Billy, Brit, Bo, Benny, anything?"

Caldwell cleared his throat. "A number of years ago, there was a Benjamin. I never knew him; a distant cousin. His name came up once in reference to a lawsuit. Turned out to be a paternity affair. By the way, should I have my attorney here for this?"

Julie watched Mr. Caldwell, who seemed unperturbed and without guile. "It's up to you. There is no accusation at this time. We are simply asking questions."

He smiled back at Julie. "Let me call my wife, see if she remembers this Benjamin character." He excused himself and left the room.

Todd crossed his legs. "What do you think, Sarge?"

Julie felt disappointed. She checked over her shoulder for the elder Caldwell. "He seems honest, unafraid. I couldn't pick up anything; how about you?"

"Unfortunately, it's a *morte finito*."

"Is that supposed to be Spanish for 'dead end'?"

"I skipped school a lot. Par-*done*." Todd laughed.

They found themselves on the street with another phone number, directions to a house in the suburbs, and an invitation from a certain Benjamin Caldwell. Todd and Julie pushed on, being met on a comfortable porch with a padded swing for two and a couple rattan chairs.

"Greetings. I spoke to Walter Caldwell; said you wanted to have a word with me about an investigation? I didn't get all of that."

Julie sat in one of the rickety chairs; Todd carefully followed suit.

"I didn't mean to frighten you. It's an important case we're working on. A possible kidnapping and what we are presently calling a murder, at this point it is simply an inquiry. We're looking into the whereabouts of someone named Bink, more than likely a derivation of a name beginning with a *B. Therefore* we are here speaking to"—she gestured toward the old fellow pedaling back and forth on the porch swing—"Benjamin Caldwell, senior?" She arched her eyebrows and smiled a "Please speak" kind of smile.

"Well, yes, you might say I'm a senior both in age and as the father of a long-lost, I guess you could say, junior Benjamin."

"Would you mind explaining that?"

"Not at all. A former . . . wife of mine became pregnant with child, the result being a little Benjie."

Todd stopped writing in his notebook.

"Where does this former Mrs. Caldwell now reside?"

"I believe with a group of hellions and heathens." The old man adjusted his shirtfront. "Sinners and nonbelievers more than likely at the corner of Hellsgate and eternity." He leaned back and smiled. "She died, rest her filthy, rotten soul, soon after giving birth."

Julie waited for the man's newly discovered glee to subside. "What happened to little Benjie?"

"Don't have a clue. Given up to the state, I suppose. Don't know, wasn't interested." He ran his hand up and down on the rusted chain holding the swing. "It's been nigh onto forty years, like a dream. Ha-ha. More like a nightmare—"

"Thank you, we've—" Julie got up to go.

"—one that keeps coming back."

"—got all we need."

"Never saw the little bastard. Cost me a sweet penny, I'll tell you."

"Let's go, Todd."

"Not even sure it were mine. Might've been about anyone's," he ranted as Todd and Julie got in their car. And just before they drove off: "We were never married, so he really was a little bastard."

Unfazed, Julie glanced at her watch. "We can still check with Child Services. Let's hustle."

"Good afternoon, miss. My partner and I have somewhat of a problem," Julie stated. She and Todd flashed their badges at the receptionist.

"Can we speak with the person in charge of Child Services? It's an emergency."

Soon a woman of Julie's age approached from down the hall. "I'm Barbara Spence; you asked for me?"

Julie explained what they needed.

"Can this wait until morning? It's four thirty. I was just leaving for my son's soccer game."

"We're dealing with an abduction, Mrs. Spence," Todd said. "We don't have the time. How far back do your records go?"

"In some cases, quite far. What was it you needed, specifically?"

"A child, a newborn, was, we think, put into your care—"

"My care? You mean the state's care, right?"

"Yes, of course. Excuse me." Julie knew to tread lightly here. "Some thirty-five years ago, a Benjamin Caldwell Jr. was, we believe, put into either an orphanage, hospital, or foster home here in Clinton or nearby. Would you have a record of this?"

"Are you all right, miss?" The woman seemed to be studying Julie closely.

"Sorry, we've been running around like crazy today. Excuse me if I seem—"

Todd interrupted. "Sergeant Worth's daughter has been abducted, Mrs. Spence. She's been gone close to two weeks; we are somewhat desperate here. Can you give us a minute?"

The woman signaled for them to follow her. "Sorry, let's get right to it."

She opened a door marked City Planning, a command office holding a number of desks with a half dozen men and women preparing to leave for the day. "Hold up, folks. I realize all of you are not with us in Child Services, but we have an emergency. Let's get together on this, please. Sarah, Jim, Roberta, get on your computers, look for a Benjamin"—she looked to Todd for confirmation—"Caldwell."

"Did you hear the name? Benjamin Caldwell. It goes back nearly forty years, get on it, please. The rest of you, if you would, go through our paper files back as far as 1970, okay?" She motioned for Julie and Todd to sit as the room took on a frenzied energy.

They had just settled in when a woman going through the paper files shouted, "Got it!" Mrs. Spence took the single sheet of paper from her and glanced at it. "Says an infant boy was brought to the Main Street Child Care Center—our former name—that occurred on February 10, 1975." She read the notes to herself and then continued out loud. "On June 1, 1980, which would be five years later, the child was put into a foster home run by husband

and wife J. T. and Gloria Gerard, ages thirty and eighteen, respectively."

"Any address?" Julie asked.

"No. Just Henry County. Things must have been fairly loose back then." She turned to a woman at a nearby desk. "Sarah, would you see if any of the old telephone directories have this fellow, J. T. Gerard?"

The woman returned, handing a note to her boss.

Mrs. Spence glanced at the memo. "A Mr. James T. Gerard, State Road 13, number 204, two miles west of Calhoun. Seems this is about the best we can do here. Hope it is of some help." She walked them out the long hallway of the city government building and wished them well.

49

The drive to Calhoun took only fifteen minutes. Todd and Julie spotted the weed-covered tin mailbox after having driven past it twice. They proceeded down a long dirt drive bordered by unsown fields, weeds, and mounds of dried cornstalks scattered along the fallow landscape. At a tree-lined opening, a group of chicken-coop-sized buildings were huddled among an orchard of scrawny crab apple trees.

A man with a shotgun greeted them, rising from a porch decorated with mismatched lawn chairs.

Todd showed his badge through the windshield as he slid out of the car. "Cover me, Sarge."

Julie unsheathed her weapon and eased open her door.

"What can I do you for?" The man, a veritable department store Santa Claus, kept his shotgun at his side.

Julie positioned herself behind the car door, her Sig just peeking over the open window.

"We're State Patrol, need to ask you a few questions."

"Well, that may be difficult. I barely graduated grade school." He laughed and set his shotgun against the newel post of the steps. "Come on up."

Julie holstered her weapon and took a position close to the man's shotgun. Todd looked to Julie, who motioned for him to proceed.

"Looking for a fellow, James T. Gerard. Would you be that gentleman?"

The heavyset fellow spread his arms wide on the divan lawn furniture. "Afraid not. J.T. got hisself burned up in a filling station accident."

"What's the *T* stand for?"

The roly-poly hulk burst out laughing in short snorts. "Stands for Tucker, like the car that Detroit dude thought up."

Julie was alerted to this Tucker being the Tuck that Venus had mentioned. "How long ago did he pass away?"

"Ah, hell's fire, I don't recall. Twenty-some-odd years, at least."

"Did you buy this property from Mr. Gerard?"

"Nope, inherited it."

"How so?"

"He were my daddy. When he went up in smoke, my ma and I got this spread. He had taken up with a hooker and left Ma and myself kinda high and very dry. About two years later, we got word he was 'toast.'" He snorted again.

Todd and Julie exchanged looks.

Julie identified herself.

"Good for you."

Another wiseacre. "We're on a case and need information about your father. Would you like to help us or be an asshole?"

The man's eyes narrowed. Todd took a step forward as Julie grabbed the shotgun, broke it open, and extracted the two shells. "Let's all be real comfy here, okay Big Guy?" she asked. "Were you brought up here on the 'spread'?"

"Yeah, with the rest of the snot-nosed brats. Dad and Gloria, my ma, took in foster kids. Buncha sorry little turds."

"Among these sorry little turds, did you ever hear the name Benjamin Caldwell?"

"Nah, don't ring no bells. Why you wanna know?"

"I'll ask the questions, Mr. Gerard."

He smiled. "Don't often get called Mister. Sounds kinda nice."

Todd moved a little closer. "How about Bink? Maybe a nickname for Benjamin?"

The man looked down at his hands as if taking a stab at coming up with something. "Look here, guys. I'm just a poor dirt farmer looking to make ends meet—"

"Yeah, we saw your fields as we came in." Julie, hands on knees, went to his face level. "Not much of a crop this year, is there?"

"I've been off my feed for a while. Couldn't tend to—"

"How's about this, Slim." Julie stayed close. "I give you fifty bucks, and you stop the bullshit and give me what I ask for."

He played with his silver beard. "I may have known Bink. Is it worth a hundred?"

"I've got sixty." Julie dipped into her pocket. She held the three twenties out in front of her.

He reached for it. She pulled back. "Talk first, Mr. Dirt Farmer."

"Bink was around for a long time. I didn't think I knew his last name, is why I paused."

"Yeah, yeah. Get on with it."

"Well, he's come from over Clinton way and grew up here on the ranch along with another group of rag tails."

"How old was he when he left the ranch?"

"Left? Well, he didn't leave so much as he disappeared."

"Ran away?"

"Nah. We were all on a sightseeing thing. 'Way Things Are Made,' they called it."

"You said 'we.'"

"Yeah, the foster kids—Bink and all the other brats. We were looking around in this warehouse place; factory, I guess. I was young— don't think on it too much—but Bink and this other kid got themselves seriously killed."

Julie didn't think that to be right. After all the running around they'd done, only to find out Bink gets himself killed. She walked the length of the porch, wondering which way to jump. Todd kept his eye on Gerard and took a seat on the porch railing.

"What?" the grizzled character asked.

"You wouldn't be putting us on, would you?" Todd asked.

"Nah, it's the God's truth. Tuck wouldn't let us look, but as I think on it, they were both pretty much waffled."

Julie moved next to Todd. "What does 'pretty much' mean?"

The scruffy hulk dropped his sporting grin when he noticed Julie's attitude. "Damn, lady, you look like you're out for bear."

"If I was, I wouldn't have far to look, would I?"

The man sucked in his stomach with effort.

"You want the sixty, keep talking, bro."

"'Bro'—that's funny."

Once again he looked at her. She raised one finger in the air as if to say "Get on with it."

"'Pretty much,' I guess, means Bink was dead. Had his brain all crushed in like a smashed pumpkin. The other idiot was on the ground moaning his guts out; forget his name. Yeah, right, he weren't killed, just fucked up. Was back on the spread after a couple months. That's all I have on the brain at the moment. About that sixty . . ."

Julie reached back into her pocket for the money. She played with it in her hands.

"Did your old man keep any records? Something to look at for names, that kind of thing?"

"Yeah, he did. After he died, Ma and I came back here. Ma burned all that rubbish, not wanting the memories, I reckon."

"Would anyone besides you have information on names of the kids here at the time?"

He shook his head. "Don't know, don't think so. Saddle, Boots, Stinky, Mirabelle, and Tucker's beloved son, Jimbo." He spread his arms wide. "Yours truly."

"What was the name of the place all this smashed melon business took place?"

"Don't recall. Someplace over close to Saint Loo-ey."

Todd walked out into the yard to answer his cell. Julie saw him hold up his arm for attention; he waved it and stepped back toward the porch while still talking. "I'll tell her, and thank you." Todd signaled for Julie to come off the porch and follow him back into the dandelion-filled yard. "That was Walker. He just heard from section commander B. J. Dalton in Jefferson City. What he said, Sergeant, and listen to me carefully—"

Julie looked at Todd's handsome face, praying he was not about to give her bad news. "They brought a girl into St. Mary's Health Center about nine this morning, suffering from exposure and malnutrition. She's alive, and she fits Cheryl's description."

She needed to be alone and staggered off into the weed-infested field, not knowing how she'd gotten there. "My God, oh, please."

50

*C*harles Clegg felt tired; his arm had kept him up most of the night. He wrapped the hurt-like-the-devil arm in a pillowcase, which then soaked with blood. He pleasured himself for a few minutes with thoughts of how and what he would do to the little bitch when he caught her. But first, priorities. He called Deedee at work.

"Hi, Dumpling. How's tricks?"

"Who is this?"

Charles thought this might not be one of his more fortunate days. Even Deedee was giving him a hard time. "It's Charlie the King. Lover extraordinaire, protector of beautiful damsels and wayward children."

"Oh, you damn fool, what is it? It's too early in the morning to be spouting all your drivel."

He would have to employ all his resolve to get through the day without making a major bungle of some kind. Were the Gods not aligned? Or was it the moon and stars—a cosmic force—that descended onto Bait Shack the previous night?

"Miss Deedee, my dear, I've been in an accident.

Could you cover for me, with Wad? Tell him I've gone to the hospital after a terrible spill down my basement stairs."

"Oh, Charles, I'm sorry I was short with you. What happened?"

"You know, I don't get it. I fell down the basement stairs and knocked myself out. Anyway, I woke about an hour ago with a welt on my head and my arm all banged up. Tell Mr. Drew I'll be out for at least a day or two. Okay?"

Charles wandered around his house. Then he gave up and headed off to the local emergency clinic. On the drive into town, he went over the events of the previous night—the shock of seeing the girl crawling out of the basement window, her puncturing his arm, the desperate drive down this country road. The hours-long search of the lake, which hadn't produced anything except a case of sniffles, and the endless hunting through the dirt lanes of the vast rolling hills and countryside. He had seen her footprints in the woods and close to the river. The search along the water bank proved trying. His arm throbbed just thinking of it. He turned off the main road and bumped his way along an unmarked dirt trail that he knew led to a road paralleling the Missouri River. He held a knowing feeling that the girl had made it to the river.

His arm ached, so he drove one-handed, resting his damaged limb in his lap. Just before an intersection of country lanes, a yellow sawhorse blocked the way. He got out and moved it to the side of the road, noticing a cattle guard had been cemented into the dirt roadway. He ignored the fresh concrete and drove across as a patrol car whipped through the intersection. The blue-and-white Crown Vic stopped, the officer signaling for him to pull over.

Charles pulled the pillowcase away from his arm, purposely breaking loose the dried blood accumulated around the wound, reopening it.

"That barrier for the cattle guard was put there for a reason. Can I see your license and registration, please."

Charles pressed his arm hard against the door, to accelerate the bleeding. "I'm hurt, sir. I'm lost, I can't find help." He raised his bloody arm up past the driver-side window.

"What the hell did you do, mister? Damn, that looks bad."

Charles let out a pitiful groan. "I'm looking for a hospital, sir. Sorry about the sawhorse business. I'm lookin' for a hospital. Did I say that already?"

The officer stepped away from the blood trickling down the outside of the door. "Stay on this Route 100 into Jefferson City. Get that arm looked after."

"Sorry again. I should have this arm seen to, right?"

He noticed the patrolman eyeing him while he pointed down the road to the west. "About twelve miles, look for Route 50 into the Whitton Expressway. It will take you right into the Health Center. You okay?"

Charles wagged his head back and forth, as if he didn't know, and then drove off.

51

Riding shotgun, Julie unclenched her fists and shifted about in the seat, unable to find a comfortable position. Calls were in to both local police in Jefferson City and her Highway Patrol contact. She had to be satisfied with the patrolman's dispatcher getting back to her as soon as they knew something.

Taking Route 65 up to 50, Todd pegged his Crown Vic on eighty-five. Nailing the gas on the interstate would still have been forty miles longer. "GPS says it goes right past St. Mary's."

"Isn't that where they took the girl?" She wouldn't say Cheryl's name; best not to let optimism get ahead of reality. After all, it was only a girl who fit Cheryl's description. But it could be her.

Todd drove with lights and siren engaged. When traffic backed up outside of Jefferson City, he cut the siren but left the lights on, passing cars in the opposite lane against oncoming traffic. Other times he snaked by on the right, close to stopped cars. They pulled into the hospital parking lot.

"Sarge, relax. I'll put you at the entrance of ER. Just hold on. Okay?"

Cars were stacked up near the emergency entrance, so Todd shot down a busy car lane and stopped three rows over from the entrance. "I'll meet you inside, go. *Go*."

Julie stumbled as she slammed the car door, squeezing her way past tight-fitting vehicles. A car door swung open on a faded grey-green station wagon, just barely allowing her to run past as the surprised driver yanked back the door. *This close to my baby and almost nailed by a car door.*

"Sorry, miss." An orderly stopped her at the entrance. "Can't let you in. Patients only."

"Who's in charge?" She flashed her badge.

"Nurse Wendy Lucasi." He pointed down the long hallway.

Julie could not help herself from running. At a desk at the corner of an intersection of hallways, a woman came to her feet upon hearing Julie's oncoming commotion. "Hold it, ma'am. This is a hospital. You can't—"

"Are you in charge?" Julie looked at the Lucasi name tag while showing her badge.

"What do you—"

"I believe my daughter has been brought here in the past hour and a half. Her name is Cheryl Worth, sixteen years old. Please."

"Let me get in touch with the ER doctor who admitted her." She held up her hand in a "stop" fashion.

Julie felt dizzy. The hospital walls sagged. She knew she would have to relax and show discipline. The nurse continued to make calls, and Julie fell into a white plastic armchair wedged up against the nurse's station. Her hands gripped her shaking knees. She tried to think if she had been told that Cheryl was definitely found. Did she do it to herself, manufacture this big premature prize because it was what she wanted to believe?

"Mrs. Worth? Sergeant Juliette Worth?" A man in a lab coat, with one hand holding a stethoscope around his neck, approached.

"Yes, do you have my daughter?" She snapped to her feet.

"I'm Dr. Nathan Ryan, head of ER." He reached across the open space and offered his hand. "To answer your question, let's take a look. Follow me."

Julie was led down a hall with a series of open rooms separated by drawn curtains, all facing yet another bustling nurse's station.

The doctor consulted a chart from the desk and stopped in front of a room with curtains drawn. "This is the young lady we saw several hours ago, listed as a Jane Doe. Before we go in—"

Julie moved his hand from the curtain and pushed past.

"Please, Officer. There are certain protocols—"

She walked to the figure in bed hooked up to an IV line and oxygen mask. Wires and monitors blinked red and yellow.

"Her internal organs are being warmed, but being careful to stay away from the extremities. Rapid warming could cause heart arrhythmia. She has a hot pack on her chest—"

"I need to see her face, now please."

"Is this your daughter?"

"I can't tell. Are those wounds to her face?"

"Yes, a number of scratches and several blackened areas most probably caused by trauma, rough deep bruising."

Julie looked at how the oxygen mask distorted the cheeks and puffed the area around the closed eyes. Darkened strands of hair made a nest of her bruised face. Julie went to the left side of the bed and started to reach under the thick cover for an arm.

"Miss, you're being extremely aggressive. Allow us to do our job."

"Listen to me, Doctor. My daughter was abducted and missing for close to two weeks. I need to find out if this is my girl. Please." Julie stood by the bed as the doctor settled beside her. "What was it you wanted to do?"

"She has a faint birthmark on her left shoulder, a star-shaped, dark image."

The doctor pulled back the sheet and looked closely at the top of the shoulder. "I don't see any—"

"More in front, close to the clavicle."

"Ah yes. Here it is, just as you said."

"Thank God. Sweetheart. Cheryl." Julie wept.

The doctor spoke from the parted curtain. "She's sedated. Rough shape when she was brought in this morning. She's doing better now, but I expect her recovery will be slow. She needs fluids. I'll be going now. I suggest you let her rest."

"Thank you, Doctor. Excuse my anxious behavior. I've been distraught and not making sense." She squeezed Cheryl's hand, noticing how cold it was, still. Outside in the hallway, she looked for Todd.

He stood in the waiting room, his cell clamped to his ear. Julie clasped her hands together and shook them in triumph over her head so Todd could see. They embraced.

Charles tried several times to put his thoughts together and do what he went there to do. He knew he could not walk into the hospital with his arm exposed. He'd spent the better part of the day driving. At times he wasn't sure what he was looking for. The episode with the policeman upset him. He did break the law; it had been a near thing. But the man was decent and, in the end, serviceable. The cop's specific directions had helped him find the hospital with no trouble. He had cash with him and intended to use an alias at the emergency room.

Rewrapping the offending limb took time, the pillowcase having stiffened from the accumulation of dried blood. Charles gritted his teeth and continued his chore. He tucked the rest of the cloth under his arm, wiped a few blood spots off the gearshift, and then checked the interior of his vehicle for any other clues to his identity in the event that he needed to abandon the car. He had reached across with his right hand to open the door when a loud whoop came from someone hurrying past his car door. Not knowing why, he slammed the door and ducked down after the woman passed. It seemed silly to him. He marked it up to just being cautious. He threw on his crumpled old fishing hat and dark glasses, and made his way toward the redcrossed main entrance.

"Walker said to stay, of course." Todd slipped his phone into his shirt pocket as he and Julie covered the length of the hospital's long marbled hallway to the entrance. "Give me your car keys. I'll get your go bag and be back by midnight at the latest. Not much else we can do until Cher can talk to us."

"Did you call the locals?"

"Yeah, I explained the situation. They're going to assign someone twenty-four/seven until she's strong enough to be moved. They want to do the right thing."

"Todd, thank you. I don't think this yahoo will come back for her, and anyway, how would he know where or what? Who knows, maybe she was just out in the woods for days." Julie stopped. The image of Cheryl's swollen face made her legs weak. "We'll know more, of course, when she comes around."

Todd smiled at Julie's nonstop jabbering. He handed her a plastic slide card with "Marriott" across the front. "I got you a room while I was waiting. It's just down the street, walking distance. See you."

"Thanks, Big Man. See you in a couple."

The night sky held a vast accumulation of streaked clouds, their wispy tails drifting west, smudging the greyish-yellow panorama. Julie watched Todd jog toward the patrol car. She breathed deep, lung-filling breaths, feeling better than she had in weeks.

Julie smiled as she opened the door for a nurse who pushed a wheelchair for a man wearing a crushed hat and cradling a heavily bandaged left arm. She wished him good evening and good luck.

Julie went back and hung out in the expansive waiting room of the hospital along with other folks in varying degrees of concern. Julie read, walked, and read again.

She visited Cheryl twice, once during visiting hours, the next time under bombardment from various nurses, orderlies, and security. The local police provided their own watch, and Cheryl had been moved to a private room.

An elderly woman whom Julie had seen earlier speaking to one of the ER nurses approached her. "Hello, dear. Don't mean to be a pest, but I noticed you speaking to one of the police officers during the dinner hour and thought maybe you could help me." She was squat, stuffed into old, baggy bib overalls.

Julie thought the elderly woman was sweet. "I'll do what I can. What is it?"

"I been here most of the day." She plopped herself

down on a well-used sofa. "Except for the occasional stroll down the street to stuff my face with a Big Mac. Aren't they nasty?" she marveled. "To get to the point, I've inquired several times about the young heifer I brung here early this morning, and the cop on duty along the hallway there"—she pointed toward the ER hall—"won't tell me diddly." She grinned.

Julie moved closer in her seat. "Let me see if I understand you—miss?" She tipped her head at the older woman.

"That would be Gran, or some call me Granny Gault; comes from a long line of Scottish men. Means a wild boar or such."

"Miss Gault, you brought in your—what?" Julie smiled. "Daughter, friend, relative? Help me out here."

"Are you a police person? You sound like it."

"Yes I am, and you?" Julie liked this woman; she seemed forthright and honest.

The old woman chuckled, putting her finger to her lips as if to tell a secret. "I'm basically just an old fart. I keep chickens and tend a couple hogs, got fruit trees and a scrabble of vegetables sprouting up. Rely mostly on my pension and spend my hours thinking about my buddy of sixty-five years, Pud Gault. But to get to it, I brought in a kid hoofing it down this old country road."

Julie took in her breath. "I was told a deputy sheriff brought in my daughter."

"Lord A'mighty, you that child's ma?"

"Excuse me, please," Julie answered, nodding, the tears starting. "Tell me what happened."

"Was making my daily trip to Ed's Eats and Stuff." She rubbed her temples and cracked her swollen knuckles. "Kind of a restaurant cafe, half-assed market." She cleared her throat. "I take a couple dozen fresh eggs to Ed every morning, about seven o'clock. I see this youngster traipsing along, and she looks flummoxed. I stop, she gets in, goes on about a dog and how her ma's gonna be pissed and something about a basement and Aunt Willy, and I'm thinking this kid is wet in the pants, and her blouse's damp, and she's going on and on like she just might be plain ill. I called Rawlins at the sheriff's, and he sirened us all the way into Jeff City to this get-sick place."

"Can I tell you something, Miss Gault?"

"It's 'Missus,' if you don't mind."

"You are a treasure, and Cheryl, my daughter, will repeat this—thank you, thank you so very much. She is, by the way, going to be fine. She'll recover."

The two of them talked for another half hour, the elderly woman promising to show Julie where she picked up Cheryl. They agreed to get together at ten o'clock the next morning at Ed's in Osage City.

Charles sat in his Nomad for nearly an hour, contemplating his next steps. What a shock when the nurse wheeled him out of the hospital and his new best friend held the door for him. How sweet, after enjoying two weeks of her daughter's company to be wished "good luck" by Mama Worth.

He watched the front entrance of the hospital until he saw the sergeant's telltale stride. She had a way of walking that would put most men to shame. He considered following but thought better of it when he saw her rest her hand on her hip. It wasn't a relaxed gesture but a comforting one that suggested an automatic pistol lived under her jacket and within easy reach.

Charles made his way back into the hospital at one

thirty in the morning. He wandered to the nurse's station, checking names on the patient board.

"Can I help you?" inquired an orderly.

"I'm looking for my cousin." He flashed a winning grin. "She was in an accident."

"Try the emergency area, buddy." He did. Charles trailed through several rooms, eyeing lumps of humanity spread out on elevated iron beds. Oxygen hissed, and tubes and wires formed nests of get-well apparatus. He came upon one young thing who lay moaning, her face and arms battered, her hair twisted into a scrambled knot, the oxygen mask distorting her features. *It could be her*, he thought. He ran his hand along her battered arm.

"What are you doing in here?" A nurse stood in the curtained entry.

"Oh, hi, I'm looking for my cousin. We were in an accident." He made a shrugging gesture with his left arm.

"Well, you can't be in here." She held the plastic curtain wide for his exit.

"Could you tell me the person's name in there?"

"No."

"What do you mean, no?"

She took his good arm and marched him toward the hospital exit. "I saw you here earlier; you had your arm stitched. A fall, wasn't it? And now you're here feeling up some kid."

"I'm injured, bitch." He tried to pull away. "What are you doing?"

She didn't answer but continued to guide him down the hall. At the wide double doors, she gave him a slight push. "If I see you back here, I'll call security. Nighty-night."

Charles thought he'd pay that particular woman a visit sometime later; get to know her a little better.

It was after one in the morning when Julie made her way to the Marriott. On her hotel room dresser, her go bag and a "Yea for our side" note from Todd. She fell exhausted on the bed, clothes and all. In the morning, she took a quick shower and returned back to the hospital. They transferred Cheryl to the third floor where Julie acquainted herself with the day-shift nurses. She approached Cheryl's room with care, knowing that her girl wouldn't be in shape for too much excitement. She neared the bed and noticed the oxygen mask removed. Julie looked down at her daughter's swollen face. She reached for her hand, and when she touched her, Cheryl's darkened eyes popped open.

"Cheryl, it's Mom."

The girl's eyes searched the room, stopping on her mother. "Hi, Ma." Her speech, slurred and soft. "Where you been?"

Julie leaned over and put her arms around her girl, feeling her daughter's strong heartbeat. Cheryl's eyelids fluttered and closed, a smile crept onto her dry lips. Behind Julie, footsteps.

"Sergeant? Dr. Ryan would like to see you." The woman in white led Julie back down the hallway to the nurse's station.

"Hope you don't mind, Sergeant. I was told you were here and wanted a word with you." The doctor gestured for Julie to follow him. They sat in a waiting room off the hall. "I would like to propose a plan that might help in your daughter's recovery." He glanced down at his chart.

"Cheryl has been through some sort of traumatic experience. Our impulse as parents is to cover our baby with love and questions and more love, etcetera. I would like to suggest a cooling-off period—no pun intended, of course." His face didn't change; he simply moved on. "Many times in these situations, the patient is inundated with questions about events that transpired, and in their attempt to be helpful, they have what might be termed a relapse. Might I institute the following?"

"Yes, of course, continue."

"An easy, nonquestioning recovery in the neighborhood of several days. Mom and Dad's gentle comfort without any 'Let's try and do better next time, sweetheart' accusations or 'Listen to your parents.' None of that kind of thing, okay?"

Julie started her trusty ten count, knowing she'd never get further than five. "Dr. Ryan, thank you for the advice. I'll take it into consideration—all except, of course, there isn't any daddy in Cheryl's life. And as far as 'accusations,' what did you have in mind?"

"Oh, I'm sorry. I forgot the story about the—abduction, was it?"

"Yes, there was an abduction." Julie wondered where this was going. "I believe I mentioned that last night."

"Well, all right then, Officer. Sometimes these tales are what keep us together as families, aren't they? We allow our loved ones their peccadilloes to cement and create a cohesiveness that in the end is a compromise but one that is harmless and maybe helps to end an abusive relationship."

Julie hadn't a clue what this jackass doctor was talking about. "I'll take your advice about going slowly; seems reasonable. But, and this is just between you and me—"

"Of course, always."

"Do not—I repeat, do not—spread any of your mis-guided bullshit to my daughter. Clear?"

"Your manner is—"

"Possibly you didn't bother to check with the police-man on duty outside my daughter's room, sir. If you had, you would have been told there is a mad motherfucker out there who kept my kid captive for two weeks, and as yet we don't know what was done to her. She is not a victim of an abusive relationship, nor does she even have a boyfriend. This fucking clown murdered my best friend during the abduction of my daughter. Your advice on relationships would be pertinent only if the diagnosis fit her circum-stances. Asshole." Julie stomped out of the waiting room, not wanting to be late for her ten o'clock meeting with Granny Gault.

Todd deposited himself in the lobby of the hospital. "Morning. How's our favorite teenager this fine day?"

Julie pulled herself together after her tête-a-tête with righteous Ryan the great philosopher. "Hello Todd-O, Cheryl's fine. Spoke a couple barely audible words to me." Julie tried to relive the moment. "Asked me where *I'd* been. Jesus, can you imagine?"

"That's funny, but she's okay for now?"

Julie caught herself drifting off, her mind back on a certain surgeon whom she thought should heal himself. "Yeah. Can we get out of here for a while? I've got an ap-pointment in twenty minutes, do you mind?"

Julie cranked up the car's GPS and instructed Todd on the twelve miles to Osage City. They made their way through the outskirts of Jefferson and Hickory Hill.

"You seem more than a little pissed. What's up?"

"Don't ask." Julie put her knee against the glove compartment door, cranked back the seat and closed her eyes.

"That bad, huh?"

"Yeah, I blew up at Cheryl's doctor. I totally lost it." She continued with a few other words to herself.

"You just said, 'that stupid asshole, bastard,' am I correct?"

Julie laughed. "Yeah, something like that. The doc said some things, then I said some things, and so forth, and that leaves you and me out here wandering in Daniel Booneville." For a while, she watched the passing scenery, settling into a new reality of Cheryl's being out of danger. "While we're in the neighborhood and things are fresh, we should do a little detective work."

They searched out Ed's Eats, and sure enough, Granny was sitting on the wood steps, corncob pipe cradled in her open palm. After introductions and refusals of coffee, they piled into the unmarked Crown Vic with Gault in the passenger-side seat, Julie in the back.

Though Julie had already primed Todd on how Gault came upon Cheryl, that didn't stop her from retelling the events of the entire day. When she exhausted herself with that story, she jumped in with another.

"But before we go too far, I want to explain about the pipe. It were Pud's, and it's just an affectation. I keep it around 'cause it feels like that old devil is back with me." She paused. "Okay. Let's get back to things. Head on out this way south, straight on the way you're headed. I met up with your baby about eight to ten mile down a ways."

For a while, they rode in silence. "And how's our baby today, missy?"

"She's fine, thank you. She recognized me, said a few words, went back to sleep."

"Coming up on our tree. Little farther, little farther. There. Pull over to your left, sir."

"Call me Todd, please."

"Okay, Todd. Pull in back of that gnarly evergreen." The old gal whipped her well-worn yellow tractor cap off her tangle of grey hair.

Once they had stopped at the side of the road, Granny turned in her seat. "I was heading west coming from back that way," she said, pointing, "when I see your youngster stumbling between that huge old monster tree up ahead and this twisted pine off your rear trunk. If you're going to get out and have a look, I'll take a pass and just sit here, okay?"

Julie and Todd got out.

"You want to look around a few minutes while I hike down there, see what's what?" Julie asked Todd.

"I'll check out the riverbed."

They parted. Julie walked along the edge of the road, not knowing exactly what she was looking for. She walked off the gravel shoulder after fifty yards. A clearing from where she stood to the river seemed a likely place for someone to have come out of the water and make their way up the country lane. Looking to a copse of thorny bushes on the sandbar, she picked up a scrap of denim on a nearby beached log. Across the moving river, there seemed to be nothing but towering cliffs.

Todd made his way through a gaggle of brush growing down to the waterside.

"Nothing of interest here, Todd-O. She must have come from this side—the side we're on, the forest. She couldn't have come off the steep cliffs; way too treacherous."

"Let's see if there's any sign of where she could have come from." Todd started back up the rise to the road.

They walked along the road edge on opposite sides of each other.

"There's a fence here! Looks like it's been bent down!" Todd called to Julie, who went ahead fifty yards.

She crossed over and trotted back to where Todd was pointing. She slid down the still-damp culvert bank and inspected the crunched wire fence.

"Look here. Where it's bent, there's a few rusted shavings. Then under and around the bend itself, it shows all silver and new."

"It doesn't mean it was Cheryl who came over this."

Todd looked at the countless bends in the top portion of the wires. "But someone recently did, that's for damn sure."

"Listen, Biggie, how's about this for a plan—since we're here and this trail is still hot, let's pursue it for a while. Would you mind taking Gault back to her truck, then meeting me back here in an hour? It will give me a chance to head in here a ways, see if there's a cabin hidden back in the woods. Who knows what I might find. What do you think?"

Todd looked up and down the road. "If there were a cabin in there"—he waved his arm at the vast forest in front of them—"there would be a road leading to it. A path, something."

"Yeah, you're right, but I'd still like to hang out, get a feeling for this jungle."

"Back soon, Sergeant." Todd headed for the car.

Julie stepped over the bent fence, wishing that she had proper hiking gear. She walked into the heavy forest, thinking a plan might be to cover as much of the area on either side of the fence opening as she could manage. She paralleled the road toward town for a hundred yards, and then went into the more heavily wooded area and turned in the opposite direction.

After a few minutes, she lost sight of the road. She drifted off her planned route and just started to veer back to her left when she spotted a recently broken branch on a large pine tree. The limb was about chest high. If the break was as new as it appeared, it would have been broken by someone about her height or Cheryl's. She took a Kleenex from her jacket pocket and dangled it on the branch before heading back toward the road.

Julie waited nearly a half hour for Todd. She paced the dirt road, seeing only one passing vehicle. A faded blue Camaro driven by a man with a crew cut and long side-burns.

He stopped across the road from Julie and sported a grin. "I could turn this buggy around and go your way, buttercup."

Julie threw out a quick "No, thank you" and kept walking. When he put the car in reverse to keep up with her long stride, she flashed her badge with her right hand and with her left pulled her short jacket away from her Sig. "I guess you didn't hear me. I said—"

He pulled away, his rear wheels spinning in the soft gravel roadway. By the time Todd arrived back, she had worked herself into a tizzy.

"What kept you, Sandman? Christ, I could have walked to Arkansas by now."

"Okay, Sarge. Keep it up and I won't give you your present."

Julie looked up at her partner. "Present? You working an angle?"

Todd reached across to the passenger seat and produced a pair of black sneakers.

"Eight, wasn't it?"

"Ah, you're too much. Where did you find these?"

"General store. Shoes laced and tied, hanging along an aisle sporting bathing trunks, workout gear, and a whole lot of other junk. Try them on." He passed her a pair of sweat socks and watched as she laced up her new sneakers. He locked the car just off the road. His new tennis shoes, a combo of red with bright green stripes.

"I marked a tree back in the woods."

"What gives?"

"Nothing big-time, just a broken branch; thought it could lead to something. Nice walkers, by the way," she said, pointing to his new shoes. "No danger of *you* getting lost. Those guys are already crying for help."

They proceeded into the tangled forest. After they came upon Julie's marked tree, they spread out like they had while looking for Cheryl and Billie back in town. They looked for footprints, handprints, disturbed underbrush. If they found a pattern of her shoe print, it could possibly lead to a house, cabin, or other dwelling.

"By the way," Julie asked, "I saw you reaching into your pocket before. What gives?"

"Just a little Daniel Boone-ism. I bought this packet of ribbons; thought I'd tie one on a tree once in a while, so we could find our way back."

"Clever, Mr. Boy Scout. Let's do it."

They spread out and scouted south through the woods. A half hour went by.

"Hey, Sarge! Hey!" Todd was on his hands and knees looking at something on the ground.

"What's up, Sherlock?"

"Sneaker print, looks like to me. Take a look."

"I'd say that's about the right size. And from the depth"—she pressed her own new sneaker next to the soft imprint—"I'd say a hundred thirty-five or a hundred forty pounds max. What do you think?"

"Yeah, right. Good call. Let's go in trail for a while. You look right, I'll look left."

Todd led the way. One of their problems was that the sun had dried most of the open area, leaving patches of soft earth under shaded areas.

They came to a bog; probably a natural spring. She paced off to her right to skirt the wet area next to half-buried brush in the trampled swampy earth. "Todd, look at this."

"What?"

"She came under here, crawling probably." Julie pointed to a tangled nest of branches. "Can you imagine my girl creeping through here at night, alone? Maybe even getting chased? That sneaker imprint, exact same shape and size as the last one. Crawling, walking, stumbling. Jesus, no wonder she's being treated for exposure." Julie turned a full circle, looking into the woods, and then walked away from Todd, not wanting him to see her crying. "Let's push on for another quarter hour, okay, Mr. Devlin?" She tried to keep it light, walking on ahead, occasionally stopping to examine a trampled bush or broken branch. A tall pine stood before her, skirting her path. A shiny object caught her eye: two D batteries nestled in a depression filled with mud. It looked as if someone had stepped on them. She called Todd and bent down to take a closer look.

She poked at the batteries with a stick. "These look

new to the environment. Someone changed batteries here recently."

Todd knelt next to her. "Probably not much of a chance for fingerprints, with all the mud, but I'll bag it anyway." He pried the two batteries out of the mud and put them in a ziplock bag.

Julie pointed at a pair of shoe prints off to the right of the water hole. "Looks like cowboy boots, men's nine or ten. Damn. Is that rain?"

"Afraid so." Todd dug into his jacket pocket for his camera.

Julie pulled off her jacket and spread it over the shoe prints. When Todd was ready, she swept the jacket away and spread a dollar bill down next to the pointy-toed impression. "We just made it."

They watched the rain obliterate the footprints.

They would follow what looked like a trail that would disappear, only to reappear some thirty yards later. The path never seemed to stay in the same direction, varying from 180 degrees east to due west. Todd found a rise and they climbed a hill that looked as if it had been hit by lightning years before. Several large trees had been knocked down, their rotten carcasses spread across the knoll. It wasn't a clear view, but through the tops of a few tall pines, they could glimpse water.

Todd clasped Julie by the shoulder and pointed through a gap in the limbs. "I'd say about a half mile at least." They looked to the east. "Nothing but pines; same to the west. The lake in front of us is at least two to three miles from where we left the car. It's too late to go all the way down to the water, but we can check with the GPS for a body of water south of the country road we were on; find out where we are, go from there. What do you say?"

"You're right. I need to get back to the hospital, check with Cher. And we should also bring Walker up to date. Thanks for today, Big Man."

They started the long trek back.

Julie sat next to Cheryl's bed, listening to her child's heavy breathing. She felt her hands and feet. Warmer. Not normal but better. The doctor left her IV still attached.

"Ma?"

"Yes, Cher, what is it?"

"Are you there? Don't leave me, please?"

"I'm here. You're safe."

"Tell Aunt Billie I'm okay, will you, please? Scoot's at the house down the street. The man called. Would you tell him not to play his music?" She tossed about in the narrow bed. "I threw up, Ma, in his face. Gross. Did I go to shop class, mom?" She squeezed her eyes shut.

Julie ran her hands up and down Cheryl's arms. "Try and forget everything, just rest."

Cheryl breathed deeply several times and then relaxed. "He smelled like garlic and dog doo."

Julie sought out the hospital administrator, requesting that a mere a five-minute audience would do. He proved to be accommodating and invited her to meet.

They chatted briefly about Cheryl's circumstances and Julie's need to have a different doctor assigned.

"I have nothing against Dr. Ryan; it's more a personality issue than anything else."

"I'll see what I can do. Nathan can be somewhat frustrating at times. I understand your daughter's situation. We want you to know we have her best interests at heart."

Julie thanked him and hustled off to meet with Todd.

"I called the captain," he said, "and explained the

tracking, trailing, and especially guessing. Walker thinks we should come back to headquarters to put together a search party. His words were 'would be a good idea.' He thinks it's a waste of time, your 'gallivanting in the woods.' Once again his words."

Julie paced around the hospital reception room like a caged animal. She looked at Todd and mouthed the word "piss."

Todd smiled. "He also said that if you had a strong feeling about this, to proceed on your own. But call for backup if anything proves out. End of message."

Julie continued around the large room, trying to keep herself in law enforcement mode, and not doing a very good job of it.

"I drove your car back." Todd threw her the keys. "Taylor's off duty, so he'll give me a lift back to the station."

"Thanks, pal. Once again I don't know how to thank you."

Julie walked her partner out front to his ride. Once settled, Todd rolled down the window. "Call, Sergeant."

52

On the way home from the hospital, Charles hired a migrant worker just outside Jefferson City. A line of Hispanic men in work clothes were milling about in front of a Home Depot parking lot. He spied one fellow standing by himself, not chatting or fraternizing. "I need a hard worker, amigo, how much?"

The man shrugged.

"How's about seven fifty an hour?" Charles asked.

The fellow nodded and got in the car.

"You speak English, friend?"

"*Poquito.*"

"What does that mean, a little? Some? What?"

The man turned in his seat back toward the other men at the gathering. "Yes, I speak. The *jefe*, head honcho there, wearing the hat, he thinks I'm loco in the head. Makes trouble for me, no English for him, *cabrón.*"

Charles didn't understand what his Mexican friend said. Maybe it didn't matter. More important was the fact that his new amigo seemed to be a loner. He drove for an hour, winding around and doubling back several times.

The guy would need to be a compass genius to figure out where he was. In the end, though, it probably wouldn't matter.

In the basement of Bait Shack, they got to work tearing down the stud-erected walls. Charles, working one-handed, wasn't much help, but he carried the long two-by-fours out back of the house, where he left them to be sawed later into chunks that could be burned. By the end of the day, the walls were down and the scraps of plasterboard stacked on the basement floor.

He fed his new friend canned sardines, scrambled eggs, and Cup Noodles. Then the two of them cleared an area for the cot. Charles explained to Rodrigo that he had at least one more full day of *más trabajo* for him. The fellow seemed to be all right with his overnight accommodation and his stand-alone toilet in the middle of the room.

The next day at a little after four, Rodrigo and Charles finished renovating the basement. The plasterboard, commode, and cot were loaded into the back of Charles's Nomad along with three heavy trash bags. Charles asked Rodrigo to help him unload as well.

Charles had paid the hospital in cash to sew up his arm, so he was short of dollars. "We'll go to ATM, *entiendes*?"

The man acknowledged by clicking his tongue twice. Charles once again drove a serpentine route even though it looked as though Rodrigo was asleep.

At the Jefferson City dump, Charles paid his five dollars, and the two of them drove to a spot where a bulldozer was parked, ready for the next day's movement of trash. Charles got into the back of the car while Rodrigo piled the trash bags in front of the dozer's shiny blade. When he returned to the tailgate, Charles, in the back pull-down-seat area of the wagon, pointed toward the dozer. "Look at those pigeons, Rodrigo. *Más bueno, sí?*"

Rodrigo's view of the hundreds of birds faded from the pale blue sky, their flapping wings morphed into dark grey ringing noises, and then black nothingness.

53

*C**heryl seemed better***—her color returned, the hot pack on her chest removed. Julie's request for a new doctor had been granted.

"Cheryl, how are you feeling?"

"Better, yes, much better. Doctor, when can I go home? Soon, I hope."

"Perhaps that should be left up to your mother. You've had a trying experience, be patient. School, for instance, should take priority, but don't rush it. I understand last night you were having difficult dreams?"

"I don't recall; don't know any of that. Mom?"

Julie stood up from her chair and moved to Cheryl's bed rail. "You were calling out. Scoot, Aunt Billie. It's stuff we can go over later, okay?"

"Yeah, sure, Ma. Wow. If I try and use my mind too much, I get this drowsy, stupid feeling." Cheryl plopped back down on her bed and turned toward the doctor.

"Is it all right if I nap now? I'm really . . . "

The doctor and Julie watched as Cheryl's breathing slowed, and she fell back to sleep.

"As far as being discharged, maybe tomorrow. Let's see how she is in the morning."

Julie walked the doctor out into the hall.

"Don't push on going back to school, not now," he advised. "You might want to consider that she see a psychiatrist. Perhaps help her to look more clearly into what happened. Anyway, nice meeting you, and I wish you the best."

Julie liked the new doctor's suggestions and mind-set. He would do. She paced the hospital corridor and then called Todd. "Hey, what's going on?"

"Not much. How's Cher?"

"Fine, good. Asleep. Says she wants to go home, so we'll see. I just wanted you to know I might be back in town tomorrow. Would you tell Walker I'll probably hang out with her for a day or so? I'll call in and let everyone know what's going on. Any thoughts on our little exploration exercise?"

"Not much, but I looked at a large-scale map of the area we were in. The water we saw might have been a river, not a lake."

"Yeah, I know. Where the cliffs were; that's the Missouri."

"But we walked south of there three miles or so. That's the Osage, and southwest of there, another ten. Lake of the Ozarks is spread out with a ton of cabins and homes. So it isn't gonna be easy, Sarge."

"She couldn't have walked that far, could she?"

"Beats me. What did the doctor say about questioning her?"

"Basically, take it easy, go slow."

"Okay. Let me know what's going on. Maybe see you tomorrow. We'll talk."

Julie would have to break the news to Cheryl about the death of Aunt Billie. Maybe the next day, on the way home. She did an inventory of her thoughts on the case—going slow didn't seem to be part of her list of goods. She determined that Cheryl's health would always come first. But somehow she would find Mr. X and serve him up a plateful of old-fashioned ass kicking.

Getting out of the hospital proved to be an ordeal, and the drive home was no easier. Cheryl pounded her hands on her thighs when her mother told her about Billie. "Was it my fault?" She watched the telephone poles whizz by. "What happened?"

"I didn't want you to find out from the news. Now that you're going home, people will talk, ask questions. How much do you remember about what went on that day?"

"You mean after he called?"

"Who called?"

"Ole Garlic Breath. I went to his house to get Scoot."

"The place at the end of the block? At the cul-de-sac?"

"Yeah. I didn't know Scooter was missing. Or did I?" She buried her face in her hands, as if willing the events to pop out of her mouth. "The guy called and said he had Scoot, and for me—us—to come get him. Aunt Billie was in the bathroom. So I went. I don't know. I fell asleep and woke up wet and walking somewhere. Aunt Billie was crying. I was in the back of an SUV. Or maybe a wagon—a station wagon. Maybe Billie was there too, I don't know."

54

L isten to me, Charles. This is where I want to be absolutely clear. Although tenured, you are not irreplaceable."

Charles's first day back at work proved to be troubling. He watched as boss Wad fussed with his tie.

"I say this because there is a manner of the vagabond spirit in your attitude which can be attractive, but—and here we are again—there is a sense of the carefree about you. As if we are hostage to your every whim. It must stop."

"Are you referring to my recent absence?" Charles exhaled carefully, not wanting, under the present circumstances, to explode.

Drew pressed his clenched fist against his desktop. "You know damn well what I'm referring to. Your cavalier attitude about this establishment, your repeated absences of late, and your lack of deference to your superiors. I want it stopped, mister."

Charles got up from his chair and took off his suit coat, and then rolled up his left shirtsleeve. While doing so, he deliberately pushed on his recent wound, forcing it to open. He exposed the bandaged long, bloody trail from elbow to wrist. "Does this look like deference to others? Does this appear as if I didn't yield to someone's opinion? I fell down my basement stairs."

"You do not have to raise your voice to me." Drew pronounced each syllable as if he were speaking to a four-year-old.

"I've been a loyal employee—"

"Yes, all the while being a brat like you were since the first day you came aboard. Take the next few days and examine your priorities, Mr. Clegg. Determine if you want to continue your relationship with Drew Box Factory. Do not come in to work, but sit in your comfortable lakefront cottage—provided, I might add, by the aforementioned box factory. Ask yourself if this company is where you want to spend the rest of your life. And if so, are you prepared to change your attitude?"

"I—"

"Come back a week from today. Ready to work with renewed character. Clear?"

Charles happily removed himself from the office. Conflicting thoughts of murder and forgiveness filled the drive back to Bait Shack. He had to change or at least put forth that appearance.

Pacing the weed-infested bank of his home, Charles looked out at the broad expanse of water. He thought of the girl. Her evil karma caused this, his wound, the attitude he had been forced to embrace. The demise of his guest quarters and the elimination of the day laborer was all on her.

Ruminating about his barrage of recent bad luck, Charles lit his outdoor incinerator, stoking it from time to time with two-by-four basement wall shards. The rug, mattress, towels, and tattered sheets had been set aside in hopes of a down-the-road revival, but they were now an ashen heap. He wondered about the missing blanket; probably caught up in the run to the garbage dump. The fan and caged light, along with the exposed toilet bowl, all gone to the dump. He painted over the fresh nail holes where the studs had been pulled away from the interior basement walls. He brought a number of boxes and other junk down the rickety stairs to fill the space left by his honeymoon suite. The basement looked like any other cluttered storage catchall.

Later, while sitting on his front porch, he thought of the girl and what she might put together of her fortnight stay. He was certain that she'd never gotten a look at him.

The Bronco would be a problem, though. He couldn't be sure if sweetie buns had seen it or not. If she hid along the road and heard him searching for her, she probably would have noticed the color or the name and maybe even the plates, though those had been stolen also.

He would get rid of it, maybe run it off a cliff, abandon it in an urban area to be taken. And then it came to him. He had the time. Why not take it back where he had borrowed, or, in fact, stolen it. Why not? It could be a soul-enlightening opportunity for redemption.

Charles spent several hours cleaning out the Bronco. Vacuuming, scrubbing the interior for fingerprints, pressure hosing the engine compartment. He would clean the car again in Tulsa before dropping it off. He wasn't sure how far law enforcement could go to track him, but he wasn't going to leave anything behind.

He knew his drive would be close to three hundred miles. A sense of relief sunk in once he settled on relinquishing the old Bronco. His "ol' hoss" had been such a burden.

With the anticipation of his trip the next morning to Oklahoma keeping him awake, Charles indulged in hot milk and toast to get to sleep.

55

Cheryl *grew more* sensitive to her surroundings. At times Julie would catch her standing in the front room by the door, as if considering whether she should go out or stay inside.

"You'll let me know, sweetheart, when you wish to speak of this." Julie waited several days before attempting to talk to Cheryl about the ordeal she'd been through. She didn't even know the right words to use when talking about her "abduction."

"Uh-huh. I will, Mother."

Her daughter's use of the word "Mother" took Julie aback. It seemed formal and distant, unlike her baby. The next morning, while Julie backed the car out of the driveway, Cheryl commented that "he smelled bad, of body odor, nasty."

Julie put the car in park and waited.

"I forced myself to be sick and threw up on him. It might have saved me from getting molested. Sorry." Cheryl gazed out the front windshield.

Julie kept silent.

"The room had been made special. No windows; more

like a cell. Kitsched up like a kid's bedroom." She made a fist and struck her knee. She dipped her head, avoiding meeting Julie's eyes. "When he called, I should have waited for Aunt Billie." She glanced down at the healing blisters on her hands. "Did I say that already?"

Julie reached across and squeezed her daughter's wrist without looking at her. She wanted to give support without emotional pressure.

"The light was always on. I figured a way to turn it off so I could sleep. Wish I could stop thinking about myself and all this junk." She rubbed at a stain on the dashboard. "I feel bad about Aunt Billie. She was with me, and then she wasn't. It poured the night he took me, and again when I got loose. I got soaking wet." Her body pulled in on itself.

Julie wanted to ask so many questions.

"I want to see Aunt Billie."

Before Julie could answer, Cheryl continued. "I'm sorry. I know she's gone. She was so afraid, Mom."

They sat, the car still in park, the engine running like a rhythmic accompaniment to Cheryl's lament.

"The phone rang at Billie's, and he said he had the dog. Ah, Scoot, is he okay?" She looked to her mother for an answer.

Julie nodded.

"He was barking. Why didn't I wait for Billie? Then I was smothered and it rained, a long ride in the back of a car—or like I said, older station buggy. How long was I gone? A week? Two?"

Julie held up two fingers.

She absorbed that and then continued. "He sang. Awful off-key down-home kind of stories, all about pretty saloon keepers who tapped beer and screwed cowboys.

Sorry. It's like he was short. I don't know why I say that."
She lost herself in her broken fingernails. "He peeked
through the food slot at all kinds of times."

They glanced at each other. Cheryl nodded.

Julie wanted to scream, but she kept quiet. After a
long, slow expelling of air, Cheryl relaxed back into her
seat. Julie once again waited, and then, after a reasonable
pause, put the car in gear and backed out of the driveway.
They were halfway into town when Cheryl spoke again.

"Did I tell you about how I got out?" She didn't wait;
just droned on. "He gave me sardines in a can. Hated them.
I bent the cans under the metal bed frame." She stopped
and closed her eyes. "Made a knife, cut my way out the
basement wall. It took days; I don't know how many. I
made up my mind not to be attacked, so whenever I heard
him come down the stairs, I hid a sharpened can in my
hair bun." She paused. "The water was so cold."

Julie never spoke, just continued to squeeze her arm.

After a less than speedy but uneventful trip, Charles arrived in the early evening in Broken Arrow, a suburb of
Tulsa. He reminisced about having been stranded in this
burg one dismal night after a boring search for compan-
ionship. He had watched a man and a woman arguing inside a house, the couple framed by a large picture window.
In the driveway, a Bronco with motor running and lights
on, ready for acquisition.

On the matter of returning the Bronco, Charles
stopped at a drugstore and called for a taxi to meet him
close to this same house, at the corner of Kenosha, just
off 193rd Avenue. He waited across from the suburban
cottage. When the cab pulled up at the corner, Charles
drove the Bronco up the driveway, swiped clean the steer-

ing wheel and radio knob, and left the SUV just as he had found it—with the engine running and lights on. He got out, jumped into the taxi, and told the driver to take him to the Greyhound bus station in Tulsa. Exhausted after the day's long drive, he felt let down after dropping off the car. He'd fulfilled his little fantasy about the vehicle but was left wanting. Maybe if he waited, even rang the doorbell, he could have completed his cautionary folktale. Seeing someone discover the long-lost Bronco, parked there laboring away, would have been priceless. It was not to be.

Julie gained permission from Captain Walker to bring Cheryl into the station house. She stayed close to her mother, walking slightly behind, her hand encased firmly in Julie's.

Over the five days since her release from the hospital, Cheryl had told her story in random sound bites. Julie asked if she would repeat it, in whole, to her superiors, assuring Cheryl that she would be by her side the whole time.

Walker cleared his throat. "Looking back, once you got outside, do you remember anything about the house exterior? Size, color, other houses close by?"

Cheryl bowed her head.

"Don't go where it will scare you," said Julie. "Just do what's comfortable."

"It's okay, Ma. I'll try." She took deep breaths. "The rain came down hard. It was dark. When I looked back at the house, it was just a silhouette."

"You say 'look back.' Cheryl, where were you when you looked back?"

"In the water."

"The rain?"

"No, the lake. After I squeezed out the window, I just ran, and the only place to go was in the water. It was so cold, but I thought I was safe. He must have known I was in there, because he cursed at me out over the lake. He looked for me."

"Could you describe the man? Did you see him clearly?" Todd asked.

"I never ever got a good look at him. He took me upstairs, out of the room, twice. Both times I was hooded. Maybe he was around my height, five foot seven, I don't know." She shook her head. "He wore clunky boots and his voice seemed to be coming from about my level."

Todd moved his chair closer. "Can you guess how long you walked that night?"

"I don't know what time it was when I got away. The TV was on upstairs. Maybe a couple hours after the news, between eleven and one in the morning. I walked to just before daylight—that is, after I got out of the water."

Thanking Cheryl and Julie, Captain Walker signaled for Todd to follow him into his office.

Sergeant Worth and her daughter left the building after a number of good wishes from the remaining officers on duty. On the way back home, Julie got a call from Todd.

"Walker and I pulled up some maps. In six or seven hours, there's no way Cheryl could have walked from any lake that we see on the map to where the old woman spotted her. We drew a circle around the area. She would have had to cover at least eight to ten miles through heavy forest to get close to where she was picked up. Is she there with you?"

"Of course."

"Ask her if she got swept up in another river besides the big one where Gault saw her. We're looking at something called the Osage; dumps into the Missouri."

Julie looked over at Cheryl, fast asleep. "I'll call you back; she's snoozing." By the time they pulled into the driveway, Cheryl had been out for nearly an hour.

"Cher, just one thing," Julie asked while they walked into the house. "They—Todd and Captain Walker—wanted to know if you think you might have crossed another river before the big one, where you slept in the cave."

Her answer, a slight shrug.

Julie hated all the interrogation of her daughter but knew it was necessary. She turned on the television to get the weather for the next day, knowing it didn't mean a damn thing to her. It was simply habit.

Several hours later, while getting ready for bed, she heard a noise outside. She grabbed her automatic, turned out the light, and slipped out the side door. The night sky melted into the hard black-outlined trees. Abstract shadows cast eerie shapes on the far side of the road. A figure moved slowly away from her, trailing a high-pitched keening, like a baby wanting a bottle. A white-sheet-like image appeared in the gap between the trees. Julie followed along the fence parallel to the form. After several yards, she slipped her weapon into the back of her slacks and quietly vaulted the fence. She crossed the road behind the retreating form. Closing in nearer to the ghostly image, she whispered, "Cheryl."

The cloth-draped figure turned. "I crossed a river, but it took me in its arms and rode me for eons. I couldn't get out of its path. Who is it, please?"

"Let's go back home, baby. Everything will be all right." Julie put her arms around her daughter, being careful not to startle her. "Shush your mind and let Mom think about all the things dancing around in your heart, okay?"

56

After a long discussion with Captain Walker about Cheryl's condition, Julie and her superior agreed that it would be best for her daughter to take some time before continuing to recall her ordeal. The troopers and support personnel extended gracious consideration.

Having agreed to temporarily put aside the restraining order, Julie allowed Bart to visit Cheryl. He arrived at her home driving a polished late-model Jaguar. "I thought we'd go to lunch, okay?"

"Of course, if it's all right with Cheryl."

"Care to join us?"

Julie stood on her front steps, looking at the man who, the last time she'd seen him, had slapped her. "Why would I do that? You're still under a restraining order for domestic violence. I've agreed to let you take Cheryl for the afternoon, but don't get any ideas about you and I being friendly. It's not going to happen."

He nodded and said something under his breath.

"Whatever that was, keep it to yourself."

"Or what?"

"Or I'll have to cuff you, read you your rights, and

drag you down to the station. Keep it to yourself." Julie opened the front door. "Cher, baby, your father's here." Cheryl came down the stairs. "Do not question her about what she's been through. Understand?"

Julie's ex agreed with a grunt. Cheryl came out of the house and gave her father a hug.

"I'll be here, hon, have fun," Julie said.

Bart looked back, and Julie mouthed the word "Prick."

Cheryl waved as she slid into the Jag. Julie watched as Bart made a U-turn in front of the house. He stopped to blip the throttle on the English roadster and sped off.

Cheryl went back to school, and, though still withdrawn, she seemed to be making progress. Julie hired a private security company that made the rounds to a variety of businesses and had them include Cheryl's school. She checked every hour and a half to two hours on her daughter's whereabouts and condition.

Though free of her restricted duty, Julie asked and received permission to continue her investigation of the long-ago abducted girls from her basement digs. She still felt a responsibility to the various aspects of her cold cases. After one of her days in her basement hideaway, Julie prepared to leave when property clerk Maddy stopped her.

"Sergeant, could I have a word with you, please?"

"Yes, of course. What is it?" Julie took the woman in. She was not unattractive, and today she appeared resplendent, with a "Forgive me, please" grin on her high-cheekboned face. In a good mood, Julie didn't want to spoil it.

"First and foremost, I'm delighted your daughter was rescued and is safe."

Rescued, my ass. She saved herself. "Thank you, Maddy, that's very kind."

"Secondly, I wish to apologize for any transgressions, arrogance, you name it—I want to apologize for it." Maddy laughed, showing her embarrassment.

"Listen, we're both professionals and have jobs to do." Julie wanted the woman to get on with it. "I appreciate your thoughts, and, once again, thank you." Julie walked away.

"Ah, oh, dammit. I forgot, one of the reasons I stopped you was Gina in dispatch gave me this BOLO to give to you. Something about a stolen car."

Julie reviewed the bulletin. "Okay. Thanks again and see you." She started to walk away and then turned. "When did this come in?"

"Geez, I don't know; it was just handed to me."

"Okeydoke, when?"

"As I said, Gina gave it to me. I don't know when it came in."

"When did she give it to you?"

"Yesterday morning."

"Yesterday morn—ah, well, fuck it. I can't win with you, can I?"

Maddy raised her arms and shrugged.

The bulletin listed a number of recovered stolen vehicles in the surrounding area. One of them, a Ford Bronco located in Oklahoma and listed as having Missouri plates, also came in as stolen two days prior.

Julie called Todd, who answered after the first ring.

"Listen, I'm at the station. A BOLO came through that lists what looks like our Bronco being picked up in Tulsa, Oklahoma. Interesting, yes?"

"Yeah. Someone might have dumped it after a certain turn of events."

"Exactly. Where are you?"

"On my way back to the station. See you in ten."

Julie contacted Walker's assistant and asked for a meeting. Once all three of them were together, Julie walked through the situation.

Walker folded his hands together and leaned back in his chair. "You want permission to go to Tulsa, right?"

"Yes, sir. We want to see it ourselves."

"I already called Tyler at FBI. He has an evidence response team doing a full workup on the car. He says they will most likely be on it all night."

"I still want to see it myself."

Walker gave Julie permission, but excluded Todd on account of "shortage of manpower." The captain talked to the authorities in Tulsa and made clearance for Julie.

"Captain, I have some vacation days unused. I'd like to go with Sergeant Worth; see if I can't help out."

"This is police work, Trooper. You mean you're willing to donate your time on this?"

"Yes, sir."

"Ahh, hell with it. Go on, get out of here, both of you. I'll fight the budget on my own. You're on duty, Devlin. Be careful, troops."

It took the partners only an hour to get themselves ready for the trip to Tulsa. Coincidentally, Bart had called the previous night to ask permission to take Cheryl to Branson for a music festival. After reciting a long list of dos and don'ts to the ex, Julie agreed.

I-44 seemed busier than usual but moving well, the

sergeant and the trooper sharing the driving. Todd, in the passenger seat, stretched his long frame. "I want this psycho prosecuted and hung out for the rest of his life," he said. "Maybe examined and studied by the feds; you know all that profiling bullshit they do. Usually I want these guys convicted and strung up. But this is different."

"You think 'strung up' is a little Wild West?"

"Maybe cart-before-the-horse cliche, since we haven't put our hands on him yet. But I want to know about this jackass's MO."

Julie motored along, keeping her own solutions of sexual offenders' transgressions to herself. If it came to a decision about justice being served either in the civilized concept accepted by most normal souls or a less orthodox method practiced by her pioneer forefathers, it would come down to a "so be it." By the book or by the Bible. "An eye for an eye sayeth the Lord." Julie thought it would be more than just an eye if she had her way.

57

I t *was close* to six in the morning when Julie and Todd walked into the large one-bay garage at the FBI office in Tulsa. The inspection of the vehicle was wrapping up, the car was lifted by four floor jacks. A dozen tired-looking FBI agents were dressed in white Tyvek suits, and most were under the car taking samples. The only one not in Tyvek was a very tall, grey-haired man in jeans and a black polo shirt with an FBI logo.

Julie extended her hand as the man approached. "Hi, I'm—"

The man smiled and cut her off. "Sergeant Julie Worth. Yes, they called and said you were here. I'm team leader, Mike Spencer."

They shook hands as Devlin introduced himself.

"Looks like you guys have had a long night," Todd said.

Everyone who heard nodded in agreement.

"But not terribly productive, I'm afraid," said Spencer. "The car was clean."

"How clean?" asked Julie, not clear what Spencer meant.

"I mean freakishly clean." He shook his head. "I've been doing this a long time, and this guy is a pro. No prints. No hair or fibers. We'll need the lab to check our filters to be sure. We superglued the interior, dusted the exterior, ran an alternate light source over the fabric, sprayed luminal for blood spatter. Nothing. I've never seen anything like it. We checked mirrors, handles, every viable surface."

Julie and Todd exchanged a look of mutual disappointment. "So we have the right Bronco, but it doesn't do us any good?"

"We did find one piece of scrap."

Julie and Todd both raised their eyebrows expectantly.

"Stuffed up under the rear passenger seat. No wonder this guy missed it. Even if he was being thorough." He held up a Bounty paper towel wrapper in a clear plastic evidence sleeve. "We'll send it to the lab for prints and enhancement first thing this morning." He handed a piece of paper to Julie. "We made a copy. Agent Ross said to make sure you got copied on everything."

"Thanks." Julie placed the paper in her portfolio.

"It's weird he would clean it like that and then leave it like he did."

"What do you mean, 'leave it'?" Julie asked.

"He left it with the lights on and the engine running." Julie and Todd exchanged glances.

"Where was this?"

"Out in Broken Arrow, a suburb east of town."

"How far is that from here?"

"About eight miles from the Civic Center." Spencer filled a Styrofoam cup with coffee and offered some to Julie and Todd. They all sat down, thinking it through.

"So, our sophisticated suspect leaves the lights on and

the engine running." Julie paused. "What the hell does that mean?"

"The guy was waiting for a buddy to pick him up, the friend pulls up, honks, the dude jumps out, and off they go?" mused Todd.

"Maybe. But that means his friend had to follow him from Missouri, doesn't it?"

The group discussed the possibilities, and after a minute, Spencer checked his watch. "Hey, it's tomorrow already. I was told the owners are coming in. They seemed pretty shocked to hear from us a decade later. Want to meet them?"

"Sure. Why not?"

"Are we releasing the Bronco?"

Spencer laughed. "Not yet. We just wanted a statement. Besides, with everything we did to that poor baby, they may never want it back. Especially after they see we've cut chunks of the upholstery out to send to the lab for DNA. Plus, the insurance company probably owns it by now."

"If they have my insurance company, they probably just got the check," Todd said.

Spencer confirmed the arrival of the owners, and he, Todd, and Julie greeted them in the reception area and guided them back to an interview room.

"Thank you for coming in at this early hour," Julie said. "We wanted a brief word with you, if you don't mind."

"Is this about the license plates?" Mrs. Everett spoke up. "Understand the car has Missouri plates on it."

"Yes and no. As I said, I'm from Missouri, and we're investigating a string of offenses that may be linked to this vehicle."

"Here in Oklahoma?"

"No, we think in Missouri. When and how did you lose the Bronco?"

"Fred and I had been out drinking, carrying on, came home, and had an argument as we pulled into the driveway. It got out of hand. I ran into the house, and a few minutes later when we looked, the Ford was gone."

"So you discover the vehicle in your drive ten years later. Were you surprised?" Todd asked.

"No, we didn't find it in our driveway. We moved from that house a number of years ago. The police called us after they ran the whatchamacallit."

"The VIN number, vehicle ID," Julie said. "Did you, all those years ago, remember having left the car running like they found it?"

The couple looked at each other and answered in unison, "Yes."

Todd and Julie drifted back into the garage to look at the Bronco one last time as the couple signed papers and affidavits in reference to their vehicle.

"Sarge, shall we pack up and head on out?"

"Yeah, Devlin. We're done."

They paid their respects to Spencer and left.

Julie took the passenger seat, barking instructions on getting to the freeway. "We're looking for 244 East, which hooks us into—stop, hold it."

"What? What's up?"

"Pull up here. On the other side of the Greyhound."

"What are you thinking? He took the bus back to Missouri?"

"Yup. Maybe our abductor took the big dog back to Kansas City, Springfield, Saint Louie, wherever. You think our friend back at the station house would check the cab records from Broken Arrow to Tulsa on the night or morning in question? I don't know if city buses would be running at that hour. Check on it and meet you back here in a half hour."

Julie got out and darted into the Greyhound station. Her brief look at the overhead schedule proved bewildering, so she confirmed comings and goings with the clerk at the ticket counter. A cab ride would have taken a half hour at the most, plenty of time to connect to a nine thirty Thursday-morning sleeper coach that left Tulsa for Saint Louis, stopping at Joplin and Springfield, and arriving in Saint Louis at seven that night.

Todd's news wasn't as good.

"The guy at the police station says that late at night most of the cabbies are independents and tend not to keep decent records. What did you get?"

"I had to do a little dipping and dodging, but after several lies, the station manager dug out his records on the Thursday morning Greyhound to Saint Louis. Halfway down the list, a tote bag checked to a certain Mr. B. Caldwell."

Todd pounded the steering wheel. "Holy shit, we got him! Well, no, we don't got him. But it sure locks up some loose ends. You think we should hang around, see if we get a description from the cabdriver?"

"I think all we get is another cap-and-glasses guy, like my half-assed description after the F-150 screwup. Let's head on home and kick it around some. We can ask the FBI to go ahead, to find and interview all the cabbies." Julie curled up in the vinyl-covered seat. "Wake me when you need me to drive; I'm gonna catch some Zs."

Julie thought about her recent proximity to her daughter's abductor. Her eyelids began their heavy descent as

Todd swerved right, cursing an errant driver. "What? What is it? Todd?"

"Nothing. Go to sleep. Sorry."

She rubbed her head where it thumped into the passenger-side window. "No, Mario Andretti, you just woke me up. Jesus, where are we, the Indy 500?"

"Sorry again."

"Do you have the old Everett address?"

"Nah, should I?"

"The dude who showed us the car—what's his name? Spencer? Give him a call and ask for the address."

Todd navigated the downtown Tulsa streets and juggled his cell.

She heard Todd thank someone and then get off the phone. "193rd Avenue. About four miles from where we are now. Are we interviewing these folks again?"

Julie stared out the side window. "No, I'm just thinking." She pulled out a map for Broken Arrow. "Get us over here." She pointed to a specific spot. "Okay?"

Todd worked his jaw like he wanted to disagree.

"What?"

"It will be nice when you join the twenty-first century, Sergeant Worth, and use MapQuest or GPS."

"Yeah, yeah. You know I know how to use it. Right now, I prefer this." She waved the multifolded paper street map at Todd's face. "Now, Mr. Devlin. If you would, please get us on a straight line, back between the Everetts' old place and the turnpike. I figure if our perp had been coming from Missouri, the obvious way would be the turnpike"—she pointed to the exit on the map—"and a straight line to the Everett house." She scanned the shops and businesses on both sides of the road.

Soon after a four-way stop, she noticed a do-it-yourself car wash. "Pull in over there, will you, Todd-O?"

"What's up? Restroom? Sandwich?"

"Nah, I just got this nutty idea."

"You want to get the car washed—do it together like a couple of newlyweds." He forced a laugh.

"Humor me, will you?" Julie walked around the four-stall car wash.

A woman carrying an infant in a belly pack washed an old VW beetle.

"Hi, ma'am. Do you know if the owner is around?"

The woman pulled the soapy brush away from her vehicle. "Nope. Never seen anyone around who looks like they know what they're doing."

"What's up? You mind telling me?" Todd drove forward without getting out.

Hands on hips, Julie continued to survey the concreted area. The four covered wash stalls were located in the very center of the square. A fenced area in the far corner of the square housed a large garbage Dumpster. "I'm going to take a look around, see what's up."

"What are you thinking?"

"I think our guy might have taken one last swipe at cleaning that Bronco, and since this place is on the way to where he left it, maybe he threw out trash, emptied ashtrays, vacuumed mats. I don't know. Just a hunch. It's the closest do-it-yourself car wash to the Everetts' house, and it's a straight line to the turnpike." Julie walked toward the fenced off garbage bin. "Wanna help?"

"Yeah, sure. I thought maybe I'd get us snacks for the trip home. There's a 7-Eleven right across the street. Back in a jiffy."

Julie laughed to herself as Todd bounced out of the driveway and cut across traffic to the convenience store.

The gate to the metal garbage receptacle was padlocked, and the chain-link fence looked formidable. On the right side of the gate, outside the enclosure and next to an alley, sat a fifty-gallon drum of detergent up against the backside of the fence. Julie climbed on top of the four-foot-tall drum and stepped easily across the wire fence onto the lid of the large Dumpster. The opposite lid had a convenient handle and opened easily to rest on the alley-side fence. She looked inside and saw the bottom of the metal Dumpster covered sparsely with trash. *Lucky for me it isn't full,* she thought. Someone had cleaned out the two small wastebaskets next to the vacuum areas and probably deposited it in the metal bin. Maybe with providence on her side, some of it might be from Mr. Yahoo's Bronco. Julie eased her way down into the shoulder-high receptacle. She kicked her way through nearly a third of the waste material before she heard Todd.

"You there! What's you doing in my garbage bin?"

Julie's head bobbed up and down. "Fuck off, Mr. Garbage Owner. What did you buy?"

"Oh, bunch of Cokes, cookies, crunchy goodies. Is there room for two in that tiny abode?"

"Yeah, sure. *Mi casa es su casa.*" She nudged a milk carton with her foot. "Nah, I'm almost done. Not much here. I'll just be a couple more minutes." Julie continued her search for she knew not what. Most of the debris turned out to be paper towels provided at the vacuum unit, newspapers, chewing gum wrappers, McDonald's Happy Meal bags, and dry pizza crusts. She looked for a date on one of the newspapers—from two days earlier. She toed through the last pile of crap when her heel caught on a roll of paper towels. Stepping on the almost fully used roll, she looked down and noticed "Bounty" printed in small letters on the edge of the paper towels. She picked it up and turned it, looking down both ends of the stiff cardboard tubing. A crumpled piece of paper fell to the metal floor. Opening it, she saw it was a grocery receipt. The faded store name and underneath that, "Miller County." It could have come from anyone's car; however, she thought it was worth checking out. She'd need a magnifying glass at least and probably an FBI lab report to make it work, but at least it was a lead.

She slipped the paper into the breast pocket of her jacket and levered herself up waist high on the downside of the bin. Todd had just started to climb the fifty-gallon drum.

"No pizza crust for you, partner. The treasure hunt is over." She had never lied to Todd about anything really serious, but she wanted to keep this little item to herself, at least for now.

58

W hat's up, sweets, did you have a good weekend?" Julie had arrived home Sunday only a
few hours before Bart dropped off Cheryl. As
soon as her daughter came through the door, Julie knew
something was cooking.

"Oh yeah, great. Concert was super, nice room at the
Branson Palace, and a nonstop monologue of complaints
from Maisie Belle."

"Who's that?"

Cheryl tugged off her jacket and wrapped it carefully
over her arm as if in imitation of someone. Then she
struck a model's pose.

"My name is Miss Maisie. But you can call me Amaz-
ing if it so pleases you. Ta-ta."

She started up the stairs.

"Is this your father's latest?"

"Latest and lastest, if you please. I have a disarmingly
throbbing cranial brow. Or headache, as the hoi polloi describe it. So if you see Master Worth, please tell him I'm
indisposed."

Cheryl's renewed sense of humor comforted Julie, but

still she felt conflicted, for it also came out of a strange weekend.

"Do men really like big knockers, Mom?" Cheryl called out from the top of the stairs. Julie smiled, but her thoughts went back to the receipt she'd retrieved from the car wash. She'd had a chance to examine it more carefully once she got back home. A partial name and "Rt. 52 Miller County" as an address.

The store name appeared to have three or four letters. A couple of the lowercased letters were discernible. "Aags" didn't make sense. Could be "Bags," but too cute for a grocery store. "Cags"? "Dags"? Possible, but didn't light any candles. She had a quick laugh when she got to *F. G* wouldn't work for a food emporium. *H* probably described some of their customers. "Mags" could be a possibility; *N* could describe the owner's wife. Julie searched the hardcopy yellow pages and Googled food-related Miller County stores for any similar names but came up blank.

She checked with Captain Walker the next day before hightailing it to Miller County. Todd hadn't fared well after the Tulsa trip, sidelined with the flu and strep throat. She would canvass the area and ask around on her own. The incorporated area took in part of Lake of the Ozarks, which spread out over several hundred square miles. Miller County bordered only a small portion of that, but it was still a lot of road to cover.

Julie started in the middle of the county and worked outward. Tuscumbia was listed as the county seat. After numerous inquiries at stores and gas stations, most of them leading to comments about the weather, an older gentleman sitting on a John Deere tractor just off the bridge over the Osage River seemed affable and, as it turned out, helpful.

"Margaret's. But everyone knows it as Mag's. Back on 52, the way you just came from, right there at the corner of 52 and County Road A, as in Adam. Right smart day, ain't it?"

She thanked the gentleman and agreed for the umpteenth time that yes, it was "right smart." Margaret's. No wonder she couldn't find it online. Mag's turned out to be pretty much as she pictured it. A frame stand-alone building with the obligatory wood-rail-enclosed porch and the rusty tin Mail Pouch chewing tobacco sign left of the front door. The fellow inside greeted her with a "Howdy" and a "What can I do you for?"

Julie introduced herself and took the plastic-encased receipt from her pocket, showing it to the down-home gentleman. "Could you tell me whether or not this is a receipt from your store?"

He pulled his steel-rimmed eyeglasses from his forehead and held them several inches from his eyes, squinting at the receipt. "Sure looks like one of ours. Named the place after my wife, Margaret, but she really goes by Mag." He moved over to the cash register and punched in one of the keys. "Would maybe be better for your evidence if you had a purchase on this here *re*-ceipt."

Julie picked up a pack of gum from the display and shoved it across the linoleum counter.

"Sure enough, ma'am, that's ours. Do we win anything? Is it like a lottery?" He grinned expectantly and then deflated. "Ah, ma'am, I was just funning with you. Didn't mean nothin'. I sit in this smelly room near to twelve hour a day. You'll have to excuse me."

Julie took her gum and started out the store, having no intention of excusing Mr. Mag's.

"I noticed something on that re-seat, ma'am."

Julie turned, ready for one more disappointing comeback.

"We don't get much of a call for one of the items on your tab there."

"And what would that be?"

"Those nasty fellows all packed up tight in the tin can."

Julie looked at her list. Mostly fruit, vegetables, and something described as "preserved meat." "Would these be sardines?"

"They could be. We got your spam and your weenies in a can, and for simple sake put them all under 'meats' that are preserved. If 'n we had the right kinda customers, we'd buy us some of that cava fish-eggs stuff. Know what I mean?"

Julie felt she understood the old coot as much as she wanted to. "Who buys most of your 'preserved fish'?"

"Oh, a whole wheelbarrow of folk, mostly older types, retirees. Can't afford steak or chicken from Splendid Farms, theys just a might better than our cat-food folk; we got a couple of them. Feel sorry about that."

"Can you give me the names of your tinned-fish people?"

The man went through a handful of names, nothing standing out. Julie wrote them all down along with any known addresses. She once again started to leave.

"There was one name I forgot. Smart fella; only gets our tinned fish on occasion. He buys it like it were going outta style, then nothing for months on end."

"Who is this fellow?" Julie stepped back on the porch.

"I won't get in any trouble tattlin', will I? What's he done?"

"I don't know if he's done a gosh darn thing. Just checking." Julie didn't think her speaking his tongue would bring the name out any sooner, but she had to try.

"That would be Mr. C, ma'am—first name, well, I don't for the life of me know. Hmm. Lives down the lakes way, I hear."

The C name resonated through Julie's brain.

"You okay, missy? You seem flustered."

Julie got as much information from the fellow as possible, making it a point to question him more thoroughly on some of his other tinned-fish customers to try to divert his attention from Mr. C, but it was not to be.

"If Mr. C comes in, I'll pretend you were never here. Would that be hunky-dory?"

She nodded her thanks. She knew the man wouldn't be able, in light-years, to keep the secret of Mr. C's sudden notoriety. She wondered what in the hell she was going to do now.

On the way back to the station house, she realized that she would have to bring Todd up to date on her findings. With luck, maybe he'd offer a helping hand when she nailed the bastard.

59

S ince Todd was still down from the flu, she went first to Walker and laid it out for her captain—all the seeming similarities that added up. She had not yet patrolled the area near the multitude of lakes, perhaps seventy miles wide, north to south.

"That's a lot of lakefront to cover, Sergeant. What will you be looking for? A mailbox that says 'I'm here'?"

She went along with the joke for a while. "I thought I'd cover the Miller County real estate tax records first, since their lake frontage seems closest to the area where Cheryl was picked up. If there's nothing, maybe a house-to-house canvass with Todd when he recoups."

"Good, keep a low profile. If you find him, don't make any moves until you've checked with me, okay?"

The folks at the Miller County seat were helpful. The warrant she'd gotten from the district judge seemed to pave the way. Since the county records didn't show whether a property was on the lakefront or not, Julie was forced to go through the whole lot.

The Cs didn't produce any Caldwells, but she figured that while there she would plow through the complete

batch. It was late afternoon when she finished. She looked
at the tax records, wondering what she'd missed. Julie went
back to the Cs, still not finding that elusive Caldwell. She
flipped over a few more of the oversized pages and came
across the Ds. Realizing her mistake, she started to close
the bulky record book when she saw the name Drew under
the heading "Business." The woman at the front desk explained, when asked, that firms doing trade in Miller
County typically received their bills at their workplace
rather than at taxed homes. Julie requested a printout from
the woman with the address and amount of yearly taxes for
the aforementioned home owned by Drew Box Factory.

Once again she checked with Walker, talking of Drew
Box Factory's ownership of this house.

"Let me think on this for a while," he said. "If Drew
in fact owns that house and put it under the company
name, there's nothing there that one could jump on. All
perfectly legal; probably a tax dodge. All companies do it."
He paused. "I'm thinking maybe give the head honcho a
call, ask him straight out, 'What's up with the house? Is it a
client perk? Company investment?' You name it; could be
a hundred reasons to have a weekend place."

"Right, sir. But what if, by chance, I was in the neighborhood and dropped by to chat. I could maybe get a better read on the situation as we discuss the place."

"Good idea, Sergeant. Nice to hear you're up to speed
on your field skills. Should I call, or do you want to?"

"If you don't mind, I'll wait til I get close by and then
pop in. Don't want to give him time to alibi out. I'll keep
you posted."

Under normal conditions, Julie's trip to the box factory would take her twenty minutes. She waited until she
was close to the factory before phoning.

"Ah, Miss Worth. Mr. Drew just this moment left for home. Can I take a message?"

"No. Maybe I can catch him. It's kind of important. What is his number?"

"Very sorry. I can't do that."

"What does he drive?"

"Well, I don't, oh . . . it's probably all right. A silver late-model Mercedes. He'll be heading toward Arnold on 141."

Julie switched on her bar lights and sped up. She was just a couple of minutes out. Nearing the factory, she doused the lights and continued past for about a mile. A silver automobile chugged along several notches below the speed limit in front of her. Approaching a gas station—a proper location to pull into—she switched her blinker back on. The driver's head bobbled up and down, from the rearview mirror to the dashboard and back again. He pulled into the Conoco lot. Julie got out of the cruiser, nudged her elbow against her Sig, and approached the car carefully. Not from any sense of danger but because, to use the old saw, she was "way out on a limb."

"Mr. Drew, sorry about the stop. It's Juliette Worth. We met a while back about your missing niece, Trudy."

"Oh yes. For a moment, I thought I'd committed some sort of crime."

Maybe, but not what you're thinking. "Could I have a few minutes of your time?"

"Well, this is sort of unusual, wouldn't you say, Sergeant?"

The passenger-side door unlocked.

"Okay. Join me here. We'll be more comfortable in my Benz."

Julie slid into the soft leather seat of the Mercedes.

"I'll get right to the point. Do you own a home in Miller County out toward Lake of the Ozarks?"

"No, no. Afraid not. That's reserved for the can't-afford-the-Caribbean crowd." He guffawed at his little joke.

Julie took out a clipboard from her portfolio case. "Says here the Drew Box Factory pays $1,600 a year on lot 762 in Miller County, Missouri. Is that a mistake?"

"Let me see that." He looked at the memo on Miller County letterhead, stationery that Julie had procured on her recent sojourn. "Huh. This can't be right. We don't have property at the lakes. Let me call David Wright, see what's up."

Julie waited while the executive on his cell switched back and forth between his comptroller and his in-house accountant.

"Dave Wright's man, Robert, says in fact we do own a property in Miller County. I'll check on this. There's no reason we would carry something like this on our books. Odd."

Drew seemed honestly at a loss as to why the property was listed as theirs. Julie got out of the Mercedes and slipped into her cruiser. She started to U-turn out of the lot when she saw the Mercedes's lights flashing on and off behind her. One good blinker stop deserved another. She reversed back to Drew's driver-side window.

"We need to talk. Do you have the time? Follow me, please." He pulled out and around her Charger and drove back toward the factory.

Julie noted that this time he pushed the speed limit, along with having his cell pressed solidly against his right ear.

When they arrived back at the factory, Drew hustled from his Mercedes, giving Julie a quick hand signal. By the time Julie got out of her cruiser, William Drew stood holding the office building door for her.

"Is there a big hurry?"

He didn't answer, just headed upstairs to his office, where a short, heavyset man waited, tapping his fingers on a stack of papers. An assistant stood next to him.

"Dave, I need an explanation of this property, right now. By the way, this is Sergeant Worth with the State Patrol. Proceed."

"When I began working here some twelve years ago"—Wright thumbed through several legal document folders—"our bookkeeping was in serious disarray. Among the equity holdings, along with this building and the factory, was the property in Miller County."

"Let me see that." Drew spread the sheaf of papers on his desk. He glanced through a large manila envelope at the bottom of the pile and pulled out a letter. "Did you see this?" He thrust it out. "That property was supposed to be transferred years ago—close to eighteen—for Christ's sake. We've paid nearly twenty-five thousand dollars in taxes. Oh, hell. Technically, it looks as though we do own this land. Technically, Miss Worth."

Miss Worth. Lovely. "So who has the rights to this property now?" She stopped herself. "Do you have a Mr. B. Caldwell working here?"

Drew turned to his comptroller. "Robert, in your perusal of the weekly payroll, does the name Caldwell mean anything to you?"

Mr. Wright's young accountant answered with a herky-jerky shake of the head.

"The name is familiar, but I'm certain he's not an employee," Wright blurted out. "Maybe one of our suppliers, vendors, that sort of thing."

Drew shot up from his desk and went to the window, looking out onto his factory grounds. "We'll have to check further on this and get back to you, Miss Worth."

Miss Worth. Again. Asshole.

"Mr. Wright, Robert, you're both excused. My apologies for keeping you late. I'll take this up with you tomorrow. Good night."

The two men, sensing that something above their pay grade had just taken place, hurried out of the office.

"Excuse the dramatics and delay in answering your questions. I suppose I'm getting old. Well, there's no supposing to it, we are all getting old." He took a long pause and gathered himself. "When you inquired about the name Caldwell, it started working on me. I never knew this person, as it was many years ago, before I was head of the business. But he was here with a group of other kids and was killed in an accident on the floor of the factory through no fault of the company."

Julie flashed back to her talk with Jimbo Gerard and his story of how his father, Tuck, had taken his foster kids on a "Way Things Are Made" trip. She was surprised to learn the accident happened at the Drew Box Factory. "Did this take place at about the time of your niece Trudy's disappearance?"

"No, years before—maybe eight to ten." Drew folded his hands as if to say, "That's it." "I don't know what else I can tell you, Miss Worth."

"This story just recently came to my attention, but I wasn't aware it took place here."

"Yes, unfortunate but true."

"And the boy was killed, is that correct?"

"Yes, Master Caldwell was killed instantly. Sorry to say."

"Do you recall the youngster's first name?"

"No, ah, Billy, Bill, Bob, it's in the records somewhere."

"Could it have been Bink?"

"Bink. Yes, maybe Bink? Sure, something like that. The name probably given to him by his pal."

"His pal?"

"Yes, Mr. Clegg, our situation manager. You met him when we had that go-around with the old-time employees who were here when Trudy went missing."

Julie had a lot to digest. She considered Mr. Drew.

He blinked as if to say "What else?" "Mr. Clegg was a young boy at the time of the incident. As part of his settlement, when he turned sixteen, the lakefront house was given to him along with lifetime employment at Drew Box. I'm sorry I didn't remember all this sooner. Guess the name Caldwell threw me."

Julie asked for the address of the house, thanked Mr. Drew, and hurried out of the drab factory, the grey brick exteriors a series of haunted looking structures. A single light glowed in the distance. A night watchman strolled toward her vehicle; his battery operated lantern swinging casually from his hand.

Julie produced her badge and ID.

The man glanced at her credentials. "How're you doing, ma'am?"

"Oh, I just had a meeting with Mr. Drew about a variety of things." She started to get back in her cruiser. "Is Mr. Clegg gone for the day?"

"Haven't seen him for a while, miss."

Strange. When asked, William Drew had been vague about Charles Clegg's work at the factory. Though annoyed about Clegg's status, he did give her an address and directions to the lakefront house. It was late, and Cheryl was staying overnight with a girlfriend, so Julie was at a loss about what to do with herself.

60

She knew the Miller County property could be at least an hour's drive, but she needed to have a look. After a quick stop for a sandwich, she took the interstate southwest to Saint James and then wrestled with the country roads west to Osage Beach. The winding route gave her time to rethink her trip. It wouldn't amount to anything—she knew that—and, being a seasoned trooper, she also knew that she had defied a number of rules that had been pounded into her head over the years.

For one thing, she had no backup. Well, she reasoned, she didn't need backup because she wasn't going to attempt an arrest. She just wanted a look-see. A warrant would have been the first of many procedural moves, but as she kept assuring herself, she wasn't attempting an arrest, simply observing. Staking out would have required an extensive explanation, and it was just for a moment, anyway. She promised herself that making a studied assessment would be a good way of explaining to Walker what she was doing.

The directions to Clegg's isolated vacation home were specific. She drove by the property slowly, noticing the last soft rays of the setting sun through the trees. It appeared that the house was buried in the woods nearly a hundred yards from the road. Julie glimpsed a patch of water from time to time. She drove down the country road for a few miles, and then turned and came back past the site again. Pulling onto a dirt path, she stopped at a wood fence just down from Clegg's locked gate. She unpacked a 12-gauge shotgun from the trunk of her Charger, loaded it, and checked that her Sig was securely buckled at her waist. She dug out her flashlight and began the walk back toward Clegg's fenced property.

It was cool out. In the distance, a heavy-voiced dog gave out a throaty threat.

She neared the gate leading to the property, climbed a decorative rail fence, and headed into the woods adjacent to the winding lane. Moving forward, she saw the outline of a structure and an early-model station wagon parked next to the tilted porch front. A country-and-western station played from a radio. Julie gripped the shotgun, circled around to the far side of the shack and came up to a window cracked open with a blind pulled down to within a few inches of the sill. Julie bent down and looked through the opening. Along with everything else, she was now a voyeur. A man seated in a worn, overstuffed chair with his back to her hummed an off-key accompaniment. She saw the throat of a guitar and a fellow's heavily bandaged left arm. He tried to make a simple half circle on the guitar neck, his arm unable to bend in such a way to form a chord. *Hey, Charlie, what happened to your arm? Get stabbed?*

She worked to subdue her urge to burst into the shack, easing back into the woods. Taking care of things now would have been preferable but she'd seen enough. The next day would be an exciting one for Mr. Clegg, whose modest cabin would be palatial compared to the eight-by-ten-foot accommodations provided by the state of Missouri.

61

I*t's after hours,"* Walker said, pissed but willing. "Where in hell's name are we going to find a judge who's available to issue a warrant?"

"Less than evidence, that's right, but more than bare suspicion." Julie stated her case with care. She knew the drill. "In this case, I'm clearly a person of reasonable caution and, more important, I believe an offense has been committed or will be."

"I love the way you paraphrase the Constitution to get your way, Trooper." Walker needed to make a decision. "Two of the three judges we've tried are either out of cell phone range or aren't answering."

"What about a magistrate?"

"Yeah, I prefer a judge, but let's try."

After a great deal of coercion, Walker made a connection, and though he was technically off duty, he accompanied Julie to the magistrate's office.

"You have your affidavit, Sergeant?"

Julie handed the man her sworn article of cause.

"It says here you observed the suspect at his home on the fourteenth, is that correct?"

"Yes." Julie glanced at Walker.

"And the reason for this search is to solidify information from a victim, of the existence of a 'special' room in the residence, correct?"

"Yes, sir."

With the warrant signed, they were on the street again. Walker grew silent. At the car door, he paused. "Today is the fifteenth. That means either you disobeyed my specific orders not to make contact with the subject or you lied to the magistrate about seeing him yesterday."

"I didn't lie, sir. And I didn't make contact, as instructed by you." She held on to the door as if its support would steady her upcoming confession. "But I did, in fact, observe him at his place of residence."

"Did he see you?"

"No, sir, he did not."

"You're positive?"

"I am."

"You're going to find yourself back in your underground office, Sergeant." Walker got into the driver's side of his car.

Julie busied herself reading the warrant.

"I specifically told you to let me know before you made contact, when you and Todd first knew about the subject." He wheeled the sedan at a slow Sunday-drive pace. "What's Devlin's status, by the way?"

"*Hors de combat.*"

"What about the fed?"

"He's in Saint Louis; had a lead on another case. Thinks he'll be back tomorrow."

"Okay. Dammit. Call the station, give dispatch a rundown on your warrant, have a couple cruisers with two officers meet us at, where?"

"Iberia. Junction of State Roads 17 and 42." She got on the phone while Walker continued his deliberate drive toward the lake country.

Two cruisers assembled just past the spot where Julie had left her car the previous day. Walker gave his people their instructions. "We don't know a whole hell of a lot about this jackass, so let's be careful. Smitty, pull your cruiser up to the gate. Detain anyone coming out. Keep in touch on channel four on your walkies. Sergeant Worth, you and Adams follow me."

The three made their way onto the property, this time walking down the rutted lane, as opposed to Julie's reconnoitering through the woods the day before.

The wagon was still parked next to the tilted porch.

Walker knocked, and they immediately heard footsteps. Clegg opened the door, facing them with a startled "What the hell?" expression.

"Mr. Charles Clegg?"

"Yes, what do you—?"

"We have a warrant to search your residence." Julie handed him a copy of the document.

"Stay out here." Walker addressed trooper Adams. "Watch our suspect."

Julie walked into the cramped living room where she had observed Charles the previous night.

Clegg stood with his back to the wall, keeping his eyes on Julie.

"How do you get to the basement?" Walker asked.

Leading them to the stairwell down to the cellar, Clegg gestured for them to proceed.

Walker shook his head. "After you, and turn on the lights. When you get to the bottom, get up against a wall."

Charles switched on the lights and descended the wood steps.

Julie and Walker followed, then paced the cool basement's interior.

"Nothing here but junk." Walker scoured the confined space, looking behind the furnace and hot water heater, inspecting an aged coal bin. "What are you smiling about, mister? Something funny?"

"No, just watching my tax dollars at work."

"Smart-ass. Sergeant, let's split. This is a dry hole." Walker signaled for Clegg to precede him up the stairs.

Julie lagged behind, but as she reached the stairs, the lights went off and then back on. Then off again. "Hey, up there, what the hell?"

"Sorry, the switch is funny." Charles's voice regained its vigor.

"I'll turn off the lights when I get up there. Leave it alone." *Asshole*. Julie took one last look around the dank space, pushing her way past a row of stacked cardboard boxes to a window tucked up tight to the ceiling. Standing on tiptoe, she had a clear view outside to the lake. It didn't look as if this dark underground catchall could have been her daughter's cubbyhole for two weeks. Julie threaded her way back through the debris, stumbling on a broom handle. She reached down to push it aside and noticed letters scratched into the floor. She stepped across, enabling her to read right side up. On her knees, Julie made out a capital letter, a scratch mark, and then "Hogar."

"Angie Hogar, here." *Christ*. This was the place, the cold, damp patch of cement and ceiling beams housing not only Angie but also her daughter and who knows how many other defenseless young women.

Upstairs, someone shouted. Julie raced up the stairs.

Captain Walker wasn't in the house. When she went to the front door, he was on his mobile handset speaking to Smitty at the front gate.

"What happened, Captain?" Julie asked.

"I turned my back, and he bolted, cracked Adams on the head, and took off across the field in that piece-of-shit wagon."

When Julie looked up, she noticed dust settling across the field as if Clegg had turned onto a utility road leading out to the main thoroughfare. Smitty, in the state cruiser, slid to a stop in front of them. Walker instructed him to take Adams to the hospital in Jefferson City, adding, "Worth and I will chase after this Clegg dickhead."

At the gate in separate cars, Julie and Walker watched as Smitty did an imitation of a rally driver on a dirt road.

"What's your best guess, Worth? Which way?"

"If he came out of the wood gate down from where we were parked, maybe there's tracks. Let's check."

Sure enough, there were skid marks where Clegg turned to avoid the parked cruiser, and then dirt and rubber tracked in the road pointing south. Walker called in a BOLO for the wagon and turned to Julie. "We'll get this guy. Rest assured."

Julie wasn't too sure.

Julie and Walker spent most of the day scouring the back roads and byways of the Missouri countryside. Julie ended up driving, as Walker coordinated a massive hunt by nearly all the troopers on duty throughout the state. Cruisers on both Interstate 70 and country roads searched for Charles Clegg.

"The problem," Walker stated, "too damn many back

roads. We can't cover them all. How much time passed between when he took off and when we were able to chase him? Five minutes? More?"

"Yeah, a little more," said Julie. "We had to wait for Smitty to come up the drive, load Adams, check out the utility road where he came out. Seven, at the rate he was driving. He could have been at least nine miles down that dusty road before we got started."

"Damn, what bad luck. What do you think set him off? Seemed relaxed to me. I didn't tell you at the time, but that piece of crap, what's his name again?"

"Clegg. Charles Clegg."

"Yeah, right. Clegg. Couldn't take his eyes off you. Looked at you like he'd never seen a woman before. Did you notice? Get a feeling from him?"

Julie ran her hands over the plastic-covered steering wheel. "I'd gotten a funny feeling from him the first time we met. It was at the factory. I told you that, didn't I?"

"Maybe, I don't recall."

"Oh, it was Todd. We had just left the factory after our series of interviews, and I got this odd sense about something Clegg said. We were leaving, and he says, 'Hope everything turns out well for you, Detective.' I told Todd the statement was off. He dismissed it, saying he meant both of us, as in 'Detectives.' At the time, I remember being tired and just dropping it. But now I get it. He was being facetious. Cheryl was in his basement right at that moment. Cocksucker."

"And when he goes to the slammer, he'll learn the true meaning of that word along with bum bruising and golden showers."

Julie wished she'd arrested the bastard when she

looked through the window. The few strident chords he'd managed on the guitar could have at least been grounds for disturbing the peace. She remembered something else.

"With the fracas at the house getting Adams to the ER, I forgot to tell you—"

"Yeah, what?"

"When I was in the basement and you went upstairs, the lights flashed on and off a few times."

"Hm. How's that pertinent?"

Julie took a moment to get her thoughts in order. She noticed of late how anything regarding her daughter and her experience tinged her thoughts of a whirlwind retaliation. She came close to acting on it while at the window of the lakeside cabin. She willed herself to be calm. "Cheryl told me that almost every day the guy would flash the lights. She thought he did it to show off his power." She cracked the steering wheel with the ball of her fist. "I'm not a vigilante, but this one, I want."

"You're lucky. You can talk about it. Lots of troops can't, Jules."

It might have been the first time Walker had ever called her Jules, and it touched her.

They called it a day. Walker broke down the concerted effort by his troopers, instructing them to pass along anything relevant to their replacements and shut it down. "We'll get him. There's always another day."

Julie picked up her vehicle at the station house and went home.

In meetings and simple office conferences over the next few days, the consensus seemed to be that their Mr. Clegg had truly gone to ground.

Julie's routine remained about the same. She continued her work on cold cases whenever time permitted and was back on her old watch. Todd was also back; their discussions about Topic A seemed to revolve around the fact that Charles Clegg probably left the state.

Over the next ten days, she flashed back to her window of opportunity. His back to her; it could have been perfect. A quick spraying of her double ought, shot into the back of his chair. No rifling—lands and grooves nonexistent in the shotgun—beyond identification. A brief check of the pulse, a few rudimentary swipes of the footprints under the windowsill. But when she thought about it later, she felt shame. She wasn't a killer. The shooting at the mall had been necessary.

T he letter, when it came, bore a Kansas postmark.

Julie stared at the crumpled envelope. She scolded herself for being so suspicious; after all, it could be one of a hundred different things: a thank-you from a traffic warning, a donation request from Hungry Children of Kansas. A long-forgotten relative.

She couldn't remember the last time she'd gotten a personal letter at the station house. Just in case, she used a letter opener and a pair of scissors to handle the envelope. She held the mailer with the point of the scissors while slitting the glued flap with her opener, pulling out one sheet of paper along with an earring. Though hammered flat, the earring looked familiar. She also noted a number of newspaper clippings glued to a piece of plain white paper.

Sometimes a complete word had been taken from a headline. Other times just a series of different letter sizes and fonts:

I have my eye on your daughter. Hope things are going well for you.

Or did I already say that? One of these days I'll pay you a visit. Can't help wondering how you found me. That tap on the shoulder in the middle of the night will be me.

Mr. C

Julie called on George Rogers, their resident forensics guy. "Rogers, I've got a letter that needs looking at. Could you come down to the basement and pick it up?"

He showed up in no time. "Hey, nice digs. How do you rate, Sarge?"

"Just one of those sliding promotional things. Being in the right place at the wrong time."

"What do you have?"

Julie explained the letter, her case, which he'd heard about, and that she knew who sent it. "Could you get this to the FBI, Detective Devlin, and Captain Walker? After you've done your thing with it, of course."

Julie thanked him and called Todd about lunch.

They ate in their favorite hamburger joint, Julie getting her obligatory turkey burger while Todd loaded up on his Double Daddies—a huge bacon-laden sandwich with two beef patties, cheese, and all the trimmings.

"You're gonna die young. You know that, don't you?" Julie asked.

"But happy as a pig in slop."

"Oink."

They talked about Charles Clegg. "Damn," exclaimed Todd. "I wished I'd been there at the warrant service."

"Yeah, me too. It would have been exciting watching you waddle down that dirt road with a greasy sandwich in your hand, chasing our Mr. C."

"Is that what you're calling him now?"

"That's what he's calling himself. I think Jackson Ross is a little annoyed we didn't wait for him. He isn't calling much," Julie said.

"Maybe he thinks you didn't want him there because you maybe want some extrajudicial remedies in this case."

Julie didn't respond.

Todd changed the subject. "So, you say, Kansas postmark. But it's easy enough to drive across the border and drop off a letter. Could you tell where in Kansas?"

"No, it was blurred. The stamp looked wrinkled, so maybe that's why the town name came out illegible. Only *Kansas* was clear."

"Probably doesn't matter; it's just a ruse, anyway."

"You think?"

They parted, agreeing to meet later. Julie took her time driving back to the station.

"This seems like a joke. No offense, Sergeant, but wouldn't you agree?" Walker opened up the conversation with Todd and Julie.

"It's not terribly original, like if some square dude read a lot of police thrillers. But to answer your question, Charles Clegg kidnapped my daughter and was responsible for the death of my best friend. Not much of a joke there."

"Well, yes. What I meant was, it's exactly the way you describe it. A copycat would be a 'dangerous man.'" He made air quotes with his fingers. "He is dangerous, but maybe not a creeper-in-the-middle-of-the-night kind of guy. As I said, a wannabe. He wishes he had the balls to walk into your bedroom in the middle of the night."

"I don't know, sir," Todd said. "He ran the sergeant off the road, had the presence of mind to scout out Thousand Pines and establish an elaborate scheme there with the dog business. He kept Cheryl locked up a couple of weeks. I think—"

Julie reached for her clipboard. "I've got some new info. Excuse me, Todd. I ran a word search on the name Clegg. Looked at some microfiche from local newspapers too. Nothing much of interest except two little items in the *Kansas City Star* newspaper's morgue. Listen to this: February 10, 1993. Blurb in the nuptials section. 'Mrs. Priscilla Linn of Kansas City, Kansas, would like to announce the engagement of her daughter, Patty, to Mr. Charles Clegg of Affton, Missouri.' Affton, by the way, is close to Drew Box Factory. It goes on, 'The couple's planned marriage will be held at the Olathe Bible Church on March 30, 1993.'"

"And . . . And *what*?" Walker asked, along with a "Get on with it" gesture.

Julie checked her anger at her boss's impatience. "The 'and what' is this: first, a brief article in the *Star,* September 18, 1993. 'Woman's body discovered in trash container behind Old Town Mall. An unidentified female in her early twenties was discovered by the driver of a Dumpster truck.' Goes on to describe the victim. Then the following day, 'Charles Clegg, husband of the previously unidentified woman left dead in a trash container on Sunday last has identified the woman as his recent bride. Police, in an earlier news conference, stated Mr. Clegg was not a suspect in what authorities are now calling a homicide. Mr. Clegg, when contacted by this reporter, said he had been across the state in Saint Louis at the time of his wife's disappearance. Authorities confirmed Mr. Clegg's alibi.'"

The room took on the somber ambiance of a funeral parlor.

"Anything else?" Walker was the first to break the silence.

"Rogers confirmed the presence of a postmark from Olathe, Kansas. The same town where Charlie and Patty were married. Coincidence? I think not." She hurried on. "Can we convict him of his wife's murder? Unlikely, but—" She leafed through her notes. "This is a duplicate of a ticket issued on September 14, 1993, by a trooper on I-70 outside of Kansas City, Missouri. It lists as the lawbreaker our Charlie boy traveling east with a broken taillight and expired insurance."

"Right, that's the day before they found the wife," Walker said.

"The ticket was issued at eleven thirty, twenty miles from location of the body. They discovered the wife eight hours later."

"There's no doubt this guy's dirty," Todd said. "But how do we find him?"

Walker held up his hand as everyone began to speak at once. "Hold it, guys. But he's had time to cross the equator. I don't know if we have a shot at him."

Julie didn't agree but kept it to herself. "Here's another carrot to chew on. Tuck Gerard, Charlie's former foster parent, and a woman thought to be his common-law wife, died in a fire at a gas station Mr. Gerard operated not far from where our Mr. Clegg was brought up. No evidence, but the locals called it suspicious." She waited. "I'm just saying."

The meeting broke up without any plan and, above all, without a revelation.

Barton, when contacted, said it would be a good time for him to take a long weekend in Chicago with Cheryl. After the usual "don't dos" to her daughter, Julie felt comfortable being separated for the three days.

Julie's cell rang.

"Sergeant Worth?"

"Yes."

"We have an APB on a break out of Western Reception, Diagnostic and Correctional Center. You're assigned a roving patrol on I-70 between Boonville and Independence until further notice. You will get continued details on your cruiser's radio within the next ten minutes from Captain Walker."

"How many escapees do we have?"

"Three was our last report."

"Am I to meet my partner on the road?"

"Detective Devlin has been sent to Kansas City to assist there. For now, you're on your own, Sergeant. Sorry."

Julie hustled into her bedroom to change, choosing her work boots, rough whipcord trousers, and a layered sweater arrangement. The last time she'd been on a fugitive hunt, she ended up in a farm's pigpen. She and Todd wrestled around with a low-life who bellowed he "weren't gonna be hauled off to no dang hoosegow."

She took other calls in her cruiser and was halfway to Columbia before Todd got through.

"Did Walker call, Sergeant?"

"Yeah, couple minutes ago. Told me all hell broke loose and that you were sent to KC—which the dispatcher already told me. Also, that I was assigned to roving patrol on Route 70. Where are you?"

"Breezing along doing a hundred, getting close to KC."

They spoke for another few minutes and then hung up, promising to keep in touch.

Contacted by the coordinator of the hunt, Julie was reassigned to Sedalia, a town just south of the interstate. She received a description of the escapees and their possible destinations, based on former places of residence, friends, and old haunts.

At close to midnight, a call came in saying the three men were cornered in an abandoned warehouse close to Cameron, Missouri. Todd called and filled her in on his being stuck with a whole cadre of law enforcement in a standoff involving hostages and SWAT. The whole nine clusterfuck yards.

Julie signed out with her dispatcher and checked in at a Motel 6. The next morning, she grabbed a Dunkin' Donuts coffee to go and headed back toward Saint Louis, recognizing the busy intersection that she and Todd passed on their way to Jefferson City. It had been the day she got news about Cheryl. Or to be more accurate, a girl fitting Cheryl's description. She thought about a couple items on her to-do list. One which, regardless of how hard she tried to convince herself of its nonrelevance in the grand scheme, was the incarceration of Charles Clegg. The second important to-do was making sure that Cheryl wasn't permanently damaged by her abduction.

Clegg's capture would lay to rest many of Cheryl's nighttime dragon fears.

Julie's thoughts turned back to Clegg and the long, complicated pursuit of the little worm. She wondered if the prick might have gone back home to the "spread," his onetime foster home in the early years—it was in the direction. She pulled her car around to head back toward Calhoun, Missouri.

The lone country road bent and straightened and then bent again. A symbolic pattern of her life since meeting up with Charles on a similar road at the other end of the state.

Her accident reminded her about country road drivers. Don't trust them passing you when they're twenty miles over the speed limit. And if they seem off, they probably are.

She went just under the limit on the long stretch of road just before the Gerard spread. A half mile past the entrance, she spotted a break in the state-owned wire fencing. Missouri highway command was responsible for an enclosure bordering its roads, to keep livestock off the thoroughfare. The opening occurred when an older tree fell across the four-foot-high wire. She drove through and then a short distance into the woods.

Once out of sight of the road, she stopped and quickly came up with a plan. It became whirling thoughts of ground formerly traveled, with the acquisition of her shotgun, the mandatory visual on her automatic. A hat, just because it happened to be there, and her cell. She considered backup, communicating to the powers that be, but settled for a stern reminder to herself. Do the job, do it right, by the book.

In truth, why wouldn't he head for home? This place where he had met best friend, Bink, and taken his name. One would hope the name change was a tribute, not merely a disguise.

Julie trod through the woods. Slash from rotted trees and overgrown vines to her left and barren land on her right where she and Todd had driven in to speak to Jimbo Gerard. She was aware of a stench long before she reached a view of the house, probably burnt garbage or a barbequed pig or fawn.

She stopped in the middle of a quiet animal path. Crows cawed their presence and gathered in a patch of reddish grass in a clearing before her. They scattered as she settled.

63

"V*iva, Las Vegas!* Oh, viva—" Charles stopped singing. He propped his guitar on his lap and watched a flock of blackbirds rise out of the pines off to his right. They seemed only moderately provoked. As they circled, he pedaled the old porch swing, remembering moments of stolen pleasure on a similar swing years earlier. Heck, maybe this same one. This spot where he and Bink would sneak around, occasionally giving the swing a shove to hear its telltale squeak. The point always to be to pester Tuck and Gloria. Miss Big Boobs.

He watched again as the crows resettled in the distant pines. He pushed his elbow against the porch swing's chain support and tried once again to make a C-flat chord on his Gibson. When the birds moved again, he thought a deer might have been foraging in the woods. Not able to complete his accompaniment, he sat down the guitar beside him on the swing and thought about his chores. He had kindling to chop, dishes to rinse, a whole shitload of laundry to swill around. But first, a back-to-work continuation of what he liked to call "Jimbo the fire king and his systematic disappearance." The pit behind the house had originally been used as a trash incinerator.

Charles stoked the still-amber remains of his early morning fire. Jimbo was slowly vanishing. Limbs and heavy objects loaded above the shoulders, along with a healthy dose of four-dollars-a-gallon premium gasoline, blazed bright.

Plastic-wrapped final remains, bagged and ready. Tears in the industrial black bags were evidence of Jimbo's attraction to all of God's creatures. Overnight, raccoon and muskrat alike, maybe a few squirrels, went to work on Charles's former tormentor.

Rekindling the blaze with a couple pine stumps, Charles once again gazed out at the murder of crows.

64

J*ulie waited for* the birds to settle and then moved once again up the incline parallel to the farmhouse. After a hundred yards, she turned to complete the right angle that would bring her to the back of the house.

She heard singing as she neared, that same familiar, nasal grieving. She recognized the poor attempts at note making, the continuous sliding up to and past the proper mark. The warble and wobble of Charles Clegg's passion.

His face glowed as he wielded a long stick, poking at a fire. She circled behind an old barn to surprise him from the back. The smell, a pungent mixture of rotting flesh and sweet pine.

"Hello, Charlie."

"What the hell?" He jumped, fighting for balance on the rocky surface surrounding the trash pit. "Who are you? What do you want?"

She took off her cap and shook out her hair, still keeping the shotgun trained on his midsection. "You left your house in such a hurry, Charles. Was it something I said? The light business, that was precious."

"I got scared, afraid you people would think I done something wrong—"

"Why would that be, Chuckie?"

"I didn't do nothing. You gotta believe me."

"Why do I 'gotta'? What reason? Can you name one?"

"What is it you think I've done? Go on, tell me."

"Murdered your wife?"

"Nope, didn't happen. I swear, I was back in my place, close to where I work, really."

"Really? What about the speeding ticket you got a couple hours before they discovered the body? The ticket was issued over two hundred miles from 'your place.' Oh, and how did you manage to get rid of Tuck? You lit his cigarette for him, and he and some woman just happened to burn up?" She waited for a response. "Do you remember Angelina Hogar? Sweet girl, nice, but now very damaged."

"Who?"

"Her name is scratched on the floor of your basement, Charlie Boy."

He shook his head, as if dismissing her. "You won't shoot me."

"Won't I? Try me. Make a funny move, brother. See what it feels like to have a double ought gnawing its way through your belly button." Julie looked at the black plastic bundle on the ground. "What's in the bag, Clegg, your lunch? By the way, where's Jimbo Gerard, owner of this mess?"

He didn't answer. Just dropped his head and shuffled his feet.

"Open it up. Now."

Charles reached down and pulled apart the yellow ties on the trash bag.

"Open it."

"I did."

"All the way." Julie motioned with the shotgun. "Whatever is in there, take it out. Do it."

Charles held the bottom of the bag and raised it to his side. "This was in the field across the way. I don't know what it is, I was just getting rid of it, I swear." The innards slipped into the fire pit, the slimy mass sizzling as it settled into the fresh coals.

"Ah, Jesus." Julie gagged.

Charles heaved the heavy mop handle at her. She tried to duck, but the lance-like weapon nicked her under her right eye as Clegg leapt across the burning pit and high-tailed it toward the barn. Blurry eyed, Julie fired her scatter gun at the bouncing figure. She saw him stumble and disappear. She turned, cranked in another round, and went in the opposite direction around the barn. Charles had crawled and then sat with his back against the outside of the flaked wood siding.

"Where are you hit, killer?"

"Don't call me that. I did what was necessary for salvation. For the human race."

Julie threw off a fake laugh. "Do you recall a young girl you abducted in the woods, coming home from school? Years ago. She would have been maybe sixteen at the time."

He said nothing.

There were probably a number of victims; how could he remember them all? "She fought with you, tore a ring from around your neck that was on a chain. Was the death of that kid salvation? Does it jog the memory, Romeo?" She watched as he slid his hand down toward his leg. "What about Lulu?"

Nothing.

"Her mom's name was Venus."

He rubbed the back of his buttocks and leg with his bloody hand.

Julie couldn't tell if he was in pain from the buckshot in his ass or his recollection of Venus Riley. "You take a nice picture, lover boy. I saw the photo booth shot of you and Venus's daughter. What did you do with her?"

"That's for me to know, and you to find out."

"Ah, well, very clever. How about this, *sweetie*? I'm going to cuff you to that water pipe next to where you're sitting. Then, because my phone doesn't get a signal in this neck of the woods, I'm gonna take a careful walk back to my car. Shouldn't take more than twenty minutes." He looked up at her, his eyes watering from the pain in his hind quarters.

"Uncomfy? We'll get you help, hon. Once I get to my car, I'll drive back toward Sedalia, looking for a phone. Probably another half hour."

"Why you doing me like this? I'm bleeding to death here."

"Why? Gee whiz, Charles. I'm telling you how I'm going to try and help you. You almost put my eye out with that damn mop handle. I'm not holding a grudge; I'm just telling you how I'm going to save your life." She squatted down next to him and nudged him in the butt with the shotgun.

He screamed.

"Well, to get back to my task. I'll wait for help to arrive and direct them back here. I'll have them follow me so they don't get lost. And don't you worry about accidents on the way back. I'll drive careful and slow. You remember how I drive, don't you, Charlie? Just below the speed limit. That way we could be back here around sunset, so the emergency guys can tend to your boo-boo."

"I should have killed you for sure on the highway that day, drowned you in that trench where you were lyin' upside down. Bitch."

"Bitch? Wow, let's talk about this. Let me make you secure with this little item." She rested the 12-gauge against the barn wall as Charles moaned. Julie cuffed his wrist to the water pipe that made a right angle out of the weathered planks from the barn. She pulled his pockets inside out. A handful of change and an earring in one pocket, a packet of Wrigley's, and a roll of singles in the other.

"What was the significance of the hammered earring you sent me?"

Clegg continued to shift from one hip to the other, his face a distorted grimace. "It were a souvenir of your sweet daughter."

"But why the deliberate flattening, the damage?"

"She left me after I treated her fair and square. Never did anything nasty to her."

"Did you try?"

He didn't answer, just moved his head away and whimpered as he leaned against the barn siding.

Julie reached over and squeezed his chin and lips. She pulled his head around to face her. "Do you have a box of loving memories somewhere?" She shook his face for a moment and then let it go. "I honestly want to try and save you, Chuck E. Cheese, because I wish for my daughter, Cheryl, to have closure. You remember her, don't you? Sixteen, blonde, five foot seven. Beautiful girl, ripped your arm up, swam away in the middle of the night. Recall? I want her to see you smarmy eyed and uptight in court.

Angie Hogar. Anyone else we can find who is alive can tell the world what a pathetic little prick you are." Julie got up from her crouched position.

"I did what I thought was right. They were undeserving, wanton whores. I mean the rest of them. I wanted the world, as you suggested, to be partially rid of the scum of the earth. Not your daughter, of course."

"That's Miss America pageant material, Chuckie."

"Please don't leave me out here alone. I'm hurtin'."

Julie gathered up her shotgun and stood over Charles. "Speaking of bitches, a person in the recent past said to me, 'You must be sure if someone is still behaving in a hostile manner toward you.' Possibly your statement to me that you should have left me to die, drown me in that wet trench. That would fall into an area of hostility toward me, agreed? Not recently, but who's to say, right?"

Charles rolled back and forth against the barn.

"I was also told, 'Consider whether a man intends to surrender, capitulate, agree with you.' Have you fallen into that category? Do you surrender?"

"It hurts all to hell. What is capit—capulat."

"It means to give up."

"Okay."

"Okay what?"

"Okay, I give in. Just get me something for the pain, bitch."

"Oh, so we're back to 'bitch.'" Julie walked around the corner of the barn, and then stopped and returned. "A millisecond could have changed your life. A little thought, a consideration here and there." She paused. "Yeah, just a millisecond here and there. I hear coyotes off in the distance, Chuckie. Maybe there's bear too. If they come sniffing around for blood, give them your speech on the scum of the earth. I hear they're very understanding."

Julie debated with herself on the way back to her cruiser. She could use the radio in her patrol car to call it in now or, as she suggested to Clegg, wait til she got to Sedalia. It would take time, but she opted for Sedalia. She would be following through on what she had promised Mr. Lowlife.

She thought of Dr. Crankenstein. "Would you consider a moment when a perpetrator asked to be forgiven?" She felt that she had done that—she had considered it.

She dabbed at the bloody swelling under her eye, savoring the walk back to the road. Crows swooped nearby, their cackles echoing like comic agreement. It sounded as though the coyotes she'd heard earlier were getting closer. She got in the car to call it in. She heard the coyotes again, even closer. Julie put down her phone and drove away as the leaves floated down to earth to match her measured pace.

Acknowledgments

My gratitude to president Louise Burke and senior editor Abby Zidle at Gallery for this opportunity. My appreciation as well to Marla Daniels for keeping everyone on track. Many thanks, also, to the rest of the talented crew: Alex Su, Philip Bashe, and Jae Song.

I am grateful to long time agent Noah Lukeman for his tenacity and wisdom. Kudos to Kevin Smith for the great insights and encouragement from the beginning.

Thanks to Lt. Kathy McKinney for needed input and to Stephan Marshall for his ideas and knowledge. And a special thank you to my wife, Betsy, for her tireless work on this project.

Keep reading for an excerpt from

Payback at Morning Peak

By Gene Hackman

ONE

Jubal hiked with abandon through the mountainous forest, cradling the Colt slide-action rifle in his slender arms, proud his father had seen fit to allow him use of the small-bore .22. Not quite eighteen, he was just under six feet, nearly as tall as his father, and did his best to dress like him—whipcord pants tucked neatly into calf-high boots. Two rabbits he'd shot that morning hung from a leather-tooled belt around his waist, a gift from pa. He thought of cleaning them himself but decided he would let ma take care of that little chore. He imagined her proud face when he returned home with them. Rabbit stew would be a welcome change from the tough buffalo meat cured in the family smokehouse.

He thought of his sister, Prudence, pouting earlier today when ma had told her to stay home, shuck peas, and tend the fire.

"Jube gets to have all the fun!" she'd said.

"Miss Prudence," ma had replied, "you're only four-teen, and it's best you tend your chores." Strict but fair.

Jubal didn't mind the company of his sister, though, as they had much in common. Much to Mother Young's concern, Pru often ventured alone into the forest to hunt berries and wildflowers.

The boy topped Morning Peak, seeing Colorado stretching out to the northern end of New Mexico's Sangre de Cristo Mountains. A late afternoon sun warmed his chapped hands while he marveled at the painted landscape, aspens shimmering as their new spring leaves caught the sun. To the west he could just barely see his family's cabin, nestled into a meadow lined with fir and limber pine. A gray smoky haze from the log structure filled the small valley, and he knew Pru had been doing her job with the fire.

The wind changed, and Jubal's eyes widened. There was too much smoke. He noticed unusual movement around the house and heard eerie sounds of strange, jubilant voices floating up through the dense valley.

His reaction was immediate. Gripping the rifle in front of him to clear the way, Jubal broke into a dead run and began to close the hefty distance to the cabin. He tore through thickets down the canyon, sharp branches ripping at his leather coat as he plowed through the brush.

Minutes later, he stopped within shouting distance of the compound, his legs on fire with exertion, his lungs needing air.

A pile of bright gingham fabric lay on the earthen courtyard. *Like a body.* The clothing looked to be his mother's, her dress cloth flapping with the breeze. Pru's horse, Butternut, lay near the well, her legs thrashing as a rush of blood flowed from her neck.

Jubal counted five men riding on horseback in the courtyard, with several more stirring around the outbuildings and barn. They all seemed determined to celebrate, shouting as if they had achieved a great victory.

Trying to control his breathing, the boy slumped behind a massive pine. He wanted this day to start over, wanted to forget the body in the yard, wanted only to run, but pa would skin him if he didn't stand as a man.

Where *was* pa?

Jubal took several more deep breaths. He moved to his stomach and started to crawl. He'd gone only a few feet when he rolled onto his back, fighting panic, his nose stung by the sharp and disagreeable scent of burnt flesh and manure.

He had to keep moving. Rising, he darted between a stand of scrub oak, then bellied down and once again crawled, hiding behind the scattered chamisa.

Laughing and drunk, the men staggered around the toolshed and outhouse. One dark-skinned fellow looked different, wearing a feathered, flat-brim leather hat with a bright yellow braided string running under his chin. He carried a bow across his back and a quiver with arrows attached to his belt. He looked familiar, the way he carried himself. The whole raft of them seemed related.

Jubal's thoughts drifted to more pleasant times. The family together, Pru laughing at his jokes, his parents sharing secrets. When was that? A lifetime ago. He forced himself back to the present. He had work to do.

He looked down at the rifle. He'd killed animals for food, but could he kill a man? He shifted on the rough ground. Maybe it didn't matter.

A wail came from the barn, growing louder as Jubal crept closer through the thicket. He caught a glimpse of the two-story structure's exterior.

And then he saw his father.

Jubal Sr., hung from a pulley outside the hayloft, arms stretched high above his head, legs dangling above the wicked flames of a fire. Charred remnants of his clothing and strips of skin swung from his chest. A chunk of red cloth, which Jubal recognized as his father's bandanna, had been stuffed into his mouth. A man with a filthy poncho wrapped around his shoulders tossed hay from the loft onto the torturous blaze.

Jubal's pa was near to death, his bare legs burned. Blood matted his neck, arms, and chest.

Then the wailing stopped, the body swaying like a pendulum. Jubal stared, looking for recognition. His father's lips were moving. With each group of words, a nod, then he would begin again. He gazed at Jubal. Did he speak? Did he call out, "Save yourself"? His eyes rolled toward the smoked sky, once again the same litany, but this time the head drooped, the shoulders and legs relaxed. The body settled into its trusses.

Jubal chambered a round in the .22, raised it, and took a long, dreadful moment to pray. His head pressed hard against the rifle's breech. He wiped the moisture from his eyes, adjusted the rear sight, and shot his father in the head.

The sound, though muffled by the crackling fire, still startled the fire-tending Mexican. He turned toward the noise as Jubal stood and pumped another round into the Colt. Trembling, he fired, his bullet catching the man in the lower stomach. The man dug his hands under his heavy leather belt, searching, then doubled over as if looking for something on the ground.

Jubal's second shot pierced his head just above the cheekbone, dropping the man like a rock from a high place.

The boy slumped to the ground, watching the remains

of his father swinging from the barn. "Help me, Pa. What have I done?"

Fifty yards off to his left, two men, their hair pulled tautly into braids on the sides of their heads, dragged tied bundles of his mother's and father's clothing. They soaked the pile of garments in lamp oil and lit it. Trailing the fiery bundle behind a crazed horseman, they made great circles around the house and barn, setting fire to the dry grasses.

"Be the man I taught you to be," his pa had once said to him. He eased to the ground, too frightened to move and yet strangely not seeming to care. Jubal looked down at the two paltry rabbits still hanging from his belt.

The men by the house stopped their whooping to look at the area of the barn, the structure now fully taken by rising flames. The cracking and popping of the dried timbers had partially covered the sound of the small-caliber .22, and Jubal was still safely unknown to them.

He watched as they cavorted in his family's vegetable garden. Others circled the lifeless form of his mother on the ground, making coarse gestures and poking their rifles at the body.

Pru. He hadn't seen her anywhere. *Where is she?*

Jubal started to pick himself up. He was sick with fear and remorse, but he'd do his damnedest.

Crouching low, he sprinted to the edge of his mother's root cellar. There he remained unseen behind the canted door, thinking how easy it would be to slither out of the clearing and into the welcoming shelter of the spruces and whitebark pines that surrounded the homestead—then run for his pitiful life.

A high-pitched scream came from the edge of the woods, beyond the burning barn. Pru was running into the clearing where their mother lay, her bonnet streaming behind her, tangled in her long blond hair. Wildflowers fell from a basket on her arm. She ran like a frightened animal, shouting to her mother.

A horseman spotted her and pursued her across the open field.

Ignoring the other men, Jubal took quick aim with his rifle and pulled the trigger. The shot went awry. The horseman scooped Prudence up in one swift powerful move, gripping her waist and swinging her up beside him. She protested loudly, beating her fists against the man's head and chest.

Jubal had very little chance for a shot now, he was afraid of hitting her. The other men honed in on Jubal's position and fired at him, bullets dancing past his head. He collapsed onto the ground and crept to where he could use the burning farmhouse as cover.

Pru was taken into the tree line from where she had just emerged. He moved along the ground. Once he was at the other side of the farmhouse, he ran into the nearby woods. All of his instincts told him to keep his head down and pursue cautiously, but he couldn't ignore his need to chase the horseman. He had lost his parents. He couldn't lose his sister.

Once in the woods, he could hear Pru's voice coming from several directions, all of her cries amplified by the reverberating valley walls. For some time he searched for her, scrambling from one tree to the next. When he was finally resigned to the idea that the horseman had moved out of the valley, he heard hoofbeats coming from the east. He ran in that direction, only to see a lone rider bolting at a gallop between the trees a hundred yards in front of him.

The man had left Pru in the woods.

Jubal quickened his pace and backtracked from where he had last seen the rider. After a lengthy search, he found her . . . her face bloody from a deep forehead wound, clothing twisted about her body. There was so much, too much blood. On his knees, he pleaded with her to speak to him. He cradled her in his arms and rocked her, trying to coax a spark of life.

The wildflower basket was still looped around her arm. Jubal gently pulled out the leaves and twigs caught in her hair. He combed her soft tresses with his fingers, then used his neckerchief to clean her face of dirt and blood.

"Jube?" She opened her eyes, trying to focus. "Tell pa a man tried to . . . hurt me."

Jubal moved her gently, thankful she was alive. "Shush, now, Pru. I'm here. You'll be all right. Try and rest."

Pru seemed to fall into a heavy sleep, a spot of blood leaked from the side of her mouth. Jubal swung his rifle over his shoulder and lifted her into his arms. They needed shelter, and so he started up the long slope toward Morning Peak.

Nearly half a mile from the house stood a group of rocks the two of them had explored in the past. Boulders as tall as their barn had split off from the cliffs above, and wagon-sized stones had fallen away to the base of these rocks, forming the makings of a cave. Jubal tried to awaken Pru while he scaled the steep terrain.

"Remember the 'Sultan's Castle'?"

"You mean the Emperor of Youngdom?" she answered slowly. "His castle?"

His eyes misted. "Yep, the very same. We're almost there."

As they reached the bouldered cave entrance, Jubal

turned sideways with his precious cargo in order to slide through the narrow gap. Once safely inside the rock-sided enclosure, he took off his coat and wrapped his sister in fleece-lined warmth. Just enough light peeked from a V-shaped opening for Jubal to see Pru's ghostly pale complexion. Dry leaves spotted the cave floor and lay in drifts against the wall. A rag doll with a clownlike smile sat on the parched vegetation. It belonged to his sister.

Jubal laid Pru on the bed of leaves and moved the doll to a pile of carefully placed rocks.

"I smell Cotton, Jube."

"What?"

"Cotton, my rag doll I used to play with. I smell her. I dabbed some of ma's lilac water on her 'cause the old stuffing got kind of dank."

Jubal took the cheery doll and passed it under his nose before he laid it next to his sister. Indeed, it smelled slightly of perfume. It had been years since he and his sister had used this stone structure as a playhouse.

"Don't tell ma." Her body heaved a long sigh of pain. "Sorry. Don't tell that I spent time here. Ma would skin me."

Jubal ran his hand softly across her face. "Are you in a lot of pain, sis?"

She nodded and held her hand to her mouth. "Jube . . . I'm not seeing too well." She cried, not like a child, but deep and steady. "My side hurts, just here. I'm bleeding something awful." She tried to touch her rib cage. "Maybe ma's pain potion, under the washbasin. The small purple bottle."

Their mother kept codeine elixir for severe pain, on a shelf in the kitchen. Jubal wondered if he could get to it or if it had even survived the fire. The men must have left the farm by now. There was still daylight, and he could be down to the farm and back in twenty minutes. "Pru, I'm going to try to get you that medicine. Will you be all right for a bit?"

"Ma," she called. "Ma, I don't feel well. I've got deep pain there. A man was with me. Make it go away."

Jubal dropped to his knees.

"Can you get me the man in the moon? He's frowning."

She was delirious. Maybe it would be a good time to get back to the cabin for medicine. She moaned, knees drawn up tight toward her chest, hands dug between her legs. Her forehead was dampened with sweat, her face flushed red. But he was afraid to leave her in such pain.

"Jubal Young, a man-child." She rolled to her side and reached a hand out toward him. "I wrote a poem for you, Jube."

"I'd like to hear it."

She tried to smile. "I don't think I can remember it all. It's about the land, the animals. . . . I gave the poem to ma to keep for your birthday. She put it away somewhere. I really need ma to help me. It's a lady's kind of thing. Please."

Jubal made up his mind. "Listen to me, Pru. I'm gonna scoot down to the house and I'll be right back. You'll be fine for a few minutes, won't you?"

She nodded, trying to smile.

Rifle in hand, Jubal ran back toward the homestead. The image of his sister lying huddled in misery, her pale face distorted, blurred him to anger. He would kill them all. He felt anguish, dizzy with it. *I will track them to the ends of the earth.*

The men had not left but were spread around the clearing, apparently looking for him. Jubal skirted the tree line and started once again to crawl. He realized the farther he went, the more he would be cut off from his sister. Never mind, he would deal with that later. First, these men.

The setting sun turned the raging fires that were once his home into a fiery pink mist. He took a last glance at the sad bundle that was his mother and continued to the root cellar. With the slide-action Colt steady on the door, he let out his breath and squeezed the trigger softly.

A man with a battered straw hat caught a round in the neck. He dropped his rifle and sat on the ground, both hands swatting at his neck as if shooing a pesky bee. Gripping his throat, he tried to squelch the bleeding. Jubal slid another bullet into the chamber, aimed, and fired it squarely into the center of his forehead. The man's sweat-stained hat spiraled backward. Arms outstretched in surrender, the renegade seemed to melt into the earth.

The other men scurried down behind his father's overturned hay wagon, several with antiquated, single-shot weapons. Jubal hit the ground as the balled rounds ripped at the earth around him. Forcing himself to be calm, he once again reloaded.

The men called out to Jubal, denouncing him, describing in detail what they would do to him. All the while bullets plowed into the ground close to Jubal.

They continued to fire, one of the younger men skipping over a pile of clothing to charge toward the root cellar. As the man drew a long-barreled .44 from his holster, Jubal's bullet caught him in the chest. Stumbling, he tried to reach Jubal, pounding his pistol at the soft earth. Moving within twenty feet, he slipped to his knees and then slowly eased to his side, as if preparing for a nap.

Several rounds splintered the root cellar's plank door, a long thin piece of wood catching Jubal in the side of the head, opening a wound. For an instant he couldn't see. He wrapped his bandanna around his forehead to stop the bleeding and fired several more shots into the distant hay wagon.

The intense pain from his gashed head gave him some welcome courage. His family had suffered, and this pain seemed to make him one with them. He thought of Pru, her bloody dress, and pa, Jubal Thaddeus Young Sr., a man striving to make a life for his kinfolk, killed now by his own son's hand. Jubal had a moment when he thought maybe his father would forgive him his death and be proud of him.

Be the man . . . , he would have said. Jubal prayed that it be so.

Jubal rose and heard what he thought was a hornet, then a high whistling sound and a shocking pain in his left hip. An arrow protruded from his body. It had not penetrated the skin of his back but stopped somewhere inside his lower waist. Jubal dropped back down on the native grasses to crawl below a small rise in the earth beyond view.

Scuttling along on his right side, he was careful so the arrow did not catch in the heavy foliage. With all the weapons in play, rifle and pistol rounds eating up the earth around him, Jubal thought it odd he would be hit by, of all things, an arrow.

His mission was too dangerous, and from the looks of the house it would be a miracle if anything survived the fire. He would have to go back empty-handed up the steep trail leading to Morning Peak and Sultan's Castle. But Jubal didn't know what else he could do for his sis.

If these men could track, and he knew at least the man with the bow could, then they would trail after him, but he knew the rocky path so well he was confident they couldn't get around him. He glanced at the farmhouse, it continued to burn.

They would follow.

He wanted them to follow.

Hours had passed since Jubal had first come upon the attack. He deemed himself safe for now, having barely made it out of the bloody grounds of the homestead, inching along on his good hip. Grasping the embedded arrow with his left hand, he clawed and elbowed with his right. The ghostlike image of a tall gray-haired man kept him going. Jubal knew him. He felt as if he were missing something, a reason. It eluded him. The figures darting about his family's property were mere phantoms without motive. His lack of memory, the why of this kept him strangely alert.

Jubal limped across an open meadow. Looking down at the protruding arrow, he thought it must have glanced off his hip bone. The length of it jutted out from his bleeding upper leg like an errant tree branch.

A stand of ponderosa pine lay ahead. He pushed on, glancing back often to see if he was followed. Not yet.

At a cliff overlooking what his sister referred to as "Young's Valley," once again he found his sister's retreat, the small opening where two large rocks formed an inverted V.

The light started to fade as Jubal eased himself into the

cave, where he was greeted by the sound of his sister's soft, forced breathing. A strand of light from a gap at the top of the boulders illuminated her pale face.

He felt remorse. His search for the medicine had not only been worthless, but he had also been rewarded with a deep wound.

He watched his sister, wondering what to do next. How to deal with his own fierce pain of the arrow was beyond him.

Prudence stirred. "What would pa say?" she asked. It was almost as if she had read his mind. "Pa once said to me, 'Prudence, when all else fails, simply smile.' It's a little harder done than said. Wouldn't you say, Jube?"

"Pa was full of sayings."

"Was?" she asked.

Jubal was happy to hear his sister once again speaking clearly, but she'd caught him off guard. He tried to cover his mistake. "Oh, I just mean he's always saying these . . . platitudes. I think that's the word. Anyhow, he's funny sometimes, right?"

Quiet for a long time, Pru worried Jubal when she finally spoke. "I'd been picking flowers." Her voice softened. "I think I was running and calling out to ma. Then, a smell like somebody's sweat. Is Butternut okay?"

Jubal didn't answer. He sat at her side, the arrow jutting out of his left hip, the blood flow fortunately stanched.

"A man was mean. He did hurtful things." Her voice began to fade. "I want ma. Please get her."

He wished he could.

Pru raised her clenched fists and made feeble striking movements into the air. She cried out.

Jubal once again stroked her forehead. "Try to relax if

you can. It will be better soon." He pushed his arm under her neck and brought her head close to his own. He kissed her softly on the cheek. Her eyes opened wide.

"I love my brother, Jubal. He's funny and kind. . . ."

Then she was gone.